THE MAKING OF DANIEL BRAUT

Arne Garborg

ARNE GARBORG (1851-1924), often described as the most naturally intellectual writer of his generation, was the first major writer to emerge from the peasant-farming community of Norway in the later nineteenth century. Breaking with a puritanical and conservative background, he moved to the capital to become a writer. Rejecting 'peasant romanticism', he described the problems of an age of rapid change: intellectual, moral and sexual confusion, and the possibility of losing one's way. These issues are explored in his novels of the 1880s, including *The Making of Daniel Braut* and *Trætte Mænd* (1891, *Weary Men*), the novel in which he grapples with the problem of decadence.

In the 1890s Garborg returned to his roots: after writing the deeply personal and compassionate work *Fred* (1892, Peace) about a farmer who, like Garborg's father, commits suicide after getting swept up in a fanatical pietistic movement, he began to draw on the folk-culture, landscape and traditions of Jæren in western Norway, to produce *Haugtussa* (1895, The Elf Maiden), his hauntingly lyrical cycle of seventy poems, and several other prose works.

A complex mix of sharp intelligence, analytic ability and a deep emotional need for roots and faith, Garborg wrote with irony but also deep compassion. He was the first writer to show that New Norwegian could function perfectly as the language of literature.

MARIE WELLS was W. P. Ker Lecturer in Norwegian at University College London until her retirement. Her main research interest has been Norwegian literature, with a special interest in the work of Henrik Ibsen. She has contributed articles to numerous journals, and is editor of *The Nineteenth-Century Discovery of Scandinavia*. Her translation of Jonas Lie's *Familjen paa Gilje* (1883, The Family at Gilje), will be published by Norvik Press in 2010.

Some other books from Norvik Press

Victoria Benedictsson: *Money* (translated by Sarah Death)
Hjalmar Bergman: *Memoirs of a Dead Man* (translated by Neil Smith)
Jens Bjørneboe: *Moment of Freedom* (translated by Esther Greenleaf Mürer)
Jens Bjørneboe: *Powderhouse* (translated by Esther Greenleaf Mürer)
Jens Bjørneboe: *The Silence* (translated by Esther Greenleaf Mürer)
Johan Borgen: *The Scapegoat* (translated by Elizabeth Rokkan)
Fredrika Bremer: *The Colonel's Family* (translated by Sarah Death)
Suzanne Brøgger: *A Fighting Pig's Too Tough to Eat* (translated by Marina Allemano)
Camilla Collett: *The District Governor's Daughters* (translated by Kirsten Seaver)
Kerstin Ekman: *Witches' Rings* (translated by Linda Schenck)
Kerstin Ekman: *The Spring* (translated by Linda Schenck)
Kerstin Ekman: *The Angel House* (translated by Sarah Death)
Kerstin Ekman: *City of Light* (translated by Linda Schenck)
Knut Hamsun: *Selected Letters* (2 vols.) (edited and translated by James McFarlane and Harald Næss)
Sigurd Hoel: *A Fortnight Before the Frost* (translated by Sverre Lyngstad) (2009)
P. C. Jersild: *A Living Soul* (translated by Rika Lesser)
Viivi Luik: *The Beauty of History* (translated by Hildi Hawkins)
Runar Schildt: *The Meat-Grinder and Other Stories* (translated by Anna-Liisa and Martin Murrell)
Amalie Skram: *Lucie* (translated by Katherine Hanson and Judith Messick)
Amalie and Erik Skram: *Caught in the Enchanter's Net: Selected Letters* (edited and translated by Janet Garton)
August Strindberg: *The Red Room* (translated by Peter Graves) (2009)
August Strindberg: *Tschandala* (translated by Peter Graves)
Hanne Marie Svendsen: *Under the Sun* (translated by Marina Allemano)
Hjalmar Söderberg: *Aberrations* (translated by Neil Smith) (2009)
Hjalmar Söderberg: *Martin Birck's Youth* (translated by Tom Ellett)
Hjalmar Söderberg: *Selected Stories* (translated by Carl Lofmark)
Helene Uri: *Honey Tongues* (translated by Kari Dickson)
Elin Wägner: *Penwoman* (translated by Sarah Death) (2009)

THE MAKING OF DANIEL BRAUT

by

Arne Garborg

Translated from the Norwegian
and with an introduction by

Marie Wells

Norvik Press
2008

Originally published in Norwegian by Fr. Nygaard, Bergen, under the title *Bondestudentar* (1883). This translation follows the text of the version included in Arne Garborg's Collected Works from 1908.

Introduction and translation © Marie Wells 2008.

The translator's moral right to be identified as the translator of the work has been asserted.

Norvik Press Series B: English Translations of Scandinavian Literature, no. 44.

No. 1 in the series: Classics of Norwegian Literature.

A catalogue record for this book is available from the British Library.
ISBN: 978-1-870041-81-2
First published in 2008 by Norvik Press.

This translation has been published with the financial support of NORLA, Norwegian Literature Abroad. Norvik Press also gratefully acknowledges the financial assistance given by Stavanger 2008, European Capital of Culture towards publication of this book.

Norvik Press
Department of Scandinavian Studies
University College London
Gower Street
London WC1E 6BT
England

Managing editors: Janet Garton, Neil Smith, C. Claire Thomson.

Website: www.norvikpress.com
E-mail address: norvik.press@ucl.ac.uk

Cover illustration: Group portrait of three students by Gustav Borgen (1916). The Norwegian Museum of Cultural History, Oslo (www.norskfolke.museum.no).

Layout: Neil Smith
Cover design: Richard Johnson

Printed in the UK by Page Bros. (Norwich) Ltd, Norwich, UK

Contents

Acknowledgements 6

Introduction 7

Translator's Note 15

The Making of Daniel Braut
1 17
2 27
3 37
4 61
5 81
6 101
7 113
8 131
9 153
10 169
11 179
12 199
13 211

Notes 235

Acknowledgements

I would like to acknowledge the help given by three friends, Alison Sinclair, Stewart Sinclair and Mark Millington, who as non-Scandinavianists took an early draft of this translation with them on holiday and read it to look out for linguistic contamination and elements that needed explanation to readers not familiar with Scandinavian culture.

I would also like to thank Professor Janet Garton, who went through the final draft with a tooth-comb, and suggested many stylistic improvements, but also found more typographical mistakes, etc. than should have been there.

For any mistakes and infelicities that remain I take full responsibility.

MW

INTRODUCTION

Marie Wells

Until 1814 Norway had been part of the kingdom of Denmark-Norway, but because Denmark ended up siding with Napoleon in the Napoleonic War, Norway was taken from Denmark and awarded to Sweden at the Treaty of Kiel in 1814. As a result of the war contact between Denmark and Norway had been severely interrupted during the period between 1807 and 1814, and Norway had already been considering breaking away from Denmark. Not surprisingly therefore the Norwegians objected to being taken from one country and handed to another, and made a bid for independence. In April 1814 leading figures in the country came together at Eidsvoll to draw up a constitution that was passed on 17 May (now celebrated as Norway's National Day). Norway was not able to hold on to its independence, but due to its vigorous defence of its rights embedded in the Constitution it became part of a twin-kingdom with Sweden rather being incorporated *into* Sweden. The king and his ministers resided in Stockholm, and were solely responsible for foreign policy, but Norway was able to have its own parliament (called the *Storting*). To begin with, however, this only met every third year and it was not until 1884 that the king's ministers had to answer to the *Storting*. Norway was also allowed to develop as an independent country with its own capital city Christiania (now Oslo) and institutions. One of these, the university, was in fact founded in 1811 and admitted its first students in 1813.

In 1815 Norway had 885,000 inhabitants and the majority of these, nearly ninety percent, lived in the country. It was not surprising therefore that the Norwegian Constitution had allocated two-thirds of the seats in the *Storting* to the country districts, but this emphasis on the country was motivated by several other factors as well. Political thinking round 1800 was influenced by the French physiocrats, and by the Romantic Movement's enthusiasm for nature, rural life and history. Moreover the Norwegian farmers were seen as the 'true' Norwegians because their life and traditions had evolved in the valleys and fjords of Norway largely untouched by the 400 years of Danish rule. Finally, during the Napoleonic War when Norway had been cut off from Denmark, the Norwegians had come to realize how important it was to achieve agricultural self-sufficiency. Thus up until about 1850 there was a certain romanticization of the farmers, something that comes out very clearly in some of the paintings by Adolf Tidemann.

Although the population started to grow rapidly after the end of the Napoleonic War, (reaching 1.33 million in 1845 and 1.7 million in 1865) agricultural production in the first half of the century managed to keep abreast of this growth due to improvements in agricultural methods, the bringing of more land into cultivation, and the introduction of the potato which, with salt herring, became the poor man's staple diet. As the towns were also growing rapidly during this period corn prices rose and it was possible for farmers to sell their produce to the townspeople, and to use the money earned to pay for new farming equipment, and to convert leasehold farms into freehold farms. From 1851 farmers were also able to borrow from the newly-established Mortgage Bank (*Hypotekbanken*). However, towards the end of the 1850s the end of the Crimean War caused a massive drop in corn prices and farmers in Norway struggled to pay off loans raised in better times. The arable farmers of Eastern Norway were particularly hard hit.

While it is true to say that in the nineteenth century the majority of the Norwegian population were farmers, this single term does not do justice to the diversity of the farming class. There were for example huge differences in wealth between the farmers in Eastern Norway and those in Western Norway. The farmers in Eastern Norway were wealthier because the land was easier to farm, the farms were larger and the farmers often owned large tracts of forest. (In this translation it is worth noting where people come from as in most cases those associated with Eastern Norway tend to be wealthier, and Stensrud, the farmer who appears in Chapter 10, is referred to as 'the estate-owner' to emphasize this). On the other hand there was a great gap between the rich and poor farmers in Eastern Norway, where the large farms often had several tenant farmers or cotters, who in return for a cottage, a small plot of land, and restricted grazing and wood-cutting rights had to work on the landlord's farm for a very low wage. The farms in Western Norway were smaller, and the farmers poorer because the land was harder to farm; on the other hand the nature of the land favoured dairy farming, which increased in value in the second half of the century, and moreover the farmers who lived near the coast could have fishing as a secondary activity.

In the middle of the century one could say that Norway was a country with two cultures. On the one hand there were the farmers whose loyalties were local and whose education did not go beyond primary level and whose language was the local dialect. On the other hand there was the official class, a tiny elite (of just under 2,000 men in 1845 out of population of 1.33 million). As it says in the novel this group ranged from 'the sheriff and teacher, through the clergyman and tax collector, the magistrate and district governor, higher and higher, more and more resplendent, right up to the king'. For many years the farmers elected men from this class, rather than members of their own class to represent them in the *Storting*, and these men, who were university educated, who spoke Dano-Norwegian and were European in their cultural orientation, had a strong sense that they formed a network of men entitled by birth and education to run the state of Norway. As a group they were not necessarily wealthy (though those at the top of the ladder were) and the growing class of the bourgeoisie, rich merchants, ship-owners, traders etc were not necessarily accepted into their ranks. It was an elite based on education and tradition.

There was therefore a huge gulf to be crossed for anyone from the farming community wanting to access education. Not only was there the barrier of language, the move from dialect to Dano-Norwegian, but the fact that education beyond primary level meant a classical education, for which one had to pay. All these issues are central to Arne Garborg's novel, *The Making of Daniel Braut*, which is set in the period 1850-1870 and concerns the difficulties that a young boy from a poor farming community in Western Norway encounters in trying to move beyond his class background.

Arne Garborg (1851-1924) was born in Jæren, the area south of Stavanger, on a farm that he himself said he used as the model for the farm Sørbraut in the novel. But the protagonist Daniel Braut is not Garborg, though they do share certain characteristics. As Garborg moved away from his farming background, so does Daniel Braut in the novel, but the motivations are different. From a young age Garborg had loved the world of books and ideas and wanted a life which revolved round these, be it through teaching or journalism, and he was involved with the latter nearly all his life, even starting two newspapers. His first novel, *A Freethinker* (*Ein fritenkjar*), was published in 1881, two years before *The Making of Daniel Braut*, in which the protagonist simply wants to get away from the misery of farming life and sees education as the only way out.

But there were also other factors governing Garborg's intellectual development, and one was the pietistic atmosphere in which he had grown up. While Garborg was still a young boy his father began to be plagued by depression and religious doubts and fears, which were exacerbated by the religious revival movements that were sweeping Norway – particularly the west coast – at the time. Garborg's father not only feared he was doomed to damnation, but when his son turned his back on the farm, which as the eldest son he should have inherited, and chose a life of letters instead, he took it as a sign of God's displeasure and in 1870 committed suicide. Garborg described this as the darkest chapter in his life, and though he had already reacted against the teaching of the state church and the clergy, his father's death was an influence on his thinking about social and cultural matters throughout his life.

The path that Garborg makes his protagonist Daniel Braut follow is very much the one that he followed. Just as Daniel is caught in the timeless situation of the country bumpkin having to deal with the snobbery and derision of the urban dwellers, with their sophisticated façade, or *frons urbana* as he learns to call it, so Garborg must have been, though by the time he became a university student in 1875 he had more experience of life behind him. Garborg also makes his protagonist about twelve year older than he was, so that he can expose him to the full force of the ferment of new ideas in all areas from education to religion and politics that were sweeping through Norway in the late 1860s and early 1870s.

Like Garborg, Daniel studies for his matriculation exams at a crammer in Christiania and like Garborg Daniel is exposed to the debate of conflicting values in culture and politics when he starts studying at the university, which Garborg started attending in 1875. However, whereas Daniel gets lost in the battle of ideas, Garborg found his way to values he truly believed in, though because he lived the conflicts of the age – those between science and religion, conservative and liberal attitudes to morality – in a deeply personal way his road to clarity in these matters was often a difficult and painful one.

The novel is therefore very much a cultural novel, a novel about the ideas and debates that dominate the period, but in the novel these are presented through representative characters to such an extent that one could sometimes almost call it a *roman à clef*. Chief among the characters who have historic counterparts are The Old Man who runs the crammer called 'The Factory', Professor Darre, who addresses the students at their matriculation festivities, the Dalesman, who also addresses the students at these festivities, and Fram, the leader of the political radicals whom Daniel subsequently meets. More information will be found about these and other characters who have historic counterparts in the notes at the end of the volume. A note is indicated by an * in the text, and may be found by looking up the relevant page number in the Notes.

Looked at from another angle the novel can also be seen as a *bildungsroman*, the story of the development of a young person from childhood to adulthood, but if this is the case it is a deeply ironic *bildungsroman* as Daniel does not gain but loses all personal integrity. Garborg himself described his novel as being fundamentally socio-economic, but in material specifically Norwegian. Looked at in this way Daniel is a victim of the socio-economic and ideological factors of the period that hinder him in his desire to achieve the goals he wants, though it also has to be said that he is seduced by a false idealism and its concomitant scorn for everyday realities.

In 1882, the year before *The Making of Daniel Braut* was published, Ibsen had published *An Enemy of the People*, his response to the furore caused by *Ghosts*, and in 1883 was working on his next play, *The Wild Duck*, which he said would take off in a new direction compared to his earlier plays. But Ibsen was twenty years older than Garborg, lived abroad and was interested in the lives and struggles of the bourgeoisie, and particularly in the lives of women in marriage, and increasingly in the influence of the unconscious, topics very different from those Garborg was interested in. Bjørnstjerne Bjørnson, Ibsen's contemporary had written stories based on the farmers in the 1850s, but at a period when the farmers were still seen in a rather romantic light as 'the true Norwegians'. In the 1880s he was interested in the conflict between religion and science and the double standard of morality, again in the bourgeoisie. Writing about the struggles of characters from the farming community, Garborg was breaking new ground with *The Making of Daniel Braut* not only with regard to subject matter but also with regard to the language in which it was written, because it was the first major novel to be written in New Norwegian, or *Landsmål* as it was called at the time, in other words the language based on the dialects, and not Dano-Norwegian. In fact Garborg was the first writer to write New

Norwegian and to show that it was a viable language for fiction.

We learn something about Daniel's subsequent career in Garborg's later novels. In *Men* (*Mannfolk*, 1886), a broadly-based novel about male-female relationships set in literary and artistic circles in Christiania, we meet him in his mid-thirties as a disgruntled and negative husband with marital problems, exacerbated by the fact that Inga Holm, the love of his youth is now happily married in Western Norway and has a large family. We also learn that after living the 'ideal life of the student' for some years Daniel finally studied for his theology exams, and when he had passed those and gained a reasonably good position as a teacher at a girls' school, he had to marry Hanna Stensrud. Unfortunately the following year Hanna's father goes bankrupt and Daniel who had married for money is deeply aggrieved. In the play *The Teacher* (*Læraren*) from 1896, Daniel has become a clergyman and attacks a young idealistic preacher and helps turn the secular authorities against him. In *The Prodigal Son* (*Heimkomin Son*, 1908) we learn that he had entered politics and become a member of the *Storting*.

Garborg's novels of the 1880s are set in Christiania and show his characters as the products of environment and inheritance, and where women are concerned, a wrong-headed education in matters of sex. The last of Garborg's Christiania novels *Weary Men* (*Trætte Mænd*, 1891) marks the beginning of his move away from the life of the capital city and is written in the form of a diary, where the protagonist writes about his life, loves, anxieties, religious longings and what he sees as the decline of society. As such it can be compared with the decadent novels that were being written elsewhere in Europe at the time, though Garborg treats his protagonist with strong irony.

An early Norwegian three-volume work on Garborg gave the following titles (translated) to the three volumes: *From Man of Jæren to European, The European, From European to Man of Jæren*, and in the 1890s Garborg did return to western Norway for his material. In *Peace* (*Fred*) from 1892 he describes with sympathy and understanding the life of a farmer who like his father gets caught up in financial and religious worries and in the end is driven to despair and suicide. This was followed in 1895 by *Haugtussa*, Garborg's great cycle of seventy poems, many of which have been set to music by Grieg, and which are permeated by his love for the landscape, traditions and folklore of Jæren. Then in 1896 came the play, *The Teacher* (*Læraren*) which shows that Garborg was not finished with religious matters, but was finding his way to a more socially-oriented Christianity. This was a theme he was to follow in his remaining works, which are also characterised by a lyricism that was impossible in the Christiania novels.

Though Garborg lived till 1924 his literary output dwindled at the begining of the twentieth century, after which time he worked as a translator into New Norwegian of such important works as Goethe's *Faust* and *The Odyssey*. He also kept a diary, which after his death was published in six volumes. Here he writes about his daily life in his winter home Labraaten outside Oslo and his summer home Knudaheio near to his childhood home in Jæren. The diary also shows him still grappling with the issues he had grappled with all his life, politics, culture, religion, the relationship between the need for national identity and wider sympathies. The fact that he received the Norwegian Government's Stipend for Artists from 1898 till his death says something about the respect in which he, and his work for New Norwegian culture, were held.

Translator's Note

By far the greatest challenge in this novel was the word *bonde*, which also makes up the first element of the original title, *Bondestudentar*. Meaning everything from poor peasant to wealthy farmer or estate owner, one has to judge from context, and one's knowledge of Norwegian history and geography how to translate the term. Not only that, one has to know the attitude of the character using the word and whether they are using it derogatively or with pride; if the former, then it has seemed best to translate *bonde* as 'peasant' and if the latter as 'farmer'.

Another challenge was posed by Garborg's irony. Though Garborg presents his protagonist in a largely ironic light, it was not always easy to determine how far he was being ironic in his treatment of some of his other characters, and here it seemed best to err on the side of caution and not overdo it.

The human aspect of the novel is timeless, but even so to this translator it seemed wisest to stick to English vocabulary that was in use in the second half of the nineteenth century.

Finally a modern translator can only be grateful for the Internet and the information it gives one access to. Even so finding information on certain nineteenth-century institutions and practises mentioned in this novel, so that one could understand them before trying to translate them was at times a time-consuming task. It was, however, also one of the challenges that made the translation of this novel enjoyable.

MW

1

'You who rise early – And sit late of an evening – With sorrow, toil and lack of faith – You would make yourself rich; – With grief you eat the bitter bread – Though God gives his children both food and clothes – While they so sweetly sle-ep.' Thus they sang at Ole Johannes Sørbraut's one raw, cold morning in April.*

Prayers were held every day in this house, for Ole Johannes was in his way a godly man. He was not one of the pietists,* and no matter how often he tried to achieve a change of heart he felt he had never managed it; so it would have to wait till he was old and had more time. Nevertheless he thought it best to abide by God's word as much as possible, so he held prayers every morning, which the whole household had to attend.

First they sang a hymn, then Ole Johannes read the prayer for the day from the prayer book, and sometimes also a passage from *The Treasure Chest*,* for Ole Johannes was good at reading. Finally he said The Lord's Prayer and 'The Lord bless you and keep you'. It was not always the case that the Kingo hymn fitted with the reading from *The Treasure Chest*, but that did not matter, for it was all God's word, and it always did one good to hear God's word.

Today, however, it so happened that the hymn and the reading went well together. They were both to the effect that you should not worry about food and clothing; Our Lord himself would take care of all such things. Did not God care for the fowls of the air which sow not, and the lilies of the field, which neither toil nor spin, and were not we much more than they? At the end *The Treasure Chest* recalled the widow in Zarephath and the quail in the wilderness, and spoke stern words about the lack of faith which meant that instead of trusting in God, we toiled and fretted about these wretched worldly things, as if it was we who could make the grass grow and the seed swell.

Little Daniel, who was now a boy of thirteen, liked both the hymn and the reading, and just wished that they could now live accordingly. But when the prayer was read, and Ole Johannes took both Lias, his eldest son, and Reinert, the farmboy, and Daniel out into the raw, cold weather to start the cycle of spring tasks, then ugh-h, Daniel could not help thinking that this was a strange way to live according to God's word.

It was blowing and sleeting, so it was really nasty to be working outside. Daniel thought about his warm bed, and about the living area at home, which his mother had probably now swept and got warm, so that it was cosy to be there. If only these grown-ups had the sense to believe what was stated so plainly in the book! Little Daniel was both amazed and annoyed. He decided that he would ask his father about this. Did people think it was *fun* to slave away like this! Or wasn't what it said in the book true? Oh, he could ask so many questions about this, he thought. But whenever he was about to, he felt shy, and today things nearly went as they usually did, that when he thought of saying or asking something, almost nothing came of it. But as Daniel stood there shivering and freezing and feeling really wretched, Ole Johannes stopped just by him with the plough when no one else was within earshot. So Daniel screwed up his courage, turned his back on his father, made a show of rubbing his arms and shivering, and said, 'It's beastly out here today'. 'Ye-s,' commented Ole Johannes, 'but if we want food for another year, then we had better be out here'. – 'Yes, but ... why does it say in the book ... what we read today?' stammered Daniel; he prodded his wooden clog with his manure fork – it felt very strange to come out with such questions. Ole Johannes was lost in wonder, even almost afraid. How could the boy come up with such things? Finally he said, as he flicked the reins over the old horses to get them moving again, 'Get along there! It says in the book, my boy, that ... get along there! Get a move on ... that if any would not work, neither should he eat. Don't you know

The Making of Daniel Braut

that? Get along there!' The horses heaved themselves slowly and reluctantly into their harness again, pulled and hauled and finally got going, as they stumbled, weak and wretched in the early spring. And Ole Johannnes staggered off behind the plough as he thought to himself, 'there's certainly a good head on that boy; he's almost too good to be a farmer'.

But Daniel was left standing, crestfallen and small, wondering how it was that the grown-ups were always right. –

– The spring cycle of work was finally finished; now it was to be school for the three to four weeks between that and haymaking. Ole Johannes did not like this school period in the middle of the early summer, for they could use the young boys at home then. And it cannot be denied that he hinted that Daniel might skip school this year. But at this Daniel was beside himself. School was the best thing he knew. When he was there he did not have to work. He could play in his Sunday clothes with his friends, and in class he held his own, so that he was happy there too. He had to go to school! So he went to his mother and whined and pleaded, and as usual Mari had to risk her arm for her boy. She managed to get what she wanted, because she knew how to get round her old man. 'You can see that the boy has a good head on his shoulders,' she said, 'and that he's bent on book learning too. Who knows what might become of him if he gets some knowledge?' – 'Oh, he's better off sticking to the station and position Our Lord has set him in,' replied Ole Johannes curtly. 'Yes, but we've seen so many of that sort,' replied Mari. 'Just look at the son of Jo Kleppe who became a clergyman! – I know we can't aim that high, but who knows what might happen.' – 'You speak as you have the wits to,' commented Ole Johannes. 'But if the boy absolutely wants to go to school, then as I see it he'd better go.' If Mari was happy at this, Daniel was even happier.

It was good to be at school. When the school came to the farm* it was made clean and warm indoors, and the schoolteacher was kind; he only beat those who got up to mischief, and Daniel was never one of those – nor Judith either. It must be splendid to be a schoolteacher. He could be indoors all day, dry and warm, and dressed in his Sunday best – and respected by all as an exceptional person. He got good food too, and school was not much more than play compared to having to trudge about in the soil. Daniel often thought to himself: if only he could be a schoolteacher!

At school one day he heard a description of work that he took note of. They were being given an explanation of the Fall, and in this it was made clear that work was a result of sin. If there had been no sin, we would not have had to work. Certainly Adam and Eve had had to work in the Garden of Eden too in a way; the Bible stated that they were placed in the Garden to *cultivate* it and watch over it. But before the Fall, work had been just like play or fun, because then nature had been so well disposed towards mankind that work went of its own accord and yielded the richest fruits for almost nothing. After the Fall, on the other hand, nature had become so contrary and difficult that it did nothing but resist mankind; work was now a burdensome servitude with sweat and toil, and even so the earth yielded so little that we could only just live off it. This Daniel thought he understood. Work was a punishment! It was like when they put bad people in the workhouse. Oh, that rogue, Adam, who for a single apple had brought all this servitude down on us; and he who had had a whole garden full of apples and cherries, so that he could eat as many as he wanted!

But, continued the teacher, should we not say that God was stern when he punished us in this way? Was it not mean of God to lay so heavy a burden on us? Daniel knew that he must not say that God did anything that was mean; he answered wholeheartedly 'no,' though he did in fact wonder how the teacher would explain this. But it turned out that the teacher here, as elsewhere, was able to explain it. No, said the teacher, it was not mean of God. On the contrary! After the Fall we needed to work, sweat and toil, because otherwise sin would gain too much power over us. There was an old saying that the devil finds work for idle hands; and wasn't that true? – Yes, – yes, it was true. If we did not have this burden laid on us, the devil would fill us with evil thoughts and tempt us to everything that was evil, to the extent that life on earth would be intolerable. At the end the teacher explained that even though work was in fact a curse, it was nonetheless a blessing. Daniel felt himself very small when faced with all this wisdom; there was probably also no point in ordinary people having ideas about anything.

He almost feared for himself because he had so little wish to work, for then the devil must easily be able to get him in his power. But before he knew where he was, he was given consolation against this anxiety. It was not just work with the hands that was work, said the teacher, far from it. 'What do you think about the clergyman? Doesn't he work?' Daniel replied 'yes,' as he knew he should. And the answer was correct. The clergyman, the tax collector, the magistrate, the district governor, in reality they all worked just as hard as us, and sometimes more so. 'And which do you think is the hardest: manual work or mental work?' Several pupils slipped up here. But Daniel knew what the teacher wanted, and answered loud and clear, 'Mental work is the hardest'. And the teacher agreed with Daniel, and even made fun of the others who had answered so thoughtlessly. They should just try using their heads like the clergyman, then they would soon feel it. Anyone who tried to sit up both day and night and read in learned books and study foreign languages, indeed even read the Bible in the original, he would soon break out in a sweat, the teacher said, and this work told much more on one's health.

Daniel was amazed, but happy too. Now he knew that he could be both a schoolteacher and a clergyman for that matter, and that the devil would not be able to get him in his power for idling. On the contrary, in fact!

He understood about work now. It was manual labour that was imposed on us as a punishment; but the work of the bigwigs, that was elevated and grand, and in addition led to prosperity. And when later, one Sunday in Church, he heard the verse of the hymn, 'Though God gives his children both food and clothes –While they may sweetly sle-ep', then he understood at once that it was the clergy and the important people whom God considered 'his children' and to whom he gave food and clothing while they lay asleep. Oh, if only he could join their ranks! If only he could become a schoolteacher!

The family at Sørbraut was not an old one; they could not trace it further back than to Ole Johannes's grandfather. But he was said to have been a strange character. He had been in the king's service, and when he came home he had become so clever that he believed he could invent a watch mechanism that would go by itself. This he did not manage, but he was said to have made many strange contrivances. His son was called Dagfinn, and he was the one Daniel was named after; he had been a treasure hunter. He had grubbed in whatever mounds there were on the farm, but had found nothing beyond some old scrap metal. And he had never bothered about the farm. Then came Ole Johannes. He had been a schoolteacher in his youth, and was considered a wise man, but quiet and unassuming in his ways. But he was a labourer as stolid as a thrall; and the word was that he had worked so hard that the farm was almost debt-free. He had three sons. The eldest, Elias – Lias as he was usually called, was a heavy boor of a man, but a toiler like his father; the next, Jeremias had gone to sea and does not concern this story; after Jeremias came a daughter, Naomi, who 'had been so fortunate as to die'; then came Judith, and then Daniel. He was thought to resemble old Dagfinn, for people said he had a good head on his shoulders; he 'was the cleverest in the house'. It wasn't just that he could read and write and do arithmetic, 'but he was so devilishly good at giving profound answers; it was almost as if he were the son of the clergyman'. But he had no desire to work; 'most of all he seemed to want to be a treasure hunter like the one he was named after'.

But even greater dreams were growing in Daniel.

The most splendid and glorious thing in the world was something that seemed like a great shining pyramid of power and splendour, which rose in the country from the sheriff and teacher, through the clergyman and tax collector, the magistrate and district governor, higher and higher, more and more resplendent, right up to the king, who stood right at the top and was clothed from head to toe in gold. Those who belonged in this pyramid were great and powerful, and fine and wise; but those who did not were like the children of Israel in Egypt, when they prepared the camp for King Pharaoh. Just to look at these servants of the king in all their splendour seemed to Daniel like a church holiday. As they stepped before the gaping crowd in their splendid clothes, straight and tall, with gleaming, polished boots, with snow-white collars and cuffs, with shining glasses over severe faces, and with gold chains and gold rings both here and there, they seemed to Daniel like a heavenly and wonderful apparition that he never tired of looking at. And how humbly people stood when these high and mighty ones appeared, and how bent and small even the wealthiest farmer became when he so much as had to speak to one of the their clerks. These were fellows who had power. And how elegantly they spoke! It was an elevated language; the very word of God in comparison to our heavy, slow peasant tongue. And how learned and wise they were. When they spoke to you, it was simply a matter of being quick to understand and quick to agree. The bigwigs liked it when people understood them immediately and said 'yes' at once, because then they did not have to repeat themselves. And if you had a different opinion, then you should never be so stupid as to utter it while they could hear; no, with the servants of the king it was important to be careful, for they did not bear the sword in vain as it said in the Catechism. That was one of the first things you had to learn, that you must never contradict an important person. And what it was like to visit these people! Daniel had been with his father to the vicarage a couple of times, so he knew. It was so clean and fine that you had to believe they washed the floor every day. The tables and chairs were made of a wood that shone, and there were flowers on the windowsills as beautiful as those in Paradise, and curtains as light and white as the evening clouds in the sky. On the walls there were pictures that were so completely different from the ones of the Virgin Mary and the Emperor Nicholas they had at home that there was no comparison. And there were shiny brass knockers on the doors, and glass cabinets with red, blue and gilded books, and a strange, large instrument that they tinkled on so beautifully that you could almost cry. Then there was the white marble head on a shelf, and so many, many fine things that he did not know the name of, and over the whole there was an air of something pure and mild and heavenly, a fine scent which he could not explain, and a gentle, soft caressing warmth that did not oppress you, or make you feel sleepy ... oh, oh; it was beyond words.

All this built itself up in Daniel's mind till it became a heaven on earth, which he scarcely dared dream that he could reach, but which he dreamt of all the same. The older he became, the more he thought that if there was a way, then he had to get out of the thralldom, away from the wooden clogs, the homespun breeches and the low, dark farmhouse. Oh, if only he were an adult!

The district was full of reports about the son of Jo Kleppe from Berg parish who had been to Christiania and 'studied his way to the priesthood'. He had struggled for many years before anything came of it, for it was said to be a tough course. Time and again he had to sit his examinations, and sometimes they went well, and sometimes not. He had sometimes been on the verge of madness, but he had persisted and had won out in the end, 'and now' thus ended the saga 'he is clergyman in the north and earns perhaps six hundred daler* a year'. That was Ashpot* who had won the kingdom; for Daniel it was like sound of the lur* that enticed you into a fairytale land.

Could something like that happen to him? Theological college was frighteningly expensive. Even a farmer as rich as Jo Kleppe had become a beggar because he had spent so much money on his son. And Daniel knew that his father, poor fellow, was not a rich man.

But more and more he dreamt of theological college. Who knows, God moves in mysterious ways. And if he really wanted it, help and guidance could come.

The local folk too helped him to dream. 'That boy could go on to great things,' he occasionally heard someone say... 'if only there was someone who would support him at school.' Great things! That had to mean becoming a clergyman. –

– A year ago, they had got a new chaplain in the parish; he was called Hirsch and came from the east. He was said to be such a

The Making of Daniel Braut

kind man, this Hirsch. When Daniel attended confirmation class, he was taught by him.*

There was something special about this man. In Christiania he had become involved with people who had led him into a completely new way of thinking. From them he had learnt something which the official classes had never known about before: 'belief in the people' and in particular belief in the farmers.

It was the farmers who possessed all the untapped energy of the land. It was in the farmers that the unexpressed ideas that were to raise up the new Norway lay dormant. Now Hirsch had come to a farming district. And even though in reality he thought that the farmers looked different from how he had imagined them, he nevertheless constantly dreamt of the spiritual energy that he believed he would find here.

Hirsch soon noticed Daniel. He liked the strongly-built boy with the placid, good-natured face, and in particular he liked his eyes. These eyes looked at you with such a gentle and trusting gaze; Hirsch was sure that it was intelligence that lay dreaming in them.

And to his great delight it became clear that the boy had talent. It was not just that he learnt things off pat, but he understood what he read, and had such a sure instinct for finding the correct answer. With growing excitement the chaplain followed the boy in his reading, and at last he was sure that this was one of those with untapped energy. He asked Daniel's teacher about him, and heard from him and other sensible people that he was a talented boy. Hirsch was as happy as if he had struck gold, and he determined that he would try to set free the latent energy. It would be a great deed. A single man who emerged strong and healthy from the mass of the people would be able to achieve more than the rest of us in the national task of regeneration. That was what, with God's help, we should see here.

After Daniel had been confirmed the chaplain got hold of his father one Sunday after church, and talked as persuasively as he could to Ole Johannes: this boy had to be helped on his way. Ole Johannes was so pleased about this that the colour rose to his old cheeks. But presumably this would be very expensive? The chaplain replied that he would teach the boy himself as far as he could, and that this would cost nothing. Then the eyes of Ole Johannes Sørbraut shone. Furthermore the chaplain said that he would speak to the sexton, so that Daniel could attend the school run by the sexton without paying. That was really very kind of the chaplain, said Ole Johannes, really inordinately kind; ... but wasn't the chaplain afraid that it could be dangerous for the boy to acquire so much worldly knowledge? No, the chaplain was of the opinion that a lot of knowledge was good for a man. It was *little* and *false* knowledge that gave people airs. Yes ... well, the chaplain presumably knew what was best. But did the chaplain think there was a chance that the boy could ... go *that* far? Yes, the chaplain thought he could go *far*. At last he grew tired of this farmer's inane objections and doubts, and said that he did not think Ole Johannes ought to set himself against this, when he saw so clearly that it was God's will; he should bear in mind that Our Lord perhaps had greater plans for the boy than he could understand. When Ole Johannes heard this, he gave in. The offer was so good that in reality he could not reject it. So Ole Johannes went home both proud and uneasy about what had been decided that day. But the chaplain was as pleased as a conqueror. It would be a glorious task to cultivate the spirit and mind of such a child of nature.

Daniel was as if drunk with joy. He went about laughing for a whole day. To think that such things could happen! That he, who was only a poor peasant-farmer's son, could be so fortunate! Oh, God bless chaplain Hirsch; he would never forget chaplain Hirsch; no, never.

One day later in the week old Ole Johannes shuffled off out into the parish to borrow some daler for school books. It was as if a solemn mood had descended on the whole house. But in the district they spoke with amazement, but mostly with a sneer, of this Sørbraut boy who thought himself so clever that he wanted to become a clergyman.

2

If chaplain Hirsch was delighted that he had discovered an example of the latent energy of the farming community he was no less pleased that he could now try out his new method.

For he knew it was a good one. It was the natural one. The one all the masters in the art of education had used. He would not stuff the boy full of letters; he would teach him the wisdom of life; cultivate his heart as well as his mind; teach him to recognize and love the life of the spirit. An uncorrupted child of nature, fostered in this manner, must surely grow to be something exceptional.

Daniel came to the chaplain in an eager but nervous state of mind. He expected a list of homework tasks as long as the church wall and questioning on them as stern as on the day of judgement. But then he was told that they should not worry about homework. And instead of questioning, the chaplain began to tell stories. He did no so much as ask Daniel to 'pay attention' so that he could 'remember it next time'. Daniel was puzzled. Could such things lead to learning and a degree?

Ah well, the chaplain presumably knew best, and knew what he was doing. This was perhaps the way fine people did things; they probably did not have to bother about slaving over homework and such things.

But when the chaplain one day said that the method he was using was *not* the regular Latin-school* method, Daniel became uneasy. He stared wide-eyed at this man who dared to go his own way and who believed himself to be wiser than both deans and bishops. Daniel would really have preferred to have been taught in the same way as a normal Latin-school boy, and he would have felt more secure if he had known that they were proceeding in the prescribed manner. But you could not say such things to the chaplain. He settled down and looked at his teacher with eyes that said, 'you know best; do with me as you think fit'.

It was the sagas that the chaplain embarked on in the first lessons. Each time Daniel brought his German grammar with him and placed it on the table in front of him like a silent prayer, for as long as he had not learnt German, he was no cleverer than any other peasant-farmer. But the chaplain let the German grammar lie there.

On the other hand he told him all the more about our ancient forefathers, and especially about the beliefs of these forefathers. They rose up before Daniel in a shining row, these mighty Norse gods, whose existence he had never known about before now. God after radiant god they rose, first three in number, then twelve – and the goddesses too, large and beautiful, with shining hair, golden tears, countenances as bright as the dawn, and eyes as clear as the pale stars. And Odin sat high up in Hlidskjalv with his ravens and looked out over the world and knew everything. But Thor drove around the heavens and slew the giants with his hammer. Balder was the gentle light god who dealt fairly with all, but who had to die on account of Loki's cunning and go down to Hel. Freyr was the god of good harvests and a mighty lord, who gave away his good sword for the love of a giant-maiden. Daniel had never heard such things; he sat and listened till he forgot his German grammar and everything else. He gazed at his teacher with eyes as gentle and trusting as the eyes of a child or a dog.

They were, thought the chaplain, a strange pair of eyes. There was something about them which for a long time he could not put into words. But finally he understood: they revealed such a gift for *faith*. And was it not precisely this gift that was needed by the age? Exhausted and sick it lay gasping for faith like a fish on land gasping for air. Through its poetry it cried out for will and faith. If it were to be saved it had to be by someone who had kept his childlike faith. The farmers had done that. The Lord had dealt so well with his people in Norway that when faith had died in the upper classes, then the lower classes could step forward and save it. It was this more than anything that made the farmers our hope for the future. All great gifts were of little worth without a strong, wholehearted faith, but with it the farmers, rich in inner resources as they otherwise were, would build the new Norway.

The chaplain carried on a long time with the 'old Nordic religion', for in that the spirit of our people was most clearly and strongly revealed, and it was through that that the spirit of the Norsemen would be woken again. And he saw that it was growing in this young mind. It was strange, it was invigorating, to see how easily this young lad recognized himself in the mental world of his forefathers.

But Daniel was lost in wonder at all the wisdom that our forefathers had laid down in their religion. He went home from these lessons lost in deep Old Norse dreams and thought to himself that these old Norsemen must have been very different fellows from the weaklings nowadays.

But one day when he told his mother what he was learning with the chaplain, she was alarmed and asked if the chaplain wanted to turn him into a heathen. He had to explain everything persuasively and at great length before she calmed down, and he never spoke of the 'the great gods' at home again. But the less he spoke, the more he dreamed.

Now and again Ole Johannes asked if he was learning much German. This put Daniel on the spot, but he hit on saying that there was a great deal you had to learn before you could start German, and Ole Johannes let himself be content with that. In the same way Daniel managed when the locals asked him the same question. If anyone wanted to know what you had to learn before you could begin German, then Daniel replied that it was 'grammar and such things', for he knew that no one would understand that.

What they dealt with most apart from the sagas was 'the mother tongue'. Here too the chaplain refused to follow the Latin-school method. They were not to 'cram grammar'. Daniel could pick up the essentials of that as they went along; it was the content, the thought, the spirit that it was important to get hold of.

According to the chaplain the treasury of great, stimulating ideas that we Norwegians had in our 'Nordic skaldic tradition'* was so rich that when we fully took possession of it, we could manage without borrowing from Germany or Rome. And when he began to go through 'the skalds' with the boy, they found spirit enough. Mostly they went through the sagas. Later writers such as Holberg* and Wessel* were quickly dealt with, even though the chaplain praised them highly, but they immersed themselves all the more in Oehlenschläger* and Grundtvig*. Daniel, who up till now had not read anything other than prayers, sermons, and *Holger Danskes Chronicle*,* was lost in wonder; could ordinary people write such deep things? But then he was told that the skalds were not ordinary people. They were inspired. Daniel thought that was reasonable.

Later they read more modern Norwegian writers and the most inspired of these was Bjørnson.* But Daniel was happiest when they reached the folktales and legends. Here the chaplain managed to find so much spirit that the whole world came alive: the mountains stood and thought and the forest told stories from the folktales; the sea sighed in long swelling waves and sang about eternal things. Far up the hillside the *hulder** blew on her lur; the little people held dances in mounds and crags; the water sprite sat under the waterfall and played his fiddle so that everything wept, and out on the pale moonless sea the beautiful mermaid lay and lured and sang till young sailors fell heart-sick with love. It must be strange to be a skald and to be able to hear such things.

Gradually Daniel absorbed all the dream-rich wisdom that his teacher lived on.

He learnt that all was not well with the country at this time. The people slumbered; they lay in a trance; they were caught in an enchantment; they had sunk into something bad and ugly which the chaplain called materialism, so that they no longer knew about spirit. And so long as this was the case, no Pentecostal wind could blow life into the dead bones lying around across the country.

Blind and confused the people grubbed in the soil, and thought only about what to put on the table. They had no vision of what true human life was, no higher ideals, no sense or feeling for the great and noble things in life; only this slave mentality for whatever filled the pot and the purse, this narrow-minded preoccupation with what was 'useful'; the chaplain had a tendency to snort when he said the word. Dull concern for one's daily bread lay like a curse over the land; it turned people into thralls, into animals; the people lay as if bewitched, smeared with troll poison under the power of Loki. It was necessary to ring the church bells to free the people from the enchantment. The spirit of the Norsemen from our forefathers' time must rise up, great deeds, stories, songs must waken the people to new life. And through all this a strong, apostolic Christian faith must glow like an engendering life force, so that hymn and folksong, saga and faith, the divine and the popular could ring out together whole and true. Then the spirit would again spread its wings; then Norway would be reborn.

Daniel thought that he understood this. Wasn't it the same that he himself had thought, even if he had not seen it so clearly or found such words for it? He felt truly happy. Never had he gazed at his teacher with more trusting eyes, and never had the teacher been more certain that here in this student there glowed a holy fire, which one day would blaze forth in song or deed to the delight of the country.

Half a year passed, but then the chaplain could no longer postpone the German. But they were not to study this in the dull Latin-school manner either, for according to the chaplain the Latin-school was on the whole a sad, empty place. It was not a school for youth; it was a school for cold rationalism, and hostility to everything that had life in it. That is why we could also unfortunately see that so many of the king's officials were on the side of the materialists in the great cultural battle. This, Daniel could not understand. Could wealthy and learned people be materialists? Well, they could if the chaplain said so. And he would have to be glad that he had been led along a better path; on the other hand he would not exactly have been averse to doing homework.

They did not pay much attention to German grammar. They began instead with a reader; the rules they would have to learn through using the language. The chaplain read aloud and translated, and Daniel did the same after him. It went well. If Daniel could not remember a word, he remembered the content and he quickly learnt to guess the meaning of many words; those that cropped up often, he learnt. Daniel thought it was going well.

The chaplain thought the same. He was pleased both with the boy and with the method; in this way life would enter into the German language itself. And he wrote in a pedagogical journal about how well things were going with the new method.

Just as the teacher was happy with the method, Daniel was happy that he could at last tell everyone that he was learning German. He paid particular attention to the words and phrases he could make use of; those he learnt so that he could have something to defend himself with at home, and something to show off with in the school run by the sexton.

At school he was considered quite a fellow, and he thrived there, among other reasons because he liked Inga Holm, the sexton's daughter. Inga was a round, sweet little thing, with a good, kind face and attractive manners. Her eyes were dreamily half closed, and bathed in a gentle sleepy gaze. It was strange how light and welcoming the school-room became when she entered. There was something special about her that Daniel never saw in the others; everything she did, if she so much as moved a finger, was so modest, so innocent, so beautiful to look at. But her eyes were like glimpses of the sun. Should she happen to look towards him he became warm, and a strange, sweet and uneasy feeling stirred in his breast. Daniel dreamt often of those eyes and when the chaplain told of Idun or Freya, then Daniel always thought of Inga. Little by little he began to wonder – and blushed scarlet at the thought – whether he perhaps loved Inga Holm?

After a while they had to start with Latin. This was not part of the method, but the time had come when the chaplain had to get on with it.

Daniel was proud. He knew that it was Latin that separated the learned from the ignorant; Latin was the narrow path that led from the everyday crowd to the heaven of the mind; no one could be a great man who did not know Latin; and now he was to learn Latin.

The next day, with Cæsar's *Bellum Gallicum* tucked respectfully under his arm, he set off for the chaplain's house.

But when he got there, he was told that the old Romans had been a nation of robbers, that the Roman literary heritage was an uninspired imitation of the Greek; that it was unnatural and pointless for us northerners to study Latin. This, Daniel could not understand. But if the chaplain said so, then it must be true, though he would have to wait till he was older to understand it.

It was, however, not long before he realised that the chaplain was right. Latin was in all ways so very much the opposite of everything we were used to, so absolutely contrary to our way of thinking that he had never seen the like. In the first place the *words* were so unreasonable. That a land should be called *terra* and a town *urbs*, made no sense. Here there was no point in trying to guess; you had quite simply to learn every single word. But the sentences were even worse. They were so tangled, and the words were thrown together in such a chaotic manner that it was almost impossible to separate them again. The predicate could come first in the sentence, and the subject could come somewhere halfway down the page; and sometimes there *was* no subject. He'd never seen anything like it! And then the grammar! Here you *had* to study the grammar. Here the method was of no use. To bring life into what was lifeless was hopeless, as the chaplain said. It was important to read with understanding; Daniel was not to cram. But he certainly had 'to look at' the grammar, and constantly at that. And Latin grammar looked pretty forbidding. Four declensions and six cases! And two to three exceptions to every rule, and then exceptions to every exception again, and so on and on. Daniel felt completely despondent.

Nor was there much life in what they were meant to read either. Daniel had expected deep thoughts and high visions, and wonderful stories of a totally new sort, but what he found were ordinary, dry everyday descriptions of some small wars and battles between Romans and barbarians in Gaul. What was so special about them? Daniel had read much better descriptions of war in *The Common Man's Companion*.*

So there was much hard work and little progress as far as Latin was concerned. But the chaplain did not worry too much about that. That this peasant lad and child of nature did so badly in Latin was surely just a sign of how contrary to our Nordic spirit the Roman manner was. And he comforted Daniel by saying that he would learn enough Latin to pass his matriculation examinations. It was not worth throwing away too much of one's youth on something that did not enrich, but rather distorted, our Nordic spirit.

To begin with things would have to progress as well they could. What Daniel learned most from were stories. The chaplain was a good story-teller, and Daniel paid attention. This was easy, and easy to remember, and if he forgot anything it was simply a matter of looking it up in the book.

And then he learnt to dream. He dreamt of the *hulder* and about Inga Holm and the two became more and more one. He dreamt of all the great and good things he would do when he became a student or a clergyman. From the skalds and the chaplain he learnt that the dreams of youth were amongst the greatest things in life. No one could really be a man if he had not dreamt in his youth. And when the chaplain told Daniel about student life, he usually said that it was the bold dreams of youth that gave this life its special quality. Happiness, songs, banter, good companionship were all part of student life, but every student in whom there was the stuff of manhood carried secretly within him beautiful dreams that gave happiness a tinge of seriousness, and play a meaning.

– So Daniel dreamed, and thought that he had the stuff of manhood in him because he dreamed; things would have to go as well as they could with his appetite for study. But if he lived high on dreams and in the bright uplifting hours at the chaplain's, he found it harder and harder to endure life at home.

There it was crowded and cramped. So dismal and dead. Everything revolved around getting food on the table. And the place was not cared for; there was no order in anything. They did not even keep things reasonably clean, and the window was hardly ever opened, so the air stank as you might expect. Nor did people bother to keep themselves clean; if they washed every Sunday, that was as far as it went. Except for religious matters, there was no thought for anything beyond the struggle for one's daily bread. They had no vision of human life. He was so alone here. He had no one to talk to. The only one could have been Judith, but what could she understand? And Lias ... well he was a dull boor who would give more for a bushel of potatoes than for all Daniel's spirit and skaldic poetry. Life here was not to be endured.

If he said anything about this sloppiness, they made fun of him. Sometimes his father became angry when the boy came along with his 'airs and graces'. Did he think he was somebody already? – The pig did not need to be very big before it grew a curl in its tail! Going off to school every day with a white collar round his neck, and so brushed and combed as if he had forgotten who he was. And if he lent his hand to however small a job, then he immediately had to dash into the kitchen to wash! Hmm, things would come to a pretty pass here in the countryside if we were all to start fussing like that.

Daniel grew angry when he heard such things, and sometimes answered back. Once at dusk he came in and found the living area full of a terrible smell. It had rained during the day, and wet clothes were hanging all round the stove, and were steaming like a kettle. 'Ugh,' said Daniel and huffed and puffed, and went over to the window, which he wanted to open even though it was blowing and raining slightly outside. He started banging and beating on the window, for it was not one of those that opened easily, and he had assumed he was alone indoors. Over in the curtained-off bed, however, lay the old man who heard and saw everything, and began to fume with anger, 'What on earth d'you think you're doing?' he hissed. Daniel jumped, but composed himself: he just wanted to open the window a bit – it was so stuffy in here. Ole Johannes remained silent for moment, he was seething and wanted to find a word that would really bite. 'So. That's meant to be *refined*, I suppose,' he said. Daniel was angry and replied that whether it was refined or not, he wanted fresh air! The old man shook with fury as he lay there. 'Huhh, just listen to him! Fresh air! Just listen! Perhaps you think I want this foul weather and cold wind in bed with me when I'm trying to sleep?' – 'If you're trying to sleep, it does you even less good to lie in this stink,' replied Daniel, and began to bang on the window again, but not as hard. Despite this, it yielded, and he left it ajar and took to his heels, while the old man lay in bed seething with fury. Then the wind caught the window and flung it wide open. Trembling, the old man crawled out of bed and slammed it shut with such a furious bang that if Daniel had been anywhere in the house he would have heard it.

After that day Ole Johannes maintained a stony silence for a long time, though to Mari he hinted that he did not think all this learning was good for Daniel. Mari understood what was behind all this and went immediately to Daniel. She begged him to remember what all this schooling was costing his father. It was not surprising if the old man felt a bit sore; *he* was the one who was forking out the money, and that was the thanks he got for it. Oh, this money, muttered Daniel. Had it amounted to much so far? Wasn't the chaplain giving him private tuition for free? *He* wasn't worried about the money, to which Mari replied that it would be shameful to let the chaplain work for absolutely nothing. They had to give him a quarter sheep or a wooden pot of butter once in a while, and be extra generous when the collection came round at the major festivals. It was the same with the sexton, so when everything was added up, including what Daniel himself needed, then it did amount to something all the same. Indeed, Ole Johannes had borrowed quite a bit in the course of the past year. Daniel felt as if he were caught in a deep bog. *Only* food bills and thoughts about food; pettiness and poverty through and through. He went out. He had to have air. How could he stand it?

But later, he did not dare do anything but be good. He adapted himself to the ways of the house, and behaved as well as he could when his father was looking. Ole Johannes smiled to himself and thought, 'that will do you good, my boy. There's no point in you getting grand too soon'. But Daniel did not like this game. He almost hated this dull slave of the soil, who could not understand a jot of anything that was elevated and noble on earth, and he went around and humming the classic verse about longing from Bjørnson's *Arne*:

> I want to fly away, so far, far away
>   Over mountain and hill top
> Here I'm so terribly trapped and at bay
> Though my courage stands as proud as a treetop.

But when his brother, Lias heard this, the dull boor said that 'Mr Daniel' could count himself lucky if he was never worse off than he was at home.

3

It was the second winter of Daniel's lessons with the chaplain.

But not much came of their time together. Hirsch had got into a dispute with the pietists who accused him of not preaching the true doctrine, and this gave him so much else to think about that he more and more forgot Daniel. Besides there was little more he could plant in this young soul and he had lost much of his early enthusiasm. Furthermore he finally understood that he could not get any further with his 'method', and not only that, but perhaps he had been wrong to make this poor boy a guinea-pig for his experiments in the art of education.

Round about Christmas word got round the district that the chaplain had applied to leave the parish. People said that he was probably tired of being here, and besides he would need a bigger parish, as he was about to be married.

Daniel did not want to believe this. It would be unforgivable of the chaplain to abandon him now, having helped him this far along the road already. And surely he was not a materialist, who could leave such a noble task because he could earn a few daler more a year somewhere else? But the rumour became more and more certain, until finally they heard that the chaplain had been called to another parish.

At this Daniel felt very depressed. He felt all vistas were closing in, and that all his hopes were tumbling to the ground like birds shot in the wing. He had sometimes dreamt that he was buried alive; now he felt that that dream had come true. He could not understand it. Was it defensible to lift a soul so high, and then let it sink into the ground again? –

– People said that Hirsch's fiancée was called Miss Rud, and that she was the daughter of a wealthy farmer in Eastern Norway. Later in the spring he would go there to get married, but then return to sort out his affairs before moving.

But Daniel's last lesson came sooner than expected. It was as if everything in him shrivelled up when he understood that this was the end. 'But you must not be despondent,' said the chaplain, 'I will take steps to make sure that one way or another you can carry on your lessons'. At this Daniel brightened. The chaplain saw it and smiled, 'You thought perhaps that I would abandon you?' he said. 'No, no,' stammered the boy.

When the chaplain returned from Christiania in the summer, Henning Massmann, the clergyman's son came with him. He had recently completed his studies and graduated from university, and was now coming home to rest for the summer till he got a post.

Massmann was a calm, taciturn fellow with a pale face, and seemed very serious. People could not make him out, because he was studying to become neither a clergyman, nor a doctor, nor a lawyer. The only thing they knew was that he had read 'an awful lot of languages', and that he was said to be 'terribly learned'. It was arranged that Daniel was to go to 'Mr Massman BA' for lessons over the summer and into the autumn.

Daniel was not particularly happy about this, for he was afraid of Massmann. Furthermore he was afraid of the vicarage. He remembered how elegant and sort of solemn it was there, and he had an almost holy respect for the old vicar. And it wasn't just that, he had even more respect for the vicar's dog. But he did go and realised he would have to be grateful that he could. He managed to get past the dog with his skin intact, and past the vicar too. Then he came to 'Mr Massmann BA', who sat calm and pale in a rocking chair reading a book and smoking a pipe.

Daniel bowed, blushed and was nervous. Massmann looked at him with icy blue eyes through cold, polished glasses: 'So, you are Daniel?' Yes, that was so. 'Good, sit here,' said Massmann, and pointed to a chair. Then came the questions. What had he read? Daniel answered as well as he could, but the whole time felt ill at ease and unhappy because he could not see whether Massmann was satisfied with his answers or not. Then came the

Latin test. As he sat there Daniel wished himself six feet under the ground and began to sweat.

'Right, Book II. Turn to ... turn to ... Chapter 18. You have presumably read Chapter 18?' – Yes, Daniel thought so, but it was a long time ago. With trembling, sweaty hands he found the place. 'Good, read on!' – Daniel read. '*Loci natura erat hæc, quem locum nostri castrisi delegerant.*' – 'Good, now translate!' – Daniel knew that he could not translate it. He could not remember a word. All the same he made it look as if he was trying. But he got nowhere. He just sat and struggled and groaned while his hands and feet moved restlessly, as did his whole body. He was up against a brick wall. It was awful. What would Mr Massmann think? 'All right,' he said, 'the subject is – ?' Daniel guessed. '*Natura*,' he replied, but when Massmann did not say 'yes,' he thought it was wrong and corrected himself: 'No, *loci*,' he said. 'Is *loci* also the subject?' asked Massmann. 'No,' whispered Daniel. 'No, certainly not,' replied Massmann. 'The subject is *natura*, and *natura* means – ?' – 'Nature' – 'Yes, of course. So what is *loci natura*?' A vague memory crossed Daniel's mind, and guessing, he answered, 'the grove – ? Nature in the grove – ,' to which Massmann made no answer, so Daniel thought it was wrong. 'No,' he whispered aloud. 'No,' confirmed Massmann with such infinite calm that Daniel went cold. 'What sort of word is *loci*? What is the nominative?' – 'Lo-cus?' Daniel was guessing. 'What does *locus* mean?' – '*Locus* – , it's the ... the same as – .' 'Hmm. Is it the same as *lucus*?' – 'No.' – 'What is *lucus*?' – '*Lucus* – , *lucus* – – .' – '*Lucus* is grove. But *locus*?' Daniel scratched behind his ear, '*locus* is – ... *locus* – hmm!' '*Locus* is place. Which case is *loci*?' – 'It's ... dative – ? – No ... it's the genitive – ?' – 'Hmm, listen here my boy,' said Massmann, 'have you studied grammar?' 'Yes, a bit ... but it's a while ago now,' said Daniel, who was dripping with perspiration. 'Yes, that's for certain,' said Massmann. 'Well, we'd better start with grammar!' And Daniel got the first and second declensions as homework.

Like a dog with its tail between its legs, Daniel slunk home. He felt so very small. This was an altogether different story.

Shivers ran through him as he thought about his new teacher. With him it was not a matter of the spirit and skaldic poetry, it was a matter of knowing one's stuff, and this hung over Daniel like a black cloud. But then he remembered that he had *homework*. An honest, proper piece of homework that he had to learn. It was strange how the thought reinvigorated him.

Now he knew what he had to do. He knew where he was with a piece of homework; a piece of homework was something he could manage! And the next time he went to Massmann, the learned man would get quite a different impression of him. He almost ran home, and began his homework at once. He was over the moon that he had homework, and realised with joy that he would finally master this grammar, which had always seemed to him so hopeless. He would be as good as a Latin-school boy as far as knowing his Madvig's *Latin Grammar* was concerned.

He set to work with a vengeance. Read and read, till the two declensions tripped off his tongue like a dance. The next time he went to Massmann he was not afraid; he had done his homework. And the hour went well. He came home quite proud; he had won. Grammar was perhaps not so lifeless as he had thought. He cast aside his dreams of the *hulder* and water-sprites, now he wanted to be learned. Learned and serious like Mr Massmann BA.

If only it hadn't been for the vicar's dog! All too often the courage of his young heart failed when he was faced with it. Each time he came or went, the large, black beast with its smouldering, red eyes came slinking up to him and would sniff him as if he were a ham bone. It was no joke dealing with it. Stories circulated round the district about people who had come off worse in meetings with it. It had bitten a piece out of the leg of a cotter who had come to the vicarage late one night and was suspected of having stolen something. Several people had complained to the vicar about the animal, but the vicar always replied that Apollo did not bite honest people. Once, however, it had attacked a man who had come to the vicarage to pay his annual dues of half a bushel of barley. The poor man had been on the list of debtors for a long time and the vicar had been after him for this half bushel both in church and in other places. Now at last he was going to make good and pay up. He had even sold a cow in order to pay the vicar and what he owed to a bank. In the bank he had been able to hand over the money without difficulty, but when he came to the vicarage he was attacked by the dog, so that he had to escape as fast as he could, and with torn breeches into the bargain.

After this the vicar had become angry and chained the dog up. But the dog did not like being chained and stood howling and whining all day long. The vicar could not stand listening to it, and eventually pronounced that this was 'unchristian cruelty to animals' and set it free. After that it wandered around as before, and whoever came to the vicarage had to manage as best they could. The only consolation was that it never bit 'honest folk'. Nevertheless Daniel was afraid. He could never be certain who a dog like that considered to be honest folk.

Things settled down, however, as Apollo got to know Daniel and he could finally come and go in the vicarage as he pleased. And it cannot be denied that Daniel was proud that the vicar's dog had finally accepted him into the noble ranks of honest folk who were not to be bothered. The vicar's dog certainly knew how to choose its people!

Strangely enough Massmann did not like this dog – he did not like dogs at all. It was a crude custom, he said, a remnant of our barbarian past, to allow such tamed, or half-tamed wolves to wander around one's property in order to scare the wits out of nervous fellow Christians; and least of all would he expect such barbarity on vicarage land. The old vicar just muttered that he could not be bothered with such 'modern ideas'.

During hay-making Daniel had to be at home, but in the autumn he and Massmann set to work again, and it went well. Daniel was happy, he felt that he was *learning* something, and Massmann was an energetic teacher who taught with enthusiasm. But just as everything was going smoothly Apollo got in the way.

It was during a tutorial hour with Massmann; Daniel was sitting at the middle of the table and could see out over the whole vicarage lawn. It was then that he saw a woman making her way towards the house in a very odd fashion. She was one of the district poor, wretchedly clad, and somewhat advanced in years. At her heels was Apollo looking very fierce and now and again tugging at her skirt. She was pitiably afraid. She did not dare to walk fast, and even less did she dare to stop or turn, so she proceeded with short, stiff, unsteady steps as if in a daze. She kept on looking around for help, but there was no one anywhere. She was alone with the dog. Daniel saw how she grew paler with every step, her mouth open, her eyes standing out large and white in her head. She looked as if she was about to faint, as if she did not know where to place her feet.

Massmann could see from Daniel that something was going on; he looked out. Then his book fell to the floor as he dashed to the door, then out through the sitting-room, the passage and the outer door. Outside, he first rescued the woman and brought her in, and then when Apollo came creeping up to him and fawning, wanting to show his master what a fine fellow he was because he had been so clever, Massmann brought out a large stick that he had been hiding behind his back and lay into the dog so that it was sent tumbling far across the grass, yelping as if it was being burnt alive. It was hideous to hear. Howling and yelping, with its tail between its legs and its back arched it ran round trying to escape with Massmann after it. – Then the vicar came out. 'Henning!' he shouted. 'Henning?' and Henning who saw that he could not reach the dog, turned to his father. His hair had fallen over his forehead and ears, and his face was white. As he stood there in front of the vicar, straight and angry, trembling with fury, he was beautiful. 'Ah, so there you are, father,' he said, and went on, 'if that dog's not chained up, I will kill it.' Daniel could not hear any more.

When Massmann came in again he was out of sorts, and Daniel had to leave. Soon after he heard that Massmann had got a post in Christiania.

Daniel was not too upset by this. He felt sure things would sort themselves out and that the new chaplain would be coming soon. As for his father, he was keener on seeing that Daniel be trained for the church than Daniel had realized, so Daniel understood that he no longer need be afraid.

– Yes, this slave of the soil wanted his son to become a clergyman. He spoke several times to Massmann about Daniel, and Massmann was encouraging. The boy learns *easily*, he said, and is doing remarkably well. But he has to go to school. With private lessons he will never get anywhere, as you can see, and he will never finish. – How far could he go? – Well; he could become a good servant of the state; one ... of the sort they want. 'Send him to the crammer in Christiania known as 'The Factory',* Ole Johannes!'

When Ole Johannes heard what 'The Factory' was, he thought this was not a bad piece of advice. But when he talked to Mari about it, she said 'no,' straight out. Advise the young boy to go alone as far as Christiania,* where he could come into contact with both Free Masons and other such dangers, that was something they would never get her to agree to! If he was to go anywhere, then they could send him to the Latin-school in town. Otherwise he could stay at home, now as before, and go to the new chaplain when *he* came.

The new chaplain came. He was a short, rosy-faced fellow with fair hair and a red beard. The first thing he did was to become acquainted with the pietists. When Ole Johannes spoke to him about Daniel, he answered briskly that he would write to the headmaster of the Latin-school and get all the necessary information; as for himself, he regretted that he would be so busy with the congregation that he would not have time for 'private tuition'.

Ole Johannes thanked him. If the chaplain could also ask about the cost and how long he would need to attend this school, that would be kind. But – and here Ole Johannes yet again raised his old and troubling doubts – ; did the chaplain *believe* that it was worthwhile giving the boy such advanced schooling? *Was* it possible for a simple farmer's son to go so far? The chaplain smiled and said that Norway had farmers' sons who had become *bishops*. At that Ole Johannes was silent. But great dreams drifted across his vision; nothing ventured, nothing gained...

From the headmaster they got 'all the necessary information'. Daniel could maybe get into the third form in the Latin-school, so he could perhaps manage to complete in three years, and the fees were not high. Furthermore there was the possibility of a free place when the boy had been at the school for a year. This Ole Johannes did not think was too bad either. In particular he liked the thought of the free place, and if the boy lived with Hans Nerstad, and if the family contributed most of what he needed as food, surely it would not be that much more expensive. Mari agreed. They would have to borrow the money; that went without saying. But the boy would have to pay it back when he got a government position.

So the end of it was that Ole Johannes went to the wholesale merchant at Neset, Jens at Larsebakken, or Jens Bakke as he called himself, and borrowed 100 daler, so that he could send his son to the school in town. And now Daniel felt he had won.

For one thing he was going to get away, and for another he was going to get to town. He had not been there many times, though he had been often enough to know what town was. With its high towers, its beautiful houses in long, shining rows, its wonderful shops full of all sorts of grand things, with its gardens and trees, with its proud, elegant people who hurried along the streets in gold and silk and shiny shoes, and who knew of neither toil nor any care worth mentioning, the town seemed to Daniel to resemble the new Jerusalem. But the approach to town seemed like Paradise. Large, white, imposing houses with entrance porches resting on white pillars, and overgrown with foliage, with light, magnificent rooms gleaming with crystal and gold like Solomon's Temple, and round them large shady gardens and hedges and sturdy wrought iron fences overshadowed by strange trees, large and wondrous like the cedars of Lebanon ... Daniel could not imagine anything more beautiful. Everything was different from the way it was at home. Things were strange, wonderful, magnificent, and only there to be beautiful. You could see that people there did not need to think about money. They had the wealth of Solomon, and they were rebuilding the glory of King Solomon.

And now he was to stay in town. Not for one day, not for two days, but for years, and he would himself become a town boy.

Smartly dressed, he would wander the streets every day, kicking the cobblestones and looking at the finery and the hubbub and the life and the stylish shops, and in the harbour the large ships with sails as wide as a field of oats, and masts as high as church towers. And he would eat town food, and walk on white floors with rugs and sit on sofas as soft as beds, and he would hear music and drum-beats during the day and the chant of the night watchman at night; he would see monkeys dancing on hurdy-gurdies and bears doing tricks at Svabbesalen dancehall, and tightrope walkers and magicians who ate fire and swallowed sabres and swords. He would get involved in unimaginably many grand things; now at last life was beginning; he was the happiest peasant-boy on earth.

No, not the happiest, because now he would not be able to be in Nes church every Sunday to see Inga Holm. But when he was a town-boy, it would be all the more splendid to come home once in a while and to appear in church before her and all the ordinary folk.

He hardly dared to look his peers in the eye any longer. He felt like a traitor towards them, because he alone was going to experience all this. They must not think that he was snooty, but the fact of the matter was that he did not belong among these peasants any longer. From the autumn he was to become a town gent, well-dressed and well-spoken; then he would be a different person.

Word of this got round the district. Daniel thought that people looked at him differently from before. And they did too. On the farms the gossip spread like wildfire, and Ole Johannes Sørbraut was so picked over, and his conduct so laid bare and analysed, that if he had heard even the half of it, he would have gone mad –

– Daniel arrived in town, and took up lodging with Hans Nerstad. But it appeared that he could not start any higher than in the second Latin form. This meant a year was lost. And even in the second form Daniel had his work cut out to catch up.

He also had other problems to deal with. His 'classmates' who saw that he was a mild-mannered boy, began to make fun of the 'peasant clodhopper' who spoke 'country dialect', and in the end they even began to make fun of his name.

He had been entered in the register as 'Daniel Olsen Sørbrød'.* It went without saying that he was called 'sourdough'. And the louts thought this joke was so good that at break-time they gathered round him and asked for 'sourdough'. How much does sourdough cost today?

Daniel was a grown lad, kind and patient, but this affected him so deeply that he almost wept. Had he done them any wrong? Couldn't they leave him alone? But this only made things worse. Daniel had thought it would be a great thing to get to know town boys, but he had never been so unhappy. It was as if, wherever he turned, he was stung by nettles and pricked by thorns.

Finally there was one boy who took pity on him and advised him to go to the headmaster to get his name changed. Since his name was Daniel Olsen, then he could be called 'Olsen' and that would be the end of the 'sourdough' nonsense. Daniel replied that if it were possible, he would like that, but it was so difficult to go to the headmaster alone. 'Well, if that's what you feel, I'll come with you,' replied the other. They went, and Daniel got what he wanted. From now, before God and the law, his name would be Daniel Olsen. But also from that day Daniel and Christian Bliland were friends. The friendship was all the stronger because they were both farmers' sons, for Christian was the son of a sexton in one of the mountain districts.

Getting a friend helped. And when the others saw that Daniel was no longer alone, but was under the protection of Christian Bliland, a boy who was not to be trifled with, they increasingly left him in peace.

But Daniel was never really happy in this school, and there was homework and revision all the time. Instead of going and kicking his heels on the streets he had to sit at home in his tiny room at Hans Nerstad's and study. All he had there was an old wooden chair with four legs and a rickety old kitchen table, and on the wall a picture of Karl Johan looking towards the door with a sour expression and an enormously long nose. And what made it worse was that he did not think the town itself was as elegant as he had imagined. It was the time of the autumn rains, and the rain was as cold and the mud as wet as at home. The white houses stood wet and dirty and streaked with coal smoke, and were not the slightest bit like Paradise.

Another thing that Daniel minded as much as all this was that his town clothes were not as they should be. When he came together with other boys he could see for himself that he was a peasant clodhopper.

It was also a slow and difficult task to change the way he spoke. That was because he was living with Hans Nerstad. In other ways he was well off there. His food was well prepared and when he was not studying he could come downstairs to the warm, quiet living room where Hans's wife sat sewing the whole afternoon; or he could go down to the general store and listen to the women of the town, who had come in to buy one shilling's worth of soap and one and half shilling's worth of starch and who discussed all the town news, or the farmers who had come in from the country with potatoes and butter, and who took coffee and tobacco in exchange.

But Hans Nerstad had been a farmer. He had owned a fairly large and prosperous farm, which his father had improved, and he had inherited some money as well. But this prosperity meant that Hans Nerstad no longer wanted to be a farmer. It was easier and finer to live in town. So he sold his farm and became a townie, setting himself up with a small general shop, where he sat year after year in a dark cellar selling herring and butter by the shilling. The store did not do particularly well, and the work was boring, so it cannot be denied that he occasionally regretted selling his farm. Recently too people had noticed that he had put on weight and grown rather red round the neck and got bags under his eyes – he had presumably taken to the bottle. He was still at bottom a farmer, and his wife too; Daniel was ashamed to affect fine speech when they could hear. –

– It was difficult for Daniel to catch up where he was lagging behind; he was no good at learning anything he did not have to go over as homework. So more and more he skipped going over what they had done in class; he would have to do it when they got to 'revision'. As a result he managed more or less all right, but he had a permanently bad conscience and felt that he did not quite belong.

The one he stuck to and constantly sought out at break time was Christian Bliland. He did not talk much, but he had books he read aloud from, mainly Ole Vig's *The People's Friend* and other such things. Here Daniel found many of the same ideas that he had learnt from the chaplain. And it was as if he believed in these ideas more now that he saw that there were others who did so too, and that they could be read about in black and white.

After that he often mentioned things that the chaplain had said, and which he knew Christian would like. He did not always say where he had got such things from; sometimes he was probably not aware of it himself.

He rarely dared to mention any ideas he had come to on his own; just when he was going to share them with Christian he would usually decide they were foolish. But sometimes he expressed them as if joking, so that he could laugh them off if Christian did not accept them. If they stood the test, Daniel was proud, and later on thought they were well said.

If he had not had Christian at this time, he would probably have forgotten all his old dreams, as the school atmosphere was *not* favourable to them. This Latin school was a strange place. All the boys were so witty and grown-up, they were able to sneer and laugh at everything. But they had probably never dreamt of anything but school grades. They knew that in this world it was a matter of *getting on*, and that was the wisdom they lived by, and it was as if knowledge for its own sake did not interest them. It was just a question of what it was easy to be good at and what it was difficult to be good at, and they dealt with the problem of the latter by more or less honest means. Indeed, those who were expert at cheating were considered fine fellows, and walked around boasting of their dirty tricks. But those who were conscientious and could be trusted to do their homework were often made fun of by the leading louts in this class of cabbage-heads.

'I've not done a single line of homework for today,' they all shouted in chorus as soon as they arrived at school in the morning, and then they argued about who had done least. But when they were questioned in class, they somehow managed all the same. Daniel was both amazed and depressed at this.

Fond of school the boys were not; they talked of being in a prison with the teachers as prison guards. They liked the headmaster least of all. They also had a great deal against the man who taught religion, a dry old rationalist, who constantly ground on about the three great wise men, Moses, Jesus, Socrates. It was the same with the history teacher, who was keen on 'survey tables' and gave the boys historical nicknames; he himself was called 'Robert the Devil'. Daniel thought that all in all the teachers were not as he had imagined. Many seemed to be no more interested in knowledge than the boys were, and their main concern seemed to be to get the lessons to pass. They began late and finished as soon as they dared. And they were forever in a bad mood; it was not often that a lesson passed without mutterings and naggings. Some teachers had their regular scapegoats, whom they called up every day and tore strips off. Others seemed to want to use mockery to beat some ability and morality into the class. Daniel was afraid of these stern gentlemen. But with his peasant respect he bowed down under them, and for the most part he did his homework just about well enough to get by. It was the same with Christian Bliland, though he took things more calmly. On the whole the teachers liked these students from the country. They had grown up under more 'patriarchal conditions' and had learnt to obey and respect their betters; they had none of this *frons urbana*, this snobbishness that made the town boys so tricky to deal with. The country lads were humble and obedient, easy to keep in harness, as schoolboys should be.

But Daniel knew now that the chaplain had been right when he spoke of the Latin school. It was 'dead' and that with a vengeance. He was sometimes so fed up that he dreamt of running away. Of going to America, or to sea. Often the only thing that kept him at his studies was the thought of the district gossip, and the thought of Inga.

Once a month Ole Johannes came to town with provisions for

his son; sometimes Mari was with him. 'I can't understand what you want to come to town for,' said Ole Johannes, but Mari had to come in and see 'poor Daniel', and would not be put off. Daniel was pleased when they came, but they were terrible country bumpkins. When he walked with them in town, he preferred not to meet any of his classmates. On the other hand there was no denying that his father was coming up in the world. He had bought himself a new cart for coming to town, and it did not look bad. And what was more he came sweeping in to town in a jacket and white collar. But mother was the same as she always had been. She was presumably too old to learn new ways. Nor, indeed, did she like it when Ole Johannes spruced himself up. Once when they were in town she began in her distress to fret and complain to Daniel about the strange ways in which Ole Johannes had been trying to better himself recently. It was if he wanted to be something more than he was before, now that he had a son in town at the Latin school. Nor did he have the same desire to work as before, but went and passed his time down at Neset or elsewhere in the district and lived a high old life. At home too, he wanted to live well and bought fine bread and coffee, and subscribed to newspapers which he read for fully half the afternoon. He now had spirits in the house as well. – Spirits – ? Yes, in case someone should come. Everything had to be so grand now, you see. Mari could not see where it would all end. But Daniel rather liked it, and told his mother that it was probably nothing to worry about. Father presumably knew what he was doing, and she should not worry. Perhaps when it came to the point he was better off than anyone realized. God help us, complained Mari, it was probably all borrowed money he was floating on now. Well, said Daniel, that was not so certain. In such matters you should never trust a farmer further than you could throw him. Mari looked at her son, looked down and sighed. She understood that there was little chance of her getting any help here.

When Daniel came home at Christmas he could see for himself that things had changed in the house. And he was pleased. Visitors had come who wanted to see 'the town lad', and all were served with food and drink. It was a solemn occasion. Daniel had to read German and Latin for the visitors, and he could see how proud the old man was when they praised the boy and wondered at all the things he had learnt. But Lias, the boor, went around grumpy and curt as if he were envious of his brother.

Here in the countryside Daniel felt himself to be a fine fellow, and he displayed himself wherever he could, especially where he hoped that Inga Holm might see him. He did not actually think of talking to her, but when he believed that she was looking at him, he stood up straight and put on a manly air, and prayed to God that she would like him.

The period from Christmas to spring dragged on interminably slowly. He was so fed up with doing homework that he sometimes thought of cheating, but he was not able. He did not have the knack, or the easy conscience of the town boys, and if he were to try, the teacher would see it immediately. However, when his dislike of school got too great it happened not infrequently that he asked Hans Nerstad to write a sick-note for him.

Instead of studying he would then sit at home and dream of Inga, to whom he would send a proposal as soon as he became a student. And he wrote poetry about his great love. It was a difficult job to write verse, but it was such fun to work on something that concerned 'her'.

It was as if the whole school was afflicted with boredom at this time. The boys neglected their work, and so did the teachers too sometimes. The homework they got was so short that the boys made no progress, and still they had to go over it time and again, because none of them had done it.

In January two new boys had joined the class; one was Ole Bentsen, the son of a sheriff, the other Peter Didriksen, the son of a shop-keeper at Neset. For a time the class tried to make fun of them, but nothing came of it. These two knew how to hold their own. They stuck together, and behaved shrewdly. Ole Bentsen was as silent and indifferent as a seal, so nothing bit on him. Peter Didriksen – who was also called Peter Dirk – knew how to speak up for himself so wittily and humorously that no one could silence him. Daniel and Christian tried for a while to keep company with these two lads, because they too were country folk, but it seemed that Ole Bentsen and Peter Dirk wanted more elevated company. They were lads who knew how to look out for themselves. They were even involved in such dangerous things as card games, perhaps even a half bottle of beer and a cigarette. But they always knew how to manage so that if things were to go wrong, *they* could not get the blame. They were workhorses of the first order, but they complained that progress was so slow, and the following autumn they cancelled their enrolment in the school and travelled to Christiania – you could pass the necessary exams both more quickly and more cheaply if you went to 'The Factory,' they said.

– Finally the time drew near for the end-of-year exams. Now it was a different story. Both boys and teachers came to and livened up, in the way that sheep in a fold become restless when a storm is brewing. Books were brought out and knowledge and work were now respected. How much had *this* person read for today and how much had *that* person read? Did Per know this and did Paul know that? What did *this* word mean and what did *that* word mean? Which prepositions governed the ablative and which the accusative or the dative? Did Per know *this* proof? Could Paul construct *that* polygon? Daniel was quite alarmed by all this knowledge. He felt that he did not know anything. Nor did he have the energy to do anything more than the set homework for each day. Not until the exam period began and he knew on which day he was to sit each exam did the urge to study really grip him. At that point he really crammed.

And he passed. He did not know much, and what he did know he was shaky in, because he was not sound in the basics. But when he sat at his exam desk he managed nonetheless. He could barely understand it himself. But from childhood on he had practised watching and listening out for the answer the teacher wanted, and that was the skill he used now, even if he was not aware of it himself.

He came ninth. There were sons of tax collectors and even sons of clergymen who came below him, something he found almost unbelievable. Ole Johannes thought the same when Daniel came home and told him, and the old man could not hide the fact that he was proud of his son.

Apart from that Ole Johannes was depressed and silent again. Daniel was puzzled by this, but Mari told him that father had used up the 100 daler before he knew it, so now he just had to set about thinking of raising a new loan. It was not easy. Ole Johannes had thought that 100 daler would last forever. But when you behaved so extravagantly, well – ? Daniel squirmed. This money question was an eternal torment.

But he comforted himself with the thought that the old man had now taken things so far that he could not stop. And what did it matter if he had to take out a new loan? The farm was presumably large enough to bear both that and much else.

All the same he preferred to avoid his father. This the old man misinterpreted, believing it was the bigwig airs and graces that were showing themselves again. And this was all the more annoying now that Ole Johannes no longer considered himself a simple peasant-farmer. He had even spent money on raising himself up in the world so that his son need not be ashamed of him. One day he said this. Daniel replied as mildly as he could that this had never been his intention. But the old man said that it was easy enough to see what the intention had been, and that he had never expected such a thing from Daniel. He had, he thought, done all he could. And if Daniel thought of putting on airs, then he should remember who it was that would have to suffer for it. Daniel maintained that he would be able to repay the money when he got a position, so it was not worth worrying about now, to which the old man replied that Daniel would not be getting a post within the next few weeks. 'No, no, whoever said I would?' replied Daniel brusquely.

So then the atmosphere at home became unpleasant again as usual. And Mari moaned constantly that things were going downhill. The work was mostly done by hired hands and the farm was falling into decline. Ole Johannes was in debt to Jens at Larsebakken, so that he now had to trade nearly everything there, selling cheap and buying dear. Nor was he so constant in his reading from the Bible anymore, preferring to lie in and sleep in the morning instead of holding morning prayers. So what else could one expect except that there would be 'little blessing in the work'? Daniel no longer had anything to say.

He comforted himself with dreaming about the future and about Inga. When he became a student everything would sort itself out, and then he would offer Inga his hand and his heart. She was too fine for farm boys. And for the others she was not rich enough, so she would have to stand free like a flower on a high mountain until he could come. –

– Daniel did not get a free school place the following year as he could not provide evidence of poverty. But he got to go to school all the same, the old man could see no other way. And however much Daniel disliked being at school, it was still better than being at home at Sørbraut. Indeed, even the old man seemed to be different when he came in to town. Daniel thought it was as if he became more youthful again. He looked ruddy and healthy and had such a gleam in his eye that you hardly recognized him. Even Hans Nerstad was glad when he saw Ole Johannes looking so lively. He nodded to Daniel and laughed quietly.

But one day later in the autumn – it was a cold day late in October with driving rain – Daniel thought that the old man looked more highly coloured than seemed natural. And his eyes, rather than gleaming, had a glazed look. Daniel could not understand it. What could be the matter?

Towards evening Ole Johannes got ready to set out for home. He was paler again then and more morose, but the strange mood remained, and as he sat in his new town-cart and spoke some parting words to Hans Nerstad, Daniel saw that his eyes were staring and fixed as if he were drunk. At this a weight descended on the boy. He went up to his room and did not know what he should do with himself. He could see his father as he sat down there staring with strange eyes, and something in his chest twisted and hurt. *Could* Our Lord allow such a thing? His father had always been a decent man who had lived by the Bible. Well, at least until recently. – Yes, but all the same – No, no. Something so awful could not happen! He said it to God as well, that this *must* not happen. A burning, sore urge to cry arose in him, but he was unable to shed any tears. He sat down by the window, and there he sat for a long time with his hand under his chin, staring out into space. –

Then one day Lias came driving into town in the new town-cart to fetch the doctor. Daniel was also to accompany them home. His father was not at all well. He had come home from town frozen through, and by the look of it had fallen asleep on the load, and in his stupor had driven the wrong way, so that he had not reached home until the early hours of the morning, when they had to carry him in. He was wet through and quite stiff. And now he lay there with a burning pain in his chest and looked so wretched and poorly that he was barely recognizable. Nor did he have his wits about him any longer. He simply lay there and raged, talking nonsense about bishops and priests and much that there was neither rhyme nor reason in. There was nothing to be done about it except realize that this was the end.

Daniel fell into a deep silence. He accompanied them home, weighed down and as sick at heart as if he were going to his own funeral. This was the end of everything. And that it should happen in this wretched way!

The Doctor said it was pneumonia, and that they should have fetched him sooner, for now there was nothing to be done. He wrote out a prescription, muttered and left. Mari went in and out weeping. She was so beside herself that it was mostly Judith who had to tend the sick man. Daniel dared hardly stay inside; it was so awful to see his father lying there, withered and grey, with wild eyes and hollow, bearded cheeks and painful, wheezing breath. But it was even worse to hear his wild talk about 'the son who would become a bishop'. Mari asked Daniel with tears in her eyes whether Father had ... whether he had had ... more than he could stand ... when he was in town. Daniel went pale, but said 'no'. 'Thank God for that,' wept Mari. The red-haired chaplain came yet again wanting to talk to the sick man about the state of his soul, but there was no point. Father would wake up for a while, but soon after he was lost in his delirium again. And it was in delirium that Ole Johannes died.

So that was that for Daniel.

It emerged that the old man had got himself deeper into debt in recent years than anyone had realized. He owed most to Jens at Larsebakken. But there were small debts in various places in town and in the district. The farm was mortgaged up to the hilt.

If they were going to clear the debt, they would have to come to an agreement with Jens, who showed himself to be not unreasonable. The only thing he wanted was that Daniel should sign a paper saying that he would repay the debt – 250 daler – as soon as he got a job in the state administration, or a different post. Mari and Lias were to stand as guarantors for Daniel and themselves be responsible for the money if he died or became ill. Interest was to be five percent a year until the debt was paid off. Daniel signed immediately. He did not think it was any concern of his, and that would be the end of all the unpleasantness. Mari appointed old Tarald Ruste, who had once been a sheriff, as her financial adviser and it was agreed that she should retain possession of the farm.

There was no hidden wealth to be found. No buried treasure. No money at the bottom of the chest. If Mari and Lias could get through by hard work and by scrimping and saving, that would be as much as could be expected.

For Daniel there was nothing. They said he would have to try to get a position in a general store. He replied, 'Well, maybe.' What would he do in a general store?

He went around as if under a dark cloud. It was the end of everything. And worst of all was to think of Inga.

Inga. Inga. What would she be thinking now? He did not dare to show himself in Nes church at this time. But every Sunday as people left the church Daniel sat on a stone behind a large bush above the path and kept a look-out for her.

It *could* not go on like this. Help *had* to come. He would go under if he did not reach his goal. Could God permit a soul to perish?

There were many rich people in town. There were people who threw away thousands upon thousands on frippery and finery. It had recently said in the paper that the merchant, Helle, had bought a pleasure yacht for 500 daler. 500 daler for a pleasure yacht! With those 500 daler Daniel could have been saved.

And what about that brother of theirs who travelled round the world free as a bird, while no one knew where he was? Perhaps he was in America ... had married a wealthy woman, owned a million, would come home, sort out the whole mess...

Or what about getting hold of the troll king. Or a pixie, or a dwarf, or something of that sort ... there was wealth enough in the earth and in old burial mounds. If only you could find it. Why couldn't Old Dagfinn Sørbraut just as well have found a lump of gold? There were many who had found gold in old burial mounds.

Tarald Ruste! *He* was held to be a wealthy man What if he were to talk nicely to him?

Oh no! He was a slave of the soil, just like the others. He was even a follower of Jaabæk*. What awareness of the life of the mind and of knowledge could one expect there?

– But the Jaabækian Tarald Ruste had been thinking about the young 'student'. What Tarald Ruse thought was that it would be a shame if the money spent so far were to be wasted. Besides, the boy was said to be bright. And it would be a good thing if we could raise servants of the state from farming stock. Those we had now were so alien and knew so little about the life of the people that it was just as if they belonged to a different nation. The sons of the farmers on the other hand, they knew what the people were up against.

He had talked a little with Daniel. He seemed to be a good lad. Tarald dropped in at the farm again later and talked more with Daniel, who did not think that he, a schoolboy, could hold opinions contrary to a man like the old sheriff. It was only when Tarald touched on Jaabæk and his savings policy, and on the fact that the state officials lived far too well, that Daniel could not totally agree. But he did not want to contradict the older man either, so he said that he had been far too busy at school to keep abreast of such matters. But when he saw that Tarald Ruste was not satisfied with this answer, he quickly added that of course thrift was a good thing. 'Yes, that is certainly something you will learn to understand,' replied Tarald Ruste.

After this, Daniel believed that he might have a hope with sheriff Ruste.

And the sheriff had hopes of Daniel. He went round wondering which other people he could bring on board to help the boy on his way. In this district there was no one, apart from the clergyman, who had money, and no one went to him for help in money matters. But there were a couple of men in town whom he could perhaps try. Helle, the merchant, was a decent man in some ways, even if he did not agree with Jaabæk. There were some who doubted whether Helle was as rich as he made himself out to be, but Tarald did not doubt it. And then there was old Finsen. He had helped a boy before. That had been someone who wanted to go to the missionary school, but who knows, perhaps he could be brought on board here too. Tarald Ruste drove into town one day and talked to these men, and it went well. Helle said 'yes,' immediately, Finsen was tougher, because he had promised God that he would use all he could spare on the mission to the Zulus. But he gave in in the end. Perhaps God could incline the soul of the young farm boy so that he too would become a missionary one day. According to Finsen one would have to leave it in God's hands. So these three men agreed that they should help Daniel Braut as far as his university entry examinations. And Helle wanted them to agree to send the boy to 'The Factory' so that he could 'get finished fast'. That would be both cheaper and better, he said; it was also what Jonas Didriksen at Neset had done with his son, Peter. This the others agreed to.

So one evening, very pleased with himself, Tarald Ruste came driving to Sørbraut with the wonderful offer, and was certainly made welcome. The whole house stood on its head for him. Daniel laughed, Mari made coffee and Judith fussed over the old sheriff as if he were an old grandfather. Even Lias smiled. Mari was not too happy that Daniel was to go to Christiania, but she could not dig her heels in now. So she just asked whether it wasn't risky to send a young boy in to town, where there were said to be so many bad people, Free Masons and atheists and...

'Far from it,' replied Tarald Ruste. Far younger boys than Daniel

The Making of Daniel Braut

had been sent in to town. Besides it was just nonsense that Free Masons killed people and sent them to Turkey. There were as many decent people in Christiania as there were here. There were Latin scholars and friends of officialdom and all sorts of riffraff as well, but that need not concern Daniel. He would be all right. With that Mari had to be content.

From now on Daniel could not settle at home. It was in Christiania that he would find everything grand and noble and beautiful on earth, and the town now built itself up in his imagination like a forest of white towers. In Christiania a whole new life would begin ... but he would stay faithful to Inga Holm all his days.

At long last the great Tuesday came when he was to leave. His mother and Lias accompanied him to town and finally they were all standing on the steamship jetty. Mari was so afraid that she might have forgotten something, 'Don't you think you might need another ball of grey wool?' But Daniel assured her that he had enough grey wool. He was just waiting for the boat to come. As soon as it had moored alongside, he scrambled on board, and said farewell to his mother and brother with a heart beating with restless joy.

The ship's bell was rung for the third time, and the boat gave out a terrifying blast on its horn and began to move slowly away from the jetty. Goodbye, goodbye, could be heard all round, and white handkerchiefs began to unfurl in the air like so many small wings. But there was no one to wave to Daniel. Old Mari had no handkerchief to wave with, she had left her tiny cotton handkerchief embroidered with red roses at home. She stood at one side of the jetty far away from the fine people, biting the corner of her shawl and looking towards Daniel with red eyes. It was so hard to think that he was going so far away. She did not want to cry where strangers could see her, but she could not help it. The crying welled up in her chest like a painful warm flood, and tears pressed their way out, forced themselves hot and burning into her eyes, as she bit the trembling lips of her pinched mouth. But when the boat had finally cast off from the jetty, and she saw 'Little Daniel' standing alone on the foredeck between all those strange people who looked totally unconcerned, then she could not contain herself any longer. She turned away, put her head in her hands, and wept, wept so her worn, old shoulders shook.

4

'Olsen, Olsinis, Olsini, Olsinem, Olsen! Olsine,' Johannes Ortvedt declined the name Olsen.

Markus Olivius Markussen roared with laughter. 'That's right,' he said, 'you do Olsen according to the third declension.' He laughed again. 'Olsen, Olsinis – oh, my word, Ortvedt is a man of ideas!'

Daniel did not like having his name declined, but he joined in the laughter as well as he could. He knew there was no point in getting angry.

'And there's Olsen the Second,' shouted Markus Olivarius Markussen, who was also a man of ideas.

A tall young fellow with drooping shoulders and a long neck entered. His face was coloured with the delicate flush of consumption.

'No thanks,' he said in a bass voice that one would not have expected from such a scarecrow. 'I should give you one in the eye for that! I'm far too tall to be "Olsen the Second!"' He put his books down and pulled Daniel by the arm out onto the floor of the room where he sang in a faltering voice and with bold, dramatic gestures;

> I – am – Olsen the Mighty, Olsen the Mighty, Olsen the Mighty
> He – is – Olsen the Second, Olsen the Second, Olsen the Second —
> – And we're both very wise men.

Markus Olivarius Markussen roared with laughter. Johannes Ortvedt chuckled in accompaniment, his eyes laughed, his beard laughed, the whole man shook with laughter, for he knew that now Markussen would continue the declension game. And

Markussen did continue it. À propos, could Olsen the Mighty decline 'Olsen'? –

More and more boys came in. One by one, two by two, newly washed and pale, weary-looking, and with sleep still in their eyes. Many muttered, 'Ugh, my head feels like lead today'. And as each one came in Ortvedt's declension was repeated, and Markus Olivarius Markussen roared with laughter.

The academic quarter of an hour was soon over*, the boys entered the room in flocks. Some found their seats silently and morosely, opened their books and shut themselves in their own world; others flocked round 'Olsines' and the great declining activity. Hans Haugum entered. 'Haugum! Haugum!' the whole flock shouted together, but Olsen the Mighty had got Daniel out onto the floor and shouted to the class in his unbelievable bass voice, 'Gentlemen! Here I stand up in the parliament of chatterers and require that one and all and all as one recognize Olsen the Second of the dynasty Swineburg as my legal and illegal successor in all things – .' He did not get any further. 'Hey, about this Olsen!' said Haugum, turning to Daniel and asking if he did not have a farm name that he could use instead. Daniel remembered his old battles with 'sourdough'. Er – no, he replied, His farm name was nothing special. 'What's the farm called?' Haugum persisted. Daniel writhed, 'oh …'. 'Perhaps it's called Tamperud like the farm I'm from?' suggested Olsen the Mighty. General laughter. 'No,' Daniel smiled. He could not understand this man from Eastern Norway, who was happy to tell such things. 'Come on, let's hear it,' said Haugum, puzzled by this man from the West who was so slow on the uptake. 'The farm's called Sør-brød' said Daniel. 'Sørbrød – that's strange. Do people really *say* 'Sørbrød' over there?' 'Er – no,' he replied, 'but that's how it's written.' 'But what do people *say*?' 'People – ? They say …' 'Presumably people say Sørbraut,' Markus Olivarius interjected authoritatively. He knew his *Landsmål*.* 'Yes,' Daniel conceded, 'they do say Sørbraut.' 'Well then, the farm's called Sørbraut,' Haugum declared with finality. 'And isn't that good enough?' – 'Sørbraut?' Daniel asked with wide eyes. Yes! Sørbraut! 'Sørbraut's a good name,' declared Markus Olivarius. 'But Sørbrød – my goodness! *Søer-brøth*' – he mimicked the Danish – 'that won't do! It's too funny!' It's the Danish tax-collectors who thought that one up. '*Søer-brøth*, oh dear!' 'Sourdough,' chuckled Johannes Ortvedt. Daniel reddened, but recovered when he saw that no one had noticed.

Markus Olivarius spoke learnedly about Norwegian farm names and Danish tax-collectors, while Haugum pursued his point. Sørbraut was a good name and a Norwegian name that Daniel *should* use, 'Isn't that so, Rud?' he shouted to a newcomer who was just putting down his books. 'Is the farm called Sørbraut?' asked Rud. 'Yes?' 'Well then there's presumably a Nordbraut as well?' They looked at Daniel, 'Ye-es,' he said, 'but it's a long way from…' 'That doesn't matter,' declared Rud. 'The farm's name is Braut. And Braut's what you ought to be called.' Rud sat down. General agreement. Finally Daniel too thought that 'Daniel Braut' sounded good, and said he would use the name himself – 'if it'll do.'

'What d'you mean "if it'll do?"' the question exploded loudly with a hollow gasping sound from the 'black hole' in the corner where Aslak Fjordan had his permanent position. 'What about Don Pedro, then? Don Pedro *de* Monsen, no less, who changed his name every time he moved, so that when they came with bills for Monsen, he was called Larsen, and when bills came for Larsen, he was called Rabbestad, and if bills came for Rabbestad, then he was called Monsen again – really!' But Aslak Fjordan could get no further.

The door was flung wide, and in walked – 'The Old Man', tall and sturdy in his long blue sleeveless coat, grave as a senator, but with a roguishness twinkling in his grey-blue eyes behind their glasses, and with a high, broad, bald pate that seemed to shine with wit and wisdom. At his heels he had a line of boys who were late. They were mainly those who belonged to the 'barrel scrapings', and who were usually absent, but who came to the Latin classes, because they were 'so much fun'. The Old Man took up his position and looked at them. There was

Isak Abrahamsen Opjorden coming in his homespun coat decorated with feathers, and hair as untidy as a crow's nest. He had been drunk and had not washed and had forgotten his books. 'Are you roaming loose like an old nag in the mountains – eh!' enquired The Old Man. Then the two young gentlemen, Wall and Presler, entered, dapper and tall, with top hats, lorgnettes, cigars and canes. They raised their hats elegantly to 'rector', performed a couple of leaps over the desks and landed in their seats with thunderous aplomb. 'Oh, my goodness!' laughed The Old Man. Next came Lars Risvold, clearly a stonemason in the making, huge and square and trusty as a chopping block, with a back like a barn door, and arms like oak. Finally, there came Bernt Bruvik, shining from soap and water, poorly shaved, but decent, serious and reliable. He bowed gravely to The Old Man, but quickly realized that he was still too early.

For now the Old Man walked over and locked the door. Many a sinner jumped where he sat, for now they all remembered that it was today that the Old Man was to be paid for October.

'Well now, boys,' he began in his jokey almost tearful way, 'now you must be kind to an old man!' It was not easy being him either, he said. There were many who wanted to attend his school and learn about compound sentences and grow up, and get a thorough drubbing with Livy. 'Ah, Livy, boys?' – but then there was this small matter of shillings, wasn't there? Indeed. They had probably been as good to him as they could be, those who had anything, but by Jove, it was needed too. He was a poor old man, and today – 'D'you know what happened to me today, boys?' – Yes today, before the devil got his shoes on, The Old Man had had 'a visit', – 'A visit from two black-clothed, polite men' ... 'and you know very well, boys, what that means – to be visited by two black-clothed, polite men early in the morning? And if you don't know, then I hope you may you never have to know. *Have* you any money, boys?'

The boys laughed, and those who had money, produced it. At all the desks waistcoat pockets and purses were turned inside out and outside in. One person had two daler, another three. Some who were rich produced the full five. The Old Man snatched at everything he was given as if he were afraid they would take it from him again. But those who had nothing remained silent and looked as if they were trying to hide. Or they went up to the desk and made their excuses as best they could.

Among the latter was one who Daniel paid particular attention to because he made his excuses so well. It was Bernt Bruvik. He told a story which could well have been made up, but as he stood there, so trustworthy and thoroughly decent, with an honest face and unfaltering eyes, confident that he could carry it off – one had to take him at his word, whether one believed him or not.

Daniel envied him his ability to manage situations. But he thought most about The Old Man. If everybody could deal with money matters in the way he did, then the world would not be such a difficult place to cope with.

– The Old Man unlocked the door again. The Latin class began.

Daniel had never dreamt that Latin classes could be like this. Latin was quite simply inspiring. Indeed, even grammar came alive. It was Haugum who said, 'The Old Man's a wizard.'

Today he got hold of Presler's cane and began to 'play'. He used the cane like a bow, and with the other hand played up and down the neck of an imaginary fiddle, as if to the most elegant dance. And he sang. 'Amo – amas – amat – amamus – amatis – amant!' – The boys sang along, at least the ones who were able to remain serious, did. 'Shall we do it once more? – Come on – amo – amas – amat – amamus – amatis – amant!' But when the lads were to do it on their own – the Old Man simply sat and 'accompanied' them – they got in a muddle. 'No, now I'll have to do it again' he said, and off he went. And when that did not help either, he threw away his 'bow', seized his nose and pinching it between two fingers, recited *amo* in a voice and with a face that made the boys hoot with laughter.

He had innumerable 'tricks' and devices. But however many

he had, and however strange they might seem, he always got something out of the boys. It was a 'method' that has not existed before or since, for the method was the man, and the man was a genius. And however things did or did not turn out for his boys later – they never spoke of any man with such warmth as Old Heltberg.

For grammar they had to manage with the textbook by Madvig. 'It'll be a different story' he said, 'when I can get my glorious grammar published, a grammar that's lying at home in a sacred desk drawer, ... for then,' he prophesied in Homeric tones 'a new era will dawn in this benighted land.' They would soon have an extract of this grammar. But they managed with the grammar they were given in class. It was truly poetic grammar. Stories and images followed one another in quick succession. Stories about 'linguistic geniuses' who had come to earth and had created the languages; about prepositions which had once stood 'neatly penned in' but later broke free, so that everything became a real tower of Babel; about the word groups of which there were not ten, but three – 'For all eternity, three!' Everything was three. There was even a very clever man who went mad because he saw that everything went in threes and now this trinity was the highest philosophical truth.

The Old Man was happiest when he was interpreting the ancient writers. Then it was if he was playing with fire, and inspired jokes, pictures and comparisons flickered and sparkled as boldly and cheerfully as in a Shakespearean comedy.

Nevertheless he was truly Norwegian, and Daniel was lost in wonder at how well he could make Latin fit with our Nordic spirit. When he spoke of 'that lad Cæsar' who came and softened up the Remi and Bellovaci in Gaul, that bunch of ruffians, who were as uncivilized as the cow on the hillside, then it was as if Daniel felt himself almost too much at home.

But he could be classical too, as when he spoke of his beloved Horace, and his life on his country estate. There they lived the ideal life. Wreathed in vine leaves they lounged at tables by the bubbling spring and drank the excellent Falerno wine to the sound of the lyre.

'That's a different story to being up in Romerike and growing potatoes, isn't it, Simon Husmo?'

Today it was Livy, and it was Lars Risvold who was being tested, so the class knew there would be fun. Lars Risvold was a good lad, but he did not know anything. He was one of those local luminaries who came in to town and struggled year after year, but got nowhere, who first of all used up and wasted the little money they had on the farm, then everything that siblings and relatives could raise, and finally everything they could borrow. At home they were considered bright sparks, and had been best in the confirmation class and so had stood at the head of the line of confirmands. The majority of these ended up at the 'The Factory'.

Today Livy was talking about *Lartem Porsinnam*. 'This is something for you, Lars,' said the Old Man. What is *Lartem* in the nominative? But Lars could not manage even this. The Old Man groaned, 'It's powerful today.' – 'It' was the troll power he fought with constantly, namely 'ignorance'. 'Yes, indeed,' he added, 'it's the worst time of year for us now. When it comes down from the hills in autumn, it is fat and it bellows, but what the devil, I'm not afraid to go into the stable with it!' He straightened himself, and carried on with Livy.

But then Lars translated *consilium* as a people's gathering. The Old Man got up and out of his seat, stomping across the floor, wringing his hands and moaning, 'God help me poor wretch that I am. It's not possible for me to live in this world. Lars, if you heard that a man called Krog had come to town, and you came walking along and saw a crow sitting on a some horse droppings, would you raise your hat and say, 'Good day Mr Krog, welcome to town?' – No – 'But that's what you are doing here, Lars! You are reading crow as Krog, Lars! Remember this, Lars! *Consilium* with an 's' is not *concilium* with a 'c'. 'Oh, what a poor wretch I am. These fellows who can't learn anything! I might just as well reserve a place at the Mangelsgård workhouse right now.' And he carried on with a tearful voice and much moaning, 'What is *consilium* with 's', Lars? What is *consilium* with 's', Lars Risvold? *Consilium* with 's' is *consultation*, Lars. It is consultation, Lars. Remember that now, and don't let an old man starve to death for your sake! – But *concilium* with 'c',' he said and straightened up, 'that's a council, a gathering of the people. It's where Cicero spoke against Catiline and Cato against Carthage. Can you remember that Lars Risvold? – Now go on, sit down, Lars! Oh! Oh! Oh! Sit down and be ashamed of yourself that you could not – oh! Oh! Oh!' The Old Man got an attack of asthma and coughed as if he were going to suffocate – 'could not distinguish between – – oh! Oh! Oh!' His coughing got the better of him.

Another came forward and things went better. But when they came further down the page, where it said *nisi, quanta vi civitates libertatem expetunt, tanta regna reges defendant** then he got stuck. He attached *tanta* to *regna*. The Old Man got up again. 'Listen here, my good Halvor Mosebø! If you were walking along a street and met first a fine lady, then a student and then a pig, and shortly after that you found a fine silk parasol lying on the ground, would you take the parasol to the pig, and say: excuse me, Sir, you seem to have dropped your parasol? No, Halvor, you would not be so stupid. You would hurry off till you caught up with the lady and then you would bow and smile, and say: excuse me, miss, you seem to have dropped your parasol. That's what you would do, isn't it, Halvor. But here you are going to the pig with the parasol, you're taking *tanta* to *regna* because *regna* lies closest. But *tanta* belongs with *vi*; *quanta vi, tanta vi*, Halvor Mosebø!' – The boys laughed, but they were paying attention, and they rarely forgot such classes.

At the end The Old Man got onto the content of what 'Tarquinius Superbus or Tarquinius the Haughty' had said, and delivered a lecture on Rome and Roman politics, which was the most inspired thing Daniel had ever heard. Finally he got up, gave a flourish with his hand, and said solemnly, 'Well, now by Jove, we're done, absolutely done, and can proceed.' At that he sat down, and went through the preparation for the next day. –

– Daniel lived in a garret in Akersgata. The room was not small, but was under a low, sloping ceiling. The small windows were set in the roof, and there were nooks and crannies everywhere. The view was of a couple of roofs and some chimneys. But Daniel was happy here. The room was warm and cosy, and the limited view meant that he felt safe and well-hidden away.

He liked the town too in a way, even though it was not as he had imagined. It was small and for the most part unrelievedly grey. It was unbelievable how primitive everywhere looked, apart from up at Homansbyen. But for Daniel everything was new and therefore splendid. The only stretch of main street that the town had, the stretch from the Storting or parliament building to the Palace, was really impressive with all its shops and trees and the palace at the top like a broad wall.

He presumed that this was how a city should look, and that those who were in charge of the building project here knew how things ought to be.

The dream of gaining access to something great or wonderful slipped away remarkably quickly. There was nothing here that resembled a fairytale. People looked very normal, and if he once in a while saw an imposing carriage, then he knew that the person sitting in it was at most a wealthy merchant.

But one thing annoyed him, and that was that people were so arrogant. He felt that almost everybody, no matter who they were, was sneering at him. If he so much as went into a shop, or wanted to buy four ounces of tobacco at a tobacconist, the men and women serving were so haughty and stuck-up that he felt both shy and embarrassed. Presumably it was because he did not speak in a refined enough way yet. But that would soon get better.

The only fun he had was on a Sunday afternoon when he could join Haugum and Aslak Fjordan and wander up and down the main street, 'Karl Johan'. Then he felt free, and happy as a tomboy he would watch all the elegant people hurrying to and fro under the overhanging roofs of the houses, like fish under a river-bank. Sometimes stylish young girls – they seemed to be proper young ladies – would pass and give him such a look that it warmed the cockles of his heart. At such moments his old fairy-tale dreams could be re-awakened. But the young ladies always went their way and he never heard from them again.

For the rest it was only rarely that he could go out and loaf around, because at the Factory you were given such an insane amount of homework, that if you wanted to keep up, you had to study day and night. And it was now that Daniel learnt to smoke, it was part of the student way of life, and so for most of the time he sat in his lodgings and read, smoked and read till his head throbbed. It was tough but it was manly. Now he could really feel that he was studying. He wrote home proudly that he was studying so hard that it was on the verge of making him ill.

From his friends of old, Daniel had Ole Bentsen and Peter Dirk, but they were now in the final year. Peter Dirk was much the same as before, conscientious and quietly funny. But Ole Bentsen had become religious since coming in to town. According to Johannes Ortvedt he had ended up living at a devout shoemaker's, 'and when he realized that he need pay only half the rent if he became a devout Christian, he naturally converted'. Daniel could see that Ole Bentsen had acquired a different manner. His quiet, fleshy face had stiffened and tautened and tried to look serious, and his small, cold, grey eyes struggled to look loving. Furthermore Daniel soon understood that Ole Bentsen was harbouring thoughts of converting him too. This was a nuisance. Daniel could not convert till he had tasted the ideal life of a student. But he dare not admit that he thought like this, and so was thoroughly uncomfortable when Ole Bentsen tried to tell him that he should give a thought to the state of his soul. Finally Bentsen understood that Daniel had got into the clutches of Hans Haugum, and he gave up. Daniel was delighted.

– The winter was long and the homework hard. You could read both night and day, and still have no hope of keeping up. Daniel grew weary. Oh, that everything in life should be so difficult! In fact studying was just the same as all toil – it was a punishment for our sins.

After a while he began to notice the teachers with whom you could 'take it easy', and so with them he took it easy. Did not

The Making of Daniel Braut

revise what the students had been told to revise and stayed away from those teachers' classes. If others could do this, so could he. He comforted himself with the fact that he had to.

Taken together, the group Daniel had joined was an odd assortment of like and unlike.

The majority were the sons of farmers and ordinary people, but amongst them one could spot the sons of the well-to-do, who had been expelled from the Latin school, or who for other reasons found it convenient to 'take the direct route' to their matriculation exam. Here green, young sixteen-year-olds sat alongside mature-bearded fellows and thirty-year-old bald pates. Worthy school teachers sat beside happy-go-lucky seamen, and religious men such as Ole Bentsen had to sit together with drunkards and mad-caps, who were perhaps doing nothing more than drifting around looking for fun. If you looked at the group as whole, it had a somewhat lost and cowed air about it, an expression of labour and toil, of bad days or drunkenness. Many went around poorly dressed, with dirty collars and cuffs, with trousers worn at the heel, and with crooked shoes and crazy hats. Over by the stove a fellow was sitting with his winter coat on, even though the stove was glowing red. The point was that he had a hole in his pants in a place ... where one should not have a hole in one's pants, and it could not be hidden in any other way. Many looked as if they were not getting enough to eat, and those who tried to keep up seemed wrapped in a perpetual fog, so that heavy and weary from overwork and sitting up into the small hours, they did not look quite themselves. The longer the winter continued, the more slowly things went. There was less and less of high spirits and joking. The 'communal spirit' of the class, which had never been strong, died away and the group split into small groups, while those who did not belong to any group, shuffled along on their own.

What they talked about most was what they had least of: money. 'Oh, if only one had some coins in one's pocket,' was the refrain that rang from morning to evening. But if they got onto 'the big questions', politics, nationality, faith, they could get involved and the discussion could become heated. From the start they had split into several camps: there were radicals and liberals, there were 'Norwegians' and 'Ultra Norwegians', there were cosmopolitans and champions of *Landsmål*. In addition to these there was a group of those who had no opinions, who 'were not interested in politics'. There were similar divisions of opinion in matters of faith: there were Grundtvigians*, mainly among those from the teachers' training colleges, while Jens Rud and a few others were considered by some to be 'neo-rationalists'.

But in the final-year class there were even said to be people who did not believe in anything. With such people things would have to take their course. It was not easy. They came to town, young and ignorant, lost their childhood faith and had nothing to put in its place, and could not always stand the loss. You could hear various stories like that. Haugum told of a certain Rødberg who had really gone to the dogs. Ortvedt thought the example of poor Olai Juberg was even worse. He was a right case. He had looked so calm and composed that you would have thought he was a real Mummy's boy, but the calmest waters hide the ugliest trolls. Now he wandered around bald and with a haggard face, and was said to be totally destroyed. Daniel grew afraid when he heard such things, and sent a secret plea up to God that this should not happen to him.

Of his classmates, it was Haugum whom he came to like best. He was a fully-grown man, and had been a schoolteacher for some years. He was involved in everything to do with the 'democratic revival'. In his group Daniel found again much that he had learnt from chaplain Hirsch, and which in fact was still alive in him. But he did not dare show any enthusiasm for his faith in the people, because neither the capitalist Finsen nor the merchant Helle would like it if they were to hear about it in some way.

The majority of those at the school were people who had had to borrow money or who had received help. It was only the occasional person who was paying for himself – Haugum, for example, had saved up a little from his years as a schoolteacher

– or who had a rich father to support him like Jens Rud. The majority lived in a state of poverty, 'some on four daler a month, some on nothing' as it was said. Daniel gained such respect for these 'masters in the art of starving' that it almost became a form of envy. He gradually began to understand that it was not only fun to be indebted, even if it was to good people.

Some of those who 'lived on loans' had a less than good reputation, and sometimes took the wrong road. Now and again they even became completely rotten – good-for-nothings who would go to the clergymen and other kind people and boast and lie, and then squander what they were given. Among several who had more or less come adrift, Rødberg in particular was mentioned.

All agreed that it was best if you could manage by yourself. The only thing was that you tended to be rather old before you reached your goal, and that it was often rather hard on your health. –

– If Haugum was the leader of the democrats, one could say with even more certainty that Jens Rud was the leader of the radicals. For a long time Daniel thought that Rud was a clergyman's son. He did not look like the son of a peasant-farmer. There was nothing broad and sturdy about him, and his face especially was far too refined and his mouth too shapely. Finally Daniel learnt that Jens Rud was the son of a well-to-do farmer from Romerike in the east. And yet he was a radical. And what's more, a champion of *Landsmål*!

Among Rud's flock was Halvor Mosebø, a small round-shouldered fellow from Telemark with a sallow face, a nose like a saddle and a pair of dark grey, melancholy eyes, which seemed tiny under the heavy, baggy eyelids, but which sometimes could have a twinkle in the corner, for Halvor Mosebø was a bright spark. Daniel took against him because he knew more history than he himself did, but it led to Daniel starting to study history again. Then there was Per Brageland, known as 'Sven Dufva',* a tall, stoop-necked fellow with two clear, frightened gazelle eyes, trusting and kind – a 'work horse', or one of the ants who toiled away in silence, in silence toiled away, chewed their way through book after book, through exam after exam till they were called to a parish up north or in the west somewhere, because they were so old, or because they had a wife and family to provide for. Jens Rud had once said of Per Brageland that 'he had a poor head, but a good heart' and from that day he was called Sven Dufva. Last but not least, Markus Olivarius Markussen was counted as one of Rud's flock, mainly because he was a *Landsmål* man. He was a broad-shouldered, fair-haired fellow from Trøndelag, energetic and quick-witted, with many interests and quick to laugh, a lively soul. He and Halvor Mosebø shared lodgings and 'argued and laughed, and argued and drank beer' and as far as possible kept their spirits up.

According to Haugum, the drunkards were mainly to be found among those who did not belong to any group, and who had no opinions. Isak Abrahamsen Opjorden was one of them, and eventually he was taken home from school. Olsen the Mighty and Simon Husmo also had their 'beer bouts', but it was only once in a while. Bernt Bruvik, who 'was always of the same opinion as the person he was talking to,' chased after every serving girl he saw, and every time he caught one the rumour was that 'he was absent from school for eight days'. –

– Every so often Daniel received a letter from Tarald Ruste telling him to save. Because what was saved, was saved, and the country was poor and the king's officials lived far too well. Lias wrote only very occasionally and to say that everything was fine, but that he could barely manage. Nobody wrote about the one thing Daniel cared about: Inga. Twice Daniel wrote to Judith trying to get her to tell him how things were at the sexton's, but the dim-wit did not understand what he meant.

Daniel got only just enough money to manage on. Sometimes the money did not arrive in time, and then Daniel had to borrow. But it was not a problem, for he knew that he could repay. And he was always saved. Fellows from Eastern Norway were the easiest to ask for such things. Those from Western Norway were more cautious.

One day Jens Rud came to him with a greeting from chaplain

Hirsch. Daniel blushed. 'Do you know Hirsch?' he asked. 'Yes, he's married to my sister,' replied Jens. 'Oh, really...?' – But Daniel felt fortified by this greeting and promised himself that he would not forget his old teacher.

Spring came later here than at home. Things began to get lighter in March, with warm sunshine and clear skies, but then in April winter returned, and when that was over and the ground began to warm up, then May came with a northerly wind which went on and on. Then finally June came – June with its white sun and its dense heat haze over the fjord and the hills. And overnight summer opened like a flower. But then it got too hot again. In town it was like a baker's oven; you could hardly breathe.

When Daniel had longed for the holiday month till he was weary of longing, the holiday month finally came. Then it was as if they had all been blown away, all the strange creatures at Heltberg's Factory. And Daniel did not linger either. It would be strange to come home as a Christiania man. –

– Inga Holm was paler now and more grown up, but no less sweet. The expression of mild longing, the air of gentle dreaminess still enveloped her like a bewitching veil. But why was she so pale, this lovely young girl? Was she unhappy? Did she harbour a yearning for which there were no words? Could she not sleep at night because she was thinking of her friend? Daniel felt his breast fill with sweet sensations at the thought that perhaps it was for him that she was secretly wasting away. But ... what if there was another? And wasn't that quite likely? Immediately everything became cold and grey and empty around Daniel. And in his breast it was equally cold and grey and empty, with small burning stabs of pain.

When he went to church he sat in the schoolteacher's pew as a sign that he had now risen above the ordinary people. And he sat there and, at a distance, put on airs for Inga Holm as he had done in days gone by. Then one day something unexpected and wonderful happened: when the service was over, the old sexton, Holm, came over to Daniel and invited him home to dinner. Daniel was delighted and blushed scarlet. 'Thank you ... thank you,' he said. Could it be Inga Holm herself who – ? With a trembling heart and together with one of the oldest schoolteachers he followed the old sexton home.

Old Holm was pleased with Daniel. As far as he could judge the boy was what he had always been – apart from in the way he spoke, of course. He had retained the sound principles he had from home, and he had not become conceited. He agreed with the sexton in everything; and Old Holm was almost proud to have such agreement from a man who could soon be considered educated.

For the most part Mons, the schoolteacher, remained silent. Only now and again would he enter the conversation with a little question about something that for a long time he had been wanting to ask informed people about. Daniel replied graciously both about things he knew about, and those he did not, and Holm the sexton and Mons the schoolteacher were lost in wonder at his wisdom. But it was mainly Hans Haugum's wisdom that Daniel was presenting them with.

He grew silent as they approached the sexton's house. Everything was so strange. Everything shone as if it were a mirage, everything he looked at seemed to stare back at him and say thanks for everything – or it pulled a face at him. Only an old hen strutted around and cackled and puffed herself up and said clearly time and again: suitor? Suitor? Suitor?

Daniel blushed and grew hot, but got inside, and greeted Inga's mother. That went reasonably well. Greeted Inga. That went badly. He could not see her clearly, a mist descended in front of his eyes, or rather he could not open them. But the worst of it was that he could not say anything. He stood there like a great dumb oaf. It was infuriating.

But at table when he had downed a glass of beer, he became bolder. Talked of this and that, reported and concocted, borrowed and lied. Only one thing mattered: that Inga should find what he said entertaining. But to his own ears what he said sounded like a vacuous noise.

After dinner there were pipes for the men. Now it turned out to be a good thing that he had learnt to smoke, and he remained sitting at the sexton's till long after the time for the evening round on the farm. Inga was sitting in such a way that he could not see her from his rocking chair, but he could feel that she was in the house, and it was so comfortable here. He had never seen such a cosy room. And such a garden and such flowers, with leaves that trembled in the summer breeze like a sweet whisper, were surely not to be found elsewhere on this earth.

Later Daniel had to make other visits. He had to go to the sheriff's, and there he had to show himself to be quite a Jaabækian. There was nothing else for it; sheriff Ruste had been so good to him. And the following Sunday he had to go to the wholesale merchant's. That was worse. There there was a dinner party, and he had to sit in a place where everyone could see him. And he was shown off. 'Hmm, our protégé,' announced Helle, 'we give him a bit of support. Want to help him on his way, you see. He's only a peasant boy, but according to the headmaster he has talent. No manners, as you can see, but they will come!' – Daniel was sweating. And things did not get any better when one of the guests who wanted to be 'pleasant' began to praise the merchant for his good deed, and to exhort Daniel to be grateful to such a 'beneficent' man. Daniel lost all his appetite. For the rest of the meal he sat and picked at his food, and listened with half an ear to a clergyman and a clerk who sat condemning Jaabæk, and complaining how difficult things were for the king's officials.

As soon as they got up from table, Daniel wanted to escape, but he was not able to do so. He was obliged to 'please stay and have coffee'. Besides, the merchant added, it would do him good to be in elegant company so that he could learn how to conduct himself. Daniel had to 'participate'. Helle had a use for his protégé. He was asked about both this and that, and when they got onto the subject of politics, the same 'pleasant' guest, pastor Ring, said that he hoped Daniel was not a Jaabækian. Daniel 'had not thought much about politics', and pastor Ring said that was good. Helle too was of the opinion that youth ought to stay away from such things. 'But he's certainly not a Jaabækian,' Helle added with a smile, 'that much faith I have in the boy!' –

At Finsen's things were different. Finsen was not concerned about politics. But he wanted to know whether Daniel had found his Saviour, and that was not an easy question to wriggle out of. Finally he got a long rigmarole about seeking your Creator in your youth. And then Finsen came out with his question: couldn't Daniel consider missionary work? 'Not, dear friend, that I want to put any pressure on you,' said Finsen – but that he could help him much more gladly if the Lord inclined him towards missionary work. Would it not be a great and beautiful thing to be involved in building Christ's church in the land of the Zulus? Would it not be a blessed task to take the message of salvation out into the world that still lay in darkness and in the shadow of death? – Daniel was in a real corner. Then he suddenly had a thought that saved him: 'Mother would not let me,' he said, and with that he escaped. And he thought he had managed well. His mother thought the same when he told her later on. –

– When he had been back in Christiania for some time in the autumn he heard that the merchant Helle had lost his money. Daniel was puzzled – but not unhappy. At least he was quit that guardian. But when shortly after that he received a letter from the sheriff saying that hereafter he would have to manage on less money than before, his happiness cooled.

At school everything went on as before, but four of the boys had left: Wall, Presler, Simon Husmo and Bernt Bruvik. The last-mentioned had, they said, married the daughter of a wealthy butcher and was to become a merchant. But two new boys had joined, two who had sat their exams the previous year and failed. One was called Gregus Johnsen; he was a long, thin fellow who, they said, was a poet. He had even written verse for *The Post*. The other was old Wonderboy. His real name was Underby, but he was widely known and had been rechristened, because for 'almost a generation' he had 'been in Christiania and failed his matriculation exams'. But however many times he failed, and however badly things went, he stuck it out and stuck it out, with a tenacity one could only wonder at. Now he was well on in years, so for fun they said that he had a son who was a student and who during the exam period had private tuition from his father, who 'wanted to help his son on his way'. It was common belief that Wonderboy would end up like the Wandering Jew and fail his matriculation exams for all eternity. –

– A new servant girl arrived in the house. She was from Western Norway and was called Berta Maria. She was a respectable girl, good-natured and kind, with a face as soft and round and as gentle and alluring as a pancake. Daniel looked at this girl and liked her. He did not dare speak to her, but he liked to look at her. Soon he was thinking of her even when he could not see her.

He wanted nothing from her. But if he had had some of Bernt Bruvik's cunning, then he would have got to know her in all decency and propriety, for then life in his lodgings would have been much more cosy. But he did not have any of Bernt Bruvik's cunning. He did not dare so much as to offer Berta Maria a theatre ticket.

But all the same, he was pleased that she was there, and in the end he thought almost as much about her as he thought about Inga. But it was in a different way, for Berta Maria was only a servant girl and Inga Holm was the ideal. Nevertheless he was surprised that she was so often in his thoughts.

– It was impossible for Daniel to manage on the money he received, and he began to run up small debts. Also next summer he would need new clothes. He wrote to the sheriff about this, but got no reply. Finally a letter came, but it was from Finsen, who wrote that God in his mercy had called the sheriff home to Him, and Finsen dared to say that the old man had passed away in peace. He did not doubt that his soul had been saved, and for that all of them, and not least Daniel, should thank God.

Yes, Daniel could go along with that. But what was going to happen about his new clothes? Finsen did not write a word about that. On the contrary he wrote that he was now the only one helping Daniel, and he would carry on until the matriculation exams, but after that it would be up to God. Because from the autumn Finsen was going to support a boy at the missionary school, and more than that he could not manage.

Daniel went cold. It seemed that it was fated that when he finally got as far as being a student, he would yet again find himself destitute.

5

'One! Two! Three! Punch! – 'One! Two! Three! Punch!' They beat time with their hands and feet, and fresh young voices shouted the words as loud as they could. The chant grew like a storm and drowned the hum and din that filled the hall like a restless sea. The celebration evening of the *russ*, those who had finished their matriculation exams*, had arrived.

From wall to wall the floor was filled with small tables and stools and every table was surrounded by *russ*, was black with *russ*. *Russ* and non-*russ*, aspiring citizens of academe and citizens of academe. But tonight they were all *russ*, young and happy, young and intoxicated, thirsty for academic freedom and punch.

Russ festivities happened only once a year, and there were no young men in town who were not at a *russ* party. But then everyone touched by academe was young. If the *russ* wanted to drink farewell to their salad days and be lifted into adult society with punch and with songs, then the adults and the old wanted punch and songs to transport them back to their youth again, that blessed time when to drink farewell to one's salad days had been the initiation into life.

The room was full, but still the odd late arrival stumbled around between trailing coat tails and feet while trying to find a seat; but the majority were seated – at the tables or on the tables. They were sitting waiting for the festivities to begin, talking, shouting, hallooing, laughing, mewing like cats, baying like dogs and shouting for punch. The whole tightly-packed room was like a sea of rising and falling fair heads and broad shoulders, of fresh youth thirsty for life.

Six hundred boots and twelve hundred stool legs stamping on

a floor, six hundred hands drumming on a hundred tables, three hundred voices, hooting, laughing, shouting, baying, and every so often through all this din a mighty rhythmic chorus: 'One! Two! Three! Punch! 'One! Two! Three! Punch!' – It came with a roar so the whole building resounded.

But there was so much youthfulness in the uproar that even the sourest schoolteacher thawed out and laughed, and eminent old professors sat and smiled as happily and benignly as if they had forgotten all their wisdom.

Daniel was as if drunk on all this merriment. He was surrounded by laughter. Wherever one turned there was fun and games, all the jokers from all the schools had come together here, and they knew their stuff. All the jests and witticisms, all the crazy questions and rapid answers and all the mangled Latin flew through the air like a pixie dance! Daniel had never felt so free as he felt here. Daily life with its toil and struggle was forgotten. People had left their thoughts and their sorrows at home. Tomorrow did not exist. Only joy existed. *This* was what it was to be a student. This was the ideal student life.

But the punch was taking its time coming, and the *russ* were impatient. Round the whole room shouts were raised for the drink of the gods. There was stamping and uproar, so it was as well to have stout ears. A young fellow with a blue band across his chest called out through a door that the punch needed time too! – but no one was listening. Who could be bothered with such prosaic nonsense?

Finally a drinks-server appeared, and shortly after several more. They carried punch jugs and glasses. Hurrah! Hurrah! All the dogs bayed, all the cocks crowed and cuckoos cuckooed, while those who had to show that they were educated, clapped or shouted. And suddenly the hall was alive with hundreds of waving hands and cuffs. Everyone wanted to be first. 'Psst! Over here!' 'Woof! Woof! Here!' 'Waiter! Waiter!' 'Jens!' 'Christian!' 'Cupbearer!' 'Ganymedes!' 'Psst! Psst!' – the hall was like a crawling anthill. But with amazing speed punch arrived on all the tables. Hans Haugum got a whole jug for himself and his flock.

Gradually as people were served the happiness became less

rowdy, more intimate, more like a small bubbling pot of conversation and laughter, with the occasional halloo in between. All were agreed that the punch was no good, too sweet and weak, just dishwater. But punch was better than no punch and what it lacked in quality they would have to make up for in quantity.

Personally Daniel thought the punch was good, but he agreed with the others, as they must know better. He put on a knowing air and said to Aslak Fjordan that this wasn't punch, merely sugar water.

But there was the *Magister bibendi*.

He was a tall young boy with black hair and an olive skin. He had a bold mouth and was not the slightest bit nervous. He was greeted with a great shout, smiled, bowed and took a swig of punch, said 'hmm' and began:

'Gentlemen! (*all right!* Hurrah!) – The day will soon come (hurrah!), when we – in all seriousness – can say farewell (cock-a-doodle-do) – to the time (rejoicing, bleating) – to the time that most of us – more than once ... ahem! Ahem! Ahem!' – The speaker had to cough. He swallowed it with a swig of punch and wanted to continue, but now the whole room had got a coughing fit. Ahem! Ahem! Ahem, sounded from all sides and corners like a church on New Year's Day, until finally someone started to sneeze – a-tschoo, a-tschoo – so it bounced off the walls. The fellow clearly wanted to make the *magister bibendi* start to sneeze, and he sneezed and sneezed more and more wholeheartedly, more and more seductively: a-tishoo, a-tishoo, but the *magister* did not allow himself to be seduced. As soon as the coughing and laughter had quietened down a bit, he launched off again as if nothing had happened, shouting out with his broad vowels and hard rolled 'r's which could have made themselves heard under a waterfall: '– say farewell to the time that most of us – probably many a time – in our schoolboy fashion (eh? Woof!) – have cursed (bravo! Bravo! Bravo!) as a time of slavery (great mewing). *Faustis avibus*, if all goes well, (hurrah) we will – in a few days – be adults (cock crows) and free men – we will be *students* – gentlemen, Norwegian students!' – Prolonged shouts of joy, hurrahs, halloos, and far back in a corner a cuckoo called.

With a host of words and images the speaker held forth about the great difference between before and now, and Daniel understood him so well. The main difference was that schoolboys had to work, but a student could do as he liked. A student worked when the spirit moved him, 'when Minerva called' (bravo!) 'and when Minerva doesn't call, gentlemen,' (then Venus does! More cock crows) – then the student has the great privilege that he can decide over his free time himself (skål! Hurrah! *Pereat rector!*). And that means that from now on we can be considered as men who have come of age.' The speaker drank. General rejoicing.

When he wanted to continue, he was unable to. All the dogs began to bark, for they understood that now he wanted to embark upon more serious matters. Woof! Woof! 'And now gentlemen,' – More barking! – 'And now,' – The barking intensified! – '*Silentium!*' bellowed the *magister* in a terrible voice, and it helped. He began to expound on the *duties* of 'having come of age', and this he was allowed to do in comparative peace. When society 'let us loose' he argued, it did so in the belief that we were grown up enough to be our own masters and disciplinarians, and we should not fail society in that belief. Finally the speaker turned to describing the true student, a description which won great approval from Daniel. First and foremost the true student was not a 'materialist'. He let the tradesman take care of everything to do with the cooking pot. The student himself, he lived for the true, the great and the beautiful. Nor was the true student a 'melancholic'. He knew that sufficient unto the day was the evil thereof and as Dr Morten Luther had said, he loved 'wine, women and song' above all else ('Hurrah!' 'What the devil!'). Finally the true student was – *betrothed*. But at this point his speech was almost lost in rejoicing and 'skåling'. Daniel drank a private skål for Inga Holm – she alone was the one he wanted to remember tonight – ; the *magister* had shouted himself hoarse before he reached the end of his speech.

And now all these men who had so recently 'come of age' began to shout their immeasurable joy from full lungs, and to stamp with their boot-heels in agreement so that the floor trembled. Then the *russ*-song was handed out to the gathering, copies fluttering through the air like butterflies. The music on the balcony started up and the song rose, roaring through the room like a mighty storm, the song of victory that now they were no longer school boys, but *russ* and that soon, *faustis avibus*, they would be students.

The song was sung once to music and after that without. It was even better then. They divided into small groups and each sang according to its own beat, then each had its own verse. Freedom reigned supreme, and joy was complete. Youth had let itself go and the old had forgotten their age. Everything in the room dissolved into song and laughter and the punch slipped down, nauseating though it was, as if it were nectar.

Eventually the singing stopped and there were great waves of clapping and stamping, first from one side then from another and finally from the whole room, and through the crash of the waves there came ear-splitting shouts for 'the author! The author!' till the room was nothing but a single urgent shout. And it lasted for a considerable time. They did not grow tired, these young lungs, and what did it matter if soft hands began to smart a bit this evening. Finally the happy author had to come forward. It was a young boy like all the other boys who leapt up onto the speaker's dais, bowed to right and left, and then disappeared again like a mirage. Prolonged merriment, but gradually quieter.

Many who thought it was too crowded indoors, or who had had enough of the ear-shattering din and tobacco smoke, retreated to the garden or to the covered balcony and settled there in small groups round tables. In the hall there was more and more breaking up into groups. The punch was beginning to warm the young heads and more and more wished to chat with good friends in confidence. Hans Haugum and Aslak Fjordan sat assessing the *russ* speech. Aslak did not think it was up to much, just the usual platitudes, but Haugum was amazed that the young fellow managed to say as much as he did in all the uproar. Daniel agreed with Haugum. It *was* amazing that so young a fellow could get up and speak so well in so large and critical a gathering.

The punch was good, and Daniel was getting warm. At first he thought about his father, but then he dismissed the thought: there was a difference between drinking punch in a gathering of *russ* and drinking corn spirits with farmers. Spirits destroyed a man, but punch was part of the ideal life of a student.

And he understood this more and more clearly as he drank. Never had he felt so pure and good, so raised above the poverty and baseness of the world. Indeed, he eventually felt so ideal that he could not worry about his pecuniary sorrows either.

The only feeling that swelled in his breast was love, love for everyone on earth and in particular for those he was together with this evening, but most of all, most of all for Inga. He would soon write a letter of proposal to her – his heart lurched so strangely when he thought about it, and he drank to her time after time in secret. He would not think about Berta Maria tonight. Tonight he was a *russ* and a *russ* should think about the ideal.

Oh, how grateful he felt towards the Almighty, who in his mercy had helped him on his way so that he – *he*, a peasant-farmer's son from Sørbraut in Nes parish – could taste the great joy of being part – if only for this one evening – of the ideal life of a student. It was true that the roots of wisdom were bitter, but the fruit by comparison was sweet, sweeter than he had expected. – A new man stood on the speaker's dais, a benign old man by all appearances, with greyish-white tufts of hair on a semi-bald head, and with eyes hidden behind a pair of strange horn spectacles. 'Professor Darre!' Hans Haugum whispered. 'Professor Darre! Professor Darre!' was whispered from ear to ear across the hall, and those out on the covered balcony and far down the garden returned with their punch glasses in their hand and with raised eyebrows. There were shouts of bravo, the whole hall shouted bravo, but more quietly, more like schoolboys shouting *vivat rector*. Daniel knew this was the Professor of Philosophy.*

Hans Haugum and Ortvedt jumped up and pushed their way forward to the dais. Daniel followed, happy and expectant. Now finally he was going to hear words of wisdom from the source itself.

Professor Darre did not speak loudly, but Daniel managed to catch most of what he said. It was something about school not being as bad as one often thought. When you were older you would see many things in a different light, and then memories from your school days would gain both meaning and life. And the professor craned his neck and peered out into the air with his horn spectacles as if he saw something in the far distance that the others could not see, and the room shouted bravo, bravo. But, said Professor Darre, don't let me digress! Tonight we are not going to be old and wise, or old and mad, as it says in one version (bravo!). Tonight we are going to be young and wild or young and mad, if you want (bravo!), and who knows, perhaps the madness of youth will prove to be the greatest wisdom (bravo!).

The professor now became more serious. He cleared his throat and entered upon a long account of the academic class, which he described as a higher sphere above ordinary life. Anyone who entered was thereby consecrated as a priest in the world of ideas. Henceforth such a person should live, not for temporal things, but for eternal things, live *the life of the spirit*, *ton bion theôn*, in the human sense of the phrase (bravo!), in short, gentlemen, in truth *live for the idea* (bravo!). A student had to free himself from everything petty and paltry that was part of ordinary life; he had, so to speak, always to be dressed in his wedding clothes, for it was a matter of being human in the highest sense of the word, to live in and for that which was in truth worthy of mankind. Out there in the everyday world man's life was fragmented, split into a thousand small tasks so that he could never concentrate on the ideal; in the endless hustle and bustle he could not hear the harmony of ideas through all the disparate voices, or see the unity of things through the day's broken play of light. But here in this world of ideas the distracting voices could not penetrate, here was serenity and peace, here the spirit found its home; here thought was not shattered and scattered by the incidental, the petty and the torn, the thoughtless, the one-sided and the temporal aspects of everyday life. Here one should, humanly speaking, see god as he was, speak to the spirit face to face (bravo!). A half drunk dog over in a corner dared to say 'woof', but was soon hushed.

Out there it was the practical tasks that counted, whatever was useful for the day, the 'bread and butter' issues if he might use such a phrase; here, liberated from all aimless wandering in what was multifarious and fragmented, it was a matter of seeking the eternal, the essentially important and true. It was into this elevated sphere, this priesthood of the intellect, that you my young friends were now entering; but you did not come empty-handed, you had your *youth*.

The Professor went on to show how extraordinarily well suited to the life of ideas the young were with their strong idealism, and their feeling for the great and the universal. When a young man entered the ideal world of the mind, it was on the one hand as if he found himself, while on the other, it was the spirit that found him or found itself in him.

Those who sat by the doors gradually began to leave, those inside drank deep of their punch – they understood that this was going to take time.

Daniel listened with deep reverence. Unfortunately he did not understand everything, but he found that reasonable, and it did not matter much either, because he knew instinctively that the professor was right.

All this about the life of the spirit he recognized from chaplain Hirsch, but here it was so much deeper and more learned. And that ordinary everyday life was just something petty he already knew.

What came last was best of all, and now even the dogs agreed with the professor.

It was all wrong, he said, that new students thought they had to study hard in their first couple of years. That was not the idea. Work could come all in good time. The difficult, head-splitting battle with the thousand individual elements that one had to learn so that the whole could emerge clearly and articulately, that was better suited to a later stage when one had more strength to immerse oneself in the individual elements without losing hold of the universal. Though it had to be said, the older generation too in these days often enough forgot the universal. They immersed themselves so deeply in a single thing that they *remained* there. Indeed, science itself was on the verge of getting stuck in the depths. It was precisely a time when all sorts of separate branches of knowledge were expanding and wanting to forget their connection with the universal. The professor asked his young friends to guard against getting sucked into this. All specialist knowledge was in itself dead and lifeless. It was not knowledge about this or that that made a man a scholar. What mattered was the vision of the whole, the examination of the great universal foundations, and the great universal *context* (bravo!). But the professor was of the opinion that one of the reasons why students could so easily lose themselves in dead, specialist branches of knowledge was that they did not know how to use their time wisely during their early years, but threw themselves into specialist studies immediately and believed that it was a matter of stuffing themselves with as much knowledge as they could. But this was precisely what they should *not* do. In their first years, they should take it easy (bravo! bravo!), and put more emphasis on living the healthy ideal life of a student – a youthful life in the light of the eternal ideals – than on reading learned books. They should use their time to reflect, to look around, to make themselves at home in their new world, gain an overview and a vision of the uplands they would later traverse. They should enjoy their youth, certainly, but enjoy it as students, as consecrated novices in the priesthood of the mind, as *cives academici*. And that was what was so wonderful about being a student; that was the true content of the joy of being a *russ*, and of the happiness and festivities here tonight (loud applause). And now the professor wanted to close with three cheers for all the young people studying, 'Hurrah! Hurrah! Hurrah!' they shouted round the room. Finally the shouting died away in a long thunderous round of clapping.

Afterwards the boys carried the professor aloft; Daniel had never seen anything like it before and thought it looked silly. But he clapped along with the others, because he had liked the last part of the speech very much indeed.

He made his way back to his table and tasted the punch. He was confident and happy. The world was a good place to be and people were kind. He had such an urge to talk to them, to speak out, to tell them his innermost thoughts and to hear their innermost thoughts in return; and most of all he wanted to talk to his dear friend Haugum. But Haugum was standing on the other side of the room talking to a strange fellow, – a large oaf, so it seemed to Daniel, and Aslak Fjordan had joined another group at another table; there he sat making such a noise that Daniel laughed to himself and thought happily that Aslak was presumably drunk already. But Ortvedt was nowhere to be seen, so Daniel sat down to wait.

There came Markus Olivarius Markussen and Halvor Mosebø weaving their way between table legs and boots. Both were unsteady and their progress was slow, but Markus Olivarius Markussen laughed aloud 'Oh my word! Heavy seas today and a confounded lot of wrecks!' he mimicked a well-known anecdote. When Halvor reached Daniel he greeted him with great heartiness, shook his hand and congratulated his 'bosom pal' nonstop, and Daniel who had never liked Halvor Mosebø was equally hearty, pulled him down on the chair beside him and laughed at Halvor's drunkenness. It was such fun to be young and to let go. And Daniel felt an irrational urge to throw his arms round Halvor and swear him eternal friendship. But Halvor was asking for punch, and there was plenty of that. They filled their glasses, said 'skål' and drank. 'Well, what do you think of – ?' Daniel wanted to ask, but Halvor began to sing in his weedy, thin voice 'Have you seen my woman, – up on the hillside, up on the hillside!' Daniel let out a guffaw, 'But what do you think of – ?' 'I'm a son of the soil, I am, you see!' said Halvor – 'A farmer's son, that's me! I'm from Telemark, I am, d'you understand!' Well that's good, said Daniel. For his part he was also the son of a farmer. 'Have you seen my woman – ! Shall we drink to our friendship?' asked Halvor. 'Oh well, *all right*' – 'Farmers' sons, both of us!' – *All right* – 'Skål – here's to you!' 'Skål – to you' – 'Eh! – what the devil has become of Markus Oliv... Do you know Markus Olivarius?' Daniel laughed; now he has already forgotten that we've drunk to our friendship, he thought. No, he did not know Markus Olivarius particularly well. 'But what did you think of the speech?' – At last he managed to ask his question. 'About the speech? Good speech, by Jove! Good speech!' – 'Yes, I thought so too. But...' – 'Yes, but there was a lot of rubbish too, by Jove' – 'Yes, many of the usual platitudes – .' 'Yes, that's true, that's true... – Do you know Markus Olivarius?' – 'No, unfortunately, not well...' – 'Fine fellow, damn it! Damnably fine fellow! Believe it or not ... we've shared lodgings for six months, and if there has fallen so much as ... so much as one cross word! – Yes, he's an amazing fellow.' – 'Indeed, that's for certain. But listen – ?' 'What?' – Daniel giggled and said, 'There is one thing you've never known...' – 'Known? I know everything, I do. So don't give me that one. D' you know in which year Philip IV...' – 'Yes, that's just it! D'you know that for a long time I was your worst enemy because you knew more history than I did?' Daniel giggled again. – 'Skål!' – 'Yes, let's have a bit to drink first...' – 'Du habst Recht my son. – Skål! – I know my history, so don't come near me on that one. – Have you seen my woman up on the hillside, up on the hillside? – What the devil has happened to Mark Oliv?' – 'Oh, he'll be on his way; he's only out on the balcony. – By the way, what did you get?' 'Me? I got – ' and Halvor banged the table with each word – : 'I got 3.4, darn it!'* – but they're going to pay for that four, they certainly are! ... but I'm as good a fellow for all that ... but they're going to pay! The pack of scoundrels! – they'll have cause to remember Halvor Mosebø! They're going to see that he's a fellow who won't let himself be fleeced with a blunt razor. Skål' – Daniel did not know what to say to this. Halvor sat looking glum, then suddenly shouted: 'Have you seen my woman?' Shortly after, he said, 'You got 2.2 didn't you?' – 'No, 3.3.' – 'Oh. – Skål, my old bosom pal! – Shall we drink to our friendship?' – Daniel laughed, 'we've just done so' – 'Du habst immer Recht,' sighed Halvor; 'I'm drunk tonight, you see! But it doesn't matter! I'm a freehold farmer, you see? A freehold farmer from Telemark! So you can't get me there! – What the devil has happened to Markus Olivarius?' – He got up and staggered out; Daniel called after him, but he did not hear.

The gathering had become more restless, people were on their feet, and there was a constant flow in and out of the doors. Among those moving backwards and forwards Daniel saw quite a few students of farming stock; strange; you could almost tell by looking at them.

Half behind him Daniel thought he heard a voice he

recognized. He turned round and saw that it was the *magister bibendi*. He stood talking to the same 'oaf' that Haugum had been talking to a while ago, and the 'oaf' was asking whether the *magister* had been afraid when he had to give his speech tonight. 'By God, you bet I was,' he replied. Daniel sat staring at him open-mouthed. The fellow had the courage to *say* that he had been afraid!

A new man mounted the speaker's dais. He spoke for 'the older generation'. He was a man with a good voice whose words sounded fine, but Daniel could find little meaning in what he said.

Yet another speaker! But this was a fellow, the likes of whom Daniel had never thought he would see in a group of ideal students. Daniel did not know what to think as the man with a long, irregular peasant-farmer's face and eyes shaded under prominent brows heaved himself up onto the speaker's dais, loose-jointed and angular in all his movements. But for this strange man the whole room began to shout 'Hurrah' and to clap, and through the uproar Daniel heard a piercing voice shout 'Long live the Dalesman'.*

So *this* was the Dalesman!

Daniel had felt a bit queer sitting there, a bit confused in his thoughts, a bit heavy over the eyes ... but now he was awake again. He flew up, felt somewhat unsteady on his feet, but worked his way towards the speaker's dais as fast as he could; he wanted to see and hear this Norwegian wild man, around whom so many tales revolved, and who wrote so scathingly and crazily in his crazy dialect in his crazy *Dalesman* newspaper.

Quite quietly and good-naturedly, but casting strange flashing glances, the Dalesman began by saying that it was really rather strange that two to three hundred young men in their twenties could sit together for a whole evening, drinking punch and having a good time, without making so much as a single speech on the subject young men were so mad about, namely ladies (Hurrah! Hurrah! Great uproar). Daniel felt a sudden stab in his chest and thought of Inga, but Berte Maria also pressed forward in his mind, and Daniel thought it would be a pity to dismiss her. But, said the Dalesman, and his voice grew stronger, if the young bachelors weren't going to do their duty, then the older generation would have to step in, for God help us all if the ladies were displeased with us! So now he would try to offer a little incense to this stern, but infinitely kind goddess, and he would like to do so on behalf of the whole assembly, just as the Catholic priests drank the wine for the sins of all their parishioners, and he hoped that by so doing none of the young men here would experience anything but goodness and kindness from the gentle sex.

They said that she was the weak one and man the strong one, and it was even written that woman was a frail vessel, but shame on it, she was stronger than anyone realised, the troll! And she had bowed and broken many a strong man with her tiny fingers, just as the *hulder*, that troll woman of the folk tales, had broken a horseshoe in two pieces with her soft, naked hands as if it were nothing.

The whole room followed his words with nods of approval, laughter and boisterous shouts, for he said everything in such an amusing way. Daniel thought it amusing in itself that this old scarecrow, half peasant and half satyr should be making a speech in praise of *women*.

And he launched into his speech in his own unique way, half joking, but serious all the same. He probably meant roughly what he said, however strange it might sound, but as he maybe was not certain that he meant it exactly as he had said it, he tended to put a twist in the tail at the end, which reminded people of the Dalesman's 'double vision'. But sometimes he uttered thoughts that were so strangely tender and beautiful that you quite forgot the *Dalesman* and saw only the poet.

Woman was *peace*, he said, – even though married men often said something different. She was peace because she was practical; she saw to what was useful, food for herself and her children, and she was therefore worried out of her mind lest her husband should get involved in trouble or violence of any sort and thereby become disabled. Therefore all who lived the life of the mind and who wanted to grapple with, and sacrifice themselves for, an idea or a cause – they should be bachelors like him, so that no one had to worry whether they sank or swam, for then there would be no problem with them.

But of course he did not intend to wish on all the handsome young men gathered here anything as perverse as that they should all remain bachelors, that would be a shame for them and for the poor womenfolk, who were all too keen on marrying, poor things, even though they constantly tossed their heads and played hard to get, so long as they were not over thirty. For woman was love, she was created for marriage, and given the way she was educated now, she was not capable of anything else either, and little enough indeed for marriage. Men too loved, we bachelors knew that, we who always loved and never won, but it was in a different way, it was like the bird of prey with skin and bones, sinews and muscles, and crooked beaks and claws. But woman loves the way she was created to love: like the wave that runs on the coal-blue sea as a rolling and eternal template for all beauty.

– 'Yes, boys, marry! But marry with sense, and don't rush off and acquire a wife before you can feed her, for then things will go wrong, as we so often see. For a woman despite all her lovingness, wants food, and she is right to do so.'

He said much about love and food which Daniel did not find very poetic. But every time he was on the verge of getting annoyed about this, there came a twist in the speech that made him laugh. And he laughed and clapped like the rest.

The speech ended with a couple of verses about how in addition to everything else good, woman was also beautiful, and that was the best thing about her. The Dalesman promptly forgot his words of wisdom that men of ideas should remain bachelors, and the end of it all was that a man of ideas should have the most beautiful woman. And now he wanted to drink a toast to woman, and that toast he particularly wanted to drink with all those here who had a lady friend, provided the affection and the lady friend were worth something. The *russ* cheered to this and drank. The Dalesman stepped down from the speaker's dais and shambled back to the table where he was sitting with his companions.

Daniel too made his way there. He wanted to hear more from this homely wise man and bard.

And the Dalesman was in an expansive mood. Riding high and

happy after his speech and the approval it won he took a swig of punch and began to preach again to his companions and whoever wanted to listen.

Yes, woman and food, he began. But this was because woman had less education than we had, for if she knew a bit more, she would realize that all this about food was not true. For it was *not* true, and many times he had lived his best moments on days when he had had no dinner. This concern for one's daily bread and butter, which was so evident now dragged down our whole life. Indeed was it not the power of food and the guanocracy* that we had to fight against even in politics? Everything revolved round food. And the best man was the one who could get hold of most guano. The whole of public life was more and more becoming a guano industry, where people were no longer interested in ideas and thought, but in good earnings, and in making money out of their knowledge, just as Per Degn, the sexton in Holberg's play *Erasmus Montanus*, made money out of the Latin he did not know. Even studying had become a trade, it was a matter of 'getting started'. Good heavens, we all had to live; he himself was a reporter of agricultural shows, but it was terrible to hear learned folk talking about all this food. They could not give a damn about the land and the people. They regarded their work like any other transaction, and instead of being public leaders they cut the umbilical cord between the people and themselves, and shut themselves up in their office cubicles and became bureaucrats. As a result the whole of the state administration ended up in the same torpor. It was this external, tangible benefit, this 'material progress' with railways, and agricultural shows, this 'tonnage' that one skipper called our true national life – in short, it was the British sausage-machine mentality and undervaluation of all things intellectual. It had gone so far that they no longer *liked* bright minds in the state administration; these 'damned geniuses' only caused trouble.

Now one of the others entered the conversation – Daniel did not usually like these fellows, they looked so arrogant and intellectually superior – : 'Well' said the man 'they're getting more and more dried up too, the genuine old bureaucrats. But it's a different story with the broad-shouldered, broad-cheeked farmers' sons – there's real marrow in them...'

'Exactly,' the Dalesman cut in again, 'culture makes people beautiful and noble, but weak and wizened, and then in the end Huns and Vandals from Asia are needed to reinvigorate the blood. But we don't take our Vandals from Asia, we take them from the farming districts and that is why our community will not go under but will rejuvenate itself, like Saturn who ate his own children. And we will always have barbarians to reinvigorate the blood of our society as long as we have these farmers and cotters, who live off coarse porridge and rancid ham and who climb all the slopes and mountains there are and more too, and who suck in air so strong that if they cast a troll spell on a townie and transported him straight from the street and took him up there he would suffocate, like the mouse in the bell jar which was filled with pure oxygen.'

The Dalesman lifted his glass and drank, then quickly began again:

'Yes, they are handsome fellows these townsfolk, with such brilliant faces that you could almost fall in love with them, or 'forliebe dich' in them as they say in German. But in ten years time all these girlishly soft faces will be as dry as the bark on a tree; every moderately gifted cat will look more brilliant than they do. And they'll be worn out and grumpy, and grey from all the paperwork and all this concern for getting the daily bread and butter. And they'll have beards so they look like old goshawks with noses like large crooked beaks and hair like moulting feathers. It is with them as with other animals, they look most lively when they're young; even the cow looks lively when she's a calf.'

A new speaker had joined them and to begin with he spoke so softly that the majority did not notice him, but then he grew in stature and his voice with him; Daniel turned to see who it was. God help us, it was Jens Rud. Someone from the Factory! Could this turn out all right ... Daniel was uneasy. But Jens managed and Daniel felt proud – we Factory students weren't at a loss either! – Jens Rud spoke on behalf of the student who was 'a son of the people'; he was the true and obvious bearer of 'the people's cause,' and there was sense in what he said. He also managed to say some warm and beautiful words about the Norwegian bard whom we had been able to welcome tonight. Loud applause. In particular Jens wanted to raise his glass to those students whose background was in the common people; it was their prime duty to be educators of the people, leaders of the people, because they knew the people best; – 'skål for the students who come from the farming communities!'

The whole room applauded; it was both beautiful and strange. Daniel was serious. He remembered his old dreams, and it was if he saw another man step forward alongside Jens Rud, a man who for a long time he had forgotten far too much: chaplain Hirsch.

Yes! He would be a bearer of the people's cause. He would be the ideal student, he would work for the things of the mind, and he would hate bread and butter concerns all his life. Oh, if only he had been rich!

The buzzing and murmuring continued in the room as before. Now and again there was a shout, laughter, part of a song, which then died away in the tobacco smoke. Daniel felt tired. He did not want to be in all this muddle any longer. He had to get out into the garden and fill his lungs with fresh air, and dream great dreams!

When he got out he found Hans Haugum and several others, among them Ortvedt, Sven Dufva and a stranger, sitting at a table under a tree. He went across, 'Oh, is it you?' said Haugum, 'Have a seat, and a glass of beer too if you want.' Daniel thanked him and sat down. Truth to tell a glass of beer would taste good now. Haugum sent Sven Dufva off in search of a glass, and then he presented 'studiosus Braut' to the stranger, Meier, a graduate', before picking up the thread of what he was saying again. – 'No,' he said addressing Meier, 'that's not the point. Endre Storr* is a man with both good intentions and bright ideas, but he believes that the economic foundation here is too meagre to support the real life of the mind, so first and foremost he wants people to pursue *that*.' 'Yes, but that's what *I* call materialism,' said Meier,* – 'this belief that the economy is the most important thing in life.' He spoke slowly and calmly; his words came one at a time, with weight and emphasis. Haugum was silent for a while, but then geared himself up again: 'Yes, there may be something in that, but – surely if you consider the material aspects as the *foundation* of things, it doesn't follow that you therefore consider them the *primary* aspect?' Meier let a huge smile light up his serious face which, surrounded as it was by a vast mass of dark hair, resembled that of an apostle, and he said, 'Let us first seek the spirit and its life, then everything else shall be added to us!' Daniel understood now that Meier was a great man, and as he at the same moment saw Sven Dufva come ambling towards them with a glass and a bottle, he grew brave, thumped the table, and said: 'Never was a truer word spoken!'

Haugum stared in amazement at his apprentice, who was stirring things up like that, but he still tried to defend Endre Storr, though he could not quite manage it. With secret delight Daniel heard how Haugum more and more had to give in to Meier's strong faith and weighty words. But strangely enough Haugum did not give up.

The beer tasted refreshingly good. Daniel felt himself strong and reinvigorated. He was on the verge of telling them about Jens Rud and his speech, when Meier started to talk about 'the cultural leader, Hirsch.' 'Yes, how are things going for him?' asked Haugum. 'Oh, things are going for him as they go for all other cultural leaders in this country, he is persecuted by inanity from above and ignorance from below, and since he will not give up, it is just a matter of time before he will be compelled to resign.'

'Chap... chaplain Hirsch,' Daniel asked with wide eyes. 'Yes, he's still a chaplain,' replied Meier. 'Yes, but ... what's he done?' 'Oh,' said Haugum casually, 'he's got into conflict with the pietists up country about the correct form of words for baptism.' Daniel was both surprised and appalled, but as he continued to listen to the conversation, the punch and his anger began to boil in him and he banged the table so it echoed, 'the pack of trolls!' – Meier smiled angelically and said, 'True enough, they're Loki's offspring.' Shortly after he got up and went into the hall; he wanted to hear what the young people were talking about when they were drunk, he said.

Haugum spoke of the Folk High School idea that was

beginning to take root and mentioned among other things that Meier wanted to be a Folk High School teacher. 'In other words, he's a good man!' shouted Daniel and thumped the table. 'Wasn't that what I said? I can nearly always tell by looking at a man what he's good for...' – 'But Haugum, Endre Storr, who's he?' asked Bragestad, in a loud, hurried voice, as if he was too shy to take part in the conversation. 'He's my landlord,' said Haugum. 'A rich devil of a merchant,' threw in Ortvedt, as if waking up; 'that Haugum always keeps in with the bigwigs, the sly dog!' 'I ended up lodging there,' said Haugum, 'because I knew his wife.' 'S-s-s; now things are getting nasty,' hissed Ortvedt in a whisper; 'Oh my' sniggered Daniel, and Sven Dufva chuckled a kindly, deep bass laugh; 'To be more exact I knew his wife's *mother*,' added Haugum. 'The devil you did!' said Ortvedt. Daniel who did not dare to say 'devil', said 'For shame!'.

They sat for a while joking about nothing in particular, and Daniel immediately raised the subject of Endre Storr again. Meier had been right in what he said about the man. Haugum could say what he wanted. Daniel had read some long articles that Endre Storr had written in *The Good Citizen*. They dealt with fertilizer and guano, and were some of the dullest things he had ever read. It was this guanocracy – this 'tonnage' as the skipper called it, indeed the whole of this British sausage machine mentality and obsession with bread and butter. ... Daniel was so eloquent that Haugum did not recognize him. But, Daniel continued, it was precisely this meaty materialism that we must fight against. We were consecrated priests in the world of the mind, as the professor had said; we were sons of the people and bearers of a great popular idea, and we had to be on our guard against people such as Endre Storr. For there was enough striving after one's daily bread in this country. People were not interested in anything great and beautiful and elevated, they only knelt and grubbed for what filled the pot and the purse; they had no sense of a true human life; this deadness of spirit lay over the country like a troll spell; the people had to be roused; a new spirit was needed in life, ideas, poetry ... Meier was a fine fellow; he had graduated and now wanted to be a Folk High School teacher, and we all ought to become Folk High School teachers, but a clergyman could also do much good. Chaplain, Hirsch, who had been his teacher was a ... was an ... outstanding man; 'Had it not been for him, I would not be sitting here now!' Daniel almost wept as a result of beer and fond thoughts. Haugum had never known there was so much fire in the boy, and he thought that it was actually true that under the farmer's cold exterior there sometimes beats the warmest heart.

Daniel, as bold as an Achilles, banged the table with his glass, and said 'skål – a skål, gentlemen for Hirsch and all like him who want to contribute to freeing the Norwegian people from the troll spell! Skål!' – 'Yes, we can go along with that toast ' said Haugum, and with deep delight Daniel heard that Sven Dufva uttered 'bravo' to himself".

In the hall they were singing in a wild chorus:

> – 'And now a skål for you my friend!
> And for all Norwegian girls!'

Love had got the upper hand. 'Oh! How happy they are!' Daniel giggled, and shortly after he began to join in:

> – 'And now a skål for you my friend!
> And for all Norwegian girls!'

– the first line was addressed to Sven Dufva, whom in friendship he thumped in the back , and the second was for ... yes, this time he included Berta Maria. And as he had been so strict about her the whole evening, he now thought of her all the more tenderly. –

'Yes – hic! – for all Norwegian girls!' he said and drank. 'We have to have women with us ... Freya ... Freya with her go-hic! – golden tears ... But!' he suddenly shouted, 'those who labour for the guan-hic!-ocracy – and write in *The Good Citizen* ... we won't have – hic – anything to do with them. Hic-hic-hic! I think I'm a bit – hic – *happy* tonight, but ... hic! It doesn't matter ... gentlemen! 'Skål for – hic! – Skål for – hic – all Norwegian girls!' –

– Haugum and Sven Dufva had no small trouble getting Daniel home that night.

6

Daniel had heard that the oral examinations were supposed to be easy, but as the time approached, he found it was a different story.

He was poorly prepared, had had too many different schools and schoolteachers. And they had all had their own way of approaching the work. Now he stood there with his head full of a jumble of things all heaped together, some things learnt, some things only half-learnt, and there was no coherence in anything.

So there was nothing for him to do but 'swot it up'. It was a matter of life and death. The people who had helped him on his way *expected* he would pass, and if he did not, then all roads would be closed to him. What he did not understand, he would quite simply have to know by heart, because when you were a student you had to know everything from beginning to end.

Day and night Daniel sat in his dark garret and studied. Sweated and studied, studied and read things over till he was dizzy. The outside world disappeared for him. He forgot both sun and soil, heaven and earth, and when he once a day went out to get something to eat, he wandered through the town as if through a large, empty dream.

And how terribly hot it was! The August sun cut through the sky like a blazing fire and the air lay heavy and torrid over the town. Outside and in were equally terrible.

Wet round the neck and with sticky hands and heavy beads of sweat on his pale brow he sat and toiled. Flies flew and whirred and buzzed nerve-shatteringly against his cheeks and ears and settled on the nearest bit of wet skin so his flesh twitched; then they flew off, came back, circled round him closer and closer, bumped against his nose, ears and head with their eternal buzz and their tickly small claws. He sweated with weariness, waved his arms round endlessly and in vain, and killed them when they held their wedding in his hair, but it did not help. And he studied. But when exhausted and worn out he tried to sleep, he was in the same desperate state, lay tossing and turning in stifling half dreams and battling with the fly hell that never ended.

It was not much cooler at night than during the day. When the August sun had scorched the roof tiles over his head from morning till evening they were like glowing iron, and the low-ceilinged garret remained as hot and steamy as a bathhouse till far into the early hours. And never did the flies buzz and dance more madly than at night.

But he could not revise outside in the fresh air either. There were so many things that distracted his eyes and thoughts out there. He sat and stared at trees and flowers and dreamt of Berte Maria and Inga Holm and all sorts of nonsense and forgot everything to do with exams. The air quivered and sparkled, there were sounds of fun and gaiety and all sorts of life so that thoughts of exams died like small trolls when the sun rises. He had to shut himself in.

So he sat shut in, struggled and read, smoked, drank water and lost his appetite. With each day that passed he felt himself more and more wretched, and every day he had to pull himself together. And the more he read, the more he had to read, or so he thought.

One day he met Sven Dufva on the street and bemoaned his lot to him. Sven Dufva said that the best remedy was to take quinine drops. 'That's what I use,' said Sven Dufva, 'and they both perk you up and make you stronger'. So Daniel bought quinine drops. And when he felt just too tired and wretched, he took some and felt better.

It was a long battle. No sooner had he finished with one subject and revised it till he was sick of it than he had to get back into harness and start the next, which was just as difficult. His health was now seriously affected. At night when he lay and could not sleep because his head throbbed and flies buzzed, and all the grammar rules danced in his head and thumped and banged about like lumberjacks after an orgy, then he would sometimes jump up in trembling terror, fearing that he was going mad.

And he who had been so happy on the day of the *russ* festivities, and had thought that the worst was over! He had not seen what was ahead of him, and he had not known that the *russ* festivities were for the *true russ*, but not for those who had broken into the kingdom of academe via the Factory.

The true *russ*, who came from solid folk, and who had dozed their way though a solid Latin school, got through the orals fairly easily, for you had to assume that such boys had learnt what they were supposed to learn, and moreover, it was in fact written work that counted for more in this country. But the university had an instinctive suspicion of the Factory-*russ*. They were people with unheard-of names, people who sometimes did not look very academic, and who, what is more, came storming into the hallowed halls like thieves and robbers through the wrong door. You really had to examine the teeth of such horses very closely indeed. They were camels trying to get through the eye of a needle, and many failed, and did not get through, whether it was because they were camels or because the eye of the needle was sometimes too narrow. It had happened more than once that after the exams a message had come to 'The Old Man' from the university saying that he had lost his right to present students for their matriculation exams, because far too many of the boys from his school had 'failed'. But it could also happen that The Old Man told the bringer of the message in no uncertain terms that he had *not* lost the right to present students, whatever it said in the regulations.*

The Factory students, and Daniel among them, were growing paler and paler round the gills with every day that passed. And one after another they became ill and lay down, one on this hillside and one on that, like tired soldiers on a march. But the Factory students were not allowed to be ill, for there was no one who believed in their illnesses. The professors shrugged their shoulders and the *russ* laughed; 'He's sick in mathematics' they said; 'He's got a pain in his Greek'. And there was a piece in *The Good Citizen* that said how strange it was that it was precisely the Factory students who fell ill during the exam period.

Hans Haugum and Markus Olivarius kept themselves upright, but Halvor Mosebø and several others were ill. Daniel too thought hard about saying he was ill. But then one day he bumped into Sven

Dufva. Sven was terribly pale, and his usually large, frightened gazelle eyes now stood out white and staring like rivets. 'Good lord, you're ill,' burst out Daniel alarmed. Sven Dufva shook his head. 'You must go to the doctor and get a certificate!' Daniel continued. Then Sven Dufva stared at Daniel, and a reddish flush spread over his face. 'No,' he said, in his deep booming voice; 'I'll never do that!' And when Daniel wanted to know the reason, Sven explained, 'You mustn't go either. They don't believe us!' The reddish flush on his face intensified and stayed.

Daniel understood the fellow and was ashamed. Sven Dufva was right. Later Haugum said the same, and also added that those who absented themselves because of illness were examined more strictly later. It was best to keep going, if you could. Daniel heaved a great sigh and said that then he too would have to try to keep going.

And he kept going. But towards the end he could not study. When he sat down to read everything started to spin for him. Nor did he dare take any more quinine drops. Haugum had said they were dangerous.

So things would have to take their course. He had recently hoped to get *laud*;* he had done well in several subjects, and in history and geography he would get 1.1. But now he would have to let go of that hope. Since he could not revise his French and German, those subjects at least would destroy his *laud*.

Strangely enough his French and German went well. And now he was certain of getting *laud*. He comforted himself with the thought of how happy they would be, all those who had helped him on his way, and how grand it would be to be able to write to Inga Holm, 'Student with top marks'. But then things went wrong in history and geography – the only subjects he knew. As examiner he got an awkward old professor, who asked about all sorts of things that were not in the textbook, and as external he got his old history teacher from the Latin school, Robert the Devil. It was this that made him become confused, because he was afraid of Robert the Devil, and when the examiner started to get awkward, Daniel got totally lost. He answered every which way, and sometimes got totally stuck. The result was that he got 3.3 instead of 1.1, and with that his *laud* disappeared out of the window.

He could not understand it. It was perverse beyond the bounds of reason. To be so close to *laud* and not to get it. And to fail in the subjects he knew best! Could God allow such things? – He stood for a long time outside the door, half expecting that the professor would come out and say that it was a mistake. Such things could not happen. Certainly he had done less well today, but the external knew that he knew his history, and God would help, for surely there was justice in the world! Was a man's whole future to suffer, just because an old professor was in a bad mood? It could not happen; it could not!

But Daniel was to see that it could. The examiner and external came out and left. They did not even look at him. They seemed to have the best of consciences. And Robert the Devil was busy ingratiating himself with the professor, fawning and smiling, and working his way into his good books...

A burning rage boiled up in Daniel, and he said 'damn' for the first time in his life.

He staggered home, sick and angry. He should have had *laud*. *Had* in fact had it, but did not get it! If only he had not been so close. And weren't history and geography his best subjects! That such things could happen! He was now to go through life with *haud* for his matriculation exam and that just because ... in fact just because he had had Robert the Devil as his external.

He threw his books at the wall and kicked at them with his boot. Then he sat down tired and depressed and gave himself over to black thoughts. Suddenly he stamped the floor. He could not rid himself of the infuriating memory. So close to *laud*, and then not to get it. Hmm. There he sat. He had finished. Finished his exams. He was a student. This was the day he had longed for so long and so earnestly. And now the day had come. But he could not think of being happy. He was angry, furious, miserable, that's what he was.

He went out, he needed to find people. Find someone to talk to. But he could not find anyone. Presumably everyone had enough with their own problems.

A heavy despondency overwhelmed the boy. He was so alone. He had companions, but no friend. Not even Berta Maria cared about him; if she had done she would not be out so often on Sunday evenings. He was the son of a poor man and had a poor man's portion of happiness. And when some time had passed, he would perhaps starve to death. Or he would have to work.

He had written to Jens at Larsebakken for an additional loan of 100 daler 'in order to be able to take the compulsory *examen philosophicum** as soon as possible', and he had shown clearly that it would be to Jens's advantage too. But would the old soil grubber understand this?

And he who had thought of proposing to Inga Holm when he became a student! What an idea! A student with *haud*, and without money! That would be a fine suitor. Then even the hens in the sexton's yard could cackle and make fun of him. Now it was unlikely that the sexton, Holm, would invite him home to Sunday dinner.

The older generation had said that poverty was a sin. That was a great big lie. Poverty was a disaster. The worst and greatest disaster on earth. –

'Hello, Braut!' it was Aslak Fjordan, who commented laughingly, 'you're not walking fast, old man!' Daniel jumped: 'Hello there' – and they started a conversation. Aslak was on his way up to see 'student' Hærland, in order 'to try to get the main elements of syntax under his belt,' he said, because Hærland was such a solid fellow where Latin was concerned. And tomorrow he was going to be examined on Latin, but, oh, heaven help him, he did not know a thing. Oh, it was all a terrible struggle. He had been ill for his Greek exam, like the other *nons*; and in mathematics he had got 6, so he would have to resit that, and so the whole show would probably go to pot.

He had been unlucky from beginning to end, and had had to endure all sorts of dirty tricks from the professors. 'What about me?' Daniel said. 'Ah, yes, but in one subject I was lucky,' Aslak continued, 'and that was history!' – 'That's just where I was...'. But Aslak was not listening. 'Have you ever heard anything like it!' Aslak had opened his world history book at random in three places, and swotted them up, and that was the sum total of the history he knew. But when he came up for the oral he got precisely those three sections. He would have got a 1 for history, had not the fool of a professor brought up the French Revolution. Now he would have a 2, but that 2 might still save his skin for these exams.

Aslak laughed and got into a better mood as he recounted his tale, and in the end Daniel could not mope any longer either. He told the story of his history test, and it was a great relief to get his misfortune out into the open. All in all it was a good thing for someone who had been buried in books for so long to meet people. The weight he had felt pressing on his chest and his whole being relaxed and melted away like mist over the forest.

When Aslak got going, it turned out that he had a whole store of exam stories, and Daniel listened to them and became heartened – there were those who had done worse than he had. Afterwards he sauntered out along the road and was not in a bad frame of mind. When all was said and done, it was good to have finished. And he would have to comfort himself with the thought that if it had not gone well, it could have gone worse.

Out here it was open and beautiful. The August air, so sparklingly clean, lay fine and blue over meadow and wood. It was so clear that you could make out the tree-tops far out on the horizon. The district of Aker with its fields and meadows turning pale gold and beautiful lay between clumps of trees and gentle slopes. Far down below Oskarshall he glimpsed the fjord, shining white in the strong sunshine, while to the west the mountain range stretched in fine wavy lines through the sun-clear air with a charming, yet powerful plasticity.

Daniel saw that it was beautiful. He had been absent from it for so long. The air out here was like wine and filled a man with courage – should he finally dare to send a letter of proposal? Or should he wait till he had taken the *examen philosophicum*?

A student ought to be engaged. And it was so hard to be alone in the world. No one was happy unless he could find a loyal heart who could accompany him with loving thoughts in his struggle. Berte Maria, poor thing, was good and kind, but she was only a servant girl. It was the ideal one had to reach out for. Oh, if only he'd had *laud*! – or money. He finally settled things for himself by saying that if Jens at Larsebakken sent money, he would propose, but otherwise it would have to wait till after he had taken the *examen philosophicum.*

He was on the verge of sinking into his financial woes again, but remembered that a true student should not think about money. It was poetic to be poor; a true student should live for ideas and let shop-keepers and peasants worry about food and money.

All in all, he would have to remember that he *was* a student! – and not go around imagining that he was still a schoolboy and peasant! He would dream of his future hopes, of the job he would one day have. It was great dreams that made for the ideal student life.

In the end it was chaplain Hirsch whom he could thank for everything, and the good man must not reach the point of regretting what he had done. And Haugum and Rud, and the other grand fellows, they would see that he was not one who thought only of bread and – for Daniel Braut was not a materialist.

In all fairness he ought to become a Folk High School teacher like Meier and Massmann. But perhaps he was not suited to that, so then he had better be a clergyman of the kind Hirsch was – at least as far as he was able.

Suddenly he remembered that he had forgotten to order an academic cap, so he turned round and hurried back into town as fast as he could. It was best to be on the safe side. He still did not feel himself fully a student. Nor did he look like a student. But when he got his academic cap with a tassel, and his certificate of admittance to the university, then surely that would help.

– Matriculation day arrived.

Daniel Braut put on his black suit and reverently placed his academic cap on his head. Now he was a student. With a thumping heart he walked over to his mirror. Now that he had reached his great goal, he would look at himself. He expected to see a transformation.

His academic cap would not sit properly. He pulled it down more towards one ear. But still it did not sit properly. He pulled it down towards the other ear, but that did not help either. Then he set it straight on his head – no better. He tried all ways; set it further back, and further forwards, a bit more askew, a bit less askew, but to no avail. It was as if the academic cap was not made for his head.

Daniel grew cold as he stood there. He tried again; put the tassel at the back, at the front, put it on his shoulder. No, it just did not look right. And his coat – his coat sat like all the coats he had had. He did not look like a student. He was a peasant in disguise.

Pale and depressed he stood and stared at himself in the mirror. He felt he had become a stranger to himself. The broad, good-natured face had become long and lean. His mouth looked stupid, and his eyes, which once had been so bright, had shrunk and become red and dead. His shoulders were bent so he looked as if he were weighed down. He would have to straighten up if he wanted to reach his full height. He had looked different in his dreams about being a student. Well, it would presumably all work out in the end. But with a chill in his heart he shambled up to the University to collect his matriculation certificate, which he now understood could not work miracles.

And when he reached the place and saw all the young urban students, who came looking so smart and as light as birds in the sun, and who wore their academic caps as stylishly and proudly as if they had been made for them, he felt himself an alien in their company. He had only one comforting thought and it was a poor one at that: the other rural students did not look much better in their academic caps than he did.

The auditorium was full of elegant gentlemen in black suits with white shirt-fronts. It was if a chill emanated from all this evening dress. It took courage to go in. Daniel felt he came like an uninvited guest to a feast; it seemed to him as if the elegant gentlemen looked with distaste at this farmer's boy who wanted to force his way into their ranks. As soon as he had sat down, the academic anthem started up and rang beautifully through the high-roofed hall. So boldly, so firmly, so confidently. Daniel was encouraged. He told himself: you have a *right* to be here; you *are* a student.

His academic cap would not have to matter. It was good to have escaped from the inanity and rawness outside and come into these pure, calm halls among the intellectual priesthood. 'Holy, holy, holy, is the student's vocation,' rang out from the choir in clear, swelling harmonies, and in his heart Daniel joined in. He raised his eyes reverently to the ceiling frieze. There he saw the gods, the old classical gods, standing thinking and pondering, moulded in plaster.

It was Professor Darre who gave the speech. He explained how knowledge was an end in itself, then he touched on a couple of points from his *russ* speech before concluding with an encomium about the ideal student life.

Daniel listened to these words of wisdom with deep and devout respect. He thought they were so right and true. But when the professor came to the bit about the ideal student life he thought to himself: if only Jens at Larsebakken would send the money.

Next the newly-fledged academic citizens were to go up and receive their matriculation certificates and make their promises. It was a long procession. The majority were town students, people with low-German names, and with this special elegant air that Daniel had wondered about all his life. But now and again a *homo novus* would tramp up, an Aslaksen or a Bragestad, and with growing unease Daniel saw how easy it was to recognize these from the others. They did not have the style. They took their certificates with stiff, clumsy hands and imagined that they bowed, but it was really only a jerk of the neck, while others bent double as if they were going to break in the middle. Daniel grew smaller and smaller as he sat there. And now it was his turn to go up. 'Mr Daniel Olsen Braut!' – he got up, moved forward as well as he could, could not see clearly, the hall seemed to be enveloped in mist and was buzzing and yet it was uncannily quiet. White collars and faces gleamed indistinctly out of the mist like large, empty eyes. He stumbled against the end of a bench, making a loud noise, so he took two steps on tiptoe, took hold of his certificate, imagined that he bowed, but it was only a jerk of the neck – and then back to his seat, sweaty, but happy that he had managed it. It was a while before he dared look up.

He began to ponder as he sat there. He recalled the Dalesman and his Huns and Vandals; there was more to it than the Dalesman had been aware of. When one of the low-Germans came, it was as if they were a different race. It was not necessarily that they were handsome; it was not necessarily that they behaved well; they could be as ugly as sin and as thick as a two short planks, – and yet! And yet one could see that they were 'masters'. In everything they did they had a confidence and self-assurance; they had what Horace called the *frons urbana*, and when it came to the point that was the true mark of culture, education. Were they born with it? Was it something one *had* to be born with? Was it not true that all were born equal and that the noblest and best were just as often born in a hut as in a castle? Could God really have arranged it so that that those who were born to wealth got all the good things, while those who were born in poverty had to bear the marks of it all their days?

Daniel did not want to believe this. Our Lord was just; all came equal from His hand. The differences that existed resulted from the fact that people grew up in unequal conditions, which could smooth themselves out in time.

And the rural students had the energy, as the Dalesman had said. As they came tramping up, heavy and serious, some of them small and solidly built, others big and broad, it was true, they did look like 'sons of the mountain'.

'Holy, holy!' rang out once more. Daniel had conquered his dark thoughts, he was now a citizen of academe, and had a certificate to prove it. And now he intended to be happy as long as he had money.

He followed Haugum to the Café Nationale; they wanted to 'mark the day'. A whole crowd had gathered in the café, where there was a party with speeches and beer. This is where the ideal student life begins, thought Daniel. There was a whole flood of festive speeches about idealism. The old spoke up for the young and the young gave speeches for the old. A town student gave a speech for the students from the country and a student from the country gave a speech for the town students, or at least those students from town who were liberal and broad-minded enough to throw in their lot with the students from the country. To this a town student responded with a speech in honour of the farmers; the farmers were the past, and the farmers were the future; the farmers were the guardians of our heritage and the farmers were the guardians of our future development; the farmers owned the land, and the farmers would carry it into the future. Skål! Long live the farmers! Hurrah! Hurrah! Daniel drank his beer and thought everything was fine. *He* had not realized that the farmer was such a fine fellow, but when a town student said it, and when people like Hans Haugum and Jens Rud agreed, then it had to be true, and then it was a fine thing to be a farmer. He strolled over to the mirror and saw that his academic cap did not sit so badly after all.

Feeling well satisfied he sauntered home. Tomorrow he would write a letter of proposal. Jens Bakke would send the money, and if he did not, well then something would turn up; the world was good and happy and people were kind.

When he got up to his room he saw that it was newly cleaned and tidied as if it were Sunday. Poor Berta Maria, she had probably done it in honour of the day. Berta Maria was kind. He would get to know her properly, poor thing; she had looked so pale lately. Was she hiding a secret love that she knew was hopeless?

Tired and heavy he lay down on the bed, and sank into beery dreams. Before he knew it, he was asleep, and that night he slept like a log. When he woke up, he had a headache. But that was part of the ideal life of a student. He would have to put up with it.

Heavy, unrecognizable steps came tramping up, the door opened and a strange woman came in with the coffee. She was a huge, red monster of a woman, with a crooked mouth and teeth like a rat. Not only that, she was round shouldered and one hip was higher than the other. Daniel stared, what was the meaning of this? 'There you are,' said the girl. 'And I was to ask if you wanted anything in town today. I'm the new maid.' 'Indeed,' said Daniel with a voice still thick from the beer, 'what's happened to the old one?' 'Uh? Who? Ha! She went into a decline as they say. She's left.' Daniel got an uneasy feeling. 'Decline?' he said. 'Ye-es. It's not for me to say anything as you can imagine, but that's what happens when a girl doesn't watch out for herself. She should've kept away from 'em good-for-nothing soldiers, and kept herself proper, like other girls. But it's none of my business as you can imagine.'

Student Daniel Braut did not write a letter of proposal that day. He did not write a letter of proposal the next day either. In fact he never wrote a letter of proposal. On the other hand he did give notice about quitting his room and moved into a garret in Fredensborg Way.

He could not stand living in his old digs any longer, and least of all could he stand the new maid.

7

Lectures began; the schoolboys had now become students.

For Daniel they were a great relief, for they distracted him. And here among all this idealistic youth he could least of all think about Berta Maria.

But the lectures were not as inspired as he had imagined. Many a time he would have said they were dull, if he had dared to say or think this way about such elevated things. But he did not dare. It was, of course, just he who did not understand them sufficiently.

The good thing here was that you did not need to do homework, and that you were not examined on it. The only thing you had to do was listen and write 'notes' if you felt like it. And if you did not want to attend lectures, there was no one keeping a register. What was more, the professors did not know their students, and everyone did what they wanted. Daniel liked this, but he did wonder how he would learn anything if he were not given homework.

In the afternoon he spent time in the company of whoever he happened fall in with. He had thought of revising both what he had learnt and what he had not learnt during his schooldays, but it would have to wait. In the evening he was often at the theatre. He was happy there, for nearly everything revolved around love, and everything was beautiful and idealized. The theatre was like a fairytale land in the midst of the prose of everyday life. There everything beautiful lived its life in peace, protected from anything that could damage or disturb it. In truth it was in the theatre that Daniel felt that he lived ideally, even though he had to sit in the gods.

– Jens at Larsebakken sent money. But the old soil-grubber sent fifty daler instead of a hundred, so he would have to save. And Daniel saved the way he had learnt to save. It was a matter of getting the fifty daler to stretch as far as possible. In time he would presumably get more.

Anyone who had helped him so far would in all likelihood carry on doing so. And now Daniel had a special reason to hope, for Jens at Larsebakken had told him that his brother Lias had got the prospecting rights to look for ore in several 'promising' mines. –

– Some evenings he went to the Student Union because he wanted to see *proper* student life. But everything there was so formal. He felt lost in the great long room among the crowd of haughty young men, so he sat and listened to people reading aloud from the newspapers or to conversations as hushed as in church. But the debate now was about an autumn ball, which some people really wanted to have, and it was strange how quick they were to twist each other's words and to make fun of each other. Daniel listened with respect to these great speakers and thought to himself that this was something he could never learn to do. But it was boring here; he just sat and longed for them to finish. Finally the toddy arrived. But it was not as in the *russ* celebrations. You had to sit bolt upright and listen to long speeches, and not until the night had worn on a bit did things grow more lively. But when they had reached that stage, they stopped.

This was presumably the ideal student life in practice? But then one evening Aslak Fjordan let out a great gasp of laughter and swore that he had never experienced anything so ridiculous. And when Haugum partly went along with this, Daniel agreed completely. They were unanimous that student life did not have the right spirit now. And when they split up Aslak invited them home to his place the following Saturday; things there would be much better than in the Union, he promised.

Saturday evening came, and Aslak kept his word. There was a whole crowd there and it was a lively gathering. A couple of guests, among them a certain Hærland – from the 'Fram' group

– were new to Daniel, but it was not long before everyone knew everyone else, and discussion quickly got going. The professors were variously criticised, but then talk turned to academic questions, and in particular to philosophy. Haugum was having difficulty with 'the transition from 'being' to 'nothingness' and asked Hærland to explain. Hærland laughed and asked whether Haugum thought such things could be 'understood', and added: 'If you can find a single Norwegian student who has learnt to understand Hegelian logic, then I'm not an honest man'. At this Aslak laughed his great laugh and said that, Goddamn it, he could well believe that, and the poet Gregus Johnson nodded.

From logic they moved on to ethics and from there to politics. Hærland and Aslak were republicans while the others were constitutional monarchists. It grew into a heated debate and the only ones who did not join the discussion were Ortvedt, who thought it too abstract, Gregus Johnsen who thought it was too prosaic, and Daniel who was happy just to listen. Besides, he was not quite sure on which side to come down. Basically he agreed with Haugum, but he would nevertheless have preferred to support Hærland who was a sharp and able debater.

After a while Aslak grew tired of the discussion and wanted to have agreement and conviviality, and so in a shaky voice he started the National Anthem.* It helped. Haugum forgot about the monarchy and the republic and sang lustily 'as it rises up'; Daniel and Gregus Johnsen joined in too, and Hærland could not restrain himself and joined in at 'With its thousand homes'.

They sang till they grew warm. One verse led to the next, and with each verse they became happier and more enthusiastic. When in firm voices they had finally sworn:

> We too, when it is required
> Will fight for its peace!

Haugum raised his glass and in elegant words proposed a toast to the fatherland. He did not have much to say, and it was not a speech, but it was sincere, and a silence fell on the gathering when the toast was drunk.

Gregus Johnsen now felt that his moment had come. He asked good naturedly if anyone had read Bjørnson's most recent poem. 'Yes' replied Ortvedt quickly, but Daniel, who was an innocent said 'no', whereupon Gregus began to recite the poem. He did so stiffly and there was not much applause, but then Haugum stood up and gave a speech for Bjørnson which won so much support that Gregus tried to gave a second speech on the topic. This speech gave Hærland the opportunity to touch on 'Scandinavianism';* Haugum opposed him, but it soon became clear that they were in fact in agreement. By now the toddy had done its work so well that the atmosphere had softened and the gathering broke into smaller groups. Ortvedt told Aslak about a drunken party that ended when the host pointed a revolver at the guests. Haugum and Hærland discussed the state of the government, and Gregus latched on to Daniel and told him about his bad luck in the exams. He had re-sat them twice, but what Daniel had to understand was that he was not cut out to pass exams. He was made for something else, which he for his part thought was more elevated. He did not know whether Mr Braut could agree with him that poetry was the highest thing in life... 'Yes, yes,' shouted Daniel, 'poetry – yes, that's just what I think too; there is nothing like it!'

Gregus was pleased to hear this. There were so many philistines nowadays, even among the students, philistines who, as he would put it, could not see that poetry was the greatest force in life. But that was something that Gregus understood, and no one would make him think otherwise. To harness him up to do exams was like ... well, he would not use the image he had thought of. People talked of intellectual development and mental discipline ... well he, Gregus, had read philosophy and other things like that, but ... these people did not understand *inspiration*. They had never felt inspiration rush through them on broad wings; indeed Gregus would say that he was *quite sure* they had not, if they thought that they could bind the spirit to rules, and say that you had to think in this way or that. It was as if the spirit did not follow its own path.

– 'Go on, sing it!' shouted Aslak Fjordan, 'sing it!' – Haugum began with his calm, gentle voice, and they all listened:

> I have borne the wings of the lark,
> I have sung its song aloud,
> I have felt that I shall rise
> To paradise one day,
> To paradise one day.

The song came at just the right moment. Haugum had to sing it again. Happy and at peace they sat and listened and dreamt again the dreams of their childhood about the angels and God the Father. It could be that in the everyday course of things they might end up doubting something or other in the teaching of the church, but at times like this all the good and happy memories rose to the surface and they believed like children. Even Hærland was swept along. With shining eyes and a warm sensation in his breast he sat and let himself slip into the blissful dreams taught him by the church. Finally he swore that the song touched the highest and deepest feelings in us, however much we tried to doubt and deny it.

After a while they embarked on a new topic: women, and this was a long chapter. They covered the whole spectrum from 'the ideal' – skål for our fiancées! '*The cool deep darkness descended*' – and went on from there till they reached the bottom. Then in a thin, faltering voice Ortvedt started to sing a song about 'Samson who loved Daliladalila, Daliladalila,' and they all joined in with gusto. Daniel, who with a sore heart was thinking of his poor Berta Maria, could not really join in. By a natural chain of thought they came to sinister matters, sickness and medical horrors, so that in the end Daniel was quite frightened. Then Aslak said 'skål!' and swallowed the rest of his glass. 'Was that my second or my third?' he laughed and poured a new one and encouraged the others to do the same. But as Ortvedt was still carrying on with his hospital stories, Aslak stood up and with a voice that could waken the dead, began '*Sing of the student's happy days*'.

This ballad too came at the right moment. Haugum got up and joined in, and soon they were all walking up and down the room and singing along, but they did not get to the end of the ballad, as one after the other they all started talking again. They had so much to talk about; in twos and threes they stood about the room and chatted, and every once in a while they had to go over to the table and drink a 'skål'. It got livelier and livelier and voices became louder and louder, like a sea when the wind gets up. Some argued about where it was best to get dinner, others about the Trinity. And now many things came up, about which they otherwise remained silent. Financial worries and sins, mistakes and foolishness were laid out as honestly and openly as if it were the Day of Judgement. Daniel could no longer carry his heartsickness alone. Gregus Johnsen let Ortvedt know that he was working on a great tragic drama that was to be called *The Emperor Caligula*. 'What the devil!' laughed Ortvedt. '*Aut Cæsar, aut nihil,*' replied Gregus. But Hærland whose good mood had now left him was explaining to Haugum in no uncertain terms that the church's teaching about the divinity of Christ was unbiblical. And they drank to friendship with each other and believed in each other and laughed great happy laughs over nothing. Once in a while they started *Sing of the student's happy days*, and then everything else was forgotten, and all joined in with: '*let us rejoice!*' – but immediately after the conversation started up again, and the ballad was never finished. The air was thick with the smell of tobacco and toddy. Haugum managed to open a window slightly, but it did not help much. Then a glass would be tapped and someone or other would stand up, red-eyed and pale, and propose a toast for something or someone or other. Finally when Hærland had grown tired of arguing with Haugum about the divinity of Christ, he made a great speech about 'the mighty ideas that like a flood were now rushing in on us from Europe'. It was almost morning by the time the gathering broke up.

But they had more evenings like this. And they sang and grew rowdy and discussed all sorts of things, argued about politics and all the big issues to the point where they sometimes almost became enemies. Often they got Aslak Fjordan and Halvor Mosebø to engage in a rhyming *stev** contest, or Hærland to narrate folktales in Sogn dialect.

When far into the night they ambled along the streets arm in arm, chatting and humming, they nearly always had a police constable following close on their heels. According to Hærland, 'He knew they were *russ*, and was hoping to get some fines'. From time immemorial it had been part of student life to be at odds with the police, but they let that quarrel lie; when they heard the constable's footsteps following them, they became as solid and serious as a committee of town councillors. The old farming-class respect for everything that smelt of 'authority' was in their blood. Daniel immediately became sober when he saw the arm of the law. Sometimes Aslak, when he had a fair amount on board, got the urge to 'have a friendly chat with that constable fellow,' whom he would like to 'cut open along his backbone' or 'knock his teeth down his throat,' but then they all hushed him up. Daniel feared for his life, for one could never know what would happen if one fell into the hands of the police.

Apart from that they could risk trying out wilder paths. Freed from all taskmasters, from the strict traditions of the farming community and quick popular condemnation, they felt they should use their freedom. Christiania nightlife seemed to them like a wild, seductive adventure; you had to get to know the unbelievable werewolf life beyond all morality and beyond the pale of human society. Thus it could happen that when they were feeling lively and high-spirited and the night was dark Ortvedt would say 'Beer upstairs,' and then they would all go to where they could get 'beer after midnight'. But it was not much fun; the adventure was not much of an adventure. It was the most wretched Christiania prose, crude and rotten-smelling like a gutter. It was unbelievable that such things could exist, and that people could be so disgustingly awful. –

Daniel soon grew tired of going to lectures. To sit up there in the dark university building for four or five hours a day listening to endless explanations of angles and categories was not much better than being at school. Nor was he learning anything. He wondered if it was not just such lectures that Professor Darre had meant when he spoke of dead specialist knowledge. And as for philosophy, – well, that was beyond comprehension, as Hærland had said.

He began to skip lectures. When it got closer to the exams, one could revise the essentials from books; that was just as good. And there were many who did that. Besides the *examen philosophicum* was easy, and did not count for much. One could use one's time more profitably. One could sit at home in peace and comfort and study human life through inspired books.

So that was what Daniel did. Not every day, because acquaintances might wonder about that, but often. And it became more and more often.

The 'inspired books' he borrowed from Gregus Johnsen in exchange for a bottle of beer every now and again. Gradually he moved on to novels. –

– But little by little his money was running out. Eventually he would have to do one of two things: look around for something where he could earn a few shillings, or start to save seriously.

He chose the saving option. You had to remain a free student as long as you could, and help would presumably come some time if you just held on. Lias would surely sell his mining prospect soon, and then everyone would be saved. And if it really came to the crunch, then it was obvious that there would be no difficulty in finding work in a town as large and wealthy as Christiania.

The only thing he could save on now was food. But that was as it should be. A philistine lived so that he could eat; a student ate so that he could live. A true student and an idealist was *meant* to live on meagre rations. And the Dalesman had lived his best days when he had had no dinner.

Daniel would try this. Two days a week he skipped dinner and lived off 'home food'. And in fact he thought he was doing well.

But his money grew less and less. He would have to cut another dinner. There was nothing else to be done and besides the good thing about eating at home was that it was so comfortable and easy. –

He became more and more lazy. In the morning he lay and read and smoked till far into the day, and when he got up he carried on in the same way.

It was so enjoyable to read about love. Nearly always he found a girl who could be Berta Maria, and one who could be Inga Holm, and then it was as if his dreams came alive. But life itself became a dream that he forgot.

He began to understand the boy who wanted to be king, and would then lie in the hayloft every day and eat sour-cream porridge. If one had a novel in addition to the porridge, and then a pipe afterwards, that wouldn't be so bad!

As time passed he developed such a strange longing for food. However indolently he lived, he was hungry all the time. This fitted ill with his need to save.

It became worse and worse. His thoughts about food were becoming so persistent that they would not leave him in peace. He could be reading the most magnificent stories about the sorrows and blessings of love, and then he would have to get up and snatch something to eat. Or he could be reading about knights and great deeds while having heated dreams of salted meat, and fatty pork and peas at the café 'Dampen'.* And then his chest would burn with hunger, and he could sense the smell of fat pork and yellow peas so clearly that he almost forgot his novel.

Sometimes he sneaked to the café 'Dampen' on days when according to his scheme he should have stayed at home. The strong, sharp smell of food from the steam kitchen got to him like a lure, and he sidled off like a drinker to the bar, even though his conscience gnawed and bit and reminded him clearly that he could not afford it.

When he reached the blessed hatch through which the food was passed out, as if from a bottomless horn of plenty ... and when he held the steaming plate in his hands so that it was no longer a dream but reality – then he threw himself over his food like an animal, arched his back like a dog with a stolen bone, and ate and ate, and sighed with happiness. He gorged soberly and systematically, so that every bit did full service, cleaned his plate and wished that he had the neck of a swan so that the joy could last a little longer. But when he had been home a while he was hungry again.

It was not as poetic to go hungry as Daniel had thought. And it was with growing alarm that he saw his money grow less from day to day. With every daler that went it was as if a bit of ground was slipping from under him, and when the last shilling had gone ... then it would be like falling into a dark abyss.

He had acquaintances, but they needed their shillings themselves. Haugum was going home at New Year to take up a position in a school. Ortvedt was going up country to be a tutor. Aslak Fjordan had presumably eaten away considerably at his bank-book already, and Hærland and Sven Dufva – lived on loans like the majority of the others. Besides his acquaintances were more and more keeping away from him. Daniel increasingly had the look of someone they feared wanted to borrow money.

He had no thoughts of dressing well; those dreams he had laid aside for the time being. His best clothes which he had had with him in his chest he would have to save as long as he could, and his everyday clothes were in a pretty poor state. His jacket had changed colour, so it was now somewhere between bottle green and ashy yellow, and hung baggily round him like a sack. His waistcoat he buttoned right up to his throat to hide his shirt which was rarely washed, because washing cost money, and round his neck he had a paper collar which was not often changed. His hair was left to grow unchecked, and long red tufts of beard grew on his chin every which way. But down towards his feet his dirty, frayed trousers hung with baggy knees over his crooked, worn boots. He consoled himself with the thought that when winter came he could hide the worst of his wretchedness under his coat.

He could no longer take part in the toddy evenings, as he could never afford to be the host. Furthermore, he got so quickly drunk now, and then was really drunk. And when he was drunk, he talked such nonsense that it was embarrassing. He was more and more alone, and more and more took to hibernating. He would have to put aside the ideal student life for the time being until he got some money.

Every day he waited for a letter from Lias about the ore mines.

But the days dragged on, and Daniel could almost calculate to the day when he would be without a shilling.

He had already had a demand for the previous month's rent. Then he had managed to get out of it somehow, but he could expect a new demand any time now. Oh, if only Lias would write.

– Then one day Lias did write. He wrote that he was going to sell the farm and go to America. He had for a while lost his senses and had prospecting fever and wasted time and money on the worst trash. Now he could not manage any longer. Jens at Larsebakken or the bank would have to take over the farm, and mother would have to live with Judith, who was going to marry a carpenter down at Neset. He himself would be leaving with the next boat.

Daniel sat and read this, and it was as if a mountain of dreams came crashing down over him with a roar and a cloud of rubble. Now he lay there. What should he do now?

Oh, why couldn't God help! He who controlled the whole world, who was all-powerful ... couldn't He have helped Lias to find some ore? Couldn't He with a word have *created* a vein of ore in the mountain where Lias had bought prospecting rights? Couldn't He have ... couldn't He have turned this letter into gold ... or this lamp to gold, or the ink-pot...

It was written that 'if any will not work, neither should he eat'. But it was not true. Hundreds of thousands of happy young men roamed the world and did nothing except mischief, and were alive all the same, lived well, lived the high life because they had a wealthy father, or a large inheritance. Why couldn't someone else have the same chance as them?

When Daniel had grown tired of thinking this way and realised that it was getting him nowhere, he heaved a great sigh and said to himself that he would have to try the last resort.

In a town like this there was enough work. It was matter of finding something he liked doing.

What could he do? Book-keeping? No. Be a teacher of music? No. Of mathematics? No. Of Latin or Greek? No. Of German or French? Hardly. He could do nothing that was of any use here.

And who should he turn to? He knew no one. No one who had money or power. He would have to look in the papers to see if there was anything there.

No. Nothing for him. For shopkeepers and servant girls there was plenty of work to be had, but for a student who could do nothing, there was nothing.

Daniel Braut was afraid.

In his need he went to Haugum. He had to think of finding something to do, he said and asked if Haugum knew of anyone who could make use of him. No, Haugum knew of no one.

It was very difficult to find work when one was not known, explained Haugum. Here there was such competition for everything, a hundred dogs for every small bone, so it was a matter of luck if one got anything. 'But go to see to the editor of the *The Farmer's Friend*,' he suggested; 'if anyone knows of anything it would have to be him' – 'Yes, but... can one go to a man like that ... and ask about such a thing?' 'Yes, of course you can! The Farmer's Friend is a kind old man, just go.'

Daniel put on his best clothes from his travelling chest, and went. But he was not feeling confident.

He was shown into a great long room, where a lot of boys were sitting each at his own table, busy with newspapers. Some were putting them in piles, others were putting them in covers, others were making transcripts. Daniel was overwhelmed by a deep respect, and remembered some words he had read somewhere, that the press was the fourth power in the land. He took off his cap and greeted people around the room; no one responded. They did not even notice him. Daniel felt very small; there was probably no point in trying here; best to go away again. But then a small boy came over to him, 'D'you wan'er speak to some'un' he asked calmly and confidently. Daniel felt embarrassed in front of the small boy. 'Yes, ... er... the editor'. 'In there, then,' he said, pointed and left. Daniel went along a passage, quietly, cautiously; the fourth power in the land, the fourth power in the land. The room was white with paper, the air full of a rustling as of harsh whispers.

Quietly and reverently Daniel knocked on the door. No reply.

The Making of Daniel Braut

He knocked again, somewhat more firmly; – 'Kem in,' said a grumpy voice, as if from a distant cellar. Daniel opened the door gingerly and went in, humble as if he was going before the king.

There was no one there. The room was not large, nor well lit. But it was ugly and untidy. In the middle of the floor was a table full of paper and old newspapers, and at the end of the table there was large willow basket full of the same. Books and packages lay scattered over the floor, while a large bookcase stood half empty, gaping and leering over some years of issues of *The Farmer's Friend* and *The Storting News*. A couple of three-legged stools stood around here and there where they had last been left. But in a small cubbyhole Daniel saw a grey back sitting bent over a desk; could *that* be The Farmer's Friend?

The grey back turned round. Daniel could see a pale, mean-eyed face with a thin, red beard surrounding heavy, puffy jaws; the mouth was broad and disgruntled, but it said nothing. Daniel felt his courage seep away. 'Are you ... the editor?' he asked, and should probably have added 'sir,' but could not manage it. 'He'll be here soon,' was the reply. Sit down!' and at that the face turned away again, so that Daniel once more saw a grey back bent over a desk.

Daniel went over to one of the stools and sat down. He was glad the grey back was not the editor, but felt nervous when he thought that the great man would soon be here ... walking in broad and majestically, pondering reforms of importance for the whole country. What could one say to such a man?

There was a knock. Daniel jumped where he sat. 'Kem in' said the grey back, and a short, lean, middle-aged man with a strangely cat-like face sidled in quickly and nimbly. He half bent his back in greeting, but quickly straightened himself when he saw that the editor was not there, and tripped with delicate steps over to the inner door. Daniel felt sure that the man was a tailor. 'Good day!' The grey back turned. 'The editor not here yet?' – 'No.' 'Will he be here soon?' – 'Oh, tomorrow.' – 'Tomorrow?' – 'Tomorrow morning some time.' 'But today I was in the office and they said he would be in this afternoon?' – 'Tomorrow morning, as I said. Look in between eleven and one.' – 'Very well, but you see it was about that piece I wrote...' – 'What piece?' – 'Oh, the one about excess and luxury ... and how wrong it all is...' – 'And – ?' – He promised it would appear, but it's taking so long. I'd like to know whether it's going to get printed soon!' – 'Hmm. You'll have to talk to the editor.' – 'And then I would like to know if I couldn't get something for it ... it's not easy to manage in times like these...' 'Look in tomorrow morning between eleven and one.' The face turned away, and in its own way the grey back showed the tailor the door. 'Very well, very well,' sighed the tailor, shifting his weight from foot to foot like a dancer, 'Tomorrow between eleven and one ... well, good day then!' He scurried out with long strides, and one could see that he had a bald patch.

Daniel felt uncomfortable sitting there. It was eerie here and he didn't expect to get anything. He ventured over to the door and asked respectfully if it was true that the editor would not be back till tomorrow? 'He'll be here soon,' growled the grey back. Was there anything *he* could help with? – Mmm – no, it was ... Was he looking for a job with the paper? Had he been sent down from the university perhaps? – No that was not what it was. 'No? Good. All the ones who fail their matriculation exams or are sent down from university come here and want to work for the newspaper. We could supply the whole of Europe with newspapermen; – so that's not an area where you should try to compete. Oh, good, there he is.'

Daniel went pale, turned and prepared to greet the editor. In through the door came a huge body in a vast winter coat; on its head it had a fur cap and on its nose a pair of large horn-rimmed glasses. Daniel bowed repeatedly. The old man did not respond, but went over to a corner and took off his galoshes and overcoat. Then with the cautious gait of an old man he advanced towards where Daniel was standing, said nothing, but stared hard at him through his glasses.

Daniel said in a rush what he wanted. The old man shook his head and said no. No, he knew of nothing. He had helped one or two on their way in the past... 'Sit down, boy!' – The old man sat himself down – 'There was even one called ... now what was he

The Making of Daniel Braut

called? ... Jacob, no, Peter, no, it was Jacob! No, that's right it was Peder, Peder ... Peder Monsen! Do you know Peder Monsen?' No, Daniel did not. – No? Well, never mind. He was a boy who knew how to make things work out for him! If he didn't borrow twenty daler, which he promised to repay when his father had sold an iron mine he had found...' And Daniel got a long story about this Peder Monsen and his ability to turn things to his advantage. The old man laughed and got into a good mood. But Daniel felt more and more disheartened. There was a knock at the door. 'Come in,' shouted the old man. 'Well, as I say, I know of nothing, my boy. You'll have to advertise. – Good evening, good evening!' he said to the new arrival, 'It's good that you've come. Sit down! Good night, my boy!' – Daniel left; he felt strangely cold, and his feet were like lead.

He went home and sat down. He did not think, just sat and felt depressed. After a while he began to dream. Perhaps there was a point in this. Perhaps God did not want him to bind himself to a job; perhaps He had help lying ready, and would send it when the need was greatest. One day when he came home hungry and weary and in total despair, there would be a letter lying on the table with a hundred daler and only the words, 'From an unknown friend. Take heart!' And when those daler had been used up, another letter of the same sort would come ... he sat and calculated how he could best use these hundred daler, but came to the conclusion that one hundred daler was far too little, and then he dreamt the dream again, but now there were two hundred daler in the letter. There was a knock on the door. Daniel jumped ... but it was only Gregus Johnsen.

The next day Daniel went up to the university to see if there were any adverts for private tutors. Yes, there was one – at a doctor's on the coast near Bergen. Daniel left immediately. Surely God could not intend him to bury himself out in the sticks.

He no longer felt calm enough to sit at home and study. Nor could he go to lectures. He had other things to think about. Mostly he wandered about the streets and dulled his frightened thoughts with dreams, and he had a secret thought that in this way he would hit on something. His good luck was perhaps waiting for him somewhere or other, if only he could find it. Food! Surely a soul could not perish for want of such a pitiful thing as food. All the heroes in poetry always got food. It was crude to ask for it. Food *had* to come. God was surely as good a poet as the others...

It would be pointless, thoughtless, indefensible to raise him up out of the life of a peasant-farmer and then to let him go again in this fashion. It cannot be denied that in his innermost thoughts Daniel almost threatened God, saying he would cease to believe in Him if He did not help him now. They were thoughts that he himself found blasphemous, but he defended them by arguing that if he were to be left helpless now, he would *have* to believe that there was no meaning in life. And how easy it should be for God! He who had every man's heart and thoughts in his hand... Daniel thought of the thousand ways in which God could do it. And sometimes an old memory of a verse of a hymn drifted through his mind ... something about God giving his children what they needed while they lay sleeping ... and what did it say in the Bible? Old Kingo wrote both about Joseph and Elijah and many others.

The hymn echoed in the ears of the boy, till he at last could hear it:

> Elijah, say, who fed you
> When the rains were so strangely withheld
> In those so difficult days of need?
> In that same hour in the land of Sidon
> God sent you a widow mild.
>
> And that you should not suffer want
> Where you walked, as God commanded,
> Doing what He required,
> Ravens brought you food:
> Bread and meat, both early and late.
>
> Joseph was sold into Egypt
> And there was cast into prison
> For his devotion to God;
> But He him raised him up and made him lord
> And brought his friends to glory and gain.

> In the lions' den, where he was thrown
> God did not Daniel abandon,
> But an angel He sent him;
> And He let food be brought him
> By his good servant Habakukk.

It was a matter of having faith – that went without saying. But he had faith. If that was what it came down to – his faith would be as firm as a mountain! But as he thought this, he felt his conscience wake and, from somewhere at the back of his mind, stick out its nose and say: there you lied.

Was that what the matter was? Did God want to bend his will through need and hardship and drive him to repentance? He was uneasy at this thought. The following day he went back to the university to take a closer look at the notice about the private tutor post; perhaps it was not worth demanding too much of God either. But when he got there the notice about the post had disappeared.

Daniel slunk home with a bowed head and heavy steps. But as he walked his dreams came to life again. When need was greatest, help was closest at hand. Perhaps ... when he got home there would be a letter on the table, a letter with a promissory note, from an unknown friend, one hundred daler, two hundred daler, five hundred, one thousand ... he did not believe it himself. But when he entered his room, he glanced uneasily towards the table, in case, despite everything, there might be something ... Good heavens! There was a letter lying there. Could it possibly be? Could God in his infinite mercy ... he tore open the letter with trembling hands, and read:

Mr Student Sørbraut

Dear cousin,

I do so want to come to Christiania. I am not happy here at home, because the prospects here are so sadly limited that in truth I can say with the poet Bjørnson here I'm consumed by a life that's so crushingly narrow though my courage's as strong and as young as the willow. Therefore I want to ask you, who are a student and acquainted with life in town, to do me the favour of finding me a position in Christiania. I don't know languages, but I have neat handwriting, can add, subtract, multiply and divide and do sums with the rule of three, as well as calculate interest and decimal fractions. My requirements would not be great, if only I could live in town...

Daniel threw the letter as far away as he could. He was tired and despondent. He could not laugh.

8

Daniel stood at the ticket window of the café 'Dampen' and shivered as he exchanged his last daler. He was blue round the nose and heavy-headed. His only thought was: that he would have to try to live as long as he could.

As he was about to enter the dining room Jens Rud came in. He was short-sighted and did not immediately recognize Daniel, who felt embarrassed and would have liked to slip away. But then Rud greeted him and asked how things were going. All right, thanks.

They entered and found a table. Rud had brought beer, and Daniel began to feel better. Rud could bring greetings from Hirsch; the trouble up there had ended, for the time being at any rate; the bishop and Ministry of Church Affairs had brought about a reconciliation, and that would presumably last a while. But you could not trust the pietists. They could talk sweetly about peace and brotherly love, but they were like the Blackfoot Indians who lay in wait along roads and paths and scalped their dear white brother as soon as there was a chance to. 'Yes, I suppose so,' replied Daniel.

'Yes, that's the sort of thing we fight about here at home,' Rud continued. 'Christening rites and old forms of words! Out in the great wide world they have other things to think about. Have you read Castelar's most recent speech?'* – No, Daniel had not. 'Well, you really must read it. That Castelar is a great man.' – 'He is?' – 'A great man!'

Later Rud spoke of the political situation in France. 'It's obvious that from now on all young people will have to be republicans,' he concluded. Daniel could not think of anything to say to this, and so replied that that seemed reasonable. 'Are you a republican?' asked Rud casually. 'Oh ... in principle I have to say – though actually I haven't given it much thought.' – 'No,' said Rud with an open, honest smile, 'one's a supporter of the free state nowadays even if one hasn't given it much thought. It's in the air, you see.' 'Yes, I suppose it is,' replied Daniel.

He sat thinking about Haugum and his counter-arguments against republicanism, but could not recall them, and in any case Rud was a clearer thinker.

After a while Rud asked, 'D'you go to the theatre much?' 'Oh – sometimes.' – 'What do you think of such management?' Daniel was surprised; he had nothing to say about the management. But then of course Rud understood these things better than he did... 'Well, there's much that could be said,' replied Daniel. 'Much that could be said?' exclaimed Rud, 'It's a scandal!' And in passionate words he explained that the way the theatre was now being managed it was the very caricature of a national theatre. He spoke so knowledgeably and authoritatively that he had to be right, and as Daniel now felt bold and full of dinner he said in complete amazement, 'That people put up with it!'

Rud smiled. 'We Norwegians are deaf' he said. 'I suppose we are,' replied Daniel. Rud continued in a low, secretive voice, 'But there's no saying how long we will put up with this situation.' – 'Oh?' – 'You mustn't say anything about it, but it could be that one of these days ... there'll be quite a commotion.' – 'A commotion?' – 'A demonstration, you understand ... when we'll all go and boo and jeer or something like that ... when it happens will you join us?' Daniel felt flattered by Rud's confidence in him and replied, 'Of course I'll join you.' Rud looked at him, 'Is that a promise?' 'Of course.' – 'Where d'you live?' – Daniel gave him his address. – 'Good, you'll get a message when the time comes. But till then, mum's the word?' – 'Trust me,' said Daniel.

As they left, Rud said, 'Coffee?' and Daniel went with him. Immediately he began to wonder whether he could perhaps find some delicate way of borrowing money for his rent. He stopped suddenly and said, 'Oh no; I don't think I can afford it. I just broke into my last daler today, so now I really have to save.' Daniel blushed slightly; he thought that Rud was bound to understand this. But, rather surprised, Rud replied, 'The coffee's on me' – 'Oh, – well – thanks then,' mumbled Daniel; he had thought that Rud had better instincts than that.

Café Nationale was the regular meeting place of the Fram* crowd, and was much frequented by 'democratic' youth. Daniel looked around for Fram , but there was no one here that he knew. Through the half-open door to the innermost room he saw a couple of fellows who might perhaps be part of the Fram crowd. They were tall and shabby and reminded him of a headline he had read in a newspaper: 'Bandits from the Apennines'; Rud made his way in that direction, and there they found Fram. He was sitting at the end of a table, writing. Rud and Daniel sat down.

Daniel could not see much of Fram apart from his incredibly long black hair, which hung down over his eyes, and which he sometimes tried in vain to sweep back from his forehead with his hand. He was dressed in a long black coat with elbows shiny from hard wear and cuffs that were slightly frayed for the same reason; he was skinny and slight. On the table in front of him stood a half-drunk cup of coffee and a cup of cloudberries. There was no writing paper; he was sitting writing on the edge of an old newspaper, and the back of a subscription proposal form had already been covered with writing and set aside. The two bandits sat reading the papers. It was quiet in the room, the only sound was Fram's pen scratching and tearing the coarse newsprint. Fram did not look up except every time he dipped into the cloudberries. Then Daniel stared at the long, open and strong face with the pale blue eyes of a child, and wondered if this really could be the terrible radical they talked so much about and whom the police, according to rumour, shadowed wherever he went, lest he start a revolution on the open street.

After a while, more of the Fram crowd drifted in, and it became livelier. One asked for coffee, another for beer, one even had a loaf of bread – he hadn't had dinner, he said. A couple came with books under their arms; they were in the habit of sitting here and reading, as they did not have the wherewithal to make a fire at home. A young, genteelly poor student asked if anyone would buy him a beer as 'he had no more credit here'; 'D'you have credit anywhere else then?' they asked. 'The devil I do,' replied the young man. The others laughed, and Strand – the one with the loaf – said that now at last Baardsen would hang himself, something he should have done long ago. The young man – Baardsen – shrugged his shoulders, 'There's no one who'll let me buy a rope on credit,' he said. 'You can have some sack cord from me,' replied Strand, 'but when you've finished with it I want it back; I'll soon need it for my own neck,' – 'Give me a piece of bread and we'll negotiate the matter,' said Baardsen. 'Damn it, I'm not half full myself! There you are, you scoundrel, you rogue; may it change to stones in your throat and your bottomless belly!' – 'Thanks,' said Baardsen.

Daniel began to feel at ease in this group; they were all bums like him, but it did not worry them. 'You there,' said Fram to one of the bandits, 'give me that rag of a paper!' – 'I haven't finished it yet,' growled the bandit. 'Give it me,' hissed Fram; he had to have something to write on! The bandit tore the paper in two and gave Fram the adverts page. During this exchange two more young men came in, whom Daniel judged to be theological students and so presumably not part of the Fram group. They sat down at one of the smaller tables over by the window, and a serving girl brought them coffee. 'Johanna!' called Fram, 'How many cups have I had now?' – 'D'you mean today?' – 'Yes?' – 'Six.' – 'Let me have one more, Johanna.' – 'Just one?' she laughed to the others with her white teeth. 'One at a time,' Fram nodded and wrote.

But when the coffee came, he put down his pen. He straightened up and looked around. Daniel noticed that he did not have a collar; then he started to drink his coffee, and when the worst of his thirst had been quenched, he turned to Baardsen and said, 'Baardsen, I'm going to tell you something. If you hang yourself, you'll be doing us a service, for you're a lout, and a lout you'll remain. But ... so be it. God has a use for all sorts;

He even has a use for theological students I imagine'. They understood immediately where he was heading; the two young theological students who were sitting over by the window, so prim and proper, were far too great a temptation for his Viking nature. One in particular must have attracted Fram's attention; he was like a theological student straight out of the theatre in his best black clothes and fluttering white necktie; the small, thin and pinched face asked God to free it from this world with every crease and corner of its mouth, and he sat as upright as if he had swallowed a long-handled axe.

These were the characters Fram wanted to pick a quarrel with. He poked fun at the students and at theology in a way that was hard for the two young theological students to listen to. To begin with it was done almost jokingly; Fram could smile as innocently as a child while uttering the sharpest words, but sometimes his eyes blazed and he became more and more bitter. Soon the boy who had swallowed the long-handled axe could not remain as tall and pale as before. He grew redder and redder, was more and more bursting with anger and zeal for the truth. Time and again it looked as if he would explode, and time and again he swallowed his anger. Finally he did explode, he could stand it no longer. Fram made the point that the clergy should be popular teachers; *they* should be like the old rationalist clergy who taught the farmers how to cultivate the earth; they were something different from these augurs of today who were as light-shy as rats, and just crept to the altar and stood and mumbled about the Mystery. This roused axe-handle. 'Excuse me' – could he take the liberty of asking who had introduced the new school reform? And was it right to call those who had done this 'light-shy'? – Daniel immediately felt respect for axe-handle. But Fram turned like a flash on the tiny theologian and said that the claim that the clergy had anything to do with new school reform was a load of humbug. He then explained in his own unique way, sometimes smiling and searching for his words, sometimes angrily and tersely that it was not the clergy who should have the credit for this; the new school reform had come about because of popular demand from below, from school-teachers and sextons. The new school reform was the fruit of meetings between schoolteachers across the country and of the spirit which had been roused by Ole Vig.* The clergy had constantly turned their eyes heavenward at this spirit, and at the meetings of school-teachers they had, if they had bothered to turn up, protested and inhibited all free expression of opinion, and had supported ignorance for all they were worth, ignorance from below, in other words the old wives' demand that Pontoppidan should be the main book in schools. That was what the clergy had done! Those who had supported the new school reforms were people like the sextons from the despised sexton-dominated district of Romsdal.* The fact that the country was now more enlightened was thanks to them and to those whom the theologians and better off called half-educated robbers, the army of labour slaves who worked from dawn to dusk for less than a daler a week in order to put food on the table, and who sweated and toiled in quite a different way from those great spreaders of enlightenment, the clergy, who in fifteen minutes performed their task of enlightenment by marrying people for five daler the pair, often with a speech that was not worth five shillings. And if anyone came and said that the teachers should be doing a better job than they were, all he could say was that the blame for this lay with none other than the theologians, since they were the people who taught at the teacher-training seminaries, where they stuffed young boys full of dogma and ridiculous training in the catechism, and on the practical side did crazy calculations on the blackboard with so and so many lines in the *regula multiplex*, or whatever these theological calculations from the seminary were called. And yet the school-teachers had done much worthwhile work, so there must have been good stuff in those doughty men that they could hold out so well against the theological murder of the intellect. 'It's natural enough,' said axe-handle, red in the face and with a trembling mouth, 'that everything that's called Christianity is murder of the intellect for Fram!, but – .' Fram flew up and went straight towards the man as if were going to teach him logic with his fists; 'Christianity! God help us for a load of rubbish. *Regula* *multiplex* Christianity! And Pontoppidan!' He would like to ask every reasonable man: what do you think of Pontoppidan? These theological blockheads wrote in their textbooks that the Catholic priests forbad people to read the Bible and that they worked against popular education; but what did they themselves do? I'll tell you, they would not allow the school-teachers to remove Latin from the curriculum of ordinary elementary schools. But elementary school Latin, that was Pontoppidan. Whether they were up in the mountain districts stuffing the youngsters with *paternoster* in Latin or were teaching lively mountain lads the fear of God by stuffing them with Pontoppidan Latin it came to the same thing: the clergy were clergy, whether they wore a dog-collar or a cape. And then they dared to come here and say that it was they who had brought popular education and a new school system! If that wasn't clergy humbug, then he did not know what was. 'Yes, by God, it's clergy humbug,' shouted the bandits from the Apennines, thumping the table.

Daniel sat staring at Fram like a bird at the fascinating snake; he was afraid, but he had to follow this argument. Now the theological student began to speak and counted up all the good things the clergy had done in the school commissions that ran the elementary schools. He was so furious that he spoke well. While he did so, Strand and Rud began to talk quietly to each other, and Rud let it be known that Daniel was 'one of ours'. Strand bowed in joking respect and said that he would 'Recommend our dear Jens Rud to consider whether in honour of the occasion they should not have a beer?' Jens Rud rang for Johanna of the coffee cups and asked for a couple of bottles of beer, which were received with shouts of 'bravo'. Meanwhile Fram and the two theologians went at it more and more heatedly. The topic of the clergyman in the school commission was abandoned and one of the two theologians tried to save himself by taking up a new position: the clergyman in his role as pastor. Fram was angry at this leap in the argument and spoke of cheating in logic and crude thinking; it was as if his eyes flashed sparks. The theologian was supported by his companion, who said that he thought the souls of parishioners would be ill served by 'popular educators' who preached about Christ being *'apparently* dead' on Easter Sunday. Fram argued that what souls needed was enlightenment, so that like King Saul they did not go around thinking that they had an evil spirit when there was something the matter with their nerves, or looking for a priest rather than the doctor when they were hypochondriacs; the theological pastor of souls was a corrupter of souls! – 'Yes, a corrupter of souls!' thundered the chorus of bandits.

The theologians grabbed their hats and left; this was too ungodly to listen to. A crowd of guests had gathered in the doorway and had stood listening to the exchange; it broke up now amidst laughter and chat, and the debate was picked up again around all the tables, but some argued about Fram. Many liked this fiery, fearless fellow, not least when he ruffled the clergy; others were annoyed with this young prophet of the people who 'thought he knew everything even though he barely had hair on his chin'. –

'Skål!' said Jens Rud. 'This, Fram is *Stud. philos*. Daniel Braut, farmer and supporter of the farmers, republican, arch-Norwegian and everything good; Skål, here's to him!' Daniel blushed; he knew he could not live up to such grand words. 'That's too much,' he said. 'Too much?' roared the bandits; 'Of beer and radicalism, one can never have too much'. 'What district are you from?' Fram asked. Daniel told him. 'They have a good dialect there,' said Fram. Daniel stared. He had never thought other than that the dialect of his district was ugly. 'I assume you're a supporter of *Landsmål*?' said one of the bandits. Daniel promptly thought that the cause of *Landsmål* was a reasonable one, and answered 'yes'. 'But,' he added quickly, 'I have not thought that much about it; but it's a thing that – .' ' – That goes without saying!' added the bandit.

A new bandit entered, a prime example of the species, with his arm in a sling, a gypsy face, unwashed and his hair uncombed. He had a scarf round his neck instead of a collar, and from top to toe he looked worn and shabby. In a surprisingly light, bright voice, he said 'For God's sake, give me some beer! I'm so thirsty.'

'Well, if it isn't the Tramp!' exclaimed the chorus. 'Whence comest thou?' asked Strand. 'That's what God once asked the Devil,' replied the Tramp, 'and like the Devil I say, "from going to and fro on the earth and from walking up and down on it."' The Tramp was given a beer which he drank, then he sat down. He said he now had a hic-story to tell, which they would give gold to hear. 'Of gold we have none,' said Strand, 'but such as we have we give you: beer.' – 'How much?' – 'We'll discuss that after.' 'You might cheat me.' – 'You might too. The "hic-story" first!' 'Payment first!' – 'Then we won't bother.' – 'Well, will I get beer afterwards?' – 'Certainly' – The Tramp pushed his empty glass forward : 'and you give me something now to wet my whistle.' – Jens poured him some. 'Thanks! If I'm going to tell a tale I have to lubricate the vocal chords now and again, you understand,' he said.

And the Tramp began. As usual, he needed some of the mammon of this world, and where the devil was he to find it this time? Then he had an idea. He went to *Pater omnipotens** and was saved. (Bravo! Laughter.) Well and good. He went to *Pater omnipotens* and confessed to him a whole lot of sins he had not committed, for those he had committed were for the Devil. But most of all he bemoaned the fact that he had got involved in that ungodly Fram group, where he had been exposed to so much cunning and deception that he had been on the verge of losing his childhood faith. (Hurrah! Hurrah for the Tramp's childhood faith!). *Pater omnipotens* was moved by the Tramp's remorse, and made a speech about the thief on the cross (laughter) before asking what he intended to do now. He replied that first of all he wanted to 'work on his salvation' (bravissimo!) and that he had then thought of studying theology (worse and worse!). Then the Pater had gone down on his knees, and the Tramp also had had to go down on his knees (ha! ha!), and Pater had prayed with burning tears for this repentant sinner and aspiring theologian. But then there was the little matter of mammon. How was one going to touch on anything so worldly after such a solemn moment? But he managed it. He asked Pater for a bible. He had such a desire to read God's word, he said, but unfortunately he had so little of the mammon of this world, that he – truth to tell – could not even afford to buy his daily bread. Then with great joy Pater took five daler out of his pocket and gave them to him, and begged him to come back whenever he felt the need. The Tramp thanked him with fair words and was so touched that he even had tears in his eyes – from all the laughter he had to contain.

The Tramp's story went down well. Everyone laughed and had fun, everyone except Jens Rud. Fram too joined the laughter for a while, but then fell silent. Daniel sided with Rud. The Tramp was given his beer and was clearly pleased with himself. Suddenly Fram turned towards him and said, 'You're scum, Mikkelsen!' – Daniel felt a surge of affection for Fram. Mikkelsen defended himself while Fram sat looking at the ceiling, apparently not listening. When the serving girl came in again, he asked: 'Have you got time to be an examiner, Johanna?' She shook her head and smiled: not now. 'Then the rest of you'll have to manage as best you can,' he said to his companions, 'but you'll have to think like grown-ups and not like school boys.' He read aloud what he had written, and wanted to know if it was written in a style that ordinary people could understand.

There was discussion about a couple of sentences, and while this was going on one of the bandits came over to Daniel, leant towards him and said, 'Excuse me Mr Braut, but you couldn't lend me a daler for eight days? I just happen to be totally out of pocket. I was due to get some money from a fellow, but he cheated me.' Then Daniel laughed, 'I'm out on the same errand myself, today.' 'Oh, I'm sorry. You're not offended?' – 'Good heavens, no.' – 'Thanks.' Soon after the bandit returned, 'Excuse me – but – it occurred to me ... I really am in a bit of a fix ... that if you manage to borrow some money today, perhaps you might have enough so that you could spare a daler, or even half a daler? You mustn't take it the wrong way – !' – Daniel was totally amazed. That's how they did things here! And he who'd been afraid to ask Jens Rud... 'If I get as much as I need myself, that'll be the limit of it – unfortunately,' he said. The bandit repeated many times, 'Please forgive me.'

Daniel stood up; now he too had the courage to go for it, and as it happened he saw Strand over in a corner talking to Rud, and it looked as if it was money they were discussing. He sauntered over; yes, Strand was getting a daler from Rud. With a voice that was meant to be calm, Daniel asked, 'Are there any more where those came from?' – he went red round the eyes. Jens looked at him and understood the situation; without a word he took a five-daler note out of his pocket and gave it to Daniel. 'Thank you, thank you...' 'Is it enough?' asked Jens. 'Yes, that's fine, thank...' He could not say any more; he was happy and ashamed, and set off as if he had stolen the five daler.

But that day Daniel had learnt that a bold fellow could struggle on for a time with the aid of small loans.

He would have to try to do that. There was no other way. He would pay them back as soon as he got a job as a private tutor; no one would be cheated. And surely he could get a job as a private tutor, just like anyone else.

– 'By the way, you couldn't spare a daler or two for a while, could you? I was due to get some money from a man, but he cheated me, and I'm in rather a tight spot!' That was roughly how the formula sounded that Daniel now lived off for a while. With a faltering tongue and going red in the face he recited his formula; he knew he was lying, and he knew he was not welcome. But ... when you had to, well ... and in his heart of hearts there lay a half-thought thought that pushed the blame onto God.

He went to lectures more often than before, as it saved on firewood. In the afternoons he mostly sat in the coffee cellar. It was warm there, and there were people there; sometimes there was even beer. He could also look in the papers to see if there was 'anything for him'. There wasn't, but then at least he had a clear conscience.

One day at the university there was an advertisement for a private tutor, and Daniel squirmed at the thought that he would have to apply for this one. But when he read it, he saw that the tutor had to know English, and he did not. So there was nothing to be done, but presumably something would come along soon that was more suitable.

He often joined the Fram crowd; things were so free and easy there, and you could learn much. Fram was unique, and sometimes Daniel was almost afraid of him. He said what he thought straight out, and whether you liked it or not, you had to listen to him. But he could be contemptuous, and not least Daniel found it irritating when he talked of 'student humbug' and this 'Latin nonsense'. 'They speak of half-educated robbers,' said Fram, 'but where do you think you find most of those? Who do you think is more 'half-educated' than all this riff-raff who do *examen philosophicum*? And cheat their way to a one or a two in, for example, philosophy. Yes, some philosophers they are! They learn their philosophy in a couple of days, then sit the exam. If they write something they've thought up themselves, they do badly, but if they write something they do not understand at all, but have read in a book, all is well. And what about astronomy? We all know these blockheads who come tumbling out in the grey light of morning to go to a private tutor to swot up a few equations which they then deceive the poor innocent professors with. They get great long lists of formulæ, which they cram for a couple of hours before the exam, and forget a couple of hours after, and never look at again. Where in life do we find as much dolled-up nonsense as among the students? Nowhere. Go out and look at these young hopefuls walking up and down Karl Johan with a swank and a swagger and a suggestive gleam in their eye, a *pince-nez* on their nose, a cane in their hand, oiled-down hair, a tassel in their cap, gloves on their hands, and a dandyism that everyone can see is their goal in life. Go out in the evening, when they wander round the outskirts of the city, in the out-of-the-way places, and in the houses; – and these very same people will one day go out into the world to preach godliness and morality and obedience to the law. Go out in the evening and look at all these lawyers, who provoke the police and are hauled in to the police station and fined. And these are the ones who are going to uphold the law. And all this futility, and futility heaped on futility the farmers have to pay for! And still they go and toss their heads and wrinkle their noses and talk of 'callous-handed farmers' and 'half-educated robbers', while at the same time saying that it is they who are the bearers of the national culture!' – Daniel had never heard anything like it. Certainly there could be some truth in it, but *say* it! And in that way!

But when Fram talked of the true student and his vocation, then he could talk so beautifully, and so clearly too that Daniel would just sit staring at him. There was a strange power in this young man, he was as fiery and angry as a prophet, and had as rich and vigorous a vocabulary as a poet, and his intellectual sharpness was like lightning. And his eyes were so clear and warm, and his face so alive and changeable. When he talked about faith Daniel would sometimes recall what was written about false prophets and the devil in the guise of an angel; because Fram was dangerous. He could twist his words so well, and make his arguments sound so reasonable that the snake in the Garden of Eden could not have done it better. Daniel listened to him with the same fascinated fear that Eve must have felt when she listened to the fair and dangerous words, 'ye shall be as gods'. Daniel knew from what he had learnt in his childhood that everything Fram said about these things was lies and poison, but nonetheless it was still as tempting to listen to as if it had been God's truth.

The theologian Ellingstad, who belonged to the group, argued against him, and Daniel thought he did well, and he felt safe when he spoke. But then Fram became like fire and coals and terrifyingly strong, sometimes almost evil, and there was no point in telling him the truth, because he turned everything inside out. Perhaps he had gone so far that God had distorted his vision, so that he should *not* be able to see. Once Ellingstad had said that he himself had doubts about many things and that he was either a fanatical high-church man or a worse freethinker than either Fram or the others. After this Daniel did not think that Ellingstad held his own against Fram as well as he had done, and he no longer felt confident when Ellingstad spoke.

There was one thing that Daniel began to think more about and that was the teaching about the Devil. He would have liked to forget about that article of faith. But then he thought that if he abandoned that one he would have to give up various other things as well, perhaps even the whole lot. It was as if the Devil was the foundation stone in the building. And so Daniel thought no more about it.

But he was certainly a republican, for that could not be particularly dangerous. And as far as he could understand Fram was right about this. Yet it was strange that so many people were against a republic. But when he became uneasy about this, he comforted himself with the thought that if it came to the crunch Fram would be man enough to defend both himself and his followers.

All sorts of people frequented this place, including various ne'er-do-wells. If there was some poor fellow who had fallen out with the world and who owned nothing and had no one to turn to, he would in all likelihood turn to Fram; and Fram could never say 'no', but lent a shilling or two to whoever asked, and never asked for it back. In this way he gathered about him a strange crowd of wrecks and good-for-nothings who followed him like long shadows; but these did not form the 'core'. The core was a small exclusive flock of idealists, urban students and students from the farming communities all mixed up together; a brave army which believed in rational thought, loved the future, had freedom as their article of faith and Bjørnson as their poet, Fram as their pathfinder and 'the new Norway' as their battle cry; they were arch-Norwegians to a man, and Europeans to a man; they were the cream of Norwegian youth.

Of his old acquaintances Daniel here met Hærland, and Gregus Johnsen and later Aslak Fjordan, Markus Olivarius, Halvor Mosebø and Sven Dufva. Daniel was noticed by the 'core' and sometimes included, because Jens Rud thought highly of him, but these thoughts Jens Rud had from his brother-in-law, chaplain Hirsch. –

– Christmas was approaching; Daniel had managed to accumulate quite a debt. His way of life had been frugal and he had gone without food more than once, but he had survived after a fashion.

But now things were getting really difficult. One after another his acquaintances left town. And with burning shame he had realized that they had recently been avoiding him; a few had even said straight out that they could not lend him any more money. He felt more and more lost and wretched. Finally, when Christmas was round the corner and he could not think of anyone else to turn to, he went to Fram. It was the most difficult thing he had done, but he did it. And was given a daler. But when that was used up, he made himself contemptible and went again. He *could not* do otherwise! He had to live! And this would be the last time. Fram had half a daler, which Daniel got. But he did not dare show himself in the core group again.

He felt ashamed, more and more ashamed. This was not an honest way of living; he could not continue in this manner. He would seriously have to look for a post. Student life would have to be set aside till later.

Every day he went into the university and looked at the notice board; every morning when he was sure he would not meet Fram he went to the coffee cellar and looked in the newspapers. There was nothing. Now when things had become serious, there was nothing. He scrimped and saved his last half daler as if he were a miser, lived on bread and water. But the half daler was soon used up all the same, so there he was, totally destitute.

It was a slushy day in January. He was cold and he was hungry. He did not have any firewood, and he decided he had better save his last crust till the next day. He walked aimlessly up and down the street, stooped and hollow, and with wet feet. He had not eaten dinner for several days. At dusk he sneaked into the coffee cellar, slinking and afraid like a hungry dog; there was no one there he knew. Should he try to see if he could get something on tick? He did not dare. One was so strangely lacking in confidence when one did not have money; he shuffled away. Wandered back and forth along the street, and wondered if there was not a single person he could go to. Then he remembered his old acquaintances, Ole Bentsen and Peter Dirk. Thank goodness! There was a way out. He was fairly certain they were in town, and that they had money. They would not say no to an old mate.

He was so happy and relieved that he set off and wanted to find them at once; they lived on Hegdehaugen. But when he got there, they were not at home. Tired and exhausted he went home and lay down. But he was so hungry that he could not sleep. Finally he had to get up and eat his last crust of bread. Then, finally, he slept. And slept heavily and for a long while.

He got up, achingly hungry, drank three glasses of water and set off. When he reached Hegdehaugen, Ole Bentsen and Peter Dirk had just gone out. They would be back some time in the late afternoon.

Daniel was so light-headed that he could barely keep himself upright. But hour after hour he wandered up and down; splashed up and down through the slushy street, until he thought they might be home. It was a sad day. Food, food, was his only thought.

With much toil and effort he reached the house; he was so weak in the knees. Thank goodness. They were at home. He breathed out as well as he could and straightened himself up. He felt so shy, standing there. There was no saying how welcome he would be; he had never spent much time with these fellows, and here he came wanting to borrow money. He would have to harden himself.

He knocked and entered. 'Good evening'. It was dark in the room; they did not recognize him. 'Good evening?' came the questioning reply. The fire was burning so merrily; it was so hot in there that Daniel felt dizzy. He advanced and shook Ole Bentsen's hand: 'Perhaps you don't recognize me?' he said; his voice sounded so strangely thin and plaintive. Peter Dirk who was lying over on the sofa, smoking, got up and lit a lamp; Ole Bentsen gradually recognized Daniel and said, 'Oh, you've become quite a stranger ... been out for a walk?' Daniel blushed and said that he lived quite a way away. He had often thought of coming up to see them, but ... time ... then he went across and greeted Peter Dirk. 'Now, how're things?' he asked. 'Oh, not so bad, thanks.' 'Please, take a seat'. He sat down.

Ole Bentsen and Peter Dirk looked at the lad, and then glanced at each other with a certain expression. They had heard

The Making of Daniel Braut

that things were not going well for Daniel Sørbraut, but now they could see it. He was yellow. There were broad sickly rings round his eyes and the dishevelled tufts of his red beard gave his face a wild, half dead look. Peter Dirk was so affected by what he saw that without thinking he asked if Daniel would like a glass of beer. 'Thanks,' said Daniel, blushing with pleasure. 'I think we have a half bottle left over from dinner,' said Peter with an uneasy glance across to Ole, who nodded. 'We have dinner at home sometimes,' he said to Daniel; 'one has to eat according to one's purse, you know.' – 'I suppose so,' said Daniel. He turned yellow again. Peter Dirk opened the bottle of beer and poured, but only for two. They don't want to drink with me, thought Daniel; but then there'll be more for me. 'For you?' Peter nodded to Daniel and Ole, 'Not for me, thanks,' said Ole. Peter took the glass and nodded to Daniel, who stood up, walked unsteadily over to the table, took the glass with shaking hand and emptied it. Good God, how good it tasted. And how good it felt! If only he had a bite of food as well ... at that moment he saw that Peter had barely touched his glass. Daniel felt ashamed, and apologized, 'A glass of beer is good when you're thirsty.' – 'Mmm, ye-es,' said Ole Bentsen.

Daniel began to talk; the beer gave him confidence, and it was important to get his companions in a good mood. Ole Bentsen sat down in the rocking chair in front of the table and said nothing. Peter Dirk lay on the sofa smoking and answered 'yes' and 'no'. They understood all too well what he wanted. He had the air that identifies the poor soul who has gone out and wants to touch someone for money, and who knows that the others have little faith in him, – this talkative, forward manner that is at the same time abject. He talked and talked about things they might like to hear, was familiar and comradely, agreed with them in everything, like the dog that wags its tail. They sat and wished him to hell and became more and more silent.

Daniel noticed how little interest they took in what he said, and as the effect of the beer subsided, he became as wretched and taciturn as before. He sat and sort of collapsed in his chair and his voice became weak and faltering. He had less and less courage to ask for money, but ... shouldn't it be possible to sit and wait till supper arrived? Then as a matter of common decency they could not do other than invite him to join them...

Ole Bentsen and Peter Dirk sat and gave each other a knowing look. Then Peter got up and looked at the clock. 'What time is it?' asked Ole Bentsen. 'Five-thirty,' replied Peter. 'Oh, that much?' said Ole, 'Well then I'd better get down to work.' 'And what about me?' said Peter. Daniel understood. He was blood-red in the face as he stood up. 'If it's that late, then ... I too had better ... go home and settle down,' he said. 'Yes, you've got quite some way to go?' suggested Ole. 'Yes,' Daniel stood and squirmed. Should he risk it? Yes, they couldn't say anything more than no ... and he *couldn't* go home empty-handed; hurrying and stumbling he set off, 'Yes, it is quite a way home, and what's more I had to go up to the 'Professor's quarter' of town ... I have an acquaintance there who owes me some money, but he was not at home today; and now I must – . But look, ... it's a long way, and dark and slushy underfoot ... you couldn't by any chance help a mate out with a couple of shillings till tomorrow, could you?' He stood fingering and twisting his cap and looked like a thief. 'Mmm ... no,' said Ole Bentsen, quietly and gently, 'I'll be darned if I have that much. I've been expecting money for several days now; I can't understand what they are thinking of, back home,' and to be on the safe side, he added, 'and what's more I'm in so much debt now that when I do get the money, it'll be gone at once. But what about you, Peter? Have you got anything?' Peter put on a humorous expression and pulled out his purse, opened it, and turned it inside out, opened his eyes wide, as if in surprise ... a button fell out. Peter Dirk whistled. Daniel laughed hoarsely and bitterly. 'Well, then...' he said with trembling lips, 'then I'll have to try the other one ... it's rather far, but ... thanks for the beer, and good to see you.' 'Likewise, and get home safely!' – 'Thanks. Good night.' – 'Good night.'

– He descended the stairs with his back bent with shame and dashed hopes. He was on the verge of tears when he got out onto the street. He had made himself act like a dog for a bone, and had not got the bone. Slowly and miserably he slouched down the street. A drunk man suddenly stood up in front of him, 'Are yu 'fraid, boy?' Daniel slipped past him. Two carefree young men came spinning along, smoking cigars that smelt dizzyingly strong; they filled the whole pavement so Daniel had to step into the street. Servant girls came carrying milk-pails and baskets full of bottles and bread. It was so painful to see. His eyes were drawn irresistibly to the baskets. Everyone had food, everybody lived well, nobody had a bite to spare for him.

He stopped outside a grocer's; the shop was full of people. With hungry eyes he looked at all the food which was passed over the counter: bread, butter, cheese, pieces of sausage, bottles of beer, quarter pounds of coffee, pearled barley, peas, pork, eggs, and he groaned with hunger. With a sad sigh he moved away from the door, but stopped by the shop window. He leant against the wall; he was so tired. His shoulders ached; his knees would soon not carry him. Oh, oh, for something to eat; even a bit of dry bread and a glass of water ... he stared with fevered eyes at all the good things displayed in the window: large jars of biscuits, boiled sweets, prunes, sugar; on a rope high up hung huge, glorious hams and cured legs of lamb, and in a basket there were loaves of bread, lovely, large loaves, baked brown and fresh; the bread of life ... he stood staring, dreaming; thought of pushing out a pane ... with a tarred rag so that the glass would not tinkle ... and of taking – *taking* the bread that lay there so golden and tempting. Then he came to; shivered and froze; pulled himself together; staggered off again. Home to bed. He was ill. If only he could sleep. If only he still had Berta Maria, he would have asked her for some food tonight. She would not have refused him. Oh, oh, oh...

He shuffled down through Homanstown with slow steps. The street was full of people; everyone was on their way home to eat. It was cold and raw. But there were lights in all the windows, and every time a door was opened a sweet smell of fresh bread and other foods wafted out from the shops like breezes from Paradise. What was he going to do tomorrow? – Go to *Pater omnipotens*? – Yes, if only he had been saved ... But perhaps ...

when he woke the postman would come with a yellow letter: 'To Mr *Stud. philos.* D. Braut there has come a promissory note for ... ten daler.' Ten daler; bread, butter, milk, no, beer; cheese, no, better a piece of sausage ... eat well ... then off to the shoemaker ... new shoes, two daler ... then dinner ... oh, oh, dinner! A good hot dinner; feel oneself good and satisfied. And then an honest pipe! – No, no. It was worse when one dreamt. Don't think of food; don't think of food...

There was something more important than food. He snorted. If they blew him up with inspiration till he was as full of it as a hot air-balloon, – he would be just as dull, so long as he had nothing to eat...

Back home in the country they were well off. There there was always the certainty of food on the table. Things could be difficult in other ways, but food was something they had. If the worst come to the worst, they could slaughter a cow. They did not starve. It was not for nothing that the older generation regarded bread as holy, and spoke of sacred oxen...

The heroes in Homer, when they were hungry they put an ox on a spit, browned it and roasted it and ate; filled themselves with tender young meat and sweet wine; it was not difficult to be a hero when things were like that. Daniel sucked on his tongue. He felt the taste of tender meat and sweet wine so clearly that his mouth watered.

He staggered on and on. Felt so hollow, so hollow that he felt he might snap in two; his shoulders ached as if they were on fire. Cigar smoke swirled around him, hot and strong; the sound of tinkling pianos drifted out from all the houses. It was painful to hear; in there people were sitting, warm and cosy. They were going to eat supper. And then have a toddy. He was frozen. He could feel the raw, snow-heavy January air right into his bones.

He had come down to Teatergate. The road was starting to go uphill again, but he was too tired to walk till he got warm. He could not go in anywhere when he did not have any money.

Up there was the Church of the Trinity. There was light there. *There* was a place he could go in and rest? There no one could chase him out because he did not have any money. And perhaps

The Making of Daniel Braut

there he would meet someone who would lend him some...

He walked in. Someone was reading from the Bible. He sank into the first empty seat he saw. Good God, how tired he was. Waves of shivering shook his body; he was so dizzy that he thought he might faint; he sank into himself where he sat, and closed his eyes. But behind his closed eyes there danced long rows of bread, golden, well-baked loaves of bread, bread in baskets, bread in crates ... if only he had a loaf of bread. Oh to be someone who would find such a loaf of bread on the table when he came home. The others sitting here, they were going home to have tea and beer for supper. With butter and three sorts of cheese. And cut meat. Perhaps even a small plate of cod first. It was easy for them to be godly. What was it they were singing? He could not distinguish the words. But each time they came to the end of a verse he thought he could clearly hear something that he now had half forgotten:

> 'Though God gives his children both food and clothes
> While they so sweetly sle-ep'.

They could sing that, but for his part he had never seen that food and clothes came while you slept. But people like this who were not part of the Fram group, and who did not live the ideal life of a student, they seemed to have plenty of everything. They looked as if they did. They were both well fed and well dressed; it paid to be godly. A young theological student entered the pulpit and began to expound something Daniel did not understand. Some things he heard; but some things got lost in the echo from all the walls that repeated every word the speaker spoke, so that the sermon seemed to have to wade through a strong counter current. And some things Daniel could not hear because his gnawing hunger distracted his thoughts.

But suddenly he started up and began to listen. The speaker was telling of the ungodly who lived wild lives and used all their worldly goods in a sinful life; and when they had squandered everything they owned, then they might take the clothes off their backs and go to the pawn-shop with them so that they could get something to sin with. The pawn-shop! That word roused

Daniel. There was a way out. He could still get food before he went to bed.

If only he had something he could pawn? – There was no point in taking his books; they were old and worn. His winter coat – he needed that far too much; and he did not have a watch. But his tasselled student cap? Yes, that ... He got up, could barely stand, but took hold of himself and set off out of the church and home for his student cap and then to the pawn shop as fast as could.

He expected to get a daler for his cap, but he did not; he got two marks. But two marks were also money. Daniel felt quite rich as he left the pawn-shop. With renewed energy and quicker steps he went to the coffee cellar and took the edge off the worst of his hunger. On his way home he bought bread and beer, and when he got home he ate again.

Good and warm and strangely exhausted he sat there and dozed; the beer he had drunk lay soft and warm round his head, almost like wool.

But his head ached.

9

The next day Daniel was ill.

His head throbbed as if someone was tightening an iron band round it. His throat was sore and it ached. A revolting taste filled his mouth, and he had a sharp little pain in his side. Fever raged through his blood. He knew that he was awake; he even lay tormenting himself with the thought that he had broken his student promise when he pawned his academic cap for food; but strange visions drifted through his brain, and sometimes his thoughts lost their footing and slipped away. He lay and drifted between wakefulness and delirium, caught in an undertow as if between consciousness and dream.

Later in the day he became worse; his fever grew stronger. Madam Henriksen, his landlady, came and saw to him; asked about one thing or another, but as she only got nonsense for an answer she left in his room whatever she thought he might need, wiped his forehead with vinegar, and allowed the servant girl to light the stove.

The room was small and the air heavy; Daniel had a terrible night; lay and tossed from dream to dream, the one worse than the other. Towards morning he finally managed to sleep for a while, and when Madam Henriksen came in mid-morning he was awake. She asked whether she should fetch a doctor. Daniel remembered his lack of money and said no; but he was afraid. Was he perhaps dangerously ill?

His headache was terrible, and the pain in his side made it difficult to breathe. Was he going to die? The thought affected him so strongly that he became numb with fear. He could see himself lying white and stiff in the black coffin, and could smell the white linen shroud and the earth in the grave. He drew his knees up to his chest in bed and tried to pray; then he thought about the life he had led. He saw all his evil, conceited thoughts rise up in his memory like ugly monsters; the coffee cellar with its drunken orgies and swearing and all its rowdiness now appeared to him like the anteroom to hell. Now he was ashamed of his dreams of leading 'the life of a student'; everything he had done and thought was sinful and shameful and wretched folly. If he were to die now, he would be damned for all eternity. Trembling with fear he grabbed hold of the bedpost and prayed, prayed with disjointed, terrified thoughts that he might live, live so that he could repent. Then the fever returned with its nonsense and confused visions.

Thus he lay for several days and dozed and hallucinated, fearful when he was awake and tormented when he dreamt. Madam Henriksen, whose heart was softened by the sight of this poor creature, did what little she could, and frightened the wits out of him with her medical talk, but comforted him when she understood that he was afraid.

Then he awoke one morning feeling better. His head felt light and strange, but did not ache as badly; he only felt the pain in his side when he breathed deeply and the fever in his blood had been quelled. And Madam Henriksen was as kind as a mother; prepared food and drink for him and simply asked him to tell her if there was anything he wanted. What was more, a shaft of sparkling sunlight came in through the window.

Now the boy thought that all was bright and fair and that a new life had awoken in him. He thought about death but without fear; he thought about God, but now as a father. Humble and weak he lay and rested, and loving thoughts flowed through him. He had walked through the valley of death and in prayer had fought for his life and his soul, but now he had won, now he was saved. With childlike trust he turned to Our Lord. He knew that his Father in heaven would help him now. His evil heart had been bowed and made meek; now Our Lord could follow his loving purpose. He prayed for forgiveness for all his sins for Christ's sake, and he saw God the

Father sitting in heaven clothed in the radiance of the sun and smiling down on his sick child. He was so moved that tears came to his eyes and that made his head ache. Now he would deliver himself totally into God's hand and let his will rule. If it was God's will that he should die, then he would follow that call without resistance, but if he was to live, then he would live as a child of God, for in the end it was the only way he could live comfortably. And if God in his wisdom had determined that he should live, then he presumably also had his angels and servants who could help him with his wretched worldly needs ... Daniel's thoughts turned to *Pater omnipotens*; and surely it was Our Lord himself who had put those thoughts into his head.

His life would start afresh now. He had never felt so happy and confident; it was the peace of God that was with him now; now he was truly saved.

Exhausted and drowsy as if from being drunk he dropped off to sleep again and slept long. Woke again in a happy state of mind and with God in his thoughts, and felt so pure, so good. He had got back some of his appetite and was given fruit gruel with which he strengthened himself, and came to the conclusion that no happiness in the world could be compared to the happiness he felt now that his sins had been washed away. This state lasted for two days. He lay in gentle, peaceful convalescent drowsiness and loved, and prayed to, God, read in the prayer book and the Bible and found such delight in God's word. He shuddered when he thought about his old sinful life amid beer bottles and doubters, and he promised God, with a little sigh that he quelled, that he would now abandon all worldly thoughts, indeed even the ideal life of a student.

A day later he got up. He did not dare go out, but Madam Henriksen brought him food and wood for his stove, and so he sat indoors and took it easy; ate and drank, tried to smoke, but his pipe tasted nasty, and read the New Testament. He did not derive quite so much pleasure from God's word today as before, and in his mind he was not quite so sure of God's grace as before, but he knew from those who were saved that the sense of grace was not always equally strong. Besides it was not

God's will that we should think only of heavenly things.

At this last thought Daniel felt relieved. He laid the New Testament aside and began to think about his worldly concerns. He would go to Pater; now that he was saved he could go to this man with a good conscience and ask for guidance and help, and do so both with regard to worldly and spiritual matters. Apart from that he would not ask for financial help. In his sinful days he had lived far too much on other people's money; now he would follow God's word, and that said that if anyone will not work, let him not eat. He would ask Pater for work. He longed to talk to this man, and believed that he already loved him in advance.

He ate well during these days and was embarrassed about it on Madam Henriksen's account. But she just seemed happy that he liked her food, and besides ... it went without saying that he would have to pay. So Daniel ate and ate with a vengeance. And he recited all the mealtime graces he could remember, both before and after eating; and it was extraordinary how these graces were answered. He had never had such good food as he had now. –

When he was strong enough to venture out he dressed in his best clothes from his trunk and went to Pater.

He was shown into a light and elegant room that faced a large garden. A small pale ray of sunshine shone through the pane-glass in the garden door, and was refracted in the glass balls of the chandelier, thus filling the room with brightness and thoughts of spring. Strange plants stood over by the window with clusters of large green leaves hanging from them, and round the walls there were pictures of Jesus with a crown of thorns, Jesus on the cross, the Norwegian-Swedish king, and a couple of Norwegian landscape paintings. In the middle of the floor under the chandelier there was a large round table with photograph albums and a bowl full of visiting cards on it. Comfortable soft chairs of various styles stood round the table, and large and small plaster figures were displayed on cupboards and shelves. A piano stood against the wall over by the window, and against the wall farthest back in the room there was a sofa,

The Making of Daniel Braut

on which Daniel now sat and waited, for the maid had said that there was a student in with Pater at the moment.

Daniel was uneasy. Today when he had come out into the fresh air his faith had grown so weak in him. He had felt such pleasure in the things of this world, and such a longing for 'the life of a student' that he almost had to force himself to keep hold of grace. How could it be? – For surely he was saved? – But he dared not say he was as happy about talking to Pater as he ought to be.

Someone was opening the office door. Daniel stood up and prepared to greet whoever it was. The door opened, and 'the student' came out backwards, bowing to someone inside, and Daniel heard a broad dialect say with great warmth and friendliness, 'The Lord be with you, dear friend!' – Daniel immediately turned pale and then straight away blood red. The unknown student was Ole Bentsen.

Ole Bentsen was neither pale nor red, but looked as if he was happy. He stopped and with a sing-song voice said 'Well fancy meeting you here? This is a pleasure. So Our Lord has found you – at last. I knew that he was working on you, and saw that he would have to use stern measures against you, for your heart was full of vainglory and would not listen to his voice. But now he has found you; I can see it in you. Welcome!' And Ole Bentsen turned to Pater, 'Here's student Daniel Braut, a good old friend of mine. Formerly he was a child of this world as were I and so many others; but now I believe that the Lord in his merciful discipline has bent him to his will.' 'Welcome, welcome', said Pater as happy as a child, while shaking his hand vigorously. 'Come dear friend! Come and let me talk with you, Daniel ... I may use your Christian name, mayn't I?' – Daniel stood there, red and quite bewitched. 'Yes, thank you, thank you', he stammered. ' Well, good-bye, my dear Bentsen!' said Pater, and Bentsen left. But Pater drew Daniel with him in to his office. 'Come! Come in, my dear young friend,' he said as he closed the door.

There was even more sun in the office. Two bright rays shone on the carpet and on the table and really lit up the room so that even the crucifix on the wall seemed to smile. 'Now, dear friend, how are you?' asked Pater. He was so warm and open in his manner that Daniel was quite moved; he had never before been greeted in this manner. He raised his gentle, pleading eyes – they were as pure and clear as in the old days – ; 'I have had a difficult time,' he said. Pater sat in midst of the sun pouring in, broad, handsome and cheerful; his face was open, as fresh and smiling as that of a child; golden, curly hair surrounded his forehead like a halo. He felt drawn to this boy who sat there so helpless and trusting; he stood up and put his hand on Daniel's shoulder and said, 'Well, if you've had a hard time then be assured that it is God's fatherly hand that has been on you, and that he will undoubtedly help you when his time comes!' He sat down again. His gentle, light blue eyes were wet with tears.

Daniel had to tell him all about his life from beginning to end. He wanted to hop over the fact that Hirsch had been his teacher, but was not subtle enough; Pater asked and Daniel had to come out with it. Then Pater laughed, 'So, you've been involved with Grundtvigianism too?' 'Yes, in a way,' replied Daniel, but he had never been a true Grundtvigian. When he told Pater about his student life, Pater wanted to know if he had been involved with the Fram group. To this Daniel replied in the same way: he had been involved in a fashion – an acquaintance had dragged him along – ; but he had never been a Fram man. Finally he told Pater about his difficult days, about hunger, poverty, and about the illness that had taught him to turn his thoughts to ... the true helper; and now he only had one wish, he said: to find some work so that he could finish his preliminary exams as fast as possible and then start on the subject that had always been in his mind: theology.

Pater liked the boy. Here again was one of these fresh, uncorrupted sons of the soil with their childlike nature and their rich gift for faith and love; here again was a man driven by the spirit to fight God's war. He asked why Daniel had chosen theology. Did he want to be an academic? – Oh no, Daniel had no thought of aiming that high; he wanted to be a clergyman. – Why? – Well, he had always thought it must be ... a great life's work ... to preach the word. – Had he felt a special *urge* to work for God's kingdom? Had he ever really felt the truth of God's word that the harvest was great but the labourers few? – It might look as if there were labourers enough, continued Pater, but *true* labourers, labourers who worked with a sense of calling and with love, of those there were few, sadly few, ... and the harvest, yes, that was great; for here there was a whole nation, a glorious, strong nation, with God's gifts in rich measure, which were to be gathered in to God's barn. Daniel looked at Pater with deep reverence; Pater had got carried away with his own thoughts.

He had great dreams for the people of Norway, and could never let go of the thought that Our Lord had chosen them for a special mission in his kingdom. He did not think much of the great cultural nations about which there was so much talk; they were all more or less corrupted and worm-eaten by immorality, self-importance and godlessness; but the people of Norway were young and uncorrupted, with a secure and simple faith and untapped energy; and when God added his blessing, which he surely would, and which in so many strange and wonderful ways he already *had shown* that he would, then we would see what he could make out of us, few though we were. It would be a strong people who could say with Joshua: 'as for me and my house, we will serve the Lord' – they would be stronger than the Philistines, stronger than all the heathens with their warhorses and wagons. It was a case of labouring while it was still day; it was important to sow and plough and water, so that the Lord could give the growth; then as the poet Landstad said 'the land over our graves would blossom like the Lord's garden.' Pater spoke passionately; time and again his eyes filled with tears, and his strong mouth quivered. Daniel was transported; he had to think of chaplain Hirsch.

But when Pater began to talk about a personal relationship to God, and the life in Christ, Daniel could no longer follow so well. He was as embarrassed as a small boy, and felt that really he did not belong here. And the more Pater spoke of 'the blessed state of grace' and the battle with the flesh, and peace in the knowledge of eternal life, the more Daniel understood that he was not saved. – 'Isn't it so,' concluded Pater, 'that this is a glorious and blessed thing, and far greater and richer than all the happiness, grandeur and glitter that our earthly life can offer? You have felt it yourself? Experienced it? – After what he had said before, Daniel did not think he could answer anything other than 'yes'. 'I am glad!' said Pater, 'I'm glad. Thank God for this, and thank him not least that he has saved you while you are still young, and saved you from getting into league with the godless!' – Those poor people! Pater felt so sorry for them; they were their own worst enemy. Without peace, without hope, without comfort and help in life and death...

Hmm, strangely enough, he had recently been visited by one of these poor creatures from the Fram group; really a prodigal son, who had tried as long as he could to sustain himself on such swill as there was; he cried so piteously over the spiritual sickness and restlessness that he had experienced as long as he had trodden those paths. But now he had returned to his father's house; and now he was happy. 'And can you imagine, he was so destitute that he barely had a shred of clothing on his body, but can you guess what he asked for? Not for money, not for food, not for clothes, no, but for a *Bible*?' – Daniel sat looking at the floor and felt as mortified as a dog; 'Yes, it's strange,' he said. 'Indeed, it's amazing', continued Pater in his profound joy. 'But that's how it is, when God gets hold of a soul, everything else becomes worthless; the soul only wants to be at peace with God, and his word, and if it has that then it wants nothing more on earth.' – 'Yes, that's what I've felt,' mumbled Daniel uncertainly. Pater stood up and filled his pipe. 'Praise and thanks be to God,' he sighed; 'He knows how to find us; He knows how to deal with us! Ah, we go round thinking we're so wise and clever; but He teaches us to see that all our wisdom is foolishness!'

Pater refreshed his pipe and changed his tone. 'You said that you thought you would like some work; wasn't that what you said, dear friend?' Yes, if that were possible, said Daniel, that was what he would like. Pater sat down again.

'Hmm, it's strange' he said with a conspiratorial smile, 'I've just heard of a post that might suit you. There you see! Our Lord is never at a loss. It's a private tutor post out in the country in an attractive district; – I don't think the post has been filled yet. Would you like me to enquire?' 'Yes, please,' said Daniel'. 'Well then, I'll do that,' said Pater. 'I think it's as if Our Lord himself had sent you ... you are just the sort I could use here. Listen, do you know the student, Bentsen?' – 'Yes, quite well.' – 'He's an amazing young man ... with such a strong faith, and so honest in his assessment of his own strengths and weaknesses ... don't you agree?' – 'Yes, I suppose so.' – 'What other students do you know?' – Daniel thought for a moment, and then mentioned Hans Haugum. Then he had to tell Pater about Hans Haugum, and he did so in such a way that he only mentioned those things that he thought Pater would like. 'Yes, it is strange,' said Pater, 'it's as if Our Lord had put everything in place for you. Student Stensrud was here just now and asked me to persevere ... and then you come. What's your name?' – 'Daniel Braut,' – 'Daniel Braut. Well, may you be a true Daniel! Come back in a couple of days; I am certain Our Lord will help you.' He patted Daniel on the shoulder and laughed, 'You're a real son of the soil, my lad! So quiet and steadfast ... a true Israelite, in whom there is no falsehood. I am fond of such lads; in fact, I'm a peasant-farmer myself; and the peasant-farmers ... the peasant-farmers they are the marrow ... "What the heart of farmer can carry, though seldom it was sown, it is our nation's honour, and our future it proclaims" as the poet Bjørnson says. – And let us give thanks to God for that. – Is there anything else I can help you with?' – Daniel turned scarlet and hesitated; 'Well – ; I don't suppose...' 'Speak out!' said Pater. 'Let me be like a father to you; don't be afraid. There is nothing more blessed than being – as it were – a hand for God's wish to help. Do you need money?' – Well, ... it couldn't be denied ... Pater smiled. 'Just today a man came and gave me ten daler, telling me to give it to a needy student ... yes, isn't it strange how he guides everything.'

Daniel was saved.

'Well, God be with you, dear Braut!' said Pater as he said goodbye and shook Daniel's hand. 'He is close to those who stay close to him. Look in in a couple of days, and then we'll see if he hasn't had a purpose in sending you here. God be with you. Good-bye, dear friend!'

Daniel left. A new visitor was waiting in the sitting room. 'Good day, good day, dear friend' said Pater heartily, 'goodbye, dear Braut!' he called equally heartily; and the door closed behind Daniel. –

– A couple of days later he received a letter from Rud saying that the following day there was going to be a meeting at five o'clock in the Café Nationale to discuss 'the matter of the theatre'.*

'What nonsense!' said Daniel and put the letter to one side. He did not want to get involved in such things now. He could sense that Pater would not like it; besides, he had things other than theatre matters to think about now.

The day after he met Rud on the street. 'Now' said Rud, 'I suppose you're coming?' – yes, ... well, Daniel was not sure; it was not that easy for him... 'I'll get the tickets', said Rud in a whisper – Yes, ... but ... he was meant to be going somewhere else tonight. 'Oh, never mind; leave serious matters till tomorrow!' laughed Jens. 'Tonight the fatherland expects every man to do his duty!' – Well, well, Daniel would have to think about it. 'Tonight at five o'clock! The Café Nationale!' said Jens and dashed off.

Daniel thought that when it came down to it this was just nonsense. But it could be fun to go along with something like this for once too. And he was not saved; so for that matter ... What's more he had in a way promised ... but then there was Pater. He was reluctant to do anything to offend such a good man.

In doubt and in two minds he went home, and in doubt and in two minds he passed the time till five o'clock, but could not come to any decision. Then he went out. He could always saunter along the street, he thought, and eventually reach a

The Making of Daniel Braut

decision. It was his intention not to get involved. But it couldn't matter if he thought some more about it. So he walked round the streets and thought; went over the same thoughts that he had had before. Finally he found himself standing outside the Café Nationale, without having got any further. He took a turn down the street and then back again; wanted to think more about it; his thoughts were the same, but his desire to join in grew.

He saw group after group come and go in; they came slinking along like conspirators. It *would* be fun to join in! The town lay as calm and secure as if nothing was the matter; the good citizens weren't dreaming of anything; but in there, in the tiny cellar, in a secret, closed-off room, young Norway sat planning revolution ... it *would* be fun to be part of it. One by one his thoughts fell silent; the wish grew; if only Rud would come and take him with him!

It was a quarter past five. If he wanted to be part of it, he would have to hurry. He had in fact promised ... and it was after all a good cause ... oh, what the hell! He hurried towards the steps, quelled all thoughts, and went in. In the café he found Jens. 'At last. In there!' said Jens; Daniel went in, '*Jacta est alea*' he thought.

But when he came out an hour later he had promised with hand on heart that he would go with them that evening and blow his whistle for all he was worth as soon as he heard the shout 'Down with the director!' coming from the stalls, and that he would not let himself be frightened by anything, but would just keep hold of his whistle and blow. And now he knew that the cause was a good one. With his passionate logic Fram had shown that the nation's theatre was being run in such an indefensible way that no Norwegian could be expected to tolerate seeing it in the hands of a clique like the one that was running it now. And Daniel had made a note of several of Fram's reasons so that he had something to defend himself with should Pater hear of the matter.

Daniel was given his whistle by Jens Rud. The majority went out and bought their own after the meeting, while some would make do with door-keys, children's trumpets and anything else that could make a noise. After the protest they were to meet up in the coffee-cellar and have a late supper.

Daniel was to sit with a group in the gods with Sven Dufva and a certain Monsen, or 'Don Pedro' as Fram called him. Most of the hooters and whistlers were to sit in the upper circle; the rest were scattered throughout the theatre. According to Jens Rud, it would be 'a first-rate concert' if everyone did their bit.

Daniel sat in the gods with pale cheeks and a thumping heart, waiting for whatever was going to happen. Behind him he had a great lump of a fellow, a butcher or someone like that, who he was not quite sure about; much worse was the fact that over in another group there was a police constable; was *he* going to get involved in the proceedings? Daniel asked his neighbour, Monsen, about this. Monsen pulled a face, 'It's none of his business to prevent the free exchange of ideas,' he said in his broad Nordfjord dialect, grinning.

The orchestra started to play. Daniel was not listening; with a thumping heart he had noticed that another police constable had sat down in the gods. He had to tell Monsen about it. Monsen sneered an ice-cold sneer and said quickly and grumpily in the deep sing-song of his dialect 'What the hell does it matter?'

Daniel was ashamed. Monsen must be a brave man.

It was as if the air in the theatre was charged with a spirit of restlessness. Nervous whispering ran along the seats like a gust of wind in dead leaves, and wherever Daniel turned he saw pale, expectant faces. The play came rushing across the boards as if in a fever; the actors forgot their lines and made one mistake after another. Every so often it was as if an electric shock struck the rows; there was a rustling of silk and stiff collars, and chignons turned this way and that like weather cocks – : was now the moment? – But young lieutenants sat sternly looking around with fierce eyes that said that if there were to be trouble they would be able to control the rabble.

But act after act went by, and everything stayed calm. People began to wonder whether they had been made fools of. And many a lieutenant who had been as severe as Mars now hung

The Making of Daniel Braut

his head: was he not going to have an opportunity to show himself as a knight to his lady. Others looked round scornfully: nothing was going to happen; we knew it!

But the old men were glad. There was no trouble; they could rest in peace; the rabble-rousers had been too weak. Christiania was loyal. It was somewhat suspicious that it was mainly students in the upper circle ... the law-abiding ones must be in the majority.

It was nearly the end of the fifth act. The restlessness started to grow again. Perhaps it was now that it was going to happen. Suddenly the whole theatre was deathly quiet. Daniel's heart started to thump. He looked down: a young man in the stalls had stood up; it was the leader.

The last line had been spoken, the curtain started to glide. Then the leader lifted his hand and with a piercing voice shouted, 'Down with the Manager!'

A sigh passed through the auditorium, a groan ... then it broke loose: A storm of whistles, howling and provocative, more and more of them came from the stalls, from the upper circle, from the gods; shrill tinkling notes from heavy door keys were added and then the crying, whining sound of the children's trumpets. But then suddenly, there was a roar, a torrent of clapping, stamping, shushing, a racket. The theatre was caught up in a whirlwind; it was like a ship in heavy seas. But the whistles, shrill and screeching, cut through the noise and din, grew sharper and sharper, whined, whistled, howled from all sides like the ride of Valkyrie, like a storm whistling through a ship's rigging. Everything was in uproar, everyone was on their feet, the air was full of clapping hands. Here and there groups of red-faced men stood in heated argument, waving their arms around, men with open mouths shouting words that no one could hear, words which disappeared in the uproar and became wind, an empty, furious pantomime – : 'Out with the lot of them!' – and then the lieutenants who stood and said 'The devil take me!' and who wanted to hit out but did not dare. But up in the upper circle and the gods a garland of faces hung over the edge looking down; they stared and laughed, stared and were amazed, stared and cursed, stared and whistled.

Daniel had taken his whistle out of his waistcoat pocket and was about to blow, but he felt uneasy. To gain courage he looked at his comrades; – Peder Monsen sat with his arms crossed and looked as if he had no intention of whistling, but Sven Dufva was blowing so hard that his cheeks were puffed like a blacksmith's bellows. Whose example should he follow? The boy was quite mesmerised. But down in the stalls he saw Jens Rud who stood blowing and staring up towards the upper circle and the gods ... he put his whistle to his lips as quickly as he could and blew, but could not hear anything. He blew harder, but still couldn't hear anything ... then he felt a fist on one of his shoulders. He jumped and as a result bit his tongue. He hardly dared to look round. 'An' wot's that s'posed to mean?' the butcher's voice shouted in his ear, as he got a blast of beery breath. Daniel said something, but could not even hear it himself. 'Wot?' roared the butcher so loudly that his face turned blue. Daniel was not happy; best to watch out. Then the butcher put his lips to Daniel's ear and shouted as if his life depended on it, 'if yer dunne shut yer damned trap, I'll call the cops, yer see if I don't.' Daniel tried to twist his way out of the man's grasp, but he sat as if held in a vice. 'Stick yer whistle in yer pocket!' screamed the butcher; both the man himself and his breath smelt of beer. What was he to do? There was no knowing what a drunken butcher could end up doing; and he certainly did not want to get involved with the police ... Daniel put his whistle in his pocket.

Don Pedro *de* Monsen sat as calmly as before and stared down into the stalls; a sardonic sneer curled his lips. But Sven Dufva whose shoulder was also held by an iron fist, had doubled up into a ball and with his elbows protecting his sides was whistling as loyally and earnestly as if his life depended on it. Daniel thought that each in their own way, both Sven Dufva and Peder Monsen, had acquitted themselves better than he had. He was ashamed.

A heavy, muffled thunder came from somewhere far off or deep down; Daniel did not know what it was and those who were whistling could not hear it; it was someone striking the great theatre gong. Then the police rushed in; there were now a lot of them down in the stalls. One whistler after the other was seized by the neck and turned out of the theatre; the whole of the upper circle was cleared, and now the gas lighting was being turned off. In the gods there was only one who ended up in the grasp of the police and that was Sven Dufva.

But Sven did not give in to the police either. He held onto the balcony railing with one hand and held his whistle in the other and blew. The constable had to use all his might to tear him loose, and then Sven had to accompany him to the police station.

– The group that was under Rud's leadership gathered as agreed in the Café Nationale; but there were fewer of them now. The most prominent in the group were disgruntled; there had been so many traitors, they said. If everyone had done what they were supposed to do it would have been a different story. Oh this damned Norwegian cowardice! Our lack of dependability and reliability! Everything had to follow the middle of the road; people never dared stick together to achieve something great. You could just see what *The Good Citizen* would have to say about that tomorrow – 'a few young people and schoolchildren ... a few children's trumpets ... the police quickly had the situation under control.'

Daniel had been in some doubt about whether he should join the others in the coffee cellar. His conscience wasn't clear ... what he had promised God ... but finally he went. If anyone asked him, he could defend himself, he thought, and besides he was not one of the saved.

'Well now,' shouted Jens Rud happily when he saw Daniel; 'finally we have a true Israelite in whom there is no guile! Did you notice him, fellows? He sat up there in the gallery and whistled like a devil; they tried to stop him, but he just turned his back, used his back and elbows and blew and blew. If everyone had done their bit as well as he did it would have been a different story. Hurrah for Daniel Braut!' – 'Hurrah! Hurrah! Hurrah! '

Daniel stood there as scarlet as a lobster and did not know what to say. When one after another came across to him and wanted to drink with him, he ducked down ... he had not deserved such praise; he had done his best, but... 'Oh nonsense,' they said. 'No false modesty at a moment like this!' And so Daniel never managed to explain the true situation. He drank; drank with all of them; his conscience was not clear; but he got drunk.

10

Autumn lay heavy on the open countryside with a dark sky and damp air, and the clouds hung down the hillsides like huge white curtains.

Daniel Braut BA looked at the cloud-enshrouded slopes and the forest which stretched over the hills as thick and black as night and remembered his old *hulder* dreams. He smiled sadly. – It was good that he had got away from the town. There was no one here to whom he owed money, and no one who could impale him with scornful eyes for having sold himself. In town they had not *said* anything, but he could see by their looks what they thought. Was it true that he had been to *Pater omnipotens* and been saved? Was it true that afterwards he had blown a whistle in the theatre – and been drunk? Or was the truth that he had *not* blown a whistle in the theatre – and *not* been drunk. But Ole Bentsen was going around saying how weak we were, and how easy it was to fall back into the old ways.

Daniel had been afraid of his comrades. He had shut himself in and revised for his exams, though he could not swot as he had done in the past because he soon got a headache. And if he tried to rest, then uncomfortable thoughts descended like a swarm of flies. What if Pater got to know that he was *not* 'a true Israelite'? What if Fram and Rud got to know that he had been 'saved'? Indeed, what if Hirsch got to know that he had become a pietist? What would the good man have to say then? What would they all say? He had behaved in such a way that no one could trust him any longer.

But the worst of it was that he had had to go and see Pater once in a while. He had been nervous going, and ashamed leaving, because with Pater he was obliged to be saved...

He had never been so unhappy; not even when he was starving.

Up here at Stensrud it was better. Though when it came to the point he was not safe here either. The thought of Hirsch gnawed at his conscience, and the thought of Pater left him perpetually uneasy. If Pater got to know that it had been humbug that he had been saved then the estate-owner would get to know it too, and then it was all too easy to imagine what would happen. It would be just as bad if the estate-owner's student son, Stensrud, found out more than he should, because he had vouched for Daniel as a tutor; but the son only knew of Daniel through Pater and Haugum; and if he heard that Braut was an old Fram man and someone who had blown a whistle in the theatre...

He had to be careful. The only thing that could save him if things were to go wrong would be if he had got the estate-owner on his side by that time. He would have to try. He behaved as well as he could when his employer was looking.

He had come here with the thought that he would atone for his sin against chaplain Hirsch through his teaching. He would teach the two small Stensrud boys to believe in the spirit of things. But as soon as he learnt that the estate-owner did not like the method that concentrated on the spirit of things, he gave it up. He would have to atone for his sin against Hirsch later; it was not up to him to have any opinions now, and so he began to teach in the way he had learnt from Massmann.

Unfortunately the boys did not have much initiative. They were dull and stupid and he did not like them. Working with them was like throwing water on a goose. Gradually Daniel slipped into the run-of-the-mill, uninspired Latin-school method; heard them recite their homework and let it go at that. But when Mrs Stensrud asked about her sons, the tutor said that there was potential in them; they had not realized it fully yet, but that would come. And he asked himself if there was anything else one could say to a mother?

Mrs Stensrud was the estate-owner's second wife; before marrying him she had been housekeeper to the old dean. She made good food and ran the house well; that was the sum of her abilities, but no one asked for more. Daniel often thought that if only he could have grown up in a house like this then he could have been quite a different fellow. And if old Ole Johannes Sørbraut had been as much of a man as the estate-owner, Stensrud – then how much unhappiness he might have been spared, and how many good things he might have had! But he would have to believe that the good Lord had a purpose with everything. He had presumably seen that it would not be good for Daniel to have too easy a life. If he had been rich, then perhaps by now he would have been a drunkard.

The estate-owner was a man of fifty-eight, calm and solid, wise and dull. In his youth he had, as he said himself, been 'a bit of an enthusiast', but age and experience had taught him to take a more balanced view of most things, and now he was the fourth deputy on the list of state officials. His money had come with his first wife, – 'and it was then that he became a moderate', said the Jaabækian school master, Borreberg, later; 'with every thousand he earned, he took a step to the right, and now he is as white as a clergyman's surplice.' He always spoke with great respect of academic education. He was not intolerant. The only thing he demanded of people was that they should be well-informed, should think for themselves, and not take their views on trust from *The People's News* or anywhere else, and that they should not let themselves be blown this way and that by every new wind of learning, or seduced by every phrase-monger. But he was correct in that. About 'the populists' he said much that Daniel would have liked to contradict if it had not been for the fact that he had to be careful.

The estate-owner had three children by his first wife, of whom the student, Stensrud, was the youngest. The next youngest was called Louise and was married to the wholesale merchant Storr in Christiania; the eldest, Miss Hanna, was still at home.

This same Miss Hanna was said to be twenty-six, but Daniel thought she must be older. She had been to school in Christiania and was a lady; dressed elegantly and did needlework and played the piano. Daniel always felt a bit embarrassed when he was with her; what was he to say to such a person? From his reading of novels he knew that there was a special art in talking to ladies! They were to have things served in a special way, and no one could do this, if he had not been taught it. But gradually he got into conversation with her, something that came about because he was allowed to borrow books from her. And once they had got to know each other, conversation flowed of its own accord. It turned out that she was not so difficult to converse with as it had appeared. What she most wanted to hear about was Christiania, and student life there. Daniel told her what he knew, made up bits where he felt it necessary to make the subject more interesting, and kept silent about the things that he thought he should not tell a young lady.

Once he happened to mention that he knew Hans Haugum, and after that he often had to talk about him because she also knew him. She said that he had visited these parts when her mother was alive as her mother had come from his part of the country and had known his parents. One day when Haugum had been mentioned Hanna said, 'He's engaged now; I suppose you know that?' She was standing by the window looking out. 'No?' said Daniel in amazement, 'When did that happen?' Quite recently, Hanna had received a letter from Louise. 'Really?' Daniel was not sure whether he liked the news or not; it came so unexpectedly.

He was not engaged yet. A couple of times during the summer he had tried to write to Inga, but had not managed it. It was as if he could not find the right words; what he wrote was so cold and empty; the sad thing was that he saw her so rarely. And love required nourishment like everything else in life.

Daniel had also begun to wonder about something strange and totally irrational. He had recently realised that he had not forgotten Berta Maria. Indeed, he wondered if the misfortune that had befallen her was not his fault! – One night after he had arrived here he had dreamt so beautifully about her. He thought she was sitting on his lap and that he had his arms around her waist. She snuggled up to him and put her hands round his neck and lay in his arms so soft and warm. And she cried with love and sorrow; he could feel her tear-wet face against his; he was so relieved and happy that he kissed her. But she asked him not to be angry with her; the bad thing she had done had happened because she loved in vain someone she could not have ... and she snuggled up to him so closely and warmly. Daniel was profoundly happy, kissed her again, and woke up. But he could still feel the tear-warm face against his, and the soft, gentle kiss; his arms were still warm with the feel of her, and he groped around in surprise that she was not there.

This dream lived on in him afterwards, and as she was in the dream that was how he remembered her. He dreamt the dream over again with open eyes and could not push it away. Such nonsense could not last, but as long as it lasted there was no point in proposing to Inga, for she would detect immediately whether he was serious. Besides, as long as he had not passed his university professional exams...

– As the autumn wore on Miss Hanna had got know 'Mr Braut BA' so well that she often accompanied him on his walks. Daniel could not deny that it was great to be seen with a lady. But it would have been even better if she had been prettier. Miss Hanna was, like her father and brother, big-boned, well padded, but pale skinned. Her face was large, her hair fair, her eyes calm and dull. Daniel guessed that she must be twenty-eight. The finest bloom of youth had disappeared; the fairytale veil, the dreaminess, the magic which no one can describe, – that was not there. He could talk to her as much as he wanted, but was untouched. Had this not been the case then perhaps he could have begun to feel at home at Stensrud.

A couple of evenings in the week there was a game of whist and a toddy, but never more than one glass and never till later than ten o'clock. Now and again the sheriff came and sometimes even the clergyman. But it was no fun. And when the estate-owner time after time sat expounding the necessity of thinking for oneself and not letting oneself be blown this way and that by every new wind of learning, or seduced by every phrase-monger, – then Daniel was sometimes afraid that he had him in mind.

For Daniel had not thought for himself. He knew that now. He had been in the habit of having the same opinion as those he was with, and when he had heard a point of view expressed cogently, then he had accepted it at face value and had forgotten what he had previously believed. More than once he had heard people say that one should think for oneself, but he had never properly taken note of it. He had been brought up in the belief that it was a matter of having the *correct* opinion, and he could not abandon that yet. What was the point of thinking for oneself if that led one astray? And one could soon end up having the wrong ideas if one had to rely on one's own wisdom. Fram and Rud and others like them, they thought for themselves, but they were rationalists. And how far would that take them?

There was little point in thinking for yourself if you were going to die. It was a matter of having the right belief. If you did not have that, you went straight to hell, however independent you were in your thinking. And here on earth it was in fact much the same: wrong-headed opinions destroyed their man.

It must be possible both to think for oneself and to have the correct opinions; that was what people meant. But how was he to get to that stage? – Once he touched on this with the estate-owner. He replied that it was a matter of *willing* what was right. If you had the will to find what was right, then you would find it, but if you let your thinking run along its own lines and did not care where it led, then you could soon end up lost. Daniel thought this sounded reasonable; that the will was important was something that he had always heard. But even so it was not quite clear; your own thoughts wanted to go their own way, and you could not rely on the will to keep them in check.

No, it was not easy to think for yourself. Take for example the matter of republicanism ... well, you could come up with reasons both for and against. And what if the reasons for and against were both equally strong? Or the reasons *for* were stronger than those against, but you did not *want* to be a republican?

Well then you looked for counter arguments until you found them. Or you examined the reasons for and found that they were not as strong as they seemed. Could you then be said to have thought independently about a free state?

But what if the free state idea was the correct one after all? There were clever people who thought that. Clever people both for and against; and both had their reasons.

Perhaps it was the starting point that was important. If you started in one place you ended up here, if you started from another, you ended up there; and whoever had no starting point kept going round in circles, like a man in thick fog.

As he went around thinking about this, he happened to remember some lectures on ethics that he had heard at the university. In these lectures the professor had explained the various forms of government in such a clear way that Daniel thought that he could never find better arguments in this matter. He had actually made notes of those lectures, but unfortunately he did not have them with him. He had lent them to Halvor Mosebø. But if he had had them here, he could have read them through carefully and then he would have had as good a body of opinions and as strong arguments as anyone could wish for. Now there was nothing he could do; furthermore he did not know where Halvor Mosebø lived.

If only everything could be like faith: that what was right and true was firmly set down. A reliable political catechism would be an invaluable guide for young people. As things were now, you were at a loss. If you tried to think without guidance, you were like a ship without a compass. It might happen that you had a great thought. But how could you *know* whether it was mad or good?

You didn't get much further if you wanted to ask others for advice. There were as many opinions as there were people, and everyone believed his opinion was the only correct one. And everyone had scores of arguments. It was no simple matter to find your way in such a Babel. –

– This was how the young graduate in philosophy wrestled with the question many a dark afternoon, and he was not happy. But when he stood looking at the high hills that appeared so beautiful, and which clothed themselves again and again in cloaks of cloud or whitish-grey drapes of mist, or at the forest which stretched over the hills as dark and endless as sorrow, then he thought of the *hulder* and Berta Maria. And he felt such a painful sense of loss. Oh, if only there was a person who understood him, who loved him! And if only there was someone he could love. He was as alone as a thief in the night.

But when he came to the supper table and heard the estate-owner and sometimes the sheriff and the clergyman sitting there commenting on everything, so sure of themselves and knowing everything, then he sighed and thought: happy are the old who have everything sorted and worked out.

The sheriff was a tall old bachelor with a stern legal face and a nose like a wedge; he was a lawyer and wanted to be considered a state official. But the clergyman was Pastor Ring, whom Daniel had met once at Helle, the merchant's. Now he had come here and had an exceptionally wealthy parish. He looked older, but cheerful and dignified. He was pleased to hear that Mr Braut was not a Jaabækian; 'That would also greatly please your old benefactor, Helle,' he said. Thank goodness Helle was on his feet again; he had started a new business that was now beginning to do well; he would soon be back to where he was before. 'Ah yes, the Lord does not forget those who do good.' Daniel sat wondering whether he could face asking Helle yet again for financial help; but it would have to be as a last resort.

It was good to be together with such grand people. If only his own concerns were in order; if only he had nothing to be afraid of. He had never imagined that a student could be in the position that he was now. Whenever the post came to the farm or the estate-owner came back from a visit to town, he never felt quite safe, and when Hanna one day said that people from town were coming to spend Christmas here he felt deeply uneasy. 'It'll come out! Just wait and see, it'll come out,' he said to himself. Sometimes he even feared that he would see his name in print – next to Fram's – in *The Good Citizen*.

But *The Good Citizen* did not print his name. All in all Daniel was surprised that the paper was not worse than it was. It also had better arguments for its position than he had imagined. It did contain various negative statements about popular movements, even a couple of acerbic things about chaplain Hirsch; but to be fair one had to remember that the paper saw all things from its own angle.

Sometimes he was struck by the thought that despite everything it was perhaps *The Good Citizen* that was right after all. It spoke so authoritatively and knowledgeably, and dismissed the 'popularists' with such force that you almost *had* to believe it. All this chatter about freedom and the people and spirit and ideas, surely it was just so many phrases? You had to take the world as it was; and this was something *The Good Citizen* understood better than the idealists.

But then one day he would bump into Borreberg, or he would suddenly remember Hirsch, Bliland, Haugum or Jens Rud; and then he saw that *The Citizen* was wrong. At least partly wrong. The others were perhaps not totally right ... oh to be able to find a middle way!

There had to be something between the two positions here. Both sides went too far; one had to be able to reconcile these opposites. And he remembered that he had heard a professor talk about 'mediating', and harmonising opposing ideas into 'a higher unity'; and went round grappling with this. He would take as his starting point the basic ideas he had from Hirsch, then he would take as much as he could from *The Good Citizen*, while being careful not to come into conflict with Pater. He would have to make sure to please Fram and Jens Rud too, for it would not be good to cross swords with them either if it came to an argument. But the more Daniel struggled with these opposites, the more confused he became.

If only he were brave! The best thing would be to resurrect his opinions from before; be a 'populist' as in olden days and defend his ideas with tooth and claw both against the estate-owner and the others. But that was inconceivable now. Here he was not his own man; others had control over his life and fate. If they would not help him on, then he was stuck. In the end he saw only one way out. He would have to hold on to his old ideas as well as he could, but keep quiet about them until he was well away from this place. It would never do to be a twenty-four year old fellow with a degree in philosophy and not have opinions of his own.

– But there was one thing he could do that would help him feel more adult, and that he did; he let his beard grow. He felt that helped quite a bit, and what's more he did not have the bother of shaving.

11

On Christmas Eve Stensrud's son, who was a student, arrived from town with his friends; the wholesale merchant, Storr, and his wife Louise accompanied them.

It was a large group and they were good-looking people. Even Storr, whom Daniel had thought must be a terrible guanocrat, was a small, quiet, brisk man, thin and nervous and with small sea-green eyes. Louise Storr was a well-built woman like her sister, but prettier. Then there were the students: the large, cheerful Bang Block, Becker the lanky, red-haired supernumerary in a government department, the tall, good-natured clerk, Petersen, with bald head and glasses, the graduate Viborg who was young and serious and as attractive as a young girl and Knutzon, the medical student with his aristocratic nose, full, soft mouth and misty grey eyes. They were all tip-top elegant young men; their white collars and smiles positively shone and their lorgnettes and eyes sparkled. Daniel walked round twisting his youthful beard and thought to himself that in this crowd even the estate-owner and his son looked like peasants.

He was no longer afraid. If people like this knew anything, they would also know how to behave and would keep quiet. Stensrud brought greetings from Pater which relieved Daniel's conscience and made him happy. If Pater had not heard anything by now, then he was unlikely to hear anything.

They could not sit down to eat until the sheriff arrived. But it would be wrong to say that the wait was boring. Conversation had started up at once, and was now raging like fire in sappy pine logs. It wasn't easy to say what they were talking about; it wasn't about the big issues of the day. But the strange thing was that the conversation was nevertheless lively. One small witticism set off others as if they were sparks from a flint. Puns and parodies shot up like rockets. It was a brilliant game of nothing, a firework display of words and social chat.

Daniel started to think about this as he wandered round. What he was hearing and seeing here was what he had always dreamt of and longed for: an aristocratic gathering, the elegant turn of phrase. 'Fram' and the others in town made fun of everything refined and called it sophisticated nonsense and empty silliness, and Aslak Fjordan could roar with laughter when he saw a real toff, but Daniel could no longer understand this. A refined manner *was* the stamp of nobility. Anyone could learn Latin, and one could always acquire an education in the things of the mind and the heart. But what really counted, when it came to the point of distinguishing the toffs from the tramps, was what Aslak Fjordan laughed at, but which *The Citizen* called a cultured manner.

Young men like this were the true students. They had sat their exams in the prescribed manner; they had the education that a student should have; they were *comme il faut* in every respect. Such students could lead the ideal life of the student. They did not drink themselves into a stupor when they were happy, and did not become wild when they were merry, and however uninhibitedly they joked and teased, they never overstepped the boundary of proper behaviour. They had wit and spirit and a cultured manner; everything they did was pleasing and elegant; but the peasant students were peasants whatever you did with them. He thought with distaste about the student life he himself had led. The constant din of argument and politics, beer and bad toddy – it was all right as far as it went, but it was not ideal, nor was it real student life.

Storr sat in the sofa chatting to Miss Hanna, while Knutzon and Viborg had started to talk to Mrs Storr. No, not to talk, but to converse, and it was amazing how elegant it sounded. Daniel took note of everything so that he could learn, and he decided that when he next returned to town he would attend dancing classes.

The others were grouped round the estate-owner. Bang Block talked amusingly, Becker was witty and sharp, and Petersen too could be witty, though he laughed at his own jokes, and now and again he looked silly with his shiny head, glasses and broad grin. But when the estate-owner started churning out his maxims it was as if a plough-horse wanted to dance with circus horses. He was clumsy and incoherent, and it was as if the others had to help him clarify what he was trying to say, and then one could see in the corner of their eyes a quick flash of laughter or scorn, and Daniel felt that even their words contained hidden barbs or critical ulterior motives. Yes, these were chaps who knew how to play the game.

The sheriff came, so now they could sit down at table. As they were doing this Daniel happened to hear an exchange between Knutzon and Viborg about Mrs Storr. 'What d'you think of her?' asked Viborg. 'Too much fat on the meat,' replied Knutzon. Daniel was taken aback, but thought he must have misheard. Later he saw Viborg whisper something to Knutzon and smile. He did not understand the smile, but afterwards he felt he no longer liked Viborg's girlishly pretty face.

At table the conversation became increasingly lively. Bang Block, Mrs Storr and the sheriff began to argue about the origins of the expression, 'spit-roast rib'. Becker who had been abroad told them about the art of 'carving' that we did not have here in Norway. Then they got into a discussion about the correct time to have dinner. Storr wanted people to adopt the English and French custom of eating at six, the others, and Mrs Stensrud in particular, defended the Norwegian dinner-time. But Storr persisted. If one ate dinner between two and three one was useless for the rest of the day; dinner should be when one was *finished* for the day. During the working day one could have a *light* lunch between twelve and one – nothing more. But if one had dinner between two and three, then one should not have lunch. That people had started to have lunch here while keeping our dinner-time was ... was barbarism. We adopted customs from abroad but adopted them raw, undigested, without thought or context; lunch in a country that had dinner at two, when lunch had its place and justification when one had dinner at six, had you ever heard anything like it? It was if savages were to put on top hats, but for the rest ... were dressed in skins, while at the same time thinking that they had taken a cultural step forward. It was not easy for Storr to say what he meant; he struggled to find words and grappled with the content, but he did manage to express his opinion. His judgements fell harshly. Our whole food culture was one of poor management and national waste. At which point the estate-owner raised his glass and bade everyone welcome.

Other subjects were raised. In his humorous way Bang Block talked about the Christmas pig, which our noble ancestors had roasted whole and eaten with hunting knives while drinking beer brewed from bog myrtle. Then when they were satisfied they threw the bones at each other. And if they got into a really merry mood they set to with swords and axes. That was quite some Christmas festivity! Petersen told some Christmas tales which he laughed at himself; the estate-owner praised education and his son told of some popular beliefs: up in the mountain districts they believed in soldiers who lived in the nether world and helped the Norwegians in time of war; it was they who caused the Swedes always to aim too high when they fired; they would march invisibly up to the Swedish soldiers and raise the barrel of their rifles when they were firing. Daniel thought the legend was beautiful, but Storr said he had never heard anything so Norwegian: take it easy and rely on the trolls for help. The sheriff wanted to compare this legend to the old one about Holger Danske; and surely no-one could deny that some years ago the Danes still tended to believe in it. 'Where was Holger Danske in 1864!'* asked Petersen laughing. 'Presumably he was shrewd and stayed at home like we did,' replied Becker. Throat-clearing round the table; then a short exchange of words, which ended with agreement that we were where we supposed to be in 1864. Daniel was surprised: was that the accepted opinion now?

They felt good sitting round the table; the convivial spirit increased. 'By the way', said the land-owner, 'how is old Jokum these days?' Oh, Jokum was fine. 'I met him a couple of days ago,' said Becker; 'father and I were out walking with Jaabæk...!' 'With Jaabæk!' screamed Petersen; 'With Jaabæk!' exclaimed Mrs Storr; 'With Jaabæk!' shouted the whole table; 'Yes,' replied

Becker calmly, 'with father's horse!' Loud laughter; Mrs Storr shuddered, 'Ugh!' Knutzon declared that old Becker, who was head of a government department, was a witty old gent. Viborg said he thought that Jaabæk ought to be told that he now stood in the stables of the head of a government department; 'Yes, indeed he ought – Jaabæk be damned!' laughed Petersen, who could also be witty. Mrs Storr felt sorry for the horse, poor thing, and feared that it probably received many an undeserved blow from the whip on account of its name. Becker did not think so. The horse may certainly have had to listen to the odd political lecture and now and again some derogatory remarks; but ... now that he came to think of it, it had once received a thorough beating on account of its name. Lieutenant Schmell had been with them on a ride in the horse-drawn sledge; then he was told the horse's name, at which point he seized the reins and the whip and stood up and shouted: 'Now, by Jove, you're in for it,' and began beating the horse till it reared up and started prancing on its hind legs. They had to restrain the lieutenant with force. But all the same you had to laugh. No, indeed, you had to laugh! But Block who liked horses said it was a shame to give a horse such a name, for a horse was an animal we liked, and if *he* ever got a horse, he would name it after one of his friends. The conversation died away in laughter; old Jokum was forgotten.

Daniel noticed this, and asked Hanna who was sitting next to him at table, what sort of a fellow this Jokum was. Oh, he was an old sea captain, replied Hanna; and he had been given the name Jokum because he was so odd. – Was he odd? – Yes, he did many odd things, and much that was wrong, which was how *The Farmer's Friend* and those people got so much to talk about. Finally he got involved in some sort of scandal – Hanna did not know much about it ... and then he got the Order of the Sword.* 'The Order of the Sword? When he had caused a scandal?' – 'Yes, so that he would leave.' – 'Oh, I see. And did he leave then?' – 'No, when he had received the honour, he thought it must because he had been such a good officer, and then he did not want to leave.' – 'Well?' – 'Well, in the end they had to give him the Order of St Olaf.' Daniel laughed, 'But did he go then?' – 'Yes, then he had to promise.' 'He must be quite a character,' laughed Daniel. But he wondered about this story. Could such things be true?

Round the table the conversation hummed like a spinning wheel. Contentment and good humour grew. It did not take much before people burst out laughing. Daniel too entered the conversation. Talked to Miss Stensrud about all sorts of things. He hardly knew himself what he talked about; he only knew one thing: looked at rightly, Miss Stensrud was beautiful.

They got up from the table with many compliments on the good food. There was laughter and liveliness and much merriment. Everything flowed uninhibitedly, even though it was all refined. And Daniel realised with growing confidence that he could hold his own in this gathering. He belonged. He could after all acquire the *frons urbana*.

Behind him, he heard someone say, 'He's an OK fellow, that estate-owner.' 'A good host!' replied the other. Daniel looked round, it was Knutzon who stood talking to Viborg. 'But he could do with a little more up *here*,' smiled Knutzon pointing to his forehead; 'but *enfin* when one has the brass...' – freedom but within strict limits; that's how it has to be, thought Daniel. At that moment the estate-owner came striding in wine-flushed and happy, 'Ladies and gentlemen, what about some dessert?' Well, the estate-owner did not quite match up, but his children...

Over dessert the conversation was more heated and more serious; they talked of the 'conveyance system'.* And here Daniel heard what he could never have imagined: that the upper class too might want to pull down those in power. Things were said about them that Daniel found almost unbelievable, and it was strange that *The Farmer's Friend* had not dragged such things out into the open. But the sheriff and the land-owner defended those in power, so there was an argument, while Storr sat smiling, saying nothing. Becker said that when you looked at this 'conveyance system', you almost wanted to join the opposition because a member of the opposition, a lawyer or someone like that found it easier to get around than a man from one of the government departments. 'Yes!' laughed Petersen, 'if only the opposition were not such stubborn mules as they are!' Now the estate-owner too had to smile ever so slightly. But Knutzon turned suddenly to Daniel and asked, 'I don't suppose you side with the opposition, do you, tutor?' 'N-no,' stammered Daniel, turning red.

After dinner, Mrs Storr played the piano. It was grand music. Daniel did not understand a thing, but clapped when the others clapped. Everyone looked kind and contented as they sat there smoking, relaxing and digesting their food, and as satisfied and lazy as gods. But the sheriff and Endre Storr sat in the sofa chatting, seemingly about music.

– So this is how things could be if you were rich. Good food and drink, peace and contentment, good company, friends and respect and everything you could wish for. And that even if you did not have more than average brains. Was it true that the estate-owner was not that bright? He looked capable of anything. But what did it matter as long as you were rich?

But those who needed people's help *had* to be clever, and they *had* to be well behaved. And submissive. Like a bad egg they had to be examined by everybody, they had to bend their necks even if it was to a gate-post. But the rich man was a free man. He counted for just as much even if he was a fool. He could get by even if he was a swine; no one could say anything. Nor did he need to be 'saved'. Stensrud's son was not saved, and was just as good a friend of Pater's for all that...

– Toddy was set out on a small table in the side room. The music ceased. The men were invited to go in and take a drop.

– 'Ah-ha; ye-es, the fourth largest fleet,' Endre Storr was heard to interject sharply, 'ye-es ... that won't ... that won't last long. Abroad they've begun selling their old wooden sailing ships and have started to build iron ships, while we trundle on investing our money in wooden ships, which they are getting rid of abroad; and then ... when iron and steam have taken over everywhere, we will be left with our old wooden sailing ships, we who rank fourth among the sea-going nations!' Daniel's jaw dropped.

'If you please, let us take a glass,' said the estate-owner, to smooth things over, and they went in. But even on the way in they argued. The sheriff tried to defend our national honour and our sailing ships, and as they stood mixing their toddy, he asked whether Storr seriously believed that we should follow suit and build iron ships. 'Follow suit?' asked Endre Storr; 'should we follow suit in anything? The only thing we have learnt from abroad is ... is how to go bankrupt!'

There was laughter at this; and they laughed confidently, because they knew that Storr had his own ideas. But Storr had got into a combative mood now, and when they were all seated he launched in again.

'Yes, it's easy to laugh', he said; 'it's easy all right. But what in the name of heaven is going to happen to a country where nobody wants to work?' – 'You exaggerate,' said the sheriff. 'Don't we want to work?' smiled the estate-owner. 'No, we don't,' replied Storr. 'We want ... we want ... to lead the good life! Take it easy ... live high on credit! That's what we want! Show me a man who when he has earned a few thousand, doesn't settle back and ... and use it up, eat it up! And if *he* doesn't use it up, then he has a son who will; just like that! And what ought to have been the basis for capital, for a large, solid business down through ... Yes, because that's how it is abroad. Do you think that the great business empires in England and America have floated down from heaven? – I'll tell you; the great business empires came about like this: a labourer or hotel bellboy earned fifty pounds; his son carried on the business and earned two hundred pounds; and that's how they worked: son took over from father, generation after generation ... they worked, you see! And in the end they had amassed capital ... wealth, power, experience! First and foremost experience! – But here? What ought to be the basis for capital, – oops! Scattered to all the four winds! If a man has a thousand daler, then his son must not work, he must study ... and so he fritters away those thousand daler, and after that he lives in debt and is a clerk! – Can I ask: where is the capital to come from, and where shall we gain the experience ... for we need both capital and experience if we are going to compete ... and where is the capital to come from if it is strangled at birth, and all those who could learn something throw themselves away and become clerks!'

Three or four voices all shouted at once and wanted to respond, but drowned each other out. The only thing Storr managed to

The Making of Daniel Braut

catch was some words of the sheriff's about our faithful hard-working farmers. 'The farmer,' shouted Storr, 'was it farmer you said? – The farmer is like us; but he's the worst of us all. He's a savage, who ... wants to lie down in the barn and eat, eat and sleep, and not give a damn about tomorrow; don't let's talk about the farmer!'

The sheriff admitted that there was something in what Storr said. The lower classes nowadays were not as content with their position in life as they should be; and it was a bad sign that the farmers had now started driving around to attend meetings of the Farmers' Friend Association instead of working. But on the whole the sheriff would like to say that across the country the farmers worked like slaves, worked so hard and conscientiously that it would be unfair to ask anything more of them. Petersen, who was the son of a District Governor over in Western Norway, said the same and there was a murmur of agreement from the whole gathering.

'My son-in-law is in the habit of using strong words,' said the estate-owner with a conciliatory smile, 'but putting that aside ... I am inclined to think that people across the country have too little idea about how to use their time. Time is money, as the English say; that's a maxim the farmer could do well to take to heart. But what is needed is *education*; education, gentlemen!' – Bravo, Bravo. – 'Well, where's the farmer to get that?' asked Storr. – From books? Well and good, but is there a single state agronomist or anyone else for that matter who can write a practical book?' (Well?) 'Don't try to tell me that. I have myself tried to write about such things, and I have seen ... seen others write; but ... well. When it comes to the point ... everyone shouts about education, but more and more I have found that all this about 'education' ... is just an empty phrase.' (Now, my good sir!) 'Yes, an empty phrase. A farmer is not *educated*. Education is not something one can acquire in a year or two through books or discussion. One has to give one's whole life to it ... one has to live in a civilised atmosphere! It is only the rich who can be educated. Education and culture ... are a luxury, an extravagance; first you have to have food, and if you have time after that, that's when you can live a cultured life. We see it too. These idealists who want to take the farmer as he plods about his work and make him into a man of culture, what happens? Clichés and nonsense! Folk High School airy-fairy fog! No, the farmer has to be *practical*, and that's something he knows how to be; practical in his field ... and if that's what you call education, Mr estate-owning Stensrud, then well and good.' Yes, of course it was practical education that the estate owner meant, and in a while it became evident that really they were all in agreement. But Daniel did not know what he should think.

The warm toddy strengthened the community spirit, and they all began to think about the country's development. When Petersen told them that in the farming districts people sat around the hearth in the long winter evenings and passed the time telling folk tales and other nonsense, instead of earning money by carving wooden clogs and making brooms, everyone found this totally mad. The sheriff even thought that this was something the government should do something about.

'Yes, that would be truly Norwegian, that would,' snapped Storr in his insistent way. 'The government! – in enlightened countries the motto is *help yourself*; here is it the government coffers and ... poor relief ... and Our Lord and ... but no-one can make an effort themselves, damn it! Government money – ? That means that a special government department would have to be set up, with an Inspector of Clogs in the Department for Ecclesiastical Affairs ... yes, and then a huge tome of reports for every quarter and objections and plans and this and that ... For heaven's sake!' he shouted to the estate-owner, 'just find people who want to buy clogs, then you'll see that the farmer will learn to make them!'

After this there was a discussion about the role of civil servants. The sheriff was annoyed about the Inspector of Clogs remark and protested and the young lawyers supported him: an educated man should not say what he had said. And Daniel agreed with them. Storr did not have much to say to this, but after they had finished he explained that when the unproductive work of the civil servants was considered the highest thing in the land, then the country was bound to become impoverished. He would like to see the best brains applying themselves to practical matters, and then the next best or mediocre brains could deal with all the record-keeping and reports. The sheriff was getting redder and redder, and Becker and Petersen called Storr a Jaabækian, while Mrs Storr sat clearing her throat, as did the estate-owner, who in the end could see no better way of ending the matter than by making a speech. He spoke in praise of the civil service and our honourable class of officials, whom we had to thank God for; and the speech ended with a skål for the sheriff, who 'represented the official class here tonight.'

The sheriff replied with a skål for the freehold farmer, our noble freehold farmer who sat secure on his plot and did not give a damn about anyone else, but who bowed to his king and those in authority; to *that* farmer the sheriff would raise his glass; *that* farmer was the backbone of our country, and *that* farmer would sort things out if it came to the crunch. There had always been amicable relations between the freehold farmer and the official class, and he did not doubt that that relationship would hold firm, even if there were – hmm – voices that – . A toast was drunk to our noble, enlightened farmer, our honoured, hospitable host, the estate-owner, Mr Stensrud. Daniel liked what the sheriff had said, and he got the feeling that when all was said and done these 'friends of the official class' were just as good friends of the people as the blockheads in the opposition.

When Mrs Storr saw that her husband intended tor reply, she hurried to ask whether any of the young people wouldn't favour them with a song. 'Yes, that would be nice,' said the estate-owner, pleased. Mrs Storr promptly sat down at the piano while Knutzon and Viborg discussed what they should sing. After some mighty chords from the piano the young men gave full voice to the Swedish song:

> Here we live the life of gods.
> And how beautiful that life is...

They sang well, artistically, with vibrato and plenty of rubato. Daniel thought it was like being at the theatre; this was what refined singing should be like. They carried on with Swedish student songs from Uppsala University, and finally a piece by Bellman*. Daniel wondered why they didn't sing something Norwegian.

People clapped after every item, and when they had finished the estate-owner gave a little speech about 'student songs'. Viborg made a speech for the Uppsala student choir,* which he thought was absolutely magical; and when the men understood that it was a matter of preventing Storr from speaking, they all started talking at once. Petersen spoke for our brother country Sweden, Knutzon for the ladies, with special address to Mrs Stensrud, Bang Block for our Danish brothers in the south, and Becker – for the peasant students. Daniel went pale. But Becker said it was a good development, and ... er ... a happy one that the peasant farmers were beginning to get a more ... er more real and thorough education. That would help them advance to ... er, er ... take up their position among the other social classes ... and ... er for example in parliament ... in a more dignified ... er ... in a more dignified way. It had become clear that there was ... er ... that the farmers did not lack ... er ... talent, and when this was properly developed and ... er ... channelled, then he was sure that the ... er ... disharmony that was ... er ... sometimes evident in relations between the ... er classes, that would ... er disappear of it own accord. He would like to raise his glass to the representative of the peasant-students whom they had the honour of having in their midst that evening, Mr ... er ... Mr ... er ... Danielsen BA ... 'Oh, I beg your pardon! ... Mr Danielsen Braut BA. To him!' Bravo! Daniel changed colour. He drank, but barely felt the ground under his feet. Now it was *his* turn to stand up and give a speech! That was the idea. It went without saying, and he could see it in the face of the others. But what could he talk about?

He remembered that the toast for king and country had not been drunk yet. He would have to propose that. If only he could find something to say on the spur of the moment! He would have to think for a while, but then someone would probably come along and take his topic. There we are; there's the sheriff. Presumably *he* will speak for king and country.

But the sheriff wanted to speak about *students*. Not about any particular class of students, for in his opinion different classes did not exist, and once they had passed their exams they were all sons of Athene and then all class distinctions ceased to exist. (Bravo! thought Daniel). The sheriff wanted to talk about the student body as whole, and in particular to remind people that they were the future officials. It was both just and necessary that employment in the service of the state should be regarded as something elevated and exceptional. We heard occasionally that to serve the state was a job that – hmm – did not count for much. From a certain quarter we had even seen the baptising of children compared to muck-spreading – hmm. But the sheriff would consider it a major disaster if the distinction between work for the state and other sorts of work should die out in people's minds. Official work should be regarded as something – yes, something ideal, if one might use that word, – as a noble life-task, which one embraced in one's youth, and pursued with energy as a lifelong task for however many years one was allotted here on earth. The state could not be satisfied with hired help and financial speculators; one could expect the servants of the state to step into the breach – when it was a matter of life and death! That was why he would like to remember the young men who were now preparing themselves for this lifelong task, and he hoped and prayed that they were preparing themselves in such a way that king and country might have a good and loyal official class. Skål! Bravo!

The sheriff drank, and his grey face shone like the full moon; tonight he was the champion of a great idea, and that did not happen often. Daniel really loved the sheriff for his speech. What he had said was as if spoken from his own heart; it was both true and a fact.

But there was Endre Storr; there was no way of preventing him any longer.

'Well, if there are going to be speeches here, then let ... let it be so. They had spoken about the farmers; he too could talk about the farmers; gladly. But not about the freehold farmer. For the freehold farmer was becoming more and more ... how should he put it ... more and more of a myth...' 'Hmm?' the sound of coughing was heard round the table. But Storr wanted to talk about the farmer living in the valleys across the country, – 'he whose farm is mortgaged to the bank, he who no longer owns the plot he is sitting on, but who toils away for the bank. Yes, it has been said that the farmer works ... that he works like a slave!' – 'Hmm!' coughed the sheriff – ; 'and it is true he does work like a slave. But that is precisely how he should *not* work; he should work with *pleasure*, that's the thing; with pleasure! But he cannot do that so long as he is a savage and hates his work ... and so long as being a state official, and working unproductively is regarded as the highest thing in the land.' 'Hmm!' said Daniel. 'But that is how it is now. And the farmer does not see or hear anything else ... and so he learns to turn his back on his work, instead of putting his heart and soul into it and thereby ... making progress. Progress! As it is now he never gets any further than to the bank. If he actually has a bit of money, then he wastes it on frippery ... and if he has a son with a bit of ability ... well then, that son is certainly not going to be a farmer. Good heavens, no. He is going to teachers' training college – to be educated; and when he has been there, then he is, of course, too refined to lend his hand to anything ... other than be all dressed up with nowhere to go; be one of the elegant crowd ... live off what the others have sweated to provide; – because that's the done thing. But live off what one has produced oneself ... that is vulgar ... and so all ability disappears from the farming community, and those that are left, the barrel scrapings, slave away for the banks ... they will become a proletariat as in England ... and that's supposed to be the freehold farmer we're to rely on when it comes to the crunch!' – Daniel felt uncomfortable sitting there; but Storr was a materialist, so one did not need to worry about what he said. And he looked round and saw that the others did not agree with him either. But Storr carried on. We talked about education ... well and good ... but ... but there was one thing that all schools and all education in the country should be have as their starting point and that was ... to imprint on the national mind-set – as if in words of flame – the good old maxim: *poverty is a crime*, poverty is shame. That should be the first commandment in the people's catechism – ; 'thou shalt not be poor'. This country had to become a nation of workers like Belgium or Switzerland; instead it was being turned into a nation of government administrators and writers after the German model. We could see it everywhere, – in our literature with all its poeticising and dreaming, all these ideas ... German romantic fog, and unhealthy, lifeless garret-room literature ... when we should be telling people the honest truth, and teaching them what it costs to live ... that this was draining the land of vitality and people. – And what about the national budget. We could see from our national budget that we were a country ruled by civil servants – and by farmers who wanted to be fine. Nearly all the money went on administration and non-productive management, and little or nothing on promotion of work and business. And if some poor wretch wanted to study to become a clergyman, then there were hundreds of patrons and scatter-brained spotters of genius ready to help him on his way (that's what you think! thought Daniel); but if there was one person who had made a useful discovery, then ... people thought he was mad. And if he set up a workshop, then the state and buyers went abroad just the same. And then ... and then we complain that we are a poor country! – Indeed. – Even Finland had a large export industry; and what did we export? Emigrants? Switzerland had industries that sent their goods all over the world; what did we produce? Aquavit and lager beer!' 'Skål, then!' shouted young Stensrud. Endre Storr came to and looked round: 'Yes, that's right, this was meant to be a toast for ... for ... yes a toast for the farmer. I'm sorry, my speech was perhaps not the most coherent, but – but, let's drink a toast to the farmer – ; that the farmer – and all of us may acquire so much culture that we learn to love work ... and that the farmer – and all of us – may learn to understand that he who produces a barrel of oats is greater than he who produces a mediocre book ... and that whoever gets two blades of corn to grow where only one grew before, he is a benefactor to his family. A toast to the farmer who works, and works with pleasure and initiative!' The toast was drunk, but no one said bravo. And Daniel thought that here was a man whom Haugum maintained was not a materialist!

Daniel had been sipping from his glass while Storr spoke so that he would have the courage to propose the toast for king and country, but now his glass was empty, and so he sauntered in to the adjoining room to fill it. For now he really *wanted* to speak. And he would have a serious word or two to say to Storr that both the sheriff and the others would like.

As he stood there mixing his drink Knutzon and Viborg came in with their glasses and sat down. 'Ugh, that Endre Storr', sighed Knutzon. 'Yes, he's a queer fish,' replied Viborg. 'That's right, tutor,' he continued, 'carry on, here we'll have to drink because by god there's nothing else to do in these parts!' 'No, there's no chance here for any other sort of adventure,' said Knutzon. 'No, there's something called morality here in the countryside,' added Viborg, laughing. 'Yes, but à propos; isn't there also something called bundling?'* – 'Good heavens, are you mad? That's only up in the more remote valleys.' – 'What do you think, Mr Tutor? You presumably know about it?' – 'No, that custom has died out in this area,' replied Daniel naïvely. They laughed drily; presumably his reply did not catch the right tone. 'I'll be damned if you can believe these peasants,' said Viborg, 'but it's understandable that you don't want to tell us, eh? You're cunning, aren't you? Eh?' – 'Oh, rubbish,' said Knutzon, 'the tutor obviously sides with the household.' They laughed and drank. Then Viborg made a couple of comments about the 'female livestock in the house', which really astounded Daniel. That people could say such things! Disrespectful and elegant at the same time; self-confident and casual, as it should be. The *frons urbana, frons urbana*...

'Goodnight gentlemen!' said the sheriff who was leaving. The ladies too came in and said goodnight; Knutzon, Viborg and Becker went over to Mrs Storr and were galant. Daniel watched them, frowning. But ... it was the cultured manner... Finally those who were leaving went out, and the estate-owner, Storr and the young Stensrud accompanied them to their sledge. The others moved back in and several gathered round the toddy table.

'That Storr is a real juggler, damn it!' said Bang Block in a low voice. 'Everything he says and does is just to make himself interesting; heavens, he *wants* to be an eccentric ... God damn it,

The Making of Daniel Braut

he ought to be a member of the opposition!' Petersen did not agree; he smiled broadly and kindly; Storr was an OK fellow, a bit naïve, but great fun. There was no lack of entertainment when he was in the party. Yes, he was fun, but he was a juggler all the same. He was of the same cloth as these other 'friends of the people'; good heavens, they were only thinking of themselves. If he had been an orator, then he would have done what Meier and others of that type did, careered round the country organizing 'Folk High Schools' – Block snorted as he said the words – and then return as a member of the Storting... 'Meier? D'you think he'll become a member of the Storting?' asked Becker. Oh, Block knew the type. Meier was once in these parts looking for a parish, and when he didn't get one, ... that's when he went off into the mountains to rouse the people!' – 'By gosh, that was some enlightenment!' said Becker. 'Is it true?' – 'It's what people say.' 'That was an interesting bit of information! The same Meier was said to be a great idealist' ... Rubbish, the same had already happened in the south. Our friend Meier was as good a lawyer Stensgård* as you could wish for, one of the same sort as these bright red fellows from the Fram group ... Daniel jumped. 'Oh, don't let's get into politics again,' begged Viborg. 'The trouble is that as soon as you get out into the country you have to get involved in politics!' – At that moment the estate-owner and the others came in again; the conversation changed topic.

Daniel was not listening to much of what was being said. He sat agonising about his toast for king and country. But every time he was on the verge of daring to do it, his courage failed him. It was no easy matter to speak in such a critical gathering. Just then the estate owner and Storr said goodnight. The estate-owner was old, Storr tired, 'But the young ones can remain sitting,' laughed the estate-owner hospitably. 'You bet we will!' said his son. The old ones left. – Was there any point in proposing a toast to king and country now? –

Block mixed a fresh glass for himself and there was a discussion about the correct way to make toddy. Becker who had been abroad told them how absinth was made, and then started talking about Paris and life there. Daniel heard about things that he could hardly believe existed in the world. From Paris the conversation turned to Christiania, and Daniel realized that he was as much a stranger to life in Christiania as to life in Paris. What he had seen was only what was common and coarse, and intended for farmers ... then Jokum cropped up again. Petersen and Becker told stories about him that were of such a kind that Daniel was not surprised that Hanna did not know about them. But what Bang Block said about 'the magnificent Mrs Harry' wasn't much better. It was strange that there could be so many things like that among the upper class.

But Viborg and Knutzon had developed a taste for teasing the good-natured tutor. As he sat there strongly built and dull with stooping shoulders, twisting his thin beard and staring straight ahead with gentle eyes, he looked so innocent that they could not contain themselves. Was it true that the tutor had led such a wild life in Christiania? Daniel gave a start; the others laughed; – yes, continued Viborg, that was the rumour in Christiania. Mr Tutor was perhaps better known than he realized, and not just for his positive achievements; 'Isn't that so, gentlemen?' – 'Yes, indeed!' said Knutzon. 'Yes, indeed' said Becker. Daniel understood that they wanted to make fun of him and became angry. 'What sort of rumour?' 'Rumour? Would Mr Tutor call what two good witnesses could vouch for, a rumour?' – 'Mr Tutor would do well to answer the questions,' said Becker. And the elegant gentlemen sat and stared at the boy with raised eyebrows and their lorgnettes in front of their eyes. Daniel found himself at a loss and knew he was the underdog; that he could get nowhere against this *frons urbana*.

He was saved by young Stensrud, who started to talk about Rødberg; did the assembled gentlemen know a certain Rødberg? He had been a tutor here on the estate last year. That was a boy who knew how to live on the wild side. But then he also had this problem that he could not tell the truth; he lied both when he had to and when he did not. But the trouble was that he could not lie consistently; one lie contradicted the other and then everything fell apart. He had managed for quite some time, had even put on a show of being religious, and got a decent clergyman to believe

The Making of Daniel Braut

in him – Daniel felt uncomfortable sitting there – ; and every time things went wrong, Rødberg did penance and the kind clergyman took the hook again. Finally he passed his matriculation exams. But when he had passed them he really let fling to such an extent with drunkenness and madness that there was no solution other than to send brother Rødberg into the country. But brother Rødberg knew how to be frail in the country too, and when he had lied so long that his lies just undid each other, then everything came out into the open and Rødberg was shown the door. – Where was he now? – In Christiania, and there were those who said that he was a police constable in the Grønland district of town. – A police constable? Could a citizen of academe fall so low? – Oh, said Stensrud, it was not easy if you were starving. – Daniel had come out in a sweat; he glanced at Stensrud with uncertain eyes and wondered if he knew anything.

'Yes, there are many like that,' said Bang Block, as he sat mixing his fifth glass. 'Did the gentlemen know a certain student called Monsen? He was another sly rogue. He had made his way with the help of lies and loans for several years, indeed for a time he had lived off an ore-mine that his brother *hadn't* found; he was on the look-out to all sides. Take a small incident like – ; last winter when they created that fuss in the theatre, 'A children's pantomime' as *The Citizen* called it ... By the way, weren't you there, tutor?' Viborg asked teasingly; he was topping up his glass frequently. Daniel shook his head, for he did not want to lie ... Oh well; this Monsen joined the whistlers and on that account was given a free ticket; but in plenty of time beforehand he had warned the police, and afterwards profited because he had *not* whistled or hooted. 'Yes, those peasants, those peasants!' laughed Petersen.

Daniel no longer felt happy among the gentlemen of culture, and as soon as he saw a chance to, he tiptoed out and went to bed.

But it was a long time before he could sleep. He lay there feeling annoyed that he had been so unable to hold his own, and now afterwards he could think of a host of good things that he should have said to those elegant gentlemen. In between he tormented himself with questions and doubts: did they know anything? – Strange words had been let slip, but surely they could not believe that he was another Rødberg, or like Peder Monsen?

What was certain was that they had made fun of him, and that he had not been able to stand up for himself. What he needed was the *frons urbana*, the urban shell, the urban boldness; if you had the right spirit and the right attitude you could do and say what you wanted.

And how stupid it was that he had not proposed a toast for king and country. If he had done so, they would have seen that he too was one of the right sort. But tomorrow, tomorrow he would do better. He would show those snooty fellows that he was no worthless creature; he would propose the toast for king and country. This thought made him calmer, and he started to rehearse the speech to himself. It went well: 'Gentlemen, in all our struggles ... there is one name which unites us ... which unites us in devotion and joy ... a name which ... when it is mentioned ... makes us forget ... everything that separates us ... and to ... reach out a brotherly hand...' – It was strange though, he thought, that none of the others had proposed a toast for king and country. Perhaps it was not the done thing? Of course it had to be done. It is only the Internationale that thinks that king and country is just some... '– to give each other a brotherly hand ... like our forefathers at Eidsvoll* ... Yes gentlemen! The glorious memories ... the sagas ... in a rosy grove in the hall of the sagas ... our glorious forefathers, the Vikings who won the whole country ... all this ... the high gods – and goddesses ... and the great heroes who wander through the pages of the sagas, the glorious Håkons ... and the glorious Olafs ... and still we have men who would risk life and limb...'

– Jokum sat at the table nodding, and on his chest he had the Order of St Olaf. But Storr the merchant stood staring at Daniel with flaming eyes and said that king and country were ... king and country were ... an empty phrase, if he could put it like that.

12

The Christmas period was long and hard going.

It passed with toddy evenings and dinner parties day after day in different parts of the district, and in between dances and all-night activities. It was an endless round, the likes of which Daniel had never seen. Endre Storr in his inimitable way said it was 'the savage who had been let loose'. However, he and the other people from town did not hold out for long and left immediately after the main Christmas festivities.

But Daniel thought everything was fine. The elegant gentlemen had since behaved reasonably towards him, and he was confident that they did not know anything. And the round of Christmas partying was something he could always cope with! He was in heaven now compared to this time last year when he was starving in town.

Just how much he had enjoyed the Christmas festivities was something he realised when they were over. It was absolutely wretched getting into harness again for the daily grind, and when he was to meet up with the small boys for the first time and test them in German he was so fed up that he could happily have fled into the woods. He would never be able to endure this struggle. He became more and more certain of it as time went on.

But he had one source of pleasure and that was that his beard looked good, and overall he thought he was more independent than he had been. He no longer had such exaggerated respect for the estate-owner, and the argumentative Endre Storr had not been able to shake his old belief in spirit and the life of the mind. One day he had even dared to engage this man in debate.

He had asked whether the merchant would admit to the proposition that only the rich could be educated? To this Storr replied 'yes' and he had good authorities to support him: thinkers 'who the tutor himself was as aware of as he was'; nor could it be denied that he had good reasons. It was *not* Daniel who won this argument, but he *knew* that Storr was wrong, the reasons *why* he would have to think about later. Storr was wrong in everything. What he stood for was totally against all that Daniel had heard and learnt. The whole of society from chaplain Hirsch to the Dalesman, from Professor Darre to Fram would unite to condemn such materialism.

He was not as bound by his old authorities as before and began to understand that all that glisters is not gold. When even a Folk High School teacher like Meier could be a financial speculator then it was not easy to see what one should believe. Perhaps *The Good Citizen* lied less often than he'd imagined. Who, for example, could know if Hirsch was the paragon he was held up to be? Hadn't he once left a task because he could get a couple of hundred more in annual salary somewhere else? – No, no, he would not think of Hirsch in that way. But the others – who among them could he trust? From Mrs Storr he had heard that Hans Haugum's fiancée was a young lady worth ten thousand a year. Who could know whether for the sake of those ten thousand daler he had not sold and betrayed the ideals of his youth?

Mrs Storr had said that Haugum was a man whom fortune smiled on. Hmm, yes; in a way. It would have been no bad thing if Inga Holm had been rich; that would have been a convenient way of getting out of poverty. Or ... if he had had some other ideals? In reality it was ridiculous to bind oneself before one had learnt the ways of the world.

He felt he had reason to believe that Hanna had nothing against him. In fact she had recently become more housewifely, both in dress and in other ways. And this had happened one day after Daniel – speaking about Mrs Stensrud – had said that he liked housewifely women. Before Christmas Hanna had mainly played Norwegian folk melodies, which he had said he liked.

After Christmas when he told her that he *adored* the Swedish student songs, she began to play those to the point that Daniel almost grew sick of them. There were several such signs, and Daniel in fact began to feel sorry for the girl. She was worth something better than to be forgotten here at home. –

– He carried on as before and kept mum about his opinions. But he did so in a different way because he did not wish to lie. When the estate-owner propounded his ideas, Daniel would state what an opponent would say: 'so-and-so says ... what's one to say to that?' – and in the end he would let the estate-owner win. It worked well. In fact Daniel was tired of politics.

More and more he longed to get back to town. Every day he would look in *The Citizen* to see if there was any position for him there. But things did not look promising. If there was anything, it was either too demanding for a student with *haud* or too little to live off. He began to dream about Lias in America. Perhaps that boor would stumble on something there; perhaps he would find gold in California; marry money and then one day send a promissory note home ... a large promissory note ... It was odd that Lias had not written yet.

Then one day he did write. Daniel saw the American stamp and tore open the letter while his heart thumped. Lias said that he had struggled a great deal, and been involved in 'many sorts of business', but that now he had come to rest for the first time, and was happy, for now he had a position as a dairyman. Daniel grimaced, and was both deflated and disappointed. A dairyman! And yet the brute wrote as proudly as if he had found gold ... talked about politics; about American 'freedom;' wrote that one had so much freedom here. Indeed! That's what they all wrote. It was utter nonsense. There was freedom enough in Norway too; if only he had money ... Daniel put the letter aside. There was no point in dreaming about a promissory note from America.

So he dreamt all the more about town, and about the cultured manner. He believed there was one thing he could acquire immediately that would help him to look more sophisticated and that was glasses. He started to complain about weak eyesight and when the estate-owner travelled to Christiania for the February winter market Daniel accompanied him to find a remedy, and got glasses. They were a great help. They took away some of his good-natured appearance and gave his face a cold gleam which made it appear sterner. Daniel looked at himself in the mirror and decided that as soon as he had grown a thicker beard no-one would be able to see that he had been a peasant.

On this trip he also saw a few old acquaintances again. One evening he was sitting in a hotel café with young Stensrud, Endre Storr and Knutzon when some fellows came in and sat down at a nearby table and began drinking toddy. There was one whom Daniel did not recognize, but the others were Aslak Fjordan, Gregus Johnsen and Strand. They were already slightly tipsy and did not look particularly respectable. Daniel turned away from them; they would not fit with the group he was now with.

Storr sat with a red-wine toddy and was expatiating about the winter market being a bad tradition. Knutzon disagreed and Daniel thought he had some very good arguments, but he finally had to give in; he could not hold out against Storr. Then Knutzon calmly admitted that what he had said he had from a man like Lampe, the merchant, and one would imagine that he knew what he was talking about. Hmm, thought Daniel, so such people too don't necessarily think for themselves. He was enjoying himself. But that they had the courage to admit it!

Storr was carrying on about the national economy. He damned the farmers who were chopping down their forests and thereby laying waste their own and the nation's capital, but perhaps we had to be ruined in order to learn the necessity of work. What we had lived off before, forestry, shipping, fishing, that was too much of a lottery that turned us into dreamers, and weakened our moral fibre. There were people along the coast who invested all their savings in ships' parts and fishing; if they were lucky they earned money, but if things went badly, then the whole project collapsed and they were left with two empty hands. This was because they had started up without a secure base; it was bound to end in poverty. But the trouble was that it destroyed initiative and the will to succeed. People learnt to trust in a stroke of luck, wanted to become rich in the twinkling of an eye, dreamed instead of working, dug for old treasure, took out prospecting rights for pyrites and mica ... Even religion was used to foster people in this barbarism. The clergy preached that people should trust in Our Lord and not worry about the morrow; that it was sinful to strive after riches; that one should be 'content with one's station in life', live like the birds of the air ... what could one expect from a nation that had been brought up in that faith? We really were a nation of seekers and dreamers. We struggled and toiled to keep body and soul together, but never got any further. Couldn't God so arrange things that they would find a lump of gold in their field? Couldn't Our Lord arrange for good fishing, good freight rates, let it rain shillings or snow daler notes? – The students laughed, Daniel too, though the colour was beginning to rise to his face. But, Storr continued, just let our farmers go to America, and then they are as if transformed. There is no one there who tells them to rely on the Lord; there they learn to help themselves, and when they have learnt that, they get on, because they know how to work. – Daniel did not get round to contradicting Storr that evening. He was right about some things, particularly in what he said about the farmers.

– Daniel heard Aslak laughing over in his corner, his voice getting ever louder; 'I agree with those who want to abolish the clergy; I'm with them on that one!' He laughed again. 'The beasts! Don't they stand up there every damned Sunday and lie for all they're worth. Do they think that we don't know that Jesus became God at the Council of Nicea three hundred years after he died!' More laughter. 'Nominated God by a simple majority? And he got the majority because the Emperor was on his side! Had the Emperor sided with Arius then, as he had several times before, then never in the world would Jesus have become God! The beasts *know* that!' – Hu, what jabbering, thought Daniel. What crudeness in thought and speech. Even the dialect was vulgar! But Gregus sat nodding, looking as if he thought Aslak was talking convincingly. Perhaps he was living off Aslak just now. Now and again he ran his fingers through his hair, then held them up in front of him and stared at them with a grim face, looking to see if any hair had fallen out ... Daniel had the impression of worn out, wretched hobos when he looked at these fellows; he turned away from them with disgust.

'Good heavens, that *he* dares to enter!' said Storr under his breath and stared at the door. Daniel followed his gaze and saw there someone whom he thought he recognized. Yes, he knew the man. It was Bernt Bruvik. 'There's a Norwegian freehold farmer,' said Storr. 'See how solid and trustworthy he looks; you could almost believe he was one of God's little angels, and yet he's a sly rogue. He's been trading for several years here in town; came into money through his wife and squandered it. Then he lived off promissory notes, cheated half the town ... for no one could doubt a face like that! But ... a few days ago he went bankrupt. It's said that the creditors are hoping for one and a half percent.'

Daniel felt he had to show his independence and say that there were rogues in town as well as in the country, and Storr agreed with that. This Bruvik could stand for the entire nation. There we were looking as if we were so utterly solid and honest, and yet all things considered, we were a bunch of dreamers. An easy-going, unreliable pack of good-for-nothings. One couldn't expect the farmers to be any better than the others; on the contrary. A great deal of culture was necessary before people learnt that it was wrong to lie, in fact, before they learnt to distinguish clearly between truth and lies. Daniel thought these were strange words, but said nothing. They went on drinking and Storr offered fresh cigars.

– 'A skål in memory of Olsen the Mighty!' shouted Aslak Fjordan and drank. 'Olsen the Mighty was an OK fellow! If I could afford it I would have travelled up there tomorrow to attend his funeral. On the other hand I had known for a long time that he had consumption.' Daniel was shocked to hear this, but then remembered that he owed Olsen the Mighty four daler, which he now would not have to repay... 'Hærland too has consumption,' said Gregus Johnsen. 'Yes, that's worse' replied Strand, 'because damn it, Hærland has one of the best brains around.' 'He could have become something big,' said Aslak. 'But things got too difficult ... too much work and too little food; a cold room and split boots; that's how it goes in the world.' – Daniel felt uncomfortable; ugh; never back to that life! Then he was struck by a thought that he promptly dismissed: it would be a relief to him if *all* his old acquaintances were to die.

As they left Aslak Fjordan was sitting arguing with Strand about Fram; it sounded as if Strand and Fram had become enemies and that Aslak believed Strand was to blame for this. But Strand swore that it was Fram who was to blame. Daniel managed to leave without being seen. The only acquaintance whom he subsequently met was one of the 'bandits' who came up to him and talked 'democratic' politics and asked to borrow half a daler; the fellow looked terrible. Daniel gave him an ort and left. –

– Up at Stensrud the days passed slowly. One day there was a position advertised in *The Good Citizen* that Daniel thought he could have managed, and which he would have applied for if he had had *laud*. As he was wondering whether there was any point in writing to Pater about this post to ask if he would put in a good word for him, he received a letter from chaplain Hirsch. It was a long letter. Daniel went cold all over when he recognized the hand-writing. He scanned the letter nervously. Did Hirsch *know* anything? –

Hirsch explained the reasons why he had not written sooner; it was mainly because he felt that Daniel ought to be free to develop completely independently. And now he believed that that time might have come.

He wrote: 'Rud has told me that since the summer you have been a tutor out in the country; and I know that there you have had time to gather yourself and reach a clear understanding about what must be the foundation of your life.' And he continued: 'I sincerely hope that you have retained your childlike faith through this struggle, for you know that it is the child who shall inherit the kingdom. And I am especially confident that you will have kept your distance from all this urban nonsense, this empty, hollow "cultured manner" or whatever it is they call it. You have too warm and genuine a nature for such things to seduce you. You must also have seen enough of urban life to know what it is worth: bold words and cold hearts, cheap fun instead of seriousness, wit instead of wisdom, dance round the golden calf and aping of pointless fashion instead of a life in love and vigour, – there in a nutshell you have the characteristics of a life that is supposed to be the most elevated, and that's not to say anything about everything that's hidden behind the façade, and which I would rather not mention. They kill every serious thought with laughter: let us eat and drink and be merry for tomorrow we die.

'I am not forgetting that there is much that is good and beautiful in town; there is both art and other things that lift and gladden the spirit, and there will always be many who live a truly human life, in the midst of all the emptiness and din. What I am talking about is what in particular is called "the urban life"; this life that makes people into dressed-up dolls and dancing masters and which kills life and heart and seriousness in an endless pursuit of frivolity, which empties people so totally of their spiritual core that they finally are incapable of having any thoughts or ideas other than those that are in fashion at the moment. And you know that as well as I do. No, as I think I taught you in my way: man is, thank goodness, more than a wooden wig stand and dressed-up doll, and life something more than being able to dance and being a lion on the dance floor. – And *that* is the greatest thing I have learnt out here in the country; that however poor and wretched and sometimes plain ugly "the life of the people" can seem when seen from "above" through a lorgnette – it is the one that contains the most truth and seriousness and compassion; it is in fact the richest and truest. There is little "form" here, but all the more content, it is the true metal which rings out; the outside may appear cold and dark, but underneath there is gold hidden, the gold of the heart.

The Making of Daniel Braut

This is where we have to start; *this* is where those of us who want to waken the spirit of the people in Norway have to start.

'You will have seen that I have had much to grapple with in recent years. When I sat dreaming in Christiania I imagined that the common people were different, and many a time I have been on the verge of losing my faith in them. It has seemed to me that they were not just caught in a trance but were turned to stone under all this lack of spirit, with their bread and butter concerns on the one hand and pietism on the other; that they were dull and worn out, rendered helpless by their long nightmare. But as I have in a way got to know the common people personally, these dark thoughts have faded away, and if we ever meet I can tell you much more about this. I have seen much that is bad, but I have found more hearts of gold, and often where one might least expect to find it.

'However, I have more and more learnt to see that the right way to rouse the common people is not to send the farmer to town, where he is often ruined and forgets both "his mother tongue and the traditions of his father"; no, the farmer must remain a farmer, and gain an education – a true education of heart and mind – on his home turf. That is why I have not helped others than you to become students; instead I have sent them to the Folk High School. This is the best and most beautiful thing that has sprung up in our northern lands in recent times; and it will achieve things – first and foremost in Norway – which foreigners and future generations will be amazed at.'

The letter stated that the chaplain intended to set up a Folk High School himself in about a year's time. He had not been able to do as much as he would have liked while he had a parish to run, but now that his father-in-law had died he would be able to afford such an enterprise. First, however, he had to go abroad for a year to rest and to learn more, but then his ideas were to be put into action. He asked whether Daniel would not join him in this.

'I won't be able to offer you a large salary, but it will be enough to manage on in the country, and when one has enough to manage on then one does not need more. And I know that you have been enthusiastic about the ideas that this enterprise is based on, and you know that the goal of man is to have something great to work for and fight for, and you will never regret that you have sacrificed yourself for such a glorious spiritual task as this. I will not try to persuade you; everyone has to take up the work he feels called to, as that's where he is most likely to find his true goal in life. You have thought of becoming a clergyman; are you sure that you will manage this heavy task in times like these? Or perhaps you are drawn to the life of a scholar? In any case, think carefully about this: that nothing is worse than to "mistake one's destiny".'* The letter ended with a warm greeting. Daniel drew a deep breath and thought partly with pleasure and partly with scorn: he doesn't know anything either.

He did not pay much attention to the first bit of the letter about urban life. In a way it might be true enough ... but what was important was to find an answer to this matter of the Folk High School.

He did not think he had a vocation to be a Folk High School teacher. He did not have the right attitude. To be out there in the country among peasant farmers teaching them the wisdom of life could be all well and good ... though the farmer perhaps needed another sort of education just as much. Scholar? No, he had never considered that. He did not care much about scholarship. In fact he could not understand the point of it. We already *had* the truth. Everything God thought it was good for us to know he had told us about in the Bible. So what were they looking for? And however long they scratched around and examined flesh and blood and dead bodies, they would never find out what life was, nor could they discover anything about the life hereafter either. What they were looking for, the Bible knew, and more than that. The more one thought about it, the more one found that the Bible had answers to all our questions. And the answers one found there would show themselves to be the best and most profound. There were certain things in the Bible that we could not understand, but that too showed that the Bible was God's word. If it had been the work of a human mind then we would have been able to understand it all. It was theology that Daniel had always thought of. It taught us how to interpret the Bible, and a theologian could know more than any one else about the things that were worth knowing. Theology was the only true philosophy; it really *knew* something, while the subject that called itself philosophy was only empty phrases. – And when he had learnt what he had to learn, then he would become a clergyman. A clergyman had a beautiful mission, and he was someone whom people needed, and whom they respected. He was the person who managed the church and was most listened to in the parish. No one could do as much as him. And in his mind's eye Daniel saw an attractive vicarage shining white among green trees, and he saw himself sitting there as master and father, and he saw a vicar's wife who – ; yes, it *was* Inga whom he saw.

No, he did not want to be a Folk High School teacher. What was more he had not done with student life. He had to go to town again. He had so much to do there; he had to study theology and other things and work his way to being able to think for himself ... As he was thinking about this he suddenly realized that Hirsch was rich now ... so surely *he* must be able help him? Especially since it was theology that he wanted to study? This thought cheered him so much that he immediately sat down to reply to Hirsch's letter.

He wrote that he had not yet got things so clear in his own mind that he could answer yes or no to the question about the Folk High School. The only thing that he was certain about was that he needed to study theology for a year or two. He explained this at length and felt that he had managed it really well. Finally he touched on his financial difficulties. It wasn't easy for someone who had only passed his *examen philosophicum* to find a job, so it could take time before he was finished, but he would have to wait and see if it couldn't be done. Daniel thought it was not worth saying any more for the time being and sent the letter.

He had to wait a long time for a reply, and was already beginning to wonder whether he should write to Helle and try him when a letter came from Hirsch. It said that Daniel should speak to Rud who would find a solution. But the chaplain did not think Daniel should sit too long studying 'in peace and quiet' because the theology we had now was the worst sort of dead German stuff that you could imagine, and very dangerous to immerse oneself in, and all things considered one learnt more from life than from books. Therefore Jens Rud would find him work in a while, but not a job that would mean he could not study at the same time.

Daniel was not too keen on this last bit, but some sort of solution was better than none. And then he would have to see what turned up. When he told Hanna that he was leaving, he could see that she minded, and he could not deny that this pleased him.

13

Daniel was happy to see Christiania again, as it lay there shimmering in the July sun, grey and sleepy, thirsting for rain. This was really the only place a student could bear to live, and he thought to himself that he would rather toil away his days as a lowly clerk in a government department here in town than bury himself in the country teaching farmers the philosophy of life.

He rented a four-daler room in Homansbyen; he wanted to live decently. Then he went to the tailor's. Paid for his old clothes and bought new ones on tick, the finest he had ever had. At the hatter's he fell for the temptation of buying a top hat, hadn't exactly thought of doing so but sooner or later he would have to. Finally he bought a pair of black gloves. So when he finally stood in front of the mirror and examined himself, the only conclusion he could come to was that he looked good. His beard had grown and his hair had become darker, but he would have to straighten his shoulders, though there were many who had stooped shoulders. He twirled his moustache and decided that when he had attended dancing classes and learnt everything that was part of the cultured manner, then he would be a thoroughly presentable gentleman.

But when he emerged onto the street in his new finery he felt that everyone was staring at him. Presumably they thought it was strange that he who was only the son of a peasant farmer wanted to strut and pretend to be a grand fellow ... he laughed drily to himself; that he could still have such ideas! He straightened up and presented the *frons urbana* as well as he could, for that was what counted. But it did not always help. People were so stuck-up and ready to sneer, so superior. But just wait. Just wait, good people. One day when he had his surplice and clergyman's ruff and they would perhaps be sitting in church listening to him proclaim judgement over them, then they would not be so likely to sneer; – uhh, if only one could become a bishop. –

– He called on the merchant Storr and was warmly received. Storr himself was not at home, but Mrs Storr was easy, behaved just like a sister towards him, and always asked him to tell about his own doings. Daniel had nothing against gratifying her in this respect, and told her everything she wanted to know. And he did not tell her anything that was not true, he could defend every word he said for he did not want to be a liar, but he was surprised himself at how well he managed it. He even admitted the *haud* he had got for his university matriculation exams, and when Mrs Storr said that *haud* was a good mark, and that her own brother had not got more, Daniel was so pleased that his eyes positively shone through his glasses. Mrs Storr became fond of those eyes because they were so deep and loyal. Then she told him how fond they had become of him at Stensrud, and when she mentioned Hanna in particular she did so in such a way that Daniel blushed. From that moment she thought she knew his heart's secret; but Daniel thought equally strongly that he knew where *he* had *her* in this matter.

He went to the *russ* festivities, for that was where his new student life was to begin; he imagined he would have a wonderful evening among fresh young people. But he quickly came to the conclusion that the *russ* this year were not as in his day. There was jollification and noise this evening as there had been then, but there was not the same joy in it. And what was meant to be fun was often, in his opinion, stupid. He wondered about this for a while, and finally found the reason: it must be because there were so many sons of farmers among the students.

He could recognize them as soon as he saw them, and he liked them less and less. The lumbering heaviness of movement and the facial features which he had once thought expressed strength, did not express strength but 'crudeness'. The urban students had none of that, but they could be just as strong for all that. And the worst of it was that the peasant students now seemed proud of their crudeness. They *made a point* of being farmers; there were even those who went dressed in their homemade country clothes. And they would stare at the urban students and at everything that was fine with such intolerable superiority ... Daniel himself experienced this and grew both angry and hot under the collar.

But the worst of it was that the urban students put up with this peasant rule and what's more made a fuss of the farming students. It even went so far that certain urban students strove to look like farmers themselves. Daniel felt sick looking at it. If things were going to carry on like this, there would soon not be anything exceptional in being a student. All these students from the farms were dragging down student life. People would soon not respect university students any more than ordinary college students.

The punch took its time coming, and when it finally did, it was not worth drinking. It was just sugar-water, like the *russ* speech, where there was much sweetness and very little of the strong stuff, much flowery language, but little to laugh at. Most of it was made up of beautiful phrases about the student as a 'son of the people', and the student as a 'a bearer of new ideas'. The *russ* greeted all this with wild enthusiasm, and Daniel himself was nearly swept along, but he remembered just in time that this was the sort of thing that educated people called empty words.

And it got worse and worse the further it went. There was one who spoke for our 'great men of the people' who were an 'expression of the Norwegian democratic spirit'; they freed the latent energy, and were popular leaders, popular poets, champions of the people, saviours of the people. Another spoke in heady words about the 'spirit of the north', which was at the heart of everything and was good for everything, then there was someone who spoke for the Folk High School movement, which was a 'daughter of the spirit of the north'. This school should rouse the people and free them, and through music free the people's princess from the power of the merman, which was materialism. Finally a young urban student got up and spoke in *Landsmål*, the language of the countryside, something which made Daniel feel both ashamed and annoyed. He did not like to hear this peasant tongue in good company, and now that through struggle and hardship he had finally worked his way out of rural life, he did not want to be caught up in it again. He got up and went into a side room. 'Three cheers for the true Norwegian language!' shouted one of the champions of *Landsmål*; 'Hurrah! Hurrah! Hurrah!' replied the whole room. Daniel thought they were mad.

He sat down at a table and tasted the punch. He felt so wretched and lonely. He did not like the farmers, but nor did he feel at home amongst the townspeople. Everything was back to front. At the moment when he finally felt he had a chance of achieving a degree of culture, the townspeople decided they wanted to be farmers! It was just as if everything he had striven for all his life was no longer worth anything. He simply could not understand it. Everything was going round in circles. Finally his anger landed on chaplain Hirsch. If that ... that ... dreamer had only taught him in the usual Latin-school way he would have become a city person sooner. But that's how it was when the poor man's son had to make his way in the world: everything depended on luck, and things developed accordingly. 'Hurrah! Hurrah! Hurrah!' sounded like a thunderclap from the next room. 'Hurrah! Hurrah! Hurrah!' louder and louder ... and then a roar and a crescendo of clapping, and out of the uproar a song worked its way ever more confidently till in the end the national anthem burst forth like storm that filled the house,

> Yes we love this country,
> As it rises up,
> Gnarled and weathered above the water,
> With its thousand homes.

Daniel sat wondering whether the people in the next room really loved their country as much as they shouted that they did. But on the other hand it was easy for those who were well off to love their country.

Somewhat later in the evening he met up with Strand and some others; one of these had a bottle of cognac, so Daniel could liven up his punch. That helped, but Strand made fun of Daniel's new image and had acquired a way of talking that was half teasing and half mocking, which Daniel did not like. You could never be sure whether what he was saying was meant to be critical or positive; it was a peasant arrogance that was worse than the *frons urbana*. Among the rest the person who most attracted Daniel's attention was a pale, fat and relaxed fellow with blonde hair and a brick red beard and large glasses. It was he who had brought the cognac. His name was Olai Juberg; could it really be he who Haugum had said was so utterly ruined? That had to be rubbish. Then there was an older man who was presented as 'Eleasar Karelius Manassesen Stormyrhals BA, otherwise known as Karl Magnus', a dark-haired, lean fellow from northern Norway; his neck and head stuck out from his sagging shoulders like those of a bird. The fourth in the group was a young *russ*, Aslak Mogen from Telemark. He was perhaps the best-looking lad Daniel had ever seen; but one could still see that he was a peasant-farmer. Daniel puzzled over this boy for a long time before coming to conclusion that he must be a descendant of one of the old rich land-owning farmers, who would soon be a myth.

Karl Magnus was speaking. He was very excited about the young man from Bergen who had spoken *Landsmål*; that's how it should be; that was the way that *Landsmål* would win through. The *russ* were a grand lot this year. They were serious people, and so many were of farming stock. Magnificent, stout fellows, tough as blocks of birch wood; wonderfully good, strong faces on the majority; and the great thing was that they were no longer ashamed of being farmers. He said he always came and examined the *russ* in the autumn, wanted to see how the harvest stood, and whether it was worth gathering in. He had such pleasure in the thought that each autumn produced new hope for the country.

But there were some who were spoken of mockingly. Like all these old fellows, who struggled on and struggled on and never got finished. They stayed in hibernation the whole year, some out in the country and others in digs, and no one knew anything about them until they came crawling out to take their matriculation exams, weird-looking and wretched, people-shy and starving, worn out and patched up, more and more disgusting with very year that passed, more and more wretched, with overgrown beards like shaggy ruffs; he laughed, yes, they had shaggy ruffs. Old Wonderboy, he had finally got through; Karl Magnus had missed him this year. But then there was Lars Risvold; he was just as tenacious. Karl Magnus had lent him money for his exam entry fees this year ... ten daler, totally wasted. 'Yes, he's living on loans now,' said Strand. 'But he remains spry,' replied Karl Magnus, 'shaves and wears a white tie ... it's the daftest thing imaginable; everyone thinks he's a theologian. He looks like a donkey in a surplice or a sheep in tails!' ... The more Karl Magnus drank, the louder he spoke, and gesticulated with arms and shoulders in unending restlessness.

Yes, there were many of these boys from the country who ended up going to the dogs, said Strand. Many never got as far as their matriculation exam, others got so far but no further; some stopped at the *Examen philosophicum* and not a few died; a difficult life and endless struggle killed many a man, and those who did win through were often worn out. 'And the majority of those were theologians,' said Olai Juberg in his slow, calm drawl. Oh yes, Karl Magnus knew many of these peasant theologians, they were easily recognizable, terrible rubbish, heavy as a keelson, with broad, dark, fanatical faces, suitable to being prison chaplains or evangelical clergy ... But that so many peasant lads ended up going that way was understandable. They were educated for it, first at primary school and later at teachers' training college. When they came in to Christiania they did not know how to study. The only thing they knew was how to learn their lessons and believe what the teacher told them, and so they studied theology. That could be all well and good, but ... the Devil take Old Nick Pontoppidan! 'And rote learning,' added Strand. 'Oh,' replied Karl Magnus, 'that's not the worst! Where Pontoppidan is concerned I think that's best, for those who make themselves believe that they *understand* Pontoppidan, they become complete idiots. They get a board in front of their eyes and a ring in their nose like a bull, so they never learn to think for themselves. No, it's the practice of catechising that's the real disaster! It's quite simply a training in being yes-men, lacking all independence. You've never seen such an abomination!' – 'Oh, when all's said and done,' said Strand 'it's all the dogma that we have to get out of our schools, if we're ever to become proper people.' – 'Skål, Strand,' said Juberg. 'Yes, church and home are the places that look after faith best,' said Karl Magnus.

'And what about you, Aslak, are you going to become a theologian?' enquired Strand.

'Not likely,' replied Aslak, and smiled like a child, 'I don't want to be any kind of state official.' 'You're right there,' said Karl Magnus. 'When someone enters public office it's as if they die. They are bound by all these 'regulations', and so they doze off, cocoon themselves like trichina worms, and eat and drink and get promoted according to seniority.' ... 'Yes that's it, and they have no respect in the community,' said Aslak, 'they're so stupid that they simply become laughing-stock. And the only things they talk about are their salary and pension, and then look at them! When you see such an old, grey, miserable, bent and worn out tax-collector or priest, it's just as if you were looking at a pair of crooked, worn-out shoes,' said Aslak, laughing lustily; the others joined in too. But Daniel was angry and no longer liked Aslak; – but it was of course impossible to say anything in a gathering like this.

He was happier when they began to tell stories from 'the Factory'. Strand and Juberg tried to outdo each other, and Daniel laughed till the tears ran down his cheeks, and told one or two stories that he himself could remember; the couple of years at Heltberg's school had been the best he had lived! Karl Magnus said The Old Man had done more for the country's democratic development than anyone realized; he mentioned in particular that so many of the students from farming stock had become lawyers and had got their degrees in the humanities. And they were some of our best people. Among others, Hærland was mentioned, and Strand said that the only thing stopping him being a 'fully grown man' was that he was not a socialist. Daniel took note of this, and Karl Magnus argued against Strand, but that was perhaps because he too was not 'fully grown up' as far as democratic politics were concerned. –

Finally Strand, Karl Magnus and Daniel went home with Olai Juberg and drank beer.

The conversation now turned to more basic topics. Strand and Juberg spoke of their 'sins', which were not few, and these fellows were not ashamed of calling a spade a spade. Daniel thought how terribly crude such things sounded when they could not talk about them with an elegant turn of phrase. He began to talk with Karl Magnus, who was now somewhat drunk and had started to tell of a great invention he was working on. It was a flying machine that he thought would be useful. He turned all his pockets inside out looking for a drawing he had made of this machine, but found instead a letter which took his thoughts in a quite different direction.

The letter was from a schoolmaster who had been dismissed because he was perhaps too fond of a jolly evening. Several times there had been problems because of him, but finally he had caused ... caused ... 'A scandal?' enquired Daniel. 'Well yes,' and then he was put out on the streets. Now he wanted to come in to the capital to seek employment here, and he was a bright fellow, but Karl Magnus knew it would be pointless. 'A fellow who has been dismissed for drunkenness!' Daniel felt sorry for the schoolmaster. But when people weren't careful...

'Yes, that's the tragedy,' said Daniel; he too was beginning to feel the effects of too much beer. 'That's the tragedy ... people want to live high ... and lead the good life ... instead of working and saving. If they earn anything it goes on frills and finery; they eat it up and drink it up ... and afterwards ... well they can always find work later. Such things can't end well. It's barbarism! The farmer is no longer the ... proud freeholder he was in olden days; his farm is mortgaged to the land bank ... it's that he toils away for; it will end in ruin. Many beautiful words had been spoken this evening about education and culture, but ... well ... the thing is people must learn to work!'

Strand sat staring at Daniel with flashing eyes, then exploded and swore that whoever said that the common people did not work was lying. And whoever said that ordinary people were living the good life was a thickhead ... It could well be that the estate owners in the wealthy farming districts lived like sheep and drank up the proceeds of the sale of their forests in champagne, but if Braut thought that the farmers were such vermin, he was in no position to talk. Daniel stared at Strand, he had never seen such eyes; they were a fiery yellow like a snake's; 'I assume I too am entitled to ... an opinion,' he stammered. 'The opinions you've acquired up in the wealthy farming districts you can keep to yourself,' replied Strand provocatively, 'and what's more Mr Braut, I don't think you've ever had more 'opinions' than you could stuff in your pocket!' Daniel was uneasy and replied, 'I've never taken sides ... I don't give a damn about politics ... one party's as good or bad as another. I've never believed in the scrimp and save politics ... the country doesn't get richer because you cut twenty daler off some wretched pension ... Perhaps everything's not gold that glisters in the Folk High School Movement either; if Meier had not got the parish he was seeking...' – 'Has Meier got a parish?' asked Strand incredulously. 'He hasn't even taken his theological exams!' shouted Karl Magnus. Daniel felt defenceless and was afraid. 'Perhaps you are trying to cast doubt on a man like Meier?' said Strand; 'Damn it, that's the most contemptible thing I've heard. Coming with downright lies to blacken a man who has given his life to helping the farmers! Meier is a man who deserves the thanks and respect of the whole country; and I think that you least of all, Mr Braut, have any right to talk about false gold.' Strand was getting more and more worked up, and in the end was so insulting and offensive that Daniel could see nothing for it but to leave. With a heavy head he tottered home; he hated Strand and the whole lot; they were an uncivilised bunch.

– Next morning he woke with a hangover and an uneasy feeling. He only had the dimmest recollection of the latter part of the previous evening and lay in agonised struggle trying to recollect it, and the more he remembered, the more he broke out in a sweat. Never in the world would he dare to go to Jens Rud now; he would have to write, and the sooner the better.

He wrote and received a written reply. Terse and matter of fact. Jens sent him a promissory note which entitled him to draw ten daler a month at Jens's lawyer. Daniel didn't think ten daler was much. Jens also promised to find work for him; there's no need for hurry thought Daniel. Finally he sent a greeting from chaplain Hirsch, who was in Germany, but was expected home in the spring. Ah, not before, thought Daniel.

From the tone of the letter, Daniel got the feeling that Jens no longer wanted to have anything to do with him. Then as something cold and shameless arose in him he said to himself, 'Very well! Just as well that they know, then I'm rid of them.'

But he wasn't happy and didn't quite like the person he had become, and he thought with horror of how beautifully Jens Rud could smile. –

– Daniel enjoyed the theological lectures. He noticed that he had forgotten various things that he had known for his matriculation exams, and much that he should have known he had never known. He would have to pull himself together and study as soon as he got time. But the subject itself he liked. What Karl Magnus had said about this sort of knowledge was just nonsense. For there was more than enough here to challenge one's thinking, and more than enough to explore. Almost daily the professors touched on profound, difficult questions, which sometimes were so enormous that he hadn't thought such things could exist in faith. But the more difficult they were, the better it was, for he was secure in the knowledge that the professors would manage to solve them in the end in the correct and prescribed manner.

On one of the first days he bumped into Haugum whom he greeted with great pleasure; for he could surely strike up with him again. But Haugum turned out to be the same as ever, but perhaps even more stubborn. He even went so far as to criticize the professors, and everything that he did not agree with was 'dull', pointless and mad. Daniel could not accept this. It was fanaticism, and he realized that he wouldn't get anywhere with Haugum, and after that they rarely talked of higher matters. Daniel could not be himself when he talked to his old friend.

He learnt that Haugum's girl friend was not as rich as she might have been; her father had invested in shipping, and had recently suffered great losses. 'Is she your first love?' asked Daniel. 'Far from it,' replied Haugum, laughing, 'I've loved so many!' – 'Yes, but seriously?' – 'Seriously, I've only loved one and she deceived me.' – After a while he continued, 'By the way, how's Hanna Stensrud? Is she not engaged yet?' – 'Not that I know of,' replied Daniel. – 'Hmm, strange, she was very good friends with a lieutenant here in town ... some say with two. But presumably they did not consider her rich enough.' Daniel became uneasy; 'Isn't she rich?' he asked. 'Oh yes, rich enough for the likes of us. – Are you perhaps considering her?' – ' No, far from it!'

Apart from Haugum the rest were more or less transformed; it was if they had acquired a new outer man; they had presumably become citizens of academe. Some had changed so much that they were hardly recognizable; this was perhaps truest of the theologians. There, for example, was Johannes Ortvedt, looking totally different; he was dressed in black, was serious, smiled, but no longer laughed. Jens Rud was studying law, but it was said that he wanted to go home and become a farmer. Markus Olivarius studied 'law, philology, theology, medicine and other sciences,' and 'knew everything that the others did not know.' Aslak Fjordan had emigrated to America, and was supposed to have said that 'it was impossible for a citizen of academe to do anything useful in this country.' Sven Dufva was out in the country resting; Gregus Johnsen was also in the country 'collecting impressions'; Rødberg was travelling round western Norway as a lay preacher. As far as Daniel could see nothing much ever came of the students of farming stock; those who got somewhere, were those who studied theology.

– At an evening lecture Daniel met his old school-friend Christian Bliland. They only just recognized each other again. They had much to talk about now and Daniel accompanied Christian back to his room. It became apparent that Christian's character and behaviour had not changed, but he had changed his opinions about various things, and Daniel was so pleased that he dared to talk about much that he otherwise did not dare mention.

They agreed about many things. Christian wanted to follow the 'popular' line, as long as he could be sure it did not lead to getting too closely involved with the Grundtvigians. 'Yes, that's precisely what I'm afraid of,' said Daniel, 'they're nearly all Grundtvigians, and many are pure rationalists!' – 'Well, the rationalists aren't so dangerous,' replied Christian calmly, 'it's the Grundtvigians with their Folk High Schools and all that – ; if they were to win acceptance among the populace ... what with their Pelagianism* and the whole of their vapid, shallow Christianity ... then God help us!' – 'That's true,' said Daniel, 'and now things have gone so far that they're even talking about taking Christianity out of the school curriculum!' 'That I can't believe,' said Christian seriously. 'Believe? I've heard it with my own ears; – from theologians!' Christian shook his head. 'And the worst of it all,' Daniel continued, 'is that I have heard that socialism is the logical consequence of these popular ideas! Socialism and communism ... isn't it awful?' Christian looked totally bemused. 'For my part,' said Daniel, calming himself, 'I've recently found it best to shun politics and suchlike, for it's not easy to know how far you can go along with it now.' – 'No,' said Christian, 'you have to watch out.' Daniel was so happy that he almost began to worry about it.

He ate supper with Christian but was given neither beer with his meal nor a toddy afterwards. In particular Christian went on about Grundtvigianism and how dangerous it was, and afterwards he spoke about the strange man they'd had as a teacher of religion at the Latin school in recent years. When Daniel was about to leave Christian asked, 'Wouldn't it be good if we prayed together this evening?' – Ow, is that how things stand, thought Daniel. 'Mmm – yes, yes gladly' he stammered.

And so he had to listen to Christian's evening prayers that were both long and tedious. Oh, it was all right for those who had got that far! For his own part he would have to wait till he was a clergyman. As long as he was here studying, he had so many other things to think about ... it wasn't that easy. For the rest, well, you could take it or leave as far as the farmers' habit of holding prayers was concerned. They were never held in the finer houses, and surely they could be just as good Christians for all that? – Daniel went as soon as the prayers were over, and did not eat supper with Christian Bliland again.

But he occasionally ate supper at Endre Storr's. Mrs Storr was always so nice and what was more, in this house he learnt the cultured manner. Daniel even grew to like Storr more and more. He was an intelligent man, and not as materialistic as he had been before. It was as if he had gained greater respect for academic training once he realized that it was from that that we could expect the greatest help in the fight against political phrasemongering. Young Stensrud and his friends were regularly at the Storrs', and Daniel got to know some of them slightly, and was pleased gradually to discover that at bottom they were not so sophisticated after all.

He also discovered something else that did him good: the majority of people did not think for themselves any more than he had done. Rather it was more usual to find that people borrowed their opinions from others, and then began to think for themselves as they grew older and as these opinions took root in them. Daniel got the feeling that he would soon be as independent in his thinking as any of the others, and Halvor Mosebø could do what he liked with his lectures in ethics.

More and more he learnt to understand that there was no point in having 'faith in the farmers'. He remembered the old fellow who used to wander between the various districts, black and dirty, and who dug the earth and thought only of what it would put in the pot, and was full of hate and scepticism towards authority, education and enlightenment ... schools he would have nothing to do with; Jensen's reading primer was just some devilment and if one tried to teach him manners he would become angry and start mocking; he had so little idea about politics that he let himself be led in circles by Jaabæk, and it was this peasant who was to be a national leader! In reality probably nobody thought that. Those who said they did had their own reasons ... help to advance the peasant-farmer? The peasant-farmer did not *want* to advance. Nor could he advance; he could not afford to. He had to struggle all his days just to put food on the table; he did not have time to learn. There was no point in talking about such things. Only those who could afford it could be educated. –

– Daniel had difficulty managing on the money he had, and it got worse. And yet he sometimes had to help others. Lars Risvold came up to his room one evening and sat down to chat ... Daniel understood only too well what he wanted, and wished the fellow to hell. But supposing the poor wretch was starving? Then he would have *that* on his conscience if he said no ... The old saying that 'poverty's a sin' was true. When it came to the point such good-for-nothings who lived by exploiting their neighbours deserved to starve. Several more poor wretches came, among them Peder Monsen who wanted to borrow a daler till tomorrow; he also took the opportunity to say that he had not told Jens Rud about the whistling concert in the theatre – hmm. Bent Bu came one evening and greeted Daniel as a 'school friend' and 'old acquaintance'. Daniel could not remember the fellow, not even his name, but dared not do other than put a brave face on it, offered him beer, said 'skål for the old days' and was in an awkward spot. But Bent Bu laughed and with great good cheer talked about his life so far.

He had gone hungry many times, and more than once had lived for several days on nothing but cold water; but for all that he was just as proud, and sometimes he lived really well. Among other things, he had written for the newspapers, concocting anecdotes and selling them to *The Post* for one mark per piece. But the best joke of all was when he engaged in debate with himself about the Folk High Schools in *The Farmer's Friend* and *The Post*. First he wrote a piece for *The Post* under the pseudonym *Audiatur et altera pars* – he laughed, – then he wrote a piece for *The Farmers' Friend*, against what he'd written and tearing himself to pieces, and got paid by both papers! What the devil did it matter who wrote for those rags so long as what was written was well written? Hmm, Daniel could not disagree. In fact he liked this brazen fellow, who was so apolitical. But the end of the story was the same: lend me a daler.

Things were soon so tight that Daniel himself had to start borrowing, and could not take part in much 'student life'.

He was on the verge of joining Olai Juberg and his kind, fellows who knew both about student life and 'Christiania love life', for Daniel believed that he ought to become familiar with such things. But money was necessary and where was he to lay his hands on that? Chaplain Hirsch had put him on starvation rations here in town.

When he collected his ten daler each month, he only just managed to appease his worst creditors and then he was broke again. It was as if he was walking in an endless circle of old and new debts, and the circle was closing in more and more, getting tighter and tighter until ... he saw all too well that this could not go on. And every day he expected Jens Rud to come and offer him a job, a terrible, dull job in a school...

– Should he make himself contemptible and propose to Hanna? She wasn't ugly. She had even had lieutenants as suitors ... and what's more she had culture and was a lady. She could play the piano and she had a feeling for poetry, quite a marked feeling for poetry ... and she could cook. If he proposed he could get financial help from the landowner, and at one stroke his debts and financial worries would be over, and he could finally have a few years of happy student life...

When he was older and had got a parish he would become a true Christian and take life seriously, and then Hanna would be entirely suitable. Inga? Yes, but if he had no money, he would be stuck here all his days, would become an eternal student or school-teacher and would not be able to marry her in any case. Besides was it certain that Inga Holm cared for Daniel Sørbraut? The whole thing was nonsense; childish dreams, boys' fancies; when life got serious there was no point in wasting time on such things.

He thought about this more and more often, but nothing became of his letter of proposal. Every time he was about to write it, he lost the urge. Instead he began to save.

One raw winter day he moved up to Hegdehaugen and rented a tiny cupboard of a room for two and half daler; after that it was 'dinner at Dampen' again. It was hard to start that again now. When he entered the large, dark dining-room, the smell of food was so strong and pungent that he immediately felt full; and then it was so 'common' and horrid there. Just after two o'clock all the wretched from the schools and the university came pouring in, not least the sons of the common people who were studying ... He had never before realized they were so ugly. And he recognized the smell of student lodgings, of stale tobacco smoke and paraffin, of coffee pots and coarse bread, of sharp curd cheese. And he saw reminders of all the wretchedness that ensues when men used to heavy labour decide to study instead of working in the fresh air. Even the food here was 'common'. He must have been terribly democratic in the days when he liked this fare. Now and again he saw acquaintances he did not want to meet, such as Hærland or Fram. He thought they looked even more wretched than before. Fram in particular was tall, gaunt and shabby with long, tangled hair hanging down over his ears and shoulders so that he looked like a communard; it seemed as if 'the great ideas' could neither feed nor clothe their man. If it came to that the pensioners and old civil servants from the government departments were better off as they at least had enough to live on, though they did not look happy as they sat there chewing over their stew and their failed hopes. They looked tired and disgruntled, grey from mounds of paper and office air, with pinched, lean, dry faces, some with bald patches, others totally bald and with grey beards ... tousleheads and former eagle-eyed departmental hawks now with moulting feathers – they formed a strange counterpart to the students. But here and there sat men from the common stock, dirty, solid working men, strong as tree trunks, eating and drinking as calmly and heartily as if they had not a care for the morrow.

Daniel sat looking at the old men till he thought he understood them. They too had had great and beautiful dreams once, and now they had to sit here and chew their stew amongst labourers and fish-wives. It was terrible to think about. And yet Jaabæk wanted to scrimp and save; scrimp and save on every shilling that a poor state official was trying to live on in his joyless old age. 'The common people?' They saw the common people all around them every day, strong, rough, full of vigour; the common people lived as well as they did, better in fact, and they had not spent a shilling on learning. An able workman could perhaps earn a daler a day, and yet he did not have creditors sucking him like leeches, or a flock of boys who had to study ... the common people lived comfortably. It was the educated who suffered hardship, and yet that peasant Jaabæk sat there in the Storting and wanted to scrimp and save ... for now it was the uncivilised who were to rule the kingdom and the country. Daniel could well understand that the rich could name their horses and dogs after Jaabæk.

The official class had to be preserved; he saw it so clearly. The uncivilized mob wanted everything to be uncivilized, that was why they sat there levelling out, levelling out and trying to stir everything into sludge. Things had gone so far that sons of farmers walked around making fun of the official class ... and in a way they were right to do so. For the official class was no longer what it once had been. But that would no longer do. There had to be some in society who raised themselves above the crowd; there had to be something that was big and noble and which had glamour and authority. A state official and his position had to be regarded as something elevated and holy; the official class was the only one that could live a civilized and cultured life here in Norway, academic education created the priesthood of the mind, and it was indefensible that these priests should starve. But the common people had to work, work and earn money. Then all would be well and return to what it was in the good old days; penny-pinching politics would die out, and the old freehold farmer would again come to power in Norway's valleys.

He saw it so clearly! And saw it in such a coherent and radiant vision; it was the greatest thought he had ever had. And now he was thinking for himself. –

– Shortly after New Year Jens Rud came and offered Daniel work. Hærland had become ill and had to have someone to stand in for him for fourteen days or so; one had to hope it was not for longer. Daniel too hoped that. He accepted the offer with not particularly warm thanks.

And the job was what he made it. The boys were difficult and bored, and school-work dull. The class periods seemed eternal whether he taught them this way or that. Karl Magnus who was a teacher at the same school sometimes came to his assistance; but every day as he wearily staggered home he swore to himself that now he would write to Hanna Stensrud. –

He had to stick it out at the school for a whole month. And as soon as he was free and had received his wages, the bills started coming in. A whole string of bills, and comrades he had borrowed from and Peder Monsen and Bent Bu who wanted to borrow from him...

When Daniel had in a fashion managed to sort all this out the postboy came with a letter. Daniel tore it open in a vague hope – ; it was from Jens at Larsebakken who had heard that Daniel now had a good teaching post at a school. Lars wished him well with this. For the rest he could just report that he had suffered various financial losses recently ... would be grateful ... just a small deduction every month ... 'Grubber!' muttered Daniel and threw the letter aside.

– This could not go on. He saw that he was not getting by. He would soon be so deep in debt that he would have to slave all his life just to pay it off. Was *that* to be the reward for his long struggle: that he should live out his life as a bonded man, never a freeholder, always toiling for others? Perhaps he would not even get as far as his theological qualifications...

And that he should accept help from Chaplain Hirsch, this man of culture who as thanks for the help wanted Daniel to work for slave wages in a job he did not like! It was insufferable to be helped on your way in the world by others. It was as if you had sold your soul. Everything you were and had been you had to thank others for; and those fellows, they *demanded* thanks. You didn't have the right to dispose over your own life, but had to remember that Peter and Paul wanted to have the returns of gratitude for the money they'd invested; and as for Chaplain Hirsch, he wanted more. Daniel worked himself into a rage

The Making of Daniel Braut

thinking about it. He would not carry on like this; he would get engaged and be his own man. Stensrud, the estate-owner would not say no when he learnt that the suitor was a man who could think for himself and who would pass his theological exams in three years time...

He had to struggle for a long time to compose his letter of proposal. Like all such letters, it had to be loving, but on the other hand he did not want to say more than he could vouch for when he met his fiancée. When he had finished writing the final version, he immediately felt despondent. It was all so awful. He had never dreamt that this was how things would turn out for Daniel Braut. And Inga Holm was not as forgotten as he had thought. Poor Inga! What if she had been waiting for him all these years? He remembered the dinner in the sexton's farm; he saw her in the sexton's cosy kitchen, sweet, young and dreamy; there was sunshine indoors and out, the leaves of the trees fluttered in the summer breeze and whispered alluring things ... He had to push away such dreams by force. Hadn't even Chaplain Hirsch married for money? Weren't such things happening every day?

There were those who married forty-year-old maids for the money, and Hanna was only about twenty-seven or twenty-eight ... and damn it all he *had* to! He stuck the letter in his pocket and hurried out of the door. Best to send it before he changed his mind.

Out on the street, an alluringly pretty young girl swept past him, shortly after another one, and then another ... fresh, virginal, blooming with youth. They were warm, happy, charming, fascinating, he sighed with a sense of loss; the world was full of beautiful maidens, maidens like lilies, maidens like newly opened rosebuds with the dew on them; but he ... well, in a few years they would be as old as Hanna Stensrud. He was a poor man's son and could not demand the best; when he had money, he would be all right ... But when he came to the post-box he immediately realized that the letter could wait till the next day.

On his way home he dropped in to see Karl Magnus as he did not feel like being alone. There he found the Dalesman sitting talking, but it sounded as if he too was in a bad mood. He was complaining about how little help he received, and how difficult it was for people like him to live in such a poor country. He considered himself the equal of any man as far as knowledge and abilities were concerned, and that in any other country he could have lived *comfortably*, but here he was a supernumerary in a government department. And finally they had taken even that from him, so now he only had his poor paper *The Dalesman* to turn to, and while there were many who wanted to read it, few were willing to pay for it. Nor could he claim damages for what he had lost on account of his honest speech* and that despite the fact that he thought he had done as much as anyone to promote Norwegian book production.

No, guano was the only thing one should produce in Norway; it was the only thing people cared about. Norway was a cowshed not a homeland for its people, and when the cow's belly was full, she was content. There was no point in offering people products they did not want, and what the hell did Norwegians care about Norwegianness, or the guanocracy about poetry? The government was hen-brained and did not understand anything that was not intellectually dead, and the farmers in the Storting were only good for being yes-men for the clergy. He laughed drily. Yes, they were statesmen indeed! They gave one hundred daler to every old clergyman who could no longer bark and their knees quaked as soon as they saw the feather in the tax collector's hat, but if someone came along who wanted to stimulate some thought in all this fat then he'd have to turn to poor relief, because why the devil wasn't he producing fat like the rest? He was sometimes tempted to believe that these muddle-heads were right when they said that the country was too small to be an independent kingdom, or that it wasn't a country, but just a collection of four hundred parishes that could never learn to think anything but poor man's thoughts. God alone knows whether our national struggle is anything but empty dreams built on grave mounds and old fairy tales.

Karl Magnus paced back and forth in an old, wide and worn cape while he listened to this. Occasionally he would stop in front of the mirror and comb his black beard; he was restless and weird. Daniel prayed God save him from ever becoming an eternal student. Now and again Karl Magnus would try to get a word in, but was seldom successful. The Dalesman wanted to hold forth. What was he to think, he asked, when he saw how little the Norwegian freehold farmer cared about his language and his country? They couldn't give a damn about the whole caboodle and emigrated to America; that was the help we got from them. So that's why he sat there in his cold garret, poor old man that he was, and wrote and wrote, and blew on his fingers so they shouldn't go numb, and laughed and was merry so he did not have to cry. And people read what he wrote and had fun and thought that the Dalesman was an amusing fellow; but they would not help him with so much as a bit of the writing so that he could find the time to work on things that would really show what he was capable of. And if there was a lad with some promise then as like as not you'd see that he'd die before he had time to mature. The ne'er do wells and the trash, they'd manage for they could always shelter under some tuft or tussock, but if there was a young tree that shot up, then it was broken by wind and weather and days of struggle, and the worst of it was that one had to say that those who were allowed to die were the lucky ones. Like this Hærland fellow. He was one of those promising fellows whom the Dalesman had hoped would help him in his struggle ... and now he lay there. The Dalesman wept. 'Hærland? Is he dying?' Daniel suddenly jumped up. 'Yes,' replied Karl Magnus. 'He's got galloping consumption!' moaned the Dalesman.

Daniel stood up and said goodnight. If Hærland died, *he* would have to take over his teaching at the school ... He rushed down to the post office again and posted his letter of proposal...

– The reply came remarkably soon. She loved him, had loved him, would love him. She was fairly confident that her father would agree; he was coming in to town soon, so Daniel could talk to him ... Daniel said to himself several times: now I have won.

He thought that the best person to talk the estate owner round would be Mrs Storr. She was kind, and she knew how to deal with the old man. Daniel went to her.

She received him graciously and with a smile, and then teasingly, 'It seems you are something of a heart-breaker.' Daniel defended himself as best he could, and asked what she thought the estate-owner would say. She hesitated for a moment, 'Well, you know papa has his fixed ideas' ... 'And I don't own anything' ... 'Well,' she smiled ... 'you'll soon have your vocational qualifications, and an official position is as good as an inheritance. But you see...' 'If there's something else,' Daniel said, and looked at Mrs Storr with eyes that seemed so firm and principled behind his glasses –, 'then I would just ask you to tell the estate-owner that what I learned from him, I have thought about, and now I can say that I ... *now I think for myself*!' Daniel Braut was sweating. Mrs Storr carried on as if she had not heard what Daniel said. 'You see, father is so *fond* of Hanna, that I am afraid he does not want to lose her; but heaven's above! He who dares, wins...' –

It was a beautiful day towards the end of May. Everything had sorted itself out in the best possible way. And the estate-owner had not wanted to hear of his son-in-law toiling away as a schoolteacher. He should sit his exams. That could be managed. And old Stensrud had been as friendly as could be.

Daniel was now on his way to dancing classes. A man who was engaged had to be able to dance, and now he could afford that sort of education too. He sauntered down the street in the spring sunshine, and decided that things had turned out well for him.

He had come so far that he felt safe. He had reached harbour after a long voyage with various detours. Had done with the chaos and confusion of youth that he had struggled with before. Now he had come to rest. Was a grown man. Knew what he wanted.

God had arranged things for the best. When he looked back over his life, he understood the meaning behind most of it. The only exception might be the *haud* for his university matriculation exams. But he forgave God for that, and the saga of his conversion he skipped over.

Rud and Haugum and that crowd would have to say what they

liked, he had such good people on his side now that he was not afraid. He would rather have the whole of the cultured public on his side than a flock of confused idealists; and he was freer now when he could wholeheartedly follow his natural urge to bow down loyally before all true authority than he was before when he was with those wanting to tear down authority. What the professor had said was true: true freedom was achieved not by following one's own counsel but by bowing down before a higher authority.

He was saved. In a few years he would have entered the splendid pyramid of power that he had always dreamt of, and which was the highest thing he knew of; then in truth he would be able to say that he had reached his ideal. He could hardly think of anything more splendid than sitting in an old vicarage and lording it over the peasants. Then he would teach the people to work, work, ... he felt sorry for the young people now who wasted their lives fighting for wild and woolly 'ideas', which for all the world could never yield anything but worn coats and broken hopes. But with the ranters who went about seducing young people and tearing down everything, and were never satisfied with anything, with them Daniel knew he felt angry. What was it they wanted? Wasn't society as well governed as one could expect?

He straightened up and looked around. Hmm, there they were again these snobs, these dandies who paraded around staring at people and sneering ... the devil only knew what they had to sneer at. But suddenly he was brought up short, there was a young girl approaching who was just like Inga Holm. Why had he not written to her first? He couldn't understand it. She who was so young and sweet, who had been the dream of his youth, the *hulder* ... no, he must not think like that. He was not allowed to. But he would go and buy Asbjørnsen's *Folktales*...

– So many beautiful young girls. Some as young and delicate as opening flowers, others rich and ample like swans ... But now he had money; now he would live the life of a student for a couple of years. God would forgive that, and no-one else need know. Hanna, she was grown-up and sensible, she would not ask more of him than was reasonable, he would write to her as often as he could. She should be glad she was getting married. He would presumably grow fond of her. If only he was over their first meeting...

It was a strange thing to be engaged. It was as if he was a different man now. There were others who had a claim on him, who owned him ... But now he could write home and tell them that he was engaged to a young lady, a rich, refined young lady; that would be something for the peasants back home to hear about, and as for Jens at Larsebakken and the merchant, Helle – he looked up at the sky and laughed.

Further down the street he saw two men walking in his direction; he gave a start and felt uneasy, for one was Jens Rud. But the other? The tall grey-haired one with a broad, black hat? Daniel stared as if he was beside himself. It could never be – For all the world it could surely never be ... chaplain Hirsch? –

Student Braut did not know what to do. He turned round, hunched his shoulders and set off with long strides, then turned into a side street.

Notes

The information in these notes is gathered from many sources including the web, encyclopedias, and relevant volumes of *Norges historie* (Cappelen 1978, 1-15) edited by Knut Mykland. However, the starting point for many searches, particularly on the models behind certain characters, was the thirty pages of notes at the back of the Norwegian school edition of *Bondestudentar*, edited by Olav Midttun (Aschehoug 1962). The translator, however, takes full responsibility for any errors.

17 Translation of part of hymn No 79 from Thomas Kingo's hymnal. Kingo (1634-1703) was a Danish bishop, poet and hymn-writer. The fragment quoted crops up several times in the novel and the complete hymn appears towards the end of Chapter 7.

17 Lutheran in its origins, pietism came to Denmark-Norway from Germany round about 1700, and was an attempt by the church and state working together to induce stricter religious observance among the subjects of the two countries, and to convert people from attending church as matter of habit to making the Christian faith a matter of personal experience and the foundation of a whole way of life. However, by the nineteenth century a feeling arose that the clergy had become too interested in preserving their own interests and authority and a new religious revival was started by Hans Nielsen Hauge (1771-1824). He had a major influence on Norwegian religious and cultural life which has lasted to the present day. He challenged the exclusive right of the clergy to preach, and he himself travelled extensively within Norway preaching and establishing brotherhoods of followers who met for religious study and prayer.

17 The widely-travelled German clergyman, Johannes Evangelist Gossner (1773-1885) wrote his collection of devotional readings,

Schatzkästchen some time in the 1820s after returning from a four-year stay in Russia. It was translated into Danish in 1845 and was widely used.

19 In country districts with a scattered population, 'rotating schools' were the norm until the 1860s. Until that time a teacher would meet up at one farm with the children of the locality for a period of a few days or weeks before moving to another nearby farm and repeating the same process until the three-month school term had ended.

24 From 1816-1875 the *speciedaler* was the highest denomination of currency. 1 *daler* = 5 *ort* = 120 *skilling* – (translated as shillings). In 1873 the *krone* and *øre* were introduced where 1 *daler* = 4 *krone* and 1 *krone* = 100 *øre*. In 1875, *daler* and shillings were discontinued.

24 Ashpot, the hero of Norwegian folktales, often the youngest son of a poor farmer, who goes out into the world and by his wit wins the hand of the princess.

24 The lur, a long wooden horn used by shepherds, is similar to the alpenhorn.

25 At a time when the teaching of the church made up a large part of what a young person had to learn in school, confirmation marked not only the completion of a young person's schooling but the transition from childhood to adulthood. To be confirmed, a young person had to learn large chunks of Erik Pontoppidan's 759 explanations of Luther's *Little Catechism*, summarised in *Truth unto Godliness*, and could be questioned on any of them. Those who did best would be at the front of the line of young people being presented to a bishop for confirmation. Pontoppidan was a Danish bishop who lived from 1698 to 1764 and who had a strong pietistic influence on religious life in Denmark and Norway.

27 The Latin-schools were originally attached to the cathedrals in Oslo, Christiansand, Bergen and Trondheim, and were intended for those going into the church. Later they also provided a Latin-based education for those who wanted to go to university.

29 The skalds were the poets in the courts of the kings and lords who ruled Norway in the medieval period and who recorded their deeds of valour in battle and their acts of generosity in friendship in intricate verse forms. Here Hirsch is using the phrase in a romantic fashion to cover all Nordic poets.

30 Ludvig Holberg (1684-1754), Dano-Norwegian dramatist, essayist and historian, sometimes considered the founder of Dano-Norwegian literature. His comedies may be compared to those of Molière, and it is with considerable justification that he can be called

'the Molière of the North'.

30 Johan Herman Wessel (1742-1785), Dano-Norwegian writer, famous for his parody of French tragedy, *Love Without Stockings*. He was also a member of the Norwegian Society in Copenhagen, and wrote many witty epigrams for it.

30 Adam Oehlenschläger (1779-1850), leading Danish poet of the High Romantic period.

30 Nikolaj Frederik Severin Grundtvig (1783-1872), leading Danish clergyman, hymn-writer, historian, educational reformer and politician. In his youth Grundtvig had been deeply influenced by his life in the countryside and his meeting with the ordinary people there. He came to believe deeply in 'the spirit of the north' as expressed in the lives of ordinary people and in Nordic mythology and folklore. He also found the classical languages and mythologies deeply alien, and believed that the Latin schools were alienating the Danes from themselves and their own identity. It was as an alternative to the exclusive Latin schools that Grundtvig conceived the idea of the Folk High Schools. These were to be open to all young adults and the students were to be given a grounding in Danish language and culture, which he saw as the foundation of modern Danish society. Furthermore the Folk High School education was not to be based on textbooks and rote learning but on active dialogue between teacher and students on topics relevant to the students' everyday lives. Grundtvig also believed that such an education would equip the students to play a larger part in Danish political and social life. The Folk High School Movement came to Norway in the early 1860s and first Folk High School, Sagatun, was started in 1864 by Olaus Arvesen and Herman Anker. As should be clear from this, chaplain Hirsch was deeply influenced by Grundtvig's ideas and was 'trying them out' on Daniel.

30 *Holger Danskes Chronicle*, a Danish compilation by Christiern Pedersen (1480-1554) of legends about Holger Danske, the Danish folk hero. The cycle of which has its origins in the French romances about Charlemagne, states that Holger Danske, whose statue sits in the vaults of Kronborg Castle, will come alive again when Denmark and Danish sovereignty are threatened. This legend is referred to ironically in Chapter 12.

30 Bjørnstjerne Bjørnson (1832-1910), poet, novelist, dramatist, newspaper editor and political activist, and contemporary of Ibsen. The author of some very popular peasant novels, which contributed to the freeing up of Norwegian literary language in the 1850s,

Bjørnson led the way in writing social dramas, though Ibsen took the form further. Bjørnson was also the author of Norway's National Anthem and during his lifetime was more influential and held in greater affection in Norway than was Ibsen.

30 The *hulder*, a figure from Norwegian folk-tales, who lures men. She is a troll, but seen from the front she appears as a beautiful young girl, and it is only when she turns round that one sees she has a cow's tail.

33 *The Common Man's Companion* (*Almuevennen*), a weekly paper, published between 1848 and 1893, the aim of which was to 'spread enlightenment among the ordinary people'. It was a good educational paper and had wide circulation.

43 The Factory is based on Heltberg's Student Factory, a crammer founded in 1846 by Henrik Anton Schjøtt Heltberg (1806-1873). The crammer ran a two-year programme for mature students to enable them to take their university matriculation exams. These were often students who had not been able to afford to go through the Latin-school system. Ibsen and Bjørnson attended the 'Factory' during the period when Heltberg was still teaching there, but Garborg did not. He did, however, know many who had studied with him, and it is generally agreed that the portrait he paints of Heltberg, 'The Old Man' in Chapter 4, is an accurate one. It was said of Heltberg that his style of teaching was the man, and the man was his style of teaching, and all his students spoke well of him. Bjørnson wrote a beautiful memorial poem on him when he died.

43 Christiania, the old name for Oslo. Named after Christian II of Denmark-Norway it was Christiania from 1624 to 1878 when the spelling was changed to Kristiania. In 1924 the capital was given back its medieval Norwegian name, Oslo.

46 'Sørbraut' would be the way that Daniel's surname – in fact the name of the farm he came from – was written and pronounced by the local people in their dialect. The Latin-school would use the 'educated' Dano-Norwegian spelling, which does not have so many diphthongs, and 'Sørbrød' is close to 'surbrød' which means 'sourdough'. When Daniel tries to use the 'educated' form of his name when he comes to the Factory in Chapter 4 he is challenged by his classmates who are not ashamed of their country dialects.

48 Ole Vig (1824-1857), a champion of popular education, much influenced by Grundtvig, and from 1852 till his death editor of *The People's Friend*, a journal containing much good educational material which was published by The Society for the Promotion of

Popular Education (*Selskapet for Folkeopplysningens Fremme*) which had been founded in 1851. He was also one of the first champions of the Folk High Schools.

57 Søren Jaabæk (1814-1894), teacher and farmer and from 1845-1891 a member of the *Storting*, where he soon became a leader of the farmers. He fought for greater democracy and extension of the franchise, and he is particularly remembered for his savings policies, which were aimed at reducing the power, numbers and pensions of the official class (which is why he is a figure of scorn for them as in Chapter 11).

62 At Norwegian universities lectures traditionally start fifteen minutes after the time given in the timetable, so if a class or lecture is down in the timetable as starting at 9.00, it will actually begin at 9.15.

62 When Norway gained its independence from Denmark in 1814, the language spoken by the educated classes was Dano-Norwegian. While there was a gradual process of 'Norwegianization' of the language, there still was a huge gap between the language of the educated and the language of the farmers who spoke their dialects. This was a major barrier to the education and the social and political integration of the farmers. In the middle of the century the philologist and poet, Ivar Aasen (1813-1896) began the huge linguistic task of creating a new Norwegian language based on the dialects, particularly of western Norway. He wrote a grammar, a dictionary, and a series of texts which showed that this new Norwegian or *Landsmål* ('country language') could be used as a written language. It was not until 1885 that *Landsmål* was given approval as an official alternative written language to Dano-Norwegian. Both written languages have been subjected to a constant process of spelling reforms etc, and since 1929 *Landsmål* has been called *Nynorsk* ('New Norwegian').

68 *Nisi ... defendant*: 'Unless kings defend their authority with as much energy as their subjects show in the quest of liberty...'

72 In religious matters Grundtvig was a liberal. He had reacted against the pietists' view that the Bible was the foundation of the Church and had come to the opinion that it was the Church itself, and its traditions, especially as expressed in baptism and communion, that was the basis of Christian faith. He believed that Christ was not to be sought in the past or in a book, but in the living community, where people bacome Christians at baptism, and where their life as Christians was nourished and sustained by the Communion. Grundtvig believed that it was through these sacraments that Christ

speaks his living word to his community.
73 'Sven Dufva', one of the poems in the poetic cycle *Fänrik Ståls Sägner*, by the Finnish poet Ludvig Runeberg (1804-1877). The poem tells of the soldier Sven Dufva, who does not know when to retreat, and the last line states that 'he had a poor head, but a good heart'.
81 Until 1883 students who had completed their secondary education came to Christiania from all over Norway to sit their matriculation exams – *Examen artium*. This was in two parts, a written part and oral part (described in Chapter 6). The *russ* festivities were also in two parts – the main festivities took place when the results of the written examination were published in the middle of August, and more subdued ones on September 2 in connection with matriculation ceremony at the university.
86 Professor Darre is based on Marcus Monrad (1816-1897) a leading cultural figure in Norway and later Professor of Philosophy. He had a brilliant mind, and diverse interests including literature, theatre and music, and he took active part in student festivities for many years, making speeches and composing student songs. Starting out as liberal in philosophical and æsthetic matters he gradually became a stern Hegelian, and wrote much on philosophical, cultural and political matters. Because of his rigidly conservative views he was considered one of the most dangerous opponents of the new progressive ideas, collectively known as The Modern Breakthrough which swept through Norway in the 1870s and 1880s.
91 Until recently the Norwegian colleges and universities used a decimal system in marking which went from 1.0 as the highest mark to 6.0 as the lowest, with 4.0 as the pass mark.
92 The 'Dalesman' is Aasmund Olavsson Vinje (1818-1870), journalist and poet, who got his nickname 'Dølen', 'The Dalesman' from the title of the weekly newspaper of that name which he started in 1858 and continued to edit until his death, and to which he was the main contributor, so that one could say it was almost a one-man paper. He was one of the first writers to use the new *Landsmål*, compiled by Ivar Aasen, and he is known for his witty and ironic style, or 'double vision' with which he could see things from two quite different angles, so one was never quite sure where he stood. He also wrote poetry and some of his poems have been set to music by Grieg.
95 A term coined by Vinje, but used in the 1860s to describe state officials who earned money on the side from various business interests. The term originated when the secretary of the Society for

the Welfare of Norway (*Selskabet for Norges Vel*) imported huge quantities of guano from South America and sold it through an agent, and was said to have made a considerable amount of money on the deal.

97 Endre Storr is based on Einar Sundt (1854-1917), the son of Eilert Sundt, Norway's first sociologist. Einar Sundt was a businessman in London and Christiania, and in 1891 he founded, and was the first editor of, *Farmand*, a business magazine inspired by the *The Economist*. In his journals Garborg wrote that he was often together with Sundt during his journalistic period and it is clear that Storr is often a mouthpiece for Garborg's ideas.

97 Meier is based on Christopher Bruun (1839-1920), a strongly idealistic character, best known as a possible model for the eponymous hero of Ibsen's play *Brand*. In 1864 Bruun volunteered to go and fight with the Danes against the Prussians, and when Ibsen criticised the Norwegians for not helping their Danish brothers, Bruun asked Ibsen why had not volunteered, to which Ibsen is said to have replied, 'We poets have others tasks'. As a young man Bruun had been inspired by Grundtvig and in addition to becoming a clergyman he started a Folk High School at Sel in Gudbrandsdalen in 1867. The school was later moved to Vonheim in Gausdal and was one of the reasons why Bjørnson moved to Aulestad in Gausdal.

103 The regulations varied according to whether students were being presented by public schools, private schools or private tutors. According to the regulations of 1840 if a student from a public or private school failed, the person presenting him had to pay a fine of 16 daler to the school library on the first occasion and double that amount if the student failed a second time. If the student failed a third time, the person presenting him would be dismissed from his post if he was paid by the state, or lose his right to present students if he taught in private school. The rules for those preparing students privately were even stronger; they lost their right to present students after the first failure.

104 *laud – laudabilis* = praiseworthy, *haud – illaudabilis* = not unpraiseworthy, *non – non contemnendus* = not to be despised. The students were examined in eleven subjects and with 1 being the highest mark and 6 the lowest, *laud* covered an aggregate up to and including 27, *haud* an aggregate up to and including 35 and *non* an aggregate up to and including 41. (When he was at university Garborg got *praeceteris* = 15).

106 *Examen philosophicum* was an examination in six to eight subjects

that all students had to pass before they could go on an take their vocational or professional exams. While philosophy was compulsory for all, students could choose according to their direction of study after that. When a student had passed that he was designated *cand. philos.*, translated in this volume as BA.

115 The Norwegian National Anthem was written by Bjørnson and in translation runs as follows:
> Yes we love our country,
> As it rises up,
> Gnarled and weathered over the water,
> With its thousand homes.

116 Scandinavianism, a mid-nineteenth-century middle-class and student movement which sought greater cultural and political unity between the Scandinavian countries in the face of growing Pan-Germanism. After Sweden and Norway refused to help Denmark when it was attacked by Prussia in 1864, the idea lost much of its validity. For details of the Dano-Prussian war in 1864 see note for page 182.

118 *Stev*, which belong to the folk tradition, are short, improvised verses which are usually half sung, and consist of four-line rhymed stanzas. In a *stev* contest one person challenges another to respond to his or her *stev* with a new four-line stanza. The aim can be to make it impossible for the other to respond.

121 *Dampen* was *Christiania Dampkjøkken*,(Christiania Steam Kitchen) founded 1857, a cheap café with a large dining area where, as the name indicates, the food was cooked by steam.

131 Emilio Castelar (1832-1899), a Spanish statesman and author, and one of the most powerful champions of Spanish republicanism from the late 1860s onwards. He was president of the first Spanish Republic from September 1873 to January 1874. The Norwegian radical Olaus Fjørtoft was enthusiastic about his ideas and published translations of several of his speeches in his radical paper *Fram* (lit. *Forward*).

133 Fram is based on Olaus Johannes Fjørtoft (1847-1878) a radical orator and journalist. He had attended Heltberg's Student Factory, and failed Latin twice before gaining admission to university. He was, however, brilliant at maths and astronomy and lived by giving private tuition in these subjects. Actively engaged in the political and cultural issues of his day firstly in the Students' Union and later in the Workers' Union, he also published his own weekly paper *Fram* for two years from 1871-1873. In the Students' Union he agitated for

The Making of Daniel Braut

students to engage actively in the new intellectual ideas and trends reaching Norway from Europe (particularly Darwinism, and all that followed from that) and to take these ideas out to the mass of the people. *Fram* championed *Landsmål*, republicanism, greater democracy and dissolution of the union with Sweden. He also wanted to do away with Pontoppidan's *Explanations*, the state church, and power of the clergy, and advocated the right of anyone to preach on the basis of Christ's own words. In the latter part of his short life he became much influenced by new international socialist and communist ideas and was thrown out of the Workers' Union. Garborg admitted to being fascinated by his ideas.

136 Ole Vig – see note for page 48.

136 In the 1850s and 1860s Møre and Romsdal had many very able sextons and they had often represented these districts in the Storting, and on a couple of occasions had been in the majority (3 out of 5).

139 *Pater omnipotens* is based on Peter Hærem (1840-1878), a graduate in theology who ran a student hostel for out-of-town students from 1871. Even in his student days he was keen on missionary work, and was the driving force behind many popular, Christian, educational and social initiatives. Garborg knew him and stayed at the hostel for one and half years. He described him as someone with an unusually cheerful and positive outlook on life, a winning manner, and someone about whom it would be hard to say a bad word. The *Pater* plays a role again in Chapter 9.

162 There was much dissatisfaction with the Christiania Theatre round about 1870, especially as it was the capital's leading theatre. Conflict arose largely because the good citizens of Christiania wanted to go to the theatre to be entertained and were willing to pay for that, while the intelligentsia saw the theatre as a place of cultural and artistic endeavour. Bjørnson had been the director there from 1865 to 1867 and during his management period had maintained artistic standards. The director who succeeded Bjørnson was Norwegian by birth but had spent most of his time in Denmark, and under his leadership the theatre was subject to much negative criticism which resulted in calls to bring back Bjørnson. During the winter season of 1869-1870 there were two 'whistle concerts', the second one provoked because the director had chosen to stage one of his own plays.

182 In February 1864 the combined armies of Austria and Prussia under Bismarck attacked Denmark in order to gain the half German-, half Danish-speaking Duchy of Schleswig for the German Confederation. After the Danish defeat at Dybbøl in Schleswig, and

the consequent occupation of the whole of Jutland, Denmark was forced by the Treaty of Vienna in October to surrender almost all of Schleswig and Holstein (which was German-speaking) to Prussia and Austria. The reason there is discussion about where the Norwegians were at the time is that the Danes believed that as a result of the movement known as 'Scandinavianism' (see page 116) Norway and Sweden would come to their aid if they were attacked. For information on Holger Danske see note for page 30.

183 The Order of the Sword is Sweden's oldest military order, founded in 1748 by King Frederik and awarded to 'Swedish Officers and foreigners for long and meritorious service in or for the Armed Forces'. The Order of St Olaf was founded by King Oscar in 1847 and is awarded for 'distinguished services rendered to the country and to mankind'.

184 The conveyance system was the term used for travel by horse-drawn carriage, boat or train in the nineteenth century. Everyone had to pay for this, but state officials and civil servants were reimbursed from public funds according to their rank and so could earn from twice to five times the cost of a journey. This the officials regarded as an additional income or perk, while the farmers who, in addition to providing the horses and boats, had to fund the reimbursement out of an annual levy based on the tax value of their land, regarded it as an extra burden on them. (I am indebted to Professor Bjarne Rogan of Oslo University for the information supplied in this note).

190 Carl Michael Bellman (1740-1795), Swedish poet and musician, and a central figure in the Swedish song tradition because of his mastery in combining words and music. Many of his songs are about 'wine, women and song', but many also have a satirical edge.

190 Uppsala was famous for its student choirs, the oldest being 'Almänna Sångern' founded 1833 and the next oldest 'Orphei Drängar' (OD), founded in 1853. Both still exist and have international reputations.

194 Bundling (*natteløperi*) was a long-standing tradition in certain Norwegian farming communities where it was difficult for young people to meet, unsupervised. Until well into the nineteenth century it was a custom at week-ends that the young men in a district would visit young girls on other farms. The girls would move up to the loft in a barn away from adults, perhaps taking some refreshments with them and await the young men. The meeting was primarily a means for young people of the opposite sex to get to know each other, and not for sex itself, as illegitimacy carried a huge stigma.

195 Lawyer Stensgård, a slippery character in Ibsen's play *The League*

of Youth who changes his opinions and political loyalties just to get ahead.
198 Eidsvoll, a town north of Christiania, where in 1814 the leading men of Norway came together to draw up the constitution which prevented Norway becoming part of Sweden as had been the intention when Norway was taken from Denmark and given to Sweden in the Treaty of Kiel (signed in January 1814) because Denmark had sided with the loser, Napoleon, in the Napoleonic War.
208 'To mistake one's destiny', a reference to Act 5 of Ibsen's *Peer Gynt*, where the Button Moulder, a sort of divine agent, comes to claim Peer's soul for his button-moulding ladle because Peer has failed to follow his divinely-given destiny which was to be 'a shining button on the waistcoat of the world'.
222 Pelagianism – also called the Pelagian Heresy, the doctrine taught by Pelagius (354?-418) that human nature was essentially good, and that man had free will and so could choose between good and evil.
230 Vinje was sacked from his job in the Department of Justice for writing articles criticising the government.

CAMILLA COLLETT

The District Governor's Daughters

(translated by Kirsten Seaver)

Written in 1854-55 and translated after 140 years into English, this is the one and only novel written by a daughter of one of Norway's best-known literary families. Camilla Collett had felt her creativity stifled and her literary ambitions thwarted by society's conventional expectations of what a woman could properly achieve; it was not until she was a widow of 42 that she could finally finish her novel, which she called 'my life's long-suppressed scream'.

In an intricate study of relationships, the novel creates a bourgeois society reminiscent of Jane Austen, in which marriage is the only respectable career for a woman. Sophie, the youngest of four daughters of a cynical and disappointed mother, struggles against society's precepts and her own conditioning to be allowed to make an independent choice; but all her surroundings can offer her by way of models are disillusioned wives, lonely spinsters or crazed old maids.

'One does not know which to admire more, the strength and variety of her characterization, the picture of provincial life in a small and remote community, the descriptions of nature with the sudden seasonal changes or the economical power of the narration .... Most powerful is the portrait of Sophie herself, a character worthy to stand beside Cathy Earnshaw in *Wuthering Heights*, published seven years before *The District Governor's Daughters*.' *London Magazine*

ISBN 978 1 870041 17 1
UK £10.95
(paperback, 312 pages)

AMALIE SKRAM

Lucie

(translated by Judith Hanson and Katherine Messick)

This ground-breaking novel from 1888 tells the story of the misalliance between Lucie, a viviacious and beautiful dancing girl from Tivoli, and Theodor Gerner, a respectable lawyer from the strait-laced middle-class society of nineteenth-century Norway. Having first kept her as a mistress, Gerner is so captivated by Lucie's charms that he marries her, only to discover that his project to turn her into a proper and demure housewife is continually frustrated by her irrepressible sensuality and lack of fine breeding. What made her alluring as a mistress makes her unacceptable as a wife. His attempts to govern Lucie's behaviour develop gradually into a harsh tyranny against which she rebels in a manner which brings misery and despair to both.

Amalie Skram, a contemporary of Ibsen, expresses the same criticism of repressive social mores and hypocrisy here as he does in plays like *A Doll's House* and *Ghosts*, although in a deeply personal way. In this novel, as in her other work, she makes an impassioned statement on the double standard, contributing to the great debate about sexual morality which engaged many Scandinavian writers in the late nineteenth century. She also presents a closely-observed realistic depiction of a lively cross-section of Kristiania society from the turn of the century, ranging from high-society fancy-dress parties and country cottages to dark and dingy tenements reeking of poverty

ISBN 978 1 870041 48 5
UK £8.95
(paperback, 168 pages)

HANS BØRLI

We Own the Forests
and Other Poems

Parallel English and Norwegian text
(translated by Louis Muinzer)

Hans Børli (1918-89) was born and lived in the wooded county of Hedmark in south-eastern Norway. His days seem to have been divided into two separate parts: by day, he lived the physically demanding life of a lumberjack, but by night he turned poet and spent the still, dark hours writing. His days, however, were an enactment of his poetry. Børli's verse is alive with his experiences of the Norwegian forests – with the moods of sky and water, with the creatures that moved in air and woodland, and with the trees themselves.

In a series of books beginning in 1945, he wrote more than eleven hundred poems. They form a poetic record of a life reminiscent in spirit, if not in form, of Walt Whitman's *Leaves of Grass*. This collection can only suggest the scope and richness of the poet's life-in-verse, but it includes many of his most admired poems. Sometimes lonely or even mystical, the finest of these poems bit deep like the blow of an axe.

ISBN 978 1 870041 61 5
UK £9.95
(paperback, 160 pages)

KJELL ASKILDSEN

A Sudden Liberating Thought

(translated by Sverre Lyngstad)

Kjell Askildsen is widely regarded as the finest short-story writer in Norway today. His reputation, based primarily on his Kafkaesque accounts of alienated individuals in a hostile environment, has grown steadily since he made his debut in the 1950s, when his first book had the dubious honour of being publicly burned by his father, who objected to its frank presentation of sexuality. One translation into French invited comparisons with Beckett (whom Askildsen has translated into Norwegian).

This collection of stories brings together works from all stages of Kjell Askildsen's career. It includes an early experimental novella, *Surroundings* (1969), about the developing tensions between four people cut off on a small island, as well as short stories from various collections, such as *Stage Settings* (1966) and the highly acclaimed *Thomas F's Last Notes for the General Public* (1983). The stories relate the struggles of ordinary people with the trivialities and absurdities of everyday life, where loneliness and despair are held at bay by grim determination and flashes of biting black humour. A few words can have a vital significance, and what is not said can be full of meaning.

'one of the few European writers who are of truly major stature'
Paul Binding, *Babel Guide: Scandinavian Fiction*

ISBN 978 1 870041 84 3
UK £9.95
(paperback, 240 pages)

JOHAN BORGEN

The Scapegoat

(translated by Elixabeth Rokkan)

Johan Borgen (1902-79) was one of the most productive and committed of twentieth-century Norwegian authors; his work spans fifty years, and as well as being an acclaimed novelist and essayist, he was active throughout his life as a journalist, literary critic and cultural personality. His style was always elegant, his wit sometimes caustic; but behind the lightness of tone lies a serious preoccupation with mankind's struggles to discover its true identity.

His novel from 1959, *The Scapegoat*, takes as its central character a figure familiar from earlier works: the splintered personality, a man in search of his own authentic self. Matias Roos is literally split in two, into an observing 'I' and an experiencing 'he'; he embarks on a journey at the beginning of the novel which takes him back into his childhood, forward into the future, and into a strange limbo of parallel time. He is a man obsessed with frontiers, the borders between countries, between war and peace, present and past, self and other; a man guilty of an unspecified crime, searching for a way to atone. Reality and fantasy merge as the novel explores with hallucinatory power his struggles to derive meaning from experience.

ISBN 978 1 870041 21 8
UK £8.95
(paperback, 187 pages)

JANET GARTON (ED.)

Contemporary Norwegian Women's Writing

This anthology presents a cross-section of Norwegian women's writing from the early 1970s to the mid-1990s, from the more directly political writings from the early part of the period to the more fantastic later ones. It ranges across many genres, including fiction, drama, poetry and essays.

Many of these texts deal with womem's attitudes to their own sexuality; some focus on women's place in society and their ability to influence the circumstances of their lives, whilst others are about women taking active control of their own desire. They include explorations of lesbianism, prostitution, incest, abuse, of mother/daughter relationships and 'jouissance'; some are angry, some are humorous. The volume is prefaced by an essay which outlines the development of women's writing in Norway during the period 1970-1995. A list of the main works and translations of the authors is also included.

Authors whose work is featured in this volume include Bjørg Vik, Liv Køltzow, Marie Takvam, Herbjørg Wassmo and Cecilie Løveid.

ISBN 978 1 870041 29 4
UK £8.95
(paperback, 253 pages)

JENS BJØRNEBOE

Moment of Freedom
Powderhouse
The Silence

(translated by Esther Greenleaf Mürer)

The three volumes of Jens Bjørneboe's personal odyssey of investigation into the inhumanity of man range through the whole gamut of human destructiveness, from religious persecution to wars to colonial exploitation, in an effort to find an answer to the problem of the evil of mankind – and, equally unfathomable, the problem of goodness in mankind.

The trilogy marks the high point of outspokenness and originality of one of Norway's most controversial modern writers. Jens Bjørneboe was an author and polemicist of fierce energy and deep conviction, who throughout his career provoked and upset the establishment with his unrelenting attacks on some of its most sacred cows: a repressive school system, a hypocritical Christianity, an inhumane prison system, power-seeking politicians, corrupt police and depraved moral guardians. With these three books, Bjørneboe turned his attention to a more general problem: the evil inherent in the human race itself. Why, his narrators ask dispairingly, does man behave so callously to his fellow creatures?

Moment of Freedom: 217 pages, ISBN 978 1 870041 41 6,
Powderhouse: 201 pages, ISBN 978 1 870041 42 3
The Silence: 201 pages, ISBN 978 1 870041 45 4
UK £10.95 each (paperback)

HELENE URI

Honey Tongues

(translated by Kari Dickson)

The honey tongues of the title belong to four friends in their thirties who have known each other since school. They make up a 'sewing circle' where no sewing is done, but much exquisite food is lovingly prepared and consumed, and increasingly bitchy gossip exchanged.

The novel follows their three-weekly meetings over six months, as they take turns to entertain each other; we are privy to their thoughts and memories and discover how apparently innocent actions are motivated by emotional hang-ups with their roots in childhood traumas. The tension builds towards a gourmet trip to Copenhagen to celebrate their friendship, where during an eight-course meal the masks drop and undisguised fear and loathing are revealed. Shocking secrets are unearthed as the balance of power subtly shifts from one member of the group to another. Brilliantly observed, this is female bonding at its worst, manipulative and psychotic, exposing the dependency and deceit behind the compassionate and affectionate facade.

ISBN 978 1 870041 72 0
UK £9.95
(paperback, 192 pages)

AUGUST STRINDBERG
Tschandala

(translated by Peter Graves)

August Strindberg (1849-1912) is best known internationally as Sweden's greatest dramatist. Less well known outside Sweden is the range of his other writings – novels, short stories, essays, journalism and poetry. *Tschandala*, the novella translated into English here for the first time, was written in 1888, the same year as the *Miss Julie* and *Creditors*.

Tschandala has an historical setting: the time is the 1690s and the location is Skåne, the southern province that Sweden annexed from Denmark in 1658. A Swedish academic, Andreas Törner, rents rooms for the summer with his family in a dilapidated manor house owned by an eccentric baroness and managed by a gipsy named Jensen. Puzzled by the peculiarities of the people and environment, Törner is eventually drawn into conflict with the Jensen, whom he suspects of criminality and incompetence. The conflict intensifies, culminating in a struggle for survival between the two men. The atmosphere and setting of the story are thoroughly Gothic: the ruinous castle, mystery and suspense, inexplicable events, strange aristocrats and gipsies, baying hounds, and unexplained noises. All of this is, however, interwoven with ideas drawn from Nietzsche and Social Darwinism.

Strindberg, in parading his prejudices so nakedly, is simultaneously revealing many of the aspects of his age that would lead to tragic consequences in the century that followed. We may find *Tschandala* morally reprehensible in its attitudes, but it cannot be denied that its author had an acute ear for the music of his time.

ISBN 978 1 870041 71 3
UK £8.95
(paperback, 136 pages)

HJALMAR BERGMAN

Memoirs of a Dead Man

(translated by Neil Smith)

'Not everyone who lives is alive; nor is death a portal that only opens in one direction'

Hjalmar Bergman (1883-1931) is widely regarded as one of the foremost Swedish novelists of the twentieth century. *Memoirs of a Dead Man*, first published in 1918, follows the efforts of Jan Arnberg, the 'dead man' of the title (although there are numerous other candidates worthy of the description among Bergman's gallery of characters), to escape the curse that has bound the fate of his family to that of the Arnfelts for generations.

The earlier efforts of Jan's father to break free of the curse by moving to America founder in a biting parody of consumer society and advertising slogans. Jan's own story culminates when he has to flee a small-town scandal in Sweden and ends up in a symbolic kingdom of death in Hamburg, a mixture of casino and high-class brothel, where the family curse is played out once more, and where he comes to realize that abdication from free will is his only option.

Although apparently realistic to begin with, Bergman's novel shifts towards a theatrical, dreamlike world of repetitions and refractions in which the fates of his characters are predetermined and acted out in a macabre mixture of comedy and nightmare. Characters presumed dead manifest themselves in incidental roles throughout the novel, casting a foreboding light on the almost biblical nature of the family curse.

ISBN 978 1 870041 65 2
UK £10.95
(paperback, 352 pages)

Norvik Press
Classics of Norwegian Literature

With the publication of *The Making of Daniel Braut*, Norvik Press is launching a distinct series of English translations of classics of Norwegian literature, which will be published within its long-running 'Series B: English translations of Scandinavian literature'. This new initiative, made possible by the support of NORLA (Norwegian Literature Abroad) and the Fritt Ord foundation in Norway, will facilitate the regular publication of translations of classic works which have been unjustly overlooked in the English-speaking world, often simply as a result of the lack of a reliable and accessible translation.

Future publications in the series will include:

Sigurd Hoel: *A Fortnight Before the Frost* (1934; translated by Sverre Lyngstad), to be published in 2009.
Jonas Lie: *The Family at Gilje* (1883, translated by Marie Wells), to be published in 2010.

Works by Johan Borgen, Ragnhild Jølsen and Alexander Kielland are under consideration for future publication. Some books already published by Norvik Press, including Camilla Collett's *The District Governor's Daughters* (translated by Kirsten Seaver) and Amalie Skram's *Lucie* (translated by Katherine Hanson and Judith Messick), will be incorporated into the series as it progresses.

For further information, or to inquire about subscriptions to this series, please contact:
Norvik Press, Department of Scandinavian Studies, University College London, Gower Street, London WC1E 6BT, England
or visit our website at www.norvikpress.com